SIGOURNEY'S QUEST

To Bob & Judi

Gordon Snider

Sigourney's Quest

Helm Publishing
For information address:
Helm Publishing
3923 Seward Ave.
Rockford, IL 61108
815-398-4660
www.publishersdrive.com

ISBN 0-9769193-6-2
Printed in the United States of America

Snider, Gordon J., 1940-
  Sigourney's Quest / Gordon Snider.
        p. cm.
  ISBN 0-9769193-6-2 (pbk. : alk. paper) 1. Women
college teachers--Fiction. 2. Tibet (China)--
Fiction. 3. Buddhist monks--Fiction. 4. Buddhism--
Fiction. I. Title.
  PS3619.N535S56 2006
  813'.6--dc22

2006003828

Author's notes

The Buddhist texts I saw in Tibet were shaped like long loaves of bread, covered in gold-colored cloth, and bound top and bottom by wooden planks painted a deep red. However, I wanted the manuscript carried by Sigourney to stimulate the reader's imagination in a way that would make the book more mysterious and tactile. Hence, the cracked leather cover, parchment paper and ancient lock. The lock is real, by the way. I purchased it from a street vendor while circumambulating around the Jokhang Monastery in Lhasa.

When I paid homage to the 17th Karmapa at the Tsurpu Monastery, he was approximately twelve. I doubt that he spoke a word of English, but I give him the ability to speak a little English in the novel to heighten the drama when Sigouney meets him. When he was fourteen, he made a dramatic escape from Tibet just as I noted in the novel. By the time I had the good fortune to meet him again in 2003, he spoke English rather well.

The diary of Anne Hopkins is based on the diary of Alexandra David-Neel who did reach the forbidden city of Lhasa in 1924 by posing as a pilgrim. She is regarded as the first western woman to see the holy city. Her journey is a remarkable one, and I recommend it to anyone who enjoyed my fictional account in Sigourney's Quest.

Tibet has always been a spiritual land, one filled with bon spirits, ancient folklore and other mysteries. When Buddhism was introduced to Tibet in the 7th century, the Tibetans simply blended its tantras with their own beliefs in animism. The two religions remain intertwined to this day. Guru Rinpoche is supposed to have founded the first Buddhist monastery at Samye, but it was actually Bhutan where legend says he arrived on the back of a flying tiger.

Sadly, the plight of the Tibetans that I describe in Sigourney's Quest was quite accurate a decade ago. It has only gotten worse. China's continual assault on Tibet's culture and its people has accelerated the process of undermining the customs and beliefs I describe in the novel, and I fear it will not be long before the fabric of the Tibetans' remarkable way of life is destroyed forever. There are support groups throughout the world that are trying to slow or reverse this process, but China mostly ignores them. If my novel in some small way builds more awareness and interest in the Tibetans' plight, I will be most gratified.

REVIEWS

Our author brings to light much about the Buddhist and the life in Tibet which was very interesting; there was not one dull page of reading in this entire novel. Good job!
If you want a book that is packed full of suspense and adventure, topped with romance, mystery, intrigue and interesting facts of a faraway place all wrapped together in a package that begs to be opened, this one is for you. I give it my highest recommendation, a book well worth your time and guaranteed to give you reading ecstasy.
Shirley Johnson, Senior Reviewer
MidWest Book Review

Reader Comments:

"I loved chapter 19, and I really can't wait to read the whole book. Let me know as soon as it's on the shelves in the bookstores."

"Gordon Snider's first novel Sigourney's Quest, is a flawlessly told tale of intrigue and suspense. I couldn't put it down."

"Absorbing and suspenseful, Sigourney's Quest won't let you down. I was sad to see it end."

"Snider is an awesome new talent. Not only is Sigourney's Quest exciting and suspenseful, it's also filled with interesting facts about Tibet. Now I know where I want to go on my next vacation."

"A compelling and expertly told tale, Sigourney's Quest will leave fans waiting for the second installment."

"Snider's first novel Sigourney's Quest is a perfect blend of history and suspense. An extraordinary and brilliant accomplishment."

"Sigourney sounds like someone I'd like to know. She has an adventurous spirit and a spiritual dimension."

"Through the descriptive, detailed writing of Gordon Snider, you experience virtual reality as Sigourney accomplishes her spiritual quest."

"You believe you are in Tibet, layered in traditional clothing and freezing as you huddle in the cave waiting for your opportunity to sneak into the monastery."

Dedication:

To my loving wife, Fe, whose encouragement and support made this novel possible.

Acknowledgments

I would like to acknowledge Himalayan Treasures & Travel, the tour operator who hired me for two photography assignments in Tibet. While much of my research for this novel took place in Tibet, the following books also provided important insights:

My Journey to Lhasa, Alexandra David-Neel,
Seven Years in Tibet, Heinrich Harrer,
Trespassers on the Rooftop of the World, Peter Hopkirk,
Invading Tibet, Mark Frutkin,
The Teachings of Buddha, edited by Jack Kornfield,
Wisdom and Compassion: the Sacred Art of Tibet, Marylin Rhie & Robert Thurman,
Into Thin Air, Jon Krakauer.

CHAPTER ONE

It was a gloomy day, one filled with uncertain light. A billowing curtain of clouds covered the mountains Sigourney Phillips had come so far to see. She stood, hands on hips, and stared at the cloud cover, willing it to depart. The clouds sat unmoving, taunting her. She felt like a jilted lover, brimming with frustrations and unfulfilled expectations. These were familiar emotions for her, but she didn't want to think about her personal life. She was beginning a daunting journey, and wanted to focus all of her energy on what lay before her.

Sigourney had spent the last two hours bouncing along the traffic-congested roads of Kathmandu Valley in Nepal to reach Nagarkot, a lookout point where, on a clearer day, one could view the distant glacial slopes and icy peaks of the Himalayas. She was greeted, instead, by a barricade of clouds so formidable, she thought her vantage point was the end of the world.

Beyond those clouds and mountains lay the remnants of an ancient Tibetan society that had concealed itself from the outside world for centuries. Tibet: the name alone was enough to fill her with promises of quixotic adventures that could stir the heart and inspire the soul. Tomorrow Sigourney would enter the mountains now hidden from her and begin a five-day trek to the holy city of Lhasa. A few weeks ago, she would never have imagined such an undertaking, but strange circumstances leading to this moment had quickly sealed her fate.

Sigourney hugged the brown valise she had just carried half-way around the world and thought about the two items tucked inside: a copy of a hundred-year-old diary written by an English woman, Anne Hopkins, who had dared to enter Tibet's forbidden interior, and an ancient manuscript that Anne had brought back with her when she fled the country. If Sigourney's information was correct, the diary would rewrite history, and the manuscript would bring new hope to a beleaguered people who were striving to retain their individual culture and identity.

As she stood there contemplating her coming ordeal, a portion of the shadowy curtain of clouds slowly parted, revealing escarpments, crags and cliffs in the mountains before her. The majestic peaks and valleys filled the opening like medieval castle walls. Sigourney had never seen anything so unyielding. The air where she stood was pleasantly warm, but she could see icy-cold tendrils streaming off the mountain crests. She shivered and took a step backward. Her mind was racing at the prospect of what lay before her. The mountains seemed to rise to greater heights as she looked at them. They stood out like sentinels, swelling their chests and folding their arms, denying her the right of passage, just as the barriers recently erected in her personal life were denying her the ability to find peace and happiness. What she saw wasn't just stone and ice. It was her husband's betrayal and the alienation of her daughter. It was loss of faith in herself and in others. Fighting back tears, she stared at the bleak landscape. How could she expect to penetrate such obstacles? Where would she find the strength?

"Stop it," she cried out, causing two nearby couples to glance at her with startled expressions. She shook her head, not caring that they were watching. She hadn't come all this way to feel sorry for herself. She had come to restore her faith in herself as a woman and as a mother. Failure wasn't an option. She *would* enter those mountains and fulfill her quest.

As she struggled with her inner demons, another sensation flooded her consciousness, sending fresh chills through her body. She had faced these mountains before! The idea was absurd--she had never traveled to this part of the world--but she couldn't shake the impression that the Himalayas were familiar territory, that she had already challenged them and survived. She could *feel* the mountains pulling at her, welcoming her back into their womb. Something waited for her there, and it made her tremble with fear and excitement.

Sigourney turned and walked away as quickly as she dared without twisting an ankle on the uneven path. Her car and driver waited for her at the bottom of a small hill, and she slipped into the back seat with a sense of relief. As soon as she was settled, the driver roared down the mountainside, ignoring her earlier pleas to drive at a more moderate speed. It was as if he, too, was in a hurry to get away. She gave up cautioning him and tried to concentrate on the landscape streaking past her window, while she sorted through the misgivings tumbling inside of her. Something had quickened her pulse back there on that hilltop, something she couldn't comprehend.

It was an awkward moment to be making the trip. The timing was all wrong, given the issues she faced back home. Yet, she felt oddly relieved to escape them. Was she running away? Her brief visit to Nagarkot had raised many questions, but none had been answered.

Her driver followed a twisting road which descended into acres of wheat and rice fields in the valley below. She watched as the women harvested crops, beads of sweat dripping down the sides of their faces. It looked like hot, uninviting work. Hiking up their colorful, long skirts and bent to their tasks, the women cut the tall stalks, stacking them in random piles. They seemed carefree and happy as they talked with one another and swung sharp knives. The children gathered the stalks and carried them from the fields in large wicker baskets strapped to their heads. Nearby, men waited to separate the golden grain and spread it on woven mats to dry in the sun.

It was an idyllic setting, and it filled Sigourney with envy. Why should they be so content with their simple lives, when she was so miserable with hers? She angrily gripped the car's door handle and braced herself against the unannounced bumps in the road. Why was life so unfair?

Sigourney tried to concentrate on her day's itinerary--she planned to attend a familiarization meeting arranged by the tour operator, followed by a visit to the Boudhanath Stupa near Kathmandu, where she hoped to catch a glimpse of Tibetan life before starting her journey--but she couldn't prevent the unwanted images of her personal life from worming their way into her consciousness. One image jostled its way through the others with maddening persistence: a young woman kissing her soon-to-be ex-husband in front of the entire English department at a university Christmas party five years ago. Sigourney had been appalled when the woman approached their table and planted the kiss on Roger's cheek. Her unsteady steps suggested the woman had been drinking, but there was something so familiar about her actions--the way she casually placed her left hand on Roger's shoulder and brushed her index finger along his neck--that Sigourney knew at once there was more between them.

She never suspected Roger of cheating on her until then. Panic overwhelmed her as she watched the woman return to her own table. Marriage had always been Sigourney's safe harbor, a place where she could retreat from life's perils, but that harbor had suddenly been threatened by a storm of uncertainty. She had scolded herself for becoming so distressed over such a small gesture, but she hadn't been able to shake the feeling that the woman was far from innocent.

Sigourney shook her head to rid herself of these unpleasant thoughts and stared at the heavy traffic now forcing her driver to slow his pace as they entered Kathmandu. The streets brimmed with wobbly rickshaws, grimy cars, diesel-belching trucks, zippy scooters and rusty bicycles, all vying for space along the narrow side-streets and two-lane roads. Horns blared as drivers tried to clear a path through the throngs of pedestrians. Sigourney covered her nose with a handkerchief against the acrid smell of diesel fumes and watched an overcrowded bus roar past with people hanging from its gaping doors. She knew the bedlam surrounding her reflected the struggles of a centuries-old culture trying to adapt to the tumultuous forces of the modern world. The result was a tilted landscape filled with animal sacrifices, sacred cows and Coca Cola signs.

By the time she arrived at the operator's office, half a dozen people were milling about inside the meeting room. Whitewashed walls, plastic chairs and a folding table holding a pot of hot water for coffee or tea comprised the room's only furnishings. A lonely map of Nepal hung on the wall near the door. It looked out of place and lost, just like her. Faces peered at Sigourney when she entered. Eyes briefly assessed her and glanced away. She touched the valise hanging from her shoulder and joined the lonely map against the wall. A few people spoke to each other, but she noted two others who appeared to be single travelers like herself: a woman with the delicate features of a song bird, who was taking quick sips of tea from a paper cup, and a man whose boyish face belied the fact that he, like Sigourney, was rushing headlong into middle age. When his eyes met hers, her shoulders tensed and she looked away.

A young man with wild, sandy hair entered the room. He introduced himself as Henri. "I will take you to the Tibetan border in the morning," he announced. "There, you will be met by your guide." He nervously pushed the hair off his forehead, "Let's begin by introducing ourselves. You'll be traveling in close quarters for the next five days, so it is good to get acquainted."

Introductions were brief. The woman with the delicate features identified herself as Marie Rose Gignoux from France. She spoke so softly, Sigourney had to strain to hear her. The boyish-looking man was an Englishman named John Henley. His merry eyes brightened like holiday cheer when he spoke, and his voice resonated with the pleasant tones of a cello. The others included,

Cameron and Beth, an American couple in their fifties, and two younger women, Jenny and Erica, who had just trekked in the Annapurnas. Jenny's pert stature and lively smile made Sigourney think of the cheerleaders she had envied in school. Her audacious charm also reminded Sigourney of the young woman she had watched kissing her husband, and she instantly disliked her.

Henri began reciting a litany of hazards the group would encounter on their journey. The Tibetan plateau was twelve thousand feet high, with five mountain passes ranging between sixteen and seventeen thousand feet. Altitude sickness could become a problem, and everyone was urged to bring medication for such a contingency. The nights were very cold. They would stay in Chinese hotels, but none had heat until Lhasa. They would need warm sleeping clothes, sweaters and jackets. Some of the hotels had no hot water, but a thermos of boiled drinking water would be available at each hotel for washing and shaving.

Sigourney tried to listen to Henri's words, but they were interrupted by memories of an angry conversation with her husband following the incident at the Christmas party.

"Why would she kiss you like that, Roger?" Sigourney demanded. They were in the car on their way home. A fine mist filmed the windshield and transformed the street lights into brightly-lit puffs of cotton candy. Roger kept his eyes fixed on the road, but she could tell from the way he clasped the steering wheel that he was agitated.

"It was just a holiday greeting for Christ's sake. She didn't mean anything by it."

"It looked awfully familiar for a holiday greeting. What's going on with her?" Sigourney tried to remain calm, but her irritation was rising.

"Nothing's going on. Peggy's been in our department since June. We work together. Tonight was no big deal."

Silence blanketed them like a heavy rain as Roger retreated to a place inside himself where Sigourney knew she couldn't reach him. It was his favorite tactic when they argued. He became emotionally absent from her, and Sigourney knew if she didn't say anything more, the silence would expand until it filled not only the car, but the house as well. She regretted her outburst, but more than a kiss had prompted it. Roger's withdrawals always made her feel sexually unattractive, a feeling that was compounded as their intimate times together became fewer and more hurried. She'd tried to talk to him about her emotions, but Roger's silence blocked her. The silence enveloped them.

She returned back to the present. Henri was warning the group to carry dried food to eat during the day and to bring plenty of bottled water. It was easy to become dehydrated at such high altitudes, he said. Seventeen thousand feet! Sigourney had never imagined being so high. The images of Roger were replaced by towering mountains bristling with avalanches and other unknown dangers. Her brief glimpse of the Himalayas had told her the journey wouldn't be easy. She was beginning to understand why.

John Henley was standing nearby, and when he caught her eye, he smiled, "This must be why they refer to travel in Tibet as 'camping in'. Sounds more like a mountain trek, doesn't it?" Sigourney nodded but said nothing. The wedding ring on his left hand was plain to see, and she had little interest in becoming too chummy with a married man.

"Oh one more thing," Henri raised his hand for silence. "The Chinese do not tolerate anyone bringing in pictures of the Dalai Lama or Buddhist artifacts." He looked at each person as he spoke. His eyes lingered on Sigourney. Could he see her guilt? She folded and unfolded her hands, then hid them behind her back. "There will be a police check point after you enter Tibet where luggage will be inspected. They pick pieces at random and search them thoroughly. If they find unwanted contraband, you may be removed from the group and detained. So, please, don't take any chances."

Instinctively, Sigourney looked down and gripped the valise containing the ancient manuscript with both hands. A chill shivered its way down her spine. Should she abort her plans? There was still time. She took a deep breath and sighed. She knew aborting the trip wasn't an option. She had committed herself to this quest, and she expected to see it through.

Glancing up, John Henley was observing her. Something in his dark-brown eyes--perhaps it was the intensity of his gaze--told Sigourney that he had noted her reaction to Henri's warning. She found his gaze discomforting and looked away.

*****

As Sigourney's driver fought his way through the city's suffocating traffic to the Boudhanath Stupa, she thought about Henri's warning. As long as the Chinese only looked through suitcases, she had nothing to worry about, but that didn't stop her heart from beating faster. *What if they wanted to see her valise? What then?*

The driver stopped in a noisy street filled with merchants' shops and pointed to a passageway lined with stalls, indicating the Boudhanath Stupa would be found through there. Street vendors cried out to Sigourney as she walked down the crowded alleyway. They reached out to her, their eager hands holding puppets, prayer wheels and other souvenirs. The raucous voices imprisoned her with their boisterous energy, forcing her to focus on the soiled pavement to keep from spinning off her axis. The odor of spices mixed with sweating bodies assaulted her until she could no longer breathe.

Bursting through the din into the unexpected hush of a large, inner courtyard, she was instantly transported from the frenzy of honking vehicles and urging voices to a place of blissful repose. A small community of Tibetan refugees had settled there, enclosing their sanctuary in a circle of shops and monasteries. The result was a serene enclave unaffected by the noise of the surrounding city.

Dominating the courtyard was a great, whitewashed dome called the Boudhanath Stupa, whose pear-shaped design reminded Sigourney of a rounded pyramid. A pair of mysterious, painted eyes stared down at her with disquieting intensity from the Stupa's peak. They were compelling eyes, and she quickly found herself lost in their hypnotic power. Where had she seen those eyes before? Why were they so memorable? Images of ancestral gods and spirits swirled before her. A world without boundaries beckoned, a world filled with infinite light and peace, and she floated in its aura like a leaf swirling on an autumn breeze. Rhythmic voices of chanting monks drifted through her consciousness, their quiet cadence lulling her into a trance-like state. She wanted to stand there forever.

"Do you know our Buddha?" The soft-spoken question snapped her back to the present, and she turned to find a smiling monk standing behind her. He was dressed in a long, magenta robe, and his hair was cropped so close, he nearly looked bald. Small wrinkles spread in web-like fashion across his sunken cheeks.

"What do you mean?" she asked in a flustered tone. His sudden appearance had startled her, yet she found his smile comforting. His eyes were filled with the same benevolence she had felt radiating down on her from the Stupa.

"You were lost in Buddha's eyes. He came from Nepal, you know."

"A prince, as I recall." Sigourney found the monk's serenity so tranquil it melted the tension in her neck and shoulders like snow in springtime.

"Yes. He grew up in great wealth many centuries before your Christ was born, but when he saw the poverty and suffering of his people, he renounced his claim to the throne and wandered for many years. After much meditation and hardship, he found his enlightenment and began the teachings of Buddhism. We worship him today as Sakyamuni, Buddha of the Present."

"I feel like I've seen those eyes before."

"Perhaps you have. . .in another life."

Sigourney had never thought about living a previous life, but when she considered the idea, it didn't seem so far fetched. *Something* was tugging at her memories. Could it be déjà vu?

Silence embraced them. Sigourney became aware of bells ringing near the courtyard's entrance and sandals scraping on the stone walkway as pilgrims circled the Stupa. She was puzzled by the monk's opening remark about knowing Buddha. She couldn't decide whether his question was meant to be spiritual or historical.

"You are traveling to Tibet?" he suddenly asked. His dark eyes never left her face.

"I leave tomorrow, overland to Lhasa."

"Yes, I thought so. Your journey will be longer than you expect and filled with hardship. Do not let it discourage you." He touched her arm in a familiar fashion, then lifted his robes and walked away.

The monk's voice echoed in her mind while she watched him disappear into a nearby monastery. She was mystified by his comment and his familiarity with her. It was as if he knew about her journey. A silly thought, she realized, but she couldn't shake the idea that he had just shared a secret. It must be nerves, she decided. The muscles in her neck had been taut all day with uncertainty about what lay before her. She rotated her head to relieve the tension that was starting to build again. The calming influences of the Stupa helped. Her body relaxed as she sensed the healing powers of Buddha's eyes wafting over her.

She turned her attention back to the whitewashed dome. Sigourney remembered an article about the importance of stupas in Tibet. They were often built in memory of a great lama or to ward off evil spirits in dangerous places, such as mountain passes. A shadow briefly crossed her face, causing her shoulders to quiver involuntarily, but when she looked up, the sky was clear. Surely there were no evil spirits around the Stupa, she thought, but she couldn't help wondering about the journey that lay ahead. The muscles in her neck tightened again.

She glanced towards a row of prayer wheels shaped like large canisters that were being turned by worshippers along a wall at the Stupa's base. Sigourney knew Tibetans believed turning the wheels released prayers into the air, spreading peace and harmony throughout the world. Colored prayer flags streaming down from the top of the Stupa also sent similar prayers fluttering on the afternoon's breezes. She turned her face towards the flags and closed her eyes, welcoming the prayers' therapeutic messages.

Unlike Nepal's Hindus, who worshipped a maddening variety of major and lesser gods, she knew Buddhists spent their lives striving to rid themselves of earthly desires in order to achieve true enlightenment, called Nirvana, a spiritual level of purity and wisdom that ended all pain and suffering. Anne Hopkins, whose diary she carried, had been a Buddhist, and Nirvana had been one of her goals when she slipped into Tibet one hundred years ago. Reaching the holy city of Lhasa had been part of her effort to achieve true enlightenment. Now, Sigourney was about to follow in her footsteps. Perhaps enlightenment awaited her in Lhasa, as well.

"This is a pleasant surprise."

Sigourney jumped at the unexpected voice. She'd been so wrapped up in her thoughts she hadn't noticed John Henley enter the courtyard. I'm a bundle of nerves, she thought.

"Looks like we're both searching for a bit of enlightenment before beginning our trip. Quite impressive isn't it?" He nodded towards the Stupa.

"Very." She cautiously returned his cheerful smile. Being so close to another man, especially a married one, put her on edge. It sparked unhappy memories of Roger. John's manner was quite disarming, however, and she realized there was no reason to react with hostility.

He pointed to several Tibetans circling the Stupa's base in a clock-wise direction. "They're circumambulating the Stupa to pray and receive blessings. I thought I would walk with them a little. Care to join me?"

Sigourney fell in step beside him. She couldn't help assessing him as they walked. Sigourney was just under six feet, but John Henley stood half-a-head taller. He had the kind of build--broad shoulders and sturdy legs--that suggested athletics had been part of his life, although his stomach was starting to show the signs of too much rich food and a less rigorous lifestyle. His hair was still dark but thinning, indicating another concession to the aging process. She estimated him to be in his forties, but his baby-smooth skin and vague good looks made it difficult to be more specific. He could be forty or fifty, which made her jealous. She knew she looked every bit of her forty-three years.

The sounds of spinning prayer wheels and mumbling voices surrounded her. Clothing whispered across the stone pavement as worshippers prostrated themselves on the ground. Everywhere Sigourney looked, she saw images of a timeless culture which thrived in the middle of Kathmandu's traffic choked streets.

"It's like a microcosm of Tibet, is it not?" John seemed to be reading her thoughts.

"Yes. I'm glad I came."

As they walked, a woman fell in stride beside Sigourney and began speaking in her native Tibetan tongue. Sigourney smiled and shook her head to indicate she didn't understand. The woman persisted. Sigourney tried to step away, but a man joined them and touched the valise hanging from her shoulder. The distant sound of chanting monks echoed in her ears, and she looked around to find their source. The chanting faded. More people gathered, smiling and talking to her as they reached out to touch the valise. John raised his eyebrows in surprise and stopped, leaving her surrounded by the jabbering Tibetans. Hands brushed her blouse. Hot, moist bodies pressed against her, robbing her of the air she needed to breathe. Her underarms were growing uncomfortably sticky. Everywhere she turned, weathered faces confronted her. Eyes sparkled. Lips moved. But, she could no longer hear them over the roaring in her ears.

Sigourney threw out her hands to fend off the Tibetans and pushed through the crowd. Free of them, she rushed back to the entrance, abandoning the Stupa and returning to the babble of the surrounding streets, where her driver waited.

She plunged into the car and sat in a daze, trying to sort through a tangle of emotions while watching the crush of humanity moving past her. What had those Tibetans wanted? Why had they surrounded her like that and touched the valise? They *knew* she carried something spiritual, and they wanted to feel its power. It had been the same with the priest. He hadn't touched her bag, but he'd known she was more than just a tourist. His departing words had spoken of hardship. Henri had warned her, as well. And what about the Tibetans? Were they warning her? Everybody seemed to understand the magnitude of her journey. Everyone but her!

You can still turn tail and run, she chided herself. If you're so afraid, why bother? No one will blame you if you go home. No one, but yourself.

Fingers raked through her hair in exasperation. She couldn't fail in her quest for lack of trying. That would mean failing both the Tibetan people and herself, which was an unacceptable option. Her journey had become more than a quest to return an ancient manuscript. It had become a quest to save herself, and she couldn't do that if she gave up.

Sigourney remembered John Henley's bemused expression when the Tibetans surrounded her, and she realized how foolish she must have looked fleeing the courtyard without saying a word to him. She had not only been silly, but impolite. It was an inauspicious way to begin her journey.

CHAPTER TWO

Sigourney had never believed in "fate," or in a pivotal moment defining one's life, but she would look back on the night her fifteen-year-old daughter, Debbie, failed to come home and realize that fate *had* intervened in her life. What else but fate would have the power to draw her to Tibet and change her life forever?

She had sat up that entire night worrying about her daughter and dueling with her guilt at not being an adequate mother. The past six months had been terrible ones for Sigourney, beginning when she discovered that her husband, Roger, was having an affair with one of his students, and she threw him out. What grand theater that had been for the neighbors! Clothing and suitcases strewn across the front lawn where she had tossed them. And in broad daylight, no less. She had never done anything so public in her life.

At first, she had resisted initiating divorce proceedings, hoping their relationship could somehow be salvaged. She knew she was in denial, but she couldn't help it. Divorce was such an ugly word, filled with arguments over property and blame. With divorce, there was no turning back. In the end, Roger moved in with his girlfriend and filed for divorce himself.

Debbie had always been a well-behaved child, but now she was mutating into a teenage devil incarnate. She sulked at home and stayed in her room behind a closed door, no longer sharing her day or talking about school. On two occasions, Sigourney had caught her lying about where she had been after school. Her grades were falling off the cliff, and she was sneaking out at night, often leaving the front door unlocked so she could return undetected. Last night, she had failed to come home at all. Sigourney had tried to reason with her, to acknowledge the pain they were both feeling, but she could no longer ignore Debbie's behavior. The time had come to confront her daughter

Morning sunlight had just broken through a layer of clouds that smelled of snow when Debbie slipped into the house. Sigourney sat at the kitchen table with a cup of cold coffee in her hands. She had spent a sleepless night listening to the wind slapping at the house's wood siding, and she was in no mood for the alibi her daughter used in her defense.

"What makes you think you can just disappear when you please?" Sigourney shouted as she rose from her chair. Her relief at seeing Debbie safe and unharmed was quickly overwhelmed by anger.

"I stayed at a friend's house." Debbie tried to sound confident, but her eyes slid away from Sigourney's accusing glare. Her tangled, blond hair reminded Sigourney of a bird's nest they had once found in the back yard. There had been two eggs in the nest, and Debbie had squealed with five-year-old delight at the discovery. She had been such a sunny child. Where had she gone? Who was this unkempt girl in stained jeans and smelly sweatshirt?

"That's not an acceptable answer, and you know it." Sigourney gripped the coffee cup with both hands in an effort to control herself, but her daughter's evasive behavior made every vein stand out in her neck. Her fury rose in hot waves.

"It's not like you care, anyway." Debbie retreated two steps and threw a long look at her mother. Her voice remained defiant, but the frown on her face showed that she was worried.

"Of course I care." Sigourney slammed the cup down, spilling cold coffee on the kitchen table. It ran in a tiny stream across the vinyl surface and dribbled over the edge, but Sigourney was too upset to stop it. Despite her desire to quell the rage boiling inside of her, frustration got the upper hand. "Do you think I would have sat up all night if I didn't care? Don't you blame me for your behavior, young lady. And don't ever pull a stunt like this again." Sigourney pointed an accusing finger at her daughter. "You're grounded until you give me a satisfactory answer about where you've been."

Debbie responded by bursting into tears, racing up the stairs to her room, and slamming the door hard enough to disturb two of the family photos hanging on the hallway wall. Sigourney absentmindedly straightened them with a shaking hand while she followed Debbie up the stairs and headed for her own bedroom. It was an ironic gesture. She had never worried about crooked picture frames or a little clutter around the house. Roger had been the one who was obsessed about cleanliness. Sigourney used to joke about her husband's meticulous nature, how he returned every item to its proper place and closed every closet door. Living with Roger had been like continuously preparing for an open house. Half the time, she'd expected to see a gaggle of real estate agents trouping up the walkway. Now that Roger was gone, the house was sliding into a less tidy relationship with its occupants, not unlike the growing discord between mother and daughter.

Sigourney was putting on her makeup when the sharp ring of the telephone jarred her from her thoughts. She glanced at the clock. Five after nine. She had a ten o'clock department meeting at the university and was tempted to let the answering machine take a message, but she worried that the call might pertain to Debbie's absence last night. She hurried to the night stand and picked up the phone.

"May I speak to Sigourney Phillips please?" The voice was formal and impersonal.

"This is Mrs. Phillips." God, why did she still use her married name?

"Mrs. Phillips, I'm Ed Townsend of Clark, Townsend and Reed. We are the attorneys representing Martha Winter's estate. I believe you knew Miss Winters?"

Sigourney sighed with relief when she realized the call wasn't about Debbie, and then grimaced with guilt at her reaction. Martha Winters had been a fellow faculty member at the university and a friend. She had died several months ago of cancer.

"I knew Martha, yes. What's this about?" She frowned, mystified that anyone would be calling her about Martha's estate.

"We've discovered a codicil to her will. Something she wrote very recently to modify the will. It was kept in a safe deposit box that was just opened. It names you as the beneficiary."

Sigourney sat down on the edge of the bed in disbelief. Martha had been an introverted woman, at least ten years older than Sigourney, and totally absorbed in her work as an anthropologist. They had sat on two university committees together and become friends, often meeting for coffee between classes. Their friendship had rarely extended beyond the campus, however, and Martha had never broached the subject of her will or estate.

"I'm not certain I understand what you're saying, Mr. Townsend. Martha wouldn't have left anything to me."

"There was a manuscript in the safe deposit box along with the codicil. It looks very old. Martha Winters left firm instructions that no one should open the manuscript but you. It's leather bound and locked. We found a key that appears to fit the lock."

"Appears. . .?" Sigourney was back on her feet, pacing the room. What was this man talking about? How could this possibly pertain to her?

"We haven't tried the key. Frankly, it's the strangest looking thing any of us has ever seen, but it seems to belong to the lock." Mr. Townsend sounded mystified, as well.

"Martha never mentioned a manuscript to me. Look, I'm sure there's been some misunderstanding." She fiddled with the phone's cord, twisting it around her index finger. She had intended to get a cordless phone but had never gotten around to it. Debbie used to laugh about the old phone and accuse her of living in the dark ages. Sigourney's mind flitted back and forth between her daughter and the strange phone call. What was she going to do about Debbie?

"No, the instructions are quite clear. I'm calling to make arrangements for you to pick it up at our offices. You'll need to provide us with a notarized document proving your identity. We have a notary on our staff, if you want to do that here."

Sigourney returned her attention to the caller. She sighed and sat down on the bed again. What could Martha have been thinking, willing something to her without so much as a peep? Did it have something to do with Sigourney's research? There was only one way to find out. She made an appointment to visit the law firm on Wednesday morning at ten.

She thought about Martha--a severe woman who always kept her gray hair pulled back off her forehead--while she flipped through the clothes in her closet, trying to decide what to wear. Their mutual interest had always been their work. Martha had done a great deal of research on the cultures in and around China, including Tibet, Bhutan and the other Himalayan countries. She had been particularly upset about China's invasion of Tibet in the 1950s. "A bunch of opportunists, that's all the Chinese were." Sigourney could picture Martha's lower lip trembling as she spoke. "Mao Tse Tung knew the world didn't care two cents about Tibet. He marched in and destroyed an ancient society, just so he could claim more land." Sigourney knew very little about the region, but as a historian, found Martha's spirited discussions fascinating.

When Martha started experiencing nose bleeds and a loss of energy, Sigourney had urged her to see a doctor. They had both been shocked by the diagnosis. Martha was told she had mesothelioma, an incurable form of cancer caused by exposure to asbestos. Martha had no idea where she might have encountered the substance, but that no longer mattered. She had only a few months to live.

They had met for coffee three more times before she left the university. Sigourney recalled their final conversation on a gray, wintry day in the university cafeteria.

"Do you believe in a hereafter?" Martha asked. She sagged in her chair, a defeated woman. Her skin had a pasty cast that made her look bedridden. Unruly strands of hair burst forth from her hairdo in uncharacteristic disarray, spilling about her moist forehead. She swatted the hair away with a quick, nervous hand.

"I'm not sure," Sigourney replied cautiously. She didn't want to say something that would upset her colleague. "You know I'm not religious."

"An afterlife doesn't need religion. Just faith."

"Yes, faith. I suppose that should be sufficient." Sigourney watched her friend sip her coffee. Steam wafted from Martha's cup and brushed her pale cheeks, enticing a slight, rosy blush to blossom in her skin. The unruly hair slipped back onto her forehead, and Martha swatted it away again.

"Yesterday, I discovered my great grandmother's diary. What a shock to find it after so many years! I plan to read it while I'm dying. She was a Buddhist, you know."

Sigourney squirmed uncomfortably at such blunt talk about dying. She knew nothing about Martha's great grandmother. Martha had never mentioned her before.

"She spent years preparing herself for a new life after death, a better life," Martha continued. "I wonder if she found it. She was an Englishwoman. Quite an eccentric, I'm told. Quite an adventurer. Anyway, I've given quite a bit of thought to the matter. . .to dying." Martha sat up straighter. Her expression grew more animated. "I never considered an afterlife as very realistic, but after finding my grandmother's diary, it makes me wonder."

Sigourney smiled in sympathy and took her friend's hand. She had never touched Martha before. Her skin was as dry as parchment and colder than she expected. Was this what it felt like to touch death? Sigourney was relieved when Martha pulled her hand away.

People suddenly began shouting around them, and Sigourney looked up in time to see a white dove swooping over their heads. It circled the room, frantically searching for a way to escape the strange voices and unfamiliar surroundings. Finally, it flew towards the light, only to bang into a window and fall to the floor. A physics professor scooped up the bewildered bird and carried it to the door, where it regained its balance and flew away. The professor made a remark about defying the laws of physics, and everyone laughed.

That was the last time Sigourney saw her colleague. Martha left the university a few days later and refused visitors. She disappeared from the world much as she had lived in it, alone.

Martha had mentioned her great grandmother's diary but said nothing about an old manuscript, and Sigourney still couldn't imagine why Martha had left it to her. Well, it would have to wait until Wednesday, when she could visit the law firm.

There were more immediate issues to contend with than Martha's will, including Debbie's disappearing act. Sigourney didn't know how much her daughter's current behavior was a reaction to her father leaving the house and how much was simply the process of becoming a full-fledged teenager. She suspected it was a combination of both, but knowing that didn't help. She had always relied on Roger to perform the role of enforcer in the house. With him gone, she was at a loss.

Sigourney picked a beige dress from the closet and began a hurried search for a pair of matching shoes. Where were they? At last, she found them hiding behind an empty shoe box. Pulling on her dress, she looked at the cluttered closet and thought about her life. One was a microcosm of the other, she decided. Both were out of control.

Debbie had doted on her father, but Sigourney had always felt close enough to discuss personal problems with her. Close enough to share feelings, if not secrets. She had believed it to be a healthy relationship. Now, she was no longer so certain. Talking didn't work any more. Talking led to shouting, and she knew that wouldn't solve anything.

Sigourney sighed again as she slipped on her shoes. She seemed to be doing a lot of that lately.

There was no point in trying to make Debbie go to school today. She was probably dead to the world by now. Sigourney continued to worry about the erosion of her relationship with her daughter. The unexpected phone call had already put her behind schedule, and she had two classes in the afternoon. Sigourney was going to have to face her day with or without an adequate night's rest. But what should she do about Debbie? The school employed a part-time psychologist. Perhaps, she could talk to him and get some help, or at least some sense of direction. Sigourney decided to call the school and try to get an appointment Wednesday morning before going to the law firm.

Her thoughts returned to Martha and how worked up she had gotten about an afterlife when she discovered her great grandmother's diary. But why had she suddenly decided to add that codicil to her will? There had to be a connection between the diary and manuscript, something Martha discovered after she'd left the university. The mystery was so intriguing, and Sigourney found herself looking forward to her meeting at the lawyers' office on Wednesday.

A blustery wind rattled the loose gutter Roger never found time to fix. The wind whispered against the bedroom window pane, and for one insane moment, Sigourney thought she heard a voice breathing her name. It was a woman's voice but not Martha's. I'm going mad, she thought. The wind pushed against the gutter again, but the voice was gone.

CHAPTER THREE

Sigourney sat with her daughter in the school psychologist's waiting room. It had taken a monumental effort to get Debbie there, but she had finally relented. She glanced at her watch. Nine was the only time she could get on such short notice, and it didn't leave Sigourney much time to make her ten o'clock appointment at Martha's law firm. She looked with dismay at her daughter, who slouched in a chair on the far side of the room. Debbie used to be meticulous in her appearance, like her father. Now, she sat in a rumpled heap of torn jeans and a discolored sweater. Her usually lovely hair spilled about her in unwashed disarray. No lipstick or other make-up brightened her sullen face. Sigourney knew she hadn't bathed that morning, but that wasn't a battle she'd been prepared to fight after their argument about seeing the school "shrink," as Debbie called him.

The psychologist, Dr. Bowen, finally appeared, sporting a gray beard, a thinning hairline and a neutral smile. He asked to speak to Debbie first, and Sigourney was left to fidget in the waiting room, wondering what her daughter was saying about her and watching the clock sprint past 9:15. Getting to her ten o'clock appointment on time didn't look promising, but she no longer cared. She was too worried about Debbie. Sigourney was about to ask the secretary if she could use the telephone to cancel the appointment when Dr. Bowen stuck his head out and asked Sigourney to join them in his office.

"So," he began after Sigourney and Debbie were seated side-by-side across the desk from him. "I understand there've been some significant changes in your lives recently. Mrs. Phillips, would you care to comment on them?" He leaned back in his chair and stared thoughtfully at Sigourney.

"If you mean my husband, we're getting divorced. He moved out six months ago." *Divorce.* There was that word again. It sounded so ugly when she said it out loud.

"He didn't *move* out. You *threw* him out. You told him to go away." Debbie stared at her feet, avoiding eye contact with either adult in the room.

"Debbie, we've had this conversation before," Sigourney couldn't control the anger in her voice. She wanted to remain calm, but the sting in her daughter's words brought tears to her eyes, and anger was the only way to hide them. She leaned forward. "You know your father wants to live with someone else. He doesn't love me anymore."

"How can you love someone who tells you to leave? It's not his fault, you know. You're the one who told him to go away." She looked at her mother with tear-streaked, accusing eyes. Her cheeks puffed in and out with each breath. "If you hadn't made him go, we'd still be a family."

"Debbie," Dr. Bowen interrupted quietly, "do you think your recent behavior has something to do with your anger towards your parents?"

"Not Dad. I'm not angry at Dad. I just don't want to be here any more. I want to live with my father." Debbie blurted this out as if it were a confession.

The words slammed into Sigourney with greater force than when she first realized she'd lost Roger. She reeled back in her chair and stared at her daughter, trying to make sense of what she'd just heard. Debbie stared down at her shoes and hunched her shoulders, withdrawing from the world and her mother.

Dr. Bowen broke the awkward silence. "It's natural to want to blame someone when parents separate, Debbie, but you mustn't do that. Your mother and father both love you. They just can't live together any more. No one person is at fault, least of all, you."

He glanced at his watch and nodded to Debbie. "Why don't you go to your ten o'clock class? I'll finish up with your mother."

Sigourney was dismayed to see it was already a quarter to ten, but she didn't want the meeting to end without some closure with her daughter. "Debbie, are you going to attend your classes today?" She tried to grasp her daughter's hand, willing Debbie to show some sign of affection.

Debbie pulled away and didn't answer.

"We discussed that before you came in, Mrs. Phillips. Debbie has promised to return to school while we sort things out, haven't you Debbie?"

A brief nod was Debbie's only response as she stood up and tromped from the room.

Dr. Bowen sat back in his chair and fiddled with a letter opener on the desk. A heavy silence blanketed the room. Sigourney could hear voices beyond the closed door, but they seemed miles away. The wounds from Debbie's words tormented her.

"Mrs. Phillips," Dr. Bowen said at last, "Debbie has very deep feelings of guilt about her father leaving. She blames you, but deep inside she's also blaming herself. Frankly, I think the other woman's young age has a lot to do with what she's feeling. It's very possible she thinks the woman is replacing her, not you. It's too soon to draw any conclusions, but I believe she's more troubled about *her* role in her father leaving than your role. And if she misbehaves enough, you'll send her to her father."

Dr. Bowen's voice sounded as if he was talking from the other end of a long tunnel. Sigourney pulled a handkerchief from her purse and dabbed at the tears which had finally escaped. "What do I do about it?"

"Sometimes the best medicine is the opposite of what one expects. 'Be careful what you wish for,' so to speak. I would recommend letting Debbie stay with her father for a little while. She's romanticized what it would be like in her mind. Reality will almost certainly be quite different. Give her a dose of that reality."

Sigourney flinched at the words raining down on her. Turn Debbie over to Roger? The idea was too absurd to even consider. She pressed her lips together and glared at the man, aware of the growing silence between them. Dr. Bowen leaned back and waited.

"You can't be serious," she finally responded in an even tone that belied the indignation seething inside of her. "Just give Debbie away? Hand her over like a piece of furniture? I think not!"

"I know it isn't easy to consider my suggestion, but it's not as crazy as it sounds." Dr. Bowen put down the letter opener and folded his hands across his stomach. "You wouldn't be giving Debbie away. It would only be for a limited period, say a month. Long enough for Debbie to realize she truly misses you, and that Mr. Phillip's new girl friend is not a substitute for her."

"And if she doesn't miss me?" Sigourney's heart fluttered unevenly, skipping beats and racing too fast. I'm going to have a heart attack, she thought wildly.

"Oh, she will. Don't worry about that. You must be patient. Anger is healthy, but you need to avoid confrontations right now." He smiled and stood up. "Please give it some thought. Discuss it with your ex-husband. In the meantime, we need to continue exploring these issues. I suggest another session next week. You can set a date with my secretary."

Sigourney stumbled from the office. Her feet felt like swollen tree stumps that she had to drag down the hall. She stared at the worn linoleum floor and tried to think what to do. Dr. Bowen's proposal seemed callous and unfair. It wasn't her fault that Roger had abandoned the family, yet Bowen was suggesting he be rewarded with temporary custody of their daughter! If he got his hands on her, would he give her back? Would he try to keep her?

Sigourney grimaced as she pictured nightmarish court scenes and lawyers battling over custody rights, but a tiny voice kept whispering in her ear that the idea wasn't so far fetched. She *had* lost control of Debbie. It didn't matter who was to blame. Perhaps a change, a brief one, would clear the air between them. The idea was so repugnant Sigourney wanted to scream, but Debbie's behavior was making her desperate. She would do anything if it helped.

Sigourney looked at a wall clock and blinked in disbelief. It was 10:15. A quarter hour had disappeared while she stood there arguing with herself. It was only a small amount of time, but it unnerved her to realize she had no idea where it had gone. Looking around, she spotted a pay phone. She would have to call Martha's law firm and reschedule.

"Mr. Townsend has gone into a meeting, but he would like to settle things as soon as possible." The voice sounded cool and professional, the opposite of how Sigourney felt. "If you come now, his assistant should be able to execute the documents with you."

Visiting the law firm wouldn't be so bad she supposed. It would take her mind off her worries, and she *was* curious about Martha's last-minute codicil and the manuscript. She was put on hold while the receptionist checked with Mr. Townsend's assistant. The cool voice returned to the line. Yes, she was available. Could Sigourney please come right away? She hurried to her car and joined the traffic making its way downtown.

The law firm of Clark, Townsend and Reed was in another league from Sigourney's divorce lawyer, whose tiny offices were crammed into a small building in one of the city's respectable but unpretentious suburbs. This outfit commanded the top floor of a new, high-rise building. She was ushered into a plush conference room, and joined by the notary public. Once the formalities were finished, a woman in her late twenties entered carrying a cardboard box that reminded Sigourney of a small pizza container.

"Mrs. Phillips, you'll need to sign these papers. After that you may take the referenced materials."

Sigourney couldn't keep her eyes off the box while she signed the documents. Curiosity had the upper hand, now, and she was anxious to see what Martha had found so noteworthy. "May I have a few minutes to look at them here?"

"Yes. Just notify the receptionist when you're finished." The woman closed the door on her way out, leaving Sigourney alone with the box containing the mysterious manuscript.

She carefully lifted the lid and stared at the tome inside. She had never seen anything like it. The manuscript's leather cover was so cracked and discolored, that she was reluctant to touch it. She lifted it from the box, and found it surprisingly solid in her hands. A musty odor rose from its surface. Sigourney had smelled similar odors when researching old texts. It spoke of a long journey through time. A solid strap attached to a bizarre-looking lock prevented her from opening the manuscript. She could see why Mr. Townsend was so intrigued by the lock. It was shaped like a small, brass box with a single slit along its edge. Leaf-shaped designs had been etched into its badly gouged surface, and a wax build-up partly obscured the images. Laying the manuscript on the table, she found the key, which consisted of a flat, rectangular piece of metal with an extension at one end forming the letter E. Lines were etched in its surface, as well, which reminded Sigourney of birds' feet imprinted in the sand. Her hand quivered as she slipped the key into the lock's opening and tried to figure out how to work the mechanism. At first, the key refused to turn, but after considerable jiggling, a rod popped out and the clasp was released.

The binding squeaked with age as she lifted the cover and stared at the first page. She saw hand-inscribed letters on yellowed parchment paper that looked older than time itself. She caressed the brittle surface of the parchment but jerked her hand away when she heard a rumbling noise that sounded like chanting voices. Her heart skipped and raced just as it had in Dr. Bowen's office. Was it her imagination? Something was there. If not voices, then a premonition that some spiritual force lay within the manuscript.

A white, #10 envelope nestled against the binding like an object from an alien world. She opened it and found a letter written in Martha's familiar, chaotic style. There was also another key, a modern one.

To my friend and associate, Sigourney:

Forgive me for being so secretive, but this letter and manuscript are for your eyes only. The manuscript recently came into my possession, which prompted me to add a codicil to my will. There are other items hidden in a safe deposit box at a bank nobody knows about. I have included the key and a pre-signed entry slip with this letter, and I have left instructions at the bank so you can have access. Just show your I.D., and you will be "in like Flynn," as they say.

By now, you must think me daft, so let me explain myself. Remember I mentioned the diary of my great grandmother, Anne Hopkins, the last time I saw you? I told you she was quite the adventurer. She wrote the diary while trekking into Tibet one hundred years ago. Great grandmother was a devout Buddhist, and she was trying to reach Lhasa in hopes of achieving Nirvana, which represents ever lasting peace to the Buddhists. Kind of like our going to heaven. I never believed in such things, but now I am no longer so sure.

My aunt rediscovered the diary while cleaning out the attic. I had been told stories about her exploits of course, but I still read the diary with amazement. It was filled with descriptions of danger and hardship that were beyond my imagination. But that is not why I added the codicil. As I read, my great grandmother began conversing with me! I was so hysterical, I wanted to flee my bed. I thought I was dead and her spirit had come for me.

Once I realized I wasn't crazy, I began listening to her. She told me about the manuscript you see before you. She was visiting one of the oldest monasteries in Tibet, when she learned the manuscript was about to be destroyed, and she was the only person who could save it. She took it and ran. Well, I suppose "ran" is too strong a verb. She trekked out of Tibet into Bhutan and brought it back to England. The manuscript sets down some of the original teachings of Buddha when Buddhism was first established in Tibet.

That would have been sometime in the 8th century! Can you imagine? I was devastated to find it had been in our family all those years, and I only learned about it, now.

My family did not have much interest in such things. They never thought about its importance to the Tibetans. It was just an odd relic that was stored away and forgotten. I asked my aunt to look for it. She found it at the bottom of a musty chest full of old clothes and other memorabilia that hadn't been opened in forty years.

Now that the manuscript has been found, great grandmother tells me it must be returned to the Tibetan monastery by you! I couldn't believe my ears. She said your spirit is linked with hers, and she needs your help. Once you complete your quest (her words), she will achieve Nirvana, and you will gain the peace and happiness you think you've lost.

I know your first reaction will be to ignore this letter as the ramblings of a dying woman. But I am not crazy! Just read the opening page of the diary. It will tell you everything. You will find it along with further instructions in the safe deposit box at the bank. Her request rests in your capable hands.

Your friend,
Martha

Sigourney stared at the letter in confusion. It was filled with such strange words. Spirits and quests. She felt compelled to read it again, just to make sense of it. *Was* Martha of sound mind when she wrote it? Claiming to hear voices was bad enough, but telling Sigourney she was somehow linked to Martha's great grandmother was more than she could swallow. Such a bizarre story argued for alerting the attorneys. Sigourney had no business getting involved in Martha's affairs if she was going "daft." There was also the issue of the secret safe deposit box. The key in question was taped to an authorization slip. She would have no trouble accessing the box, but doing so would circumvent the law. Her instincts told her to turn the whole matter over to Mr. Townsend and let Martha's heirs deal with her great grandmother's wishes.

But when she rose to summon Mr. Townsend's assistant, her hand brushed against the manuscript, and monk voices peeled in her head like church bells. She gasped and sat back down. Her hand burned as if touched by a flame. What was the matter with her? Was she hearing voices, too? *Now, I'm acting hysterical.* She took deep breaths to calm herself.

Sigourney stared at the law books against the far wall and tried to decide what to do. Martha had never been a flighty person. If anything, she'd always been too straight-laced in her conduct and too literal in her views. She was perfectly sane the last time Sigourney saw her, and there was no reason to believe she had been otherwise when she died. Besides, something was going on with the manuscript. Her skin crawled, just thinking about the voices she'd heard.

Martha wanted her to look at the diary, and she supposed it would do no harm. She could still turn everything over to Martha's lawyers, if she felt the need to. But there was an underlying current running through Martha's letter that told her the manuscript and Anne Hopkins' story might be more than small incidents lost in the backwaters of history. She sensed a vein of historical gold waiting to be discovered in those old documents, and while she knew it would be awkward to leave the country at that moment, her pulse rate rose at the thought of what she might unearth. She'd had these instincts before, and they had often led her to important discoveries.

Sigourney stood up, wrapped her arms around her precious package and nodded to the receptionist on her way out. She had set the morning aside to learn what Martha wanted, and the bank with the safe deposit box was nearby. It would take only a few minutes to find out if her intuition was right or wrong.

*****

Sigourney sat in one of the bank's cubicles with a metal box in front of her. When she lifted its lid, she discovered a small, leather-bound book with an envelope lying on top. The diary! She started to reach for it, but decided to open the envelope first. She was shocked to find a stack of fifty, one-hundred-dollar bills inside. Five thousand dollars! She dropped the money on the table, then quickly stuffed it back inside the envelope. What was she supposed to do with so much money? There was a note inside, and she recognized Martha's familiar handwriting scrawled across a single piece of paper.

Hi Sigourney:
Thank you for doing as I asked. You cannot imagine how grateful I am. Great grandmother says the future of Tibetan Buddhism may depend on you completing this quest. You know the Chinese government is trying to undermine Tibet's culture and its deep ties to Buddhism. This manuscript is terribly important to the Tibetans in their struggle against China's increasing influence over their country. She asks you to read the opening page of her diary. Please do so before continuing with my letter.

Sigourney picked up the diary with trembling hands and opened the cover. She stared at the inscription.

My Quest for Nirvana: A Journey to Lhasa
By Anne Hopkins 1899

The date struck her as odd. It meant the diary was one hundred years old, but that wasn't what bothered her. Sigourney could feel her pulse rising again. There was something about the year that tugged at her, but she couldn't put her finger on it. She read the opening page.

I am writing this first entry before my trip begins. How great are my expectations and fears for the journey I am about to undertake! I do not know why, but I sense something of great importance will occur. My karma tells me I shall be tested in a strange way.

I consider myself a modern woman free of the superstitions that afflict so many females in my society, but I could not resist the temptation to visit a "seer" to learn more about my anxious feelings. She was much younger than I expected, not past her middle thirties, and quite pretty with her raven hair and dark, Arabian skin. She told me something strange. She said I would perform a great deed, but my reward would go unfulfilled for three generations, and would only come about when my future karma, in the form of a woman, completed the circle I had started. What devilish words! I wanted to rush from the place at once and ignore her foretelling, but I was drawn into her web like a fly to a spider.

Tell me more, I demanded. She laughed and took my hand. Do not crowd your fate, she said. Give it freedom, or it will become unbalanced and dangerous. Is there nothing more you can say, I asked? The woman's black pupils narrowed until she appeared cross-eyed. Her head began to shake, and I thought she was having a fit. Her shaking subsided, however, and she looked at me normally again. You had a daughter named Serenity, she said. She will come to you again in your future in the guise of a white bird. She will show you the woman who is destined to complete your circle of life. You must recognize this woman and ask for her help. Otherwise, you shall walk the earth forever without achieving your goal. The woman will need your help, as well. She will have a daughter whom she fears losing but can find again by helping you fulfill your destiny. Be ready for her when she comes. Your fates are intertwined.

I left the establishment badly shaken. The seer's words were nearly too much for me, and I regretted going to that stupid woman. She is most certainly a charlatan. They all are. But, how did she know my daughter's name? And, she spoke of her in the past tense, which meant she knew Serenity was dead. I thought about canceling my trip but quickly scolded myself for acting like a silly woman in need of smelling salts.

Whatever lies ahead is part of my karma, and I shall be ready for it.

Sigourney stared at the page, trying to make sense of it, but the words blurred until she could no longer read them. What was this woman saying? That Sigourney was the spirit of Anne Hopkins? What utter nonsense! She slammed the cover shut and banged the book down on the table. *Someone is playing a cruel hoax on me.* She studied the manuscript's binding with suspicion but could find no evidence of tampering. She knew enough about old books to believe it was genuine, and that the page she'd just read hadn't been inserted recently. If it was a hoax, it was one played long ago. She rubbed the backs of her hands to calm herself and returned her attention to Martha's letter.

Remember the white dove in the cafeteria, Sigourney? Great grandmother says it was Serenity coming for you. It all fits, don't you see? Your problems with Debbie, the white bird, and the fact that I am third generation. Now, you know why I am asking you to undertake this quest. It is your fate, your karma, just as it is mine to die before knowing the outcome. Learning about my great grandmother and the link between her spirit and yours has given me great solace. It has given me faith in an afterlife. You told me once that you had lost faith in your own life because of Roger. I believe this quest is your chance to find that faith again, just as I have found mine.

The money in the envelope will cover your traveling expenses to Tibet. One last request. Great grandmother asks that you not read any more of her diary before you leave. She wants you to read it during your trip. Sort of like traveling with her, I suppose. Oh, I nearly forgot the most important thing. You must return the manuscript to the Samye Monastery, which is near Tibet's capital, Lhasa. Great grandmother stressed that no one else should see it, not even the monks in the other monasteries. She said there are too many spies. Also, you must go overland. It is too risky trying to smuggle the manuscript in by air. If the Chinese discover it, they will destroy it. Join a tour group out of Kathmandu in Nepal. That will be much safer.

Good luck. I hope we will meet again in another life.
Martha.

Smuggle. Spies. Risky. These were barbaric words that leapt off the page like snarling beasts. Sigourney stood up, nearly tipping over her chair, ready to march straight back to Clark, Townsend and Reed. Martha was asking too much, rambling on about spirits and voices from the past, and asking Sigourney to put herself at risk. When she put her hand on the diary, however, it felt warm to her touch. Holding the diary stirred something in her, just as the manuscript had when she first examined it. She stared at the inscription, and her impulse to return to the law firm vanished. She needed time to digest what she had just read. She needed to sit down with a cup of strong coffee in her kitchen and sort things out.

Sigourney hated to admit it, but leaving the bank, she found herself wondering what the weather was like in Tibet that time of year.

Sitting in her kitchen nook, she slowly turned the pages of the manuscript. It smelled like moldy cheese and felt dry to her touch, attesting to its years in hiding. Was the manuscript really part of Buddha's original scriptures? She could feel the history of a thousand years pulsating beneath her finger tips. The parchment crackled with age, and at first she feared the pages might crumble at her touch. A silly thought, she realized. The binding was firm and the pages sturdy. It had been handled with great care during its long journey through history. Sigourney knew there must be quite a story behind its rescue, and she was tempted to open the diary to learn what had happened. It would be easy to rationalize doing so, but that would violate Martha's trust. She left the diary closed.

Her field of expertise was European history from the 1300's through the 1500's, including the social and religious revolutions of those periods, and the Florentine and Roman renaissances that followed. That was long before Anne Hopkins' time. Sigourney knew very little about English adventurers invading Tibet. Still, it seemed likely she would have read something about this bold woman, *if* her journey had been made public. She should have made headlines in England's press, but there was not so much as a whisper in anything Sigourney could recall reading. The woman was a shadow taunting her from the pages of time.

Sigourney began to tackle the practical issues of Martha's request. She had a divorce to settle and a rebellious daughter on her hands. Her life was a mess, and traveling half-way around the world to deliver an old religious book to a monastery would only complicate things. Yet, even as she scolded herself for considering the idea, she was drawn to it. She was a historian, after all, and the manuscript and diary had historical importance. Returning the manuscript to Tibet would give her the chance to explore an event that had gone undocumented until now.

The year on the diary drew her attention again. She knew little about Tibet. Most of her information had come from her discussions with Martha. But, there was something about the specific year that continued to disturb her, and she needed to know why.

Her quickest source of information would be her fellow historian at the university, Brad Paxton. Asia was his specialty, and he had done extensive research on China and the Himalayan countries. Brad wasn't her favorite colleague. He had an inflated ego and acted superior to everyone, including Sigourney. He also competed directly with her for grants, making him impossible to ignore. Their areas of specialty bumped against each other like two wayward ice bergs and, on several occasions, Brad had used the historical trading and political ties between East and West as a pretext for venturing into her territory. Of course, if she *did* go to Tibet, she would be stepping onto his turf, which would be quid pro quo.

He knew much more about Tibet than she did, however, and on impulse she reached for the kitchen phone.

"Dr. Paxton." His stiff, formal voice always made her teeth grind.

"Brad, it's Sigourney. I was hoping you could refresh my memory about something. Wasn't the first westerner to reach Tibet's holy city of Lhasa a British military officer named Younghusband?"

"Correct." A tinge of condescension crept into his voice.

"Colonel Younghusband. He invaded Tibet with a contingent of British soldiers and reached Lhasa by force, although there really wasn't much resistance from the Tibetans. They were Buddhists, after all, with little interest in violence, and their weaponry was almost primitive."

"When did he do that, reach Lhasa I mean?"

"1904. Why?" Suspicion crept into Paxton's voice.

Sigourney's chest expanded and contracted like an accordion, and it took several heartbeats before she could regain her breath. *That* was why the date had struck her as so odd. She was holding the diary of a woman who claimed to have entered Tibet in 1899. If she reached Lhasa, she did it five years before Younghusband, making her the first westerner to see the holy city, and nobody knew about it! Sigourney was sitting on a potentially remarkable discovery.

"Just curious." She tried to sound casual, but her jaw ached from the tension of concealing her excitement. "I spoke to someone who got their facts wrong."

"Funny you should mention Tibet. I'm on my way there later this month." The self-important tone in his voice told Sigourney that their department chair, David Brosnan, had approved a research grant. Her warning systems went on alert.

"Why Tibet?" She knew she didn't sound casual anymore, but she didn't care.

"To research the monasteries for records of traders and others traveling through the region. There were many such visitors over the centuries from India, China and other neighboring countries. The monasteries often kept records of such visits, and I'm going to document as many of them as I can, including the westerners who tried to reach Lhasa before and after Younghusband."

Sigourney's systems flashed code red. If Brad started his research first, he might stumble across evidence of Anne Hopkins' journey and her arrival at the Samye Monastery. Sigourney shuddered at the idea of Brad finding that record before her. The image of his sanctimonious face returning in triumph swept away any remaining doubts about making the trip. Not only could she retrace the footsteps of a remarkable woman who had achieved greatness and chosen to hide it, she would beat Brad to an important discovery.

She hung up the phone and paced the room. Her thoughts were spinning like a whirling dervish. Martha said taking the journey, the "quest," would help Sigourney regain her faith in herself and her life. A discovery of this magnitude would certainly be a big step in that direction. The connection to Anne Hopkins mystified her. She had said they were spiritually linked, that the incident with the white dove proved it. And what about the manuscript? It seemed possessed. How else to explain those chanting voices? Finally, there was the date on the diary. A date that would rewrite the history books. A date that cried out to her like a lost child.

And what about her child? The thought of leaving Debbie, even for a week or two, struck such a discordant note on her guilt cords, she was overcome with self-reproach. Yet, the thought of her daughter's recent behavior churned her stomach so badly, she wanted to scream. How could she care so much for her daughter and be so upset by her at the same time? It wasn't healthy. She didn't know how to control such conflicting emotions. Sigourney was swimming in a powerful riptide that was robbing her of her strength and ability to think rationally. Perhaps, Dr. Bowen was right. He had suggested, no recommended, letting Debbie spend time with Roger. What better opportunity than now? Sigourney would be gone, beyond the reach of any temptation to change her mind, and she wouldn't have to face an empty house when she came home at night. If Dr. Bowen was right, a short separation would be good for them both.

She'd been so flustered when she left Dr. Bowen's office, she hadn't made another appointment. Roger could do that. It might be good for him to attend at least one session. The more she thought about Dr. Bowen's recommendation, the more sense it made. Sigourney had nothing to lose. She had no daughter. No husband. No hope for her life. Anything would be an improvement over the emptiness she felt. Maybe, losing herself in Tibet *could* help her find herself again. Maybe, going to Tibet could help her reconnect with her daughter. Living with her father and his girlfriend might change Debbie's tune. Or it might not. It was a chance she would have to take, if she followed Dr. Bowen's advice.

If she was going to go at all, she had to leave before Brad got wind of her plans. That meant getting her department head's approval, and David would only do that if she offered something substantial. She couldn't tell him about the manuscript, but the diary would do the trick. He'd be as intrigued by the date on the diary as she was. She would have to find some way to validate Anne Hopkins' story, however. It was likely that her visit and the manuscript's disappearance would have been documented at the Samye Monastery, just as Brad suggested. If she could find that record, she would have her proof.

Leaving before the end of the spring semester meant making arrangements for her two classes, but they were graduate research courses where the students worked in independent study groups. They were capable of continuing their research while she was gone, and her teaching assistant could meet with them to check their progress. David's biggest objection would be money, but Martha had solved that problem with her five thousand dollar gift.

Sigourney picked up the manuscript and stared at its parched cover. She half-expected it to speak to her, but it remained silent. It was such a special book! A bewitching book, which embraced Sigourney with its promise of redemption and rebirth. *I must take you back,* she thought. Relief flooded through her. The waves that had been crashing over her head subsided, and she found herself floating effortlessly in a new world filled with promise and purpose.

Sigourney began making mental notes of the things she had to do. Tackling David was at the top of the list. It was too late today, but she would be ready for him tomorrow. She would make a copy of the diary, so she wouldn't risk damaging or losing the original and buy a proper carrying case, a valise, for both the manuscript and diary. She would call Roger tomorrow after her meeting with David. *My God, am I really serious about this?* She knew she was. The decision had been made, she was going to Tibet.

CHAPTER FOUR

Sigourney took the diary to the university and copied it the next morning, then dropped by David's office at lunch time, when she knew he would be hiding behind closed doors. Lunch hour was a good time to broach new subjects with David. He was generally relaxed and in a good mood. When she knocked, he mumbled "come in" and quickly swallowed a mouthful of sandwich.

"Sig." He gave her a big smile as she sat down by his small conference table. Sigourney hated the name Sig, but she had never been able to convince David to use her full name and had stopped trying. The room reminded her of a garage sale. Papers, books, memos and computer disks lay in random piles on every surface, including the floor behind his desk. All that was missing were the for-sale signs. Sigourney had once been offered this office, but she'd declined. The political intrigues involved in running a university department could be brutal, and she'd known it wasn't for her. She admired David for his survival instincts, though. He'd lasted three years and seemed to be gaining momentum. There were rumors he might become the Assistant Dean.

"I don't usually see you here at this hour. What's up?" David had been sitting behind his desk, but he unraveled his lanky frame and joined her at the table. At six-foot-four, he'd been a good college basketball player but had lacked the skills to make it in a top-rated program.

"David, I want to propose a little trip." She raised her hand to fend off his immediate objection about money. "It won't cost the department a cent. Someone has already paid for it. I can't say who, but it has nothing to do with university funding."

"Summer break will be here soon, and you don't have anything scheduled again until fall. What's the problem?"

"Can't wait until summer. I'd like to leave at once."

David raised both eyebrows. Sigourney knew the signals. One eyebrow indicated interest. Two showed concern.

"I have a diary that could rewrite the history books about the first westerner to reach Lhasa." She laid the original diary on the table.

David leafed through a few pages and whistled. "Is this date correct? This Anne Hopkins claims to have entered Tibet a hundred years ago? Where did you get this?"

"The same place I got the money. There's a real possibility this woman reached Lhasa five years before Younghusband led his British army there. I need to go to Tibet and verify her story. There's a way I can do that." Sigourney stopped and took a deep breath. It was time for a little salesmanship. "It would be an important discovery for our department and for the university. But I should go now, before anyone else learns about it."

David rubbed his chin and shifted in his chair, signaling his interest. "Brad will be going there in a few weeks. It's really his area of expertise. Why not wait and go with him? You two could collaborate on this." David liked to challenge the department's professors to compete against one another. He believed it kept everyone on their toes and stimulated more research.

Sigourney stiffened and shot him a withering glare. "This is my find, David," she said firmly. "Anne Hopkins was an

Englishwoman, which puts her in *my* area of expertise. Brad has no role in my proposed research, just as I have no role in his."

"You won't endear his friendship if you go charging into Tibet just before he does."

"Brad and I are not friends, and you know it." Sigourney spoke through gritted teeth, putting equal emphasis on each word. "I don't much care what he thinks. I have something very specific to go on, and I need to pursue it before anyone interferes with my research." Her message was clear, and she knew David understood it.

"How long would you be gone?" Sigourney had to suppress a smile. When David began asking practical questions, it meant he had bought into the proposal.

"My guess would be a week. Two at the most. My students are doing their own research, and my assistant can look after them while I'm gone." There was nothing more she could think to say. She stared at David and waited.

David stood up and returned to his desk, signaling that their meeting was over. "You haven't given me much to go on, Sig, but I trust your instincts. If this is as important as it looks, I have no problem with it."

Now, it was Sigourney's turn to smile. Until that moment, the idea of traveling to Tibet had seemed more abstract than real. Knowing that she was really going made her heart flutter with hope. Hope for herself and for a better future with Debbie when she returned.

Sigourney stood up and faced her boss across the desk. "One more thing, David. No one needs to know about this diary until I get back" She shot him her most steadfast look. "Please don't reveal my project to Brad."

"Brad's going to know you're gone, Sig. It won't take him long to figure out where. I'll do my best to keep the diary under wraps until you return, so you'll have time to publish your findings."

"Good," she replied with satisfaction. "It's settled then. I'll meet with my students and assistant tomorrow."

"Be sure you give me your itinerary before you leave, in case I need to get hold of you. And keep in touch. Let me know how you're doing."

"I'll call you from Lhasa, collect." She grinned at his pained expression and left. She skipped down the hallway like a school girl, causing students to turn their heads and stare. Her response to David's consent surprised her. She wasn't sure why she felt so giddy. All she knew was that for the first time in six months she had hope. Life was suddenly worth living, again.

*****

Her first call was to her travel agent, who promised to have arrangements ready the next day, including plane reservations and a tour operator in Kathmandu who could prepare an itinerary into Tibet on short notice.

Her next call was to her attorney. "Mr. Hansen, I have to leave the country in a few days. How does that affect the divorce proceedings?"

"It could delay things. I'm waiting for confirmation from your husband's lawyer and the judge right now. The hearing could be set as early as next week. Can't your trip wait?"

She could hear annoyance in his voice, but waiting was no longer an option. She had already stirred the pot by telling David, and a little inconvenience to Roger wasn't her concern anymore. He could wait a few more weeks to be legally free of her.

"No, it can't. Contact Roger's lawyer and tell him to put off the hearing for at least two weeks. I'll call Roger and give him the good news." Sigourney paused and took a deep breath. "One more thing. Debbie will be living with Roger while I'm gone, but I want her back when I return. Make that clear. I don't want Roger to think he has any legal grounds for a custody suit."

There was a moment of silence before Mr. Hansen responded. "Has he suggested such a tactic?"

"No, but I don't trust him." Sigourney tensed. She didn't like Hansen's hesitation.

"I'll prepare a document outlining your wishes." It wasn't as forceful a reply as she wanted to hear, but there was no turning back. Not if she wanted to pursue her discovery before Brad Paxton got his egotistical nose into the middle of things.

"Please do," she said and hung up.

She dialed Roger's office in the English Department and got his recording. When she heard his voice, anger rose like bile in her throat, and she had to take several deep breaths to calm herself long enough to respond at the beep. "Roger, call me at home tonight. I'm leaving town, and I'm sending Debbie your way." There, she thought, that ought to get his attention.

Sigourney's upbeat mood returned. She was taking control of her life again. Tibet gave her a sense of direction and purpose. She hadn't felt so good about herself in months.

She decided to swing by Debbie's school and meet her at the end of classes. The old Debbie would have enjoyed finding her mother waiting for her; the current one would probably accuse her of spying and sulk all the way home. It was a risk Sigourney would have to take. She wanted to talk to Debbie before Roger called, and she couldn't take the chance that her daughter would disappear, again, after school.

Debbie's reaction when she saw her mother was right on cue. Her face glowered with anger and mistrust. "What are you now, my jailer?" she demanded in a defiant tone.

Sigourney tried to smile and maintain her composure. She wanted so badly to have a real discussion with Debbie about what she was doing and why. She wanted Debbie to know she loved her and would never abandon her. But the scowl on her daughter's face shattered Sigourney's equilibrium. Her nostrils flared. She clenched her teeth to keep from snapping back. Frustration engulfed her and angered her even more. This isn't what I wanted, she thought. Why can't I talk to my own daughter, anymore?

Sigourney knew her only hope was to take a tough stance. "You're getting your wish. Get in the car." She noted Debbie's confusion at her cryptic remark as she turned and headed for the parking lot.

"Hey, wait a minute," Debbie called out, hurrying after her mother. "What's going on?"

"I'll tell you in the car." She knew Debbie's curiosity would get the best of her.

"*Mother.*" Her daughter's grating voice screeched in Sigourney's ears. A dull throbbing began to pound against her forehead. She kept telling herself that Debbie wasn't to blame. She had to be patient with her daughter, try to reason with her. It was just so damn hard! She ignored Debbie's entreaty and beeped her car to unlock the doors.

"Get in," she demanded, settling into the driver's seat. Debbie hesitated, then reluctantly followed suit.

Sigourney waited until they were clear of the parking lot and out on the main thoroughfare. Driving the car calmed her. Be patient, she told herself. Be understanding. "Debbie, you've said you want to live with your father. Dr. Bowen thinks that's a good idea. Let you reconnect with your father. So, you're going to get your chance."

"What? When?"

"Right away. Tomorrow or the next day at the latest."

Silence. Sigourney kept her eyes on the road and held her breath.

"Oh, sure. Now you're throwing me out too, right?" The angry edge to Debbie's voice couldn't hide her surprise or bewilderment.

"This isn't for keeps. Just for a little while. A few weeks at most. At least while I'm gone on a trip."

More silence. Sigourney could hear the wheels turning in her daughter's head. For all her bluster about wanting to go to her father's place--a two bedroom apartment that he shared with his new girlfriend--the consequences of actually leaving home were not something she had considered. Would she be pleased? Would she want to come back home? Sigourney had worried over these questions ever since making her decision earlier that day.

"Okay, fine. Like I really care. I'll go to dad's tonight." Debbie tried to sound tough, but Sigourney could hear the hurt tone in her voice. She reached for her daughter's hand, which was instantly pulled away.

"Tonight might be too soon, honey, and I don't want to see you go until it is necessary. You can do what you want, though. I'll leave that up to you and your father."

"Why are you leaving me?" A gulp of air and a shaky voice replaced the tough exterior of a few moments ago.

"I'm not leaving you, Debbie. I'll never leave you. I love you too much to do that." Sigourney peeked at her daughter to see her reaction.

Debbie blinked and shifted uncomfortably in her seat. She said nothing.

"Something's come up, is all," Sigourney continued, "and I have to go to Tibet. I thought it would be a chance for you to spend time with your father, like you wanted."

"Tibet, where's that?" Debbie asked, ignoring Sigourney's last remark. "Oh, I think I know. Somewhere in Asia?" Curiosity crept into her voice.

"Good guess. China to be precise. I'm waiting to hear about the final travel arrangements, but I expect to leave by the weekend. It'll be a tough trip. Maybe even a little bit dangerous." She wanted to peak her daughter's interest, but the moment quickly passed.

"Whatever." Debbie slumped down in her seat and looked out the window.

Sigourney knew that signal. It meant the conversation was over, and any further dialogue would be useless. She said nothing more, and they drove home in silence.

Roger was even less understanding than Debbie. "Come on, Sigourney, we need to get the divorce over with. It'll be better for everybody." She knew that meant it would be better for Roger. "I'm just getting settled into my new place," he complained. "Things are still in chaos around here. It might be upsetting for Debbie to visit right now. She should get to know Bethany better, before they're thrown together like that."

Bethany! The name sounded like someone spitting on the sidewalk. Sigourney's eyes stung with sudden tears. She had to fight back the urge to get up from the kitchen table and throw the telephone across the room. She ran her fingers through her hair, instead, and dried her tears with a paper napkin.

"Cut the crap, Roger. Dr. Bowen thinks it's a good idea, and you have no choice. I *am* taking this trip."

Sigourney marveled at her new-found toughness. Had she changed that much in one day? Probably not, but she could feel new muscles developing in her self-confidence. After a brief verbal tussle, it was agreed that Debbie would join her father the following evening.

Getting a visa for Tibet on such short notice was difficult, but her travel agent said the land operator should be able handle it, as long as Sigourney went with an authorized tour group. One was being formed that would leave in a few days. Her agent would look into it. She faxed a list of items for Sigourney to pack: several layers of clothing, dust masks, sun block with a 40+ UVA rating, tablets to disinfect drinking water, cough medicine to combat dry air and dust, moisturizing creams, diarrhea medicine, lip balm, Diamox for acute mountain sickness, toilet paper and a flashlight, among other things.

It was a daunting list, one that suggested how difficult the journey would be. Sigourney had done most of her traveling in Europe, where she stayed in comfortable inns and hotels. Diamox sounded like something for mountain climbers. She had never been higher than the roof of a tall building, and she prayed she could cope with Tibet's demanding conditions. In a few days, she would find out.

CHAPTER FIVE

In a moment of self indulgence, Sigourney pulled out her personal credit card and paid for an upgrade to business class on her Thai Air flight to Nepal. She had always made the trips to Europe in the back of the plane, where she was invariably sandwiched between large people and surrounded by restless children. This time, she was handed a hot towel and offered a glass of champagne before takeoff, and it felt like she was sitting on top of the world. The allusion would soon become reality, for she would be traveling to the "rooftop of the world," a euphemism used to describe Tibet's unusually high altitudes.

Once they were airborne and dinner was served, she settled back in her spacious seat and pulled out the copy she'd made of Anne Hopkins' diary. Before opening it, she brushed her hand over the rough edges of the manuscript nestled inside the valise. It wasn't unusual for antiquities to be lost or hidden away, the victims of random, historical events, but it amazed her to think how long the manuscript had languished in obscurity and that she was about to return it to its rightful place. The book vibrated under her fingertips, as if the words so painstakingly recorded over a thousand years ago were speaking to her, telling her their fates were intertwined. Sigourney had never given much credence to fate, but since taking possession of the manuscript, she had found herself thinking more and more about hers. She found the idea disquieting and quickly placed the valise under her seat.

Sigourney had been dying to read Anne's account of her adventures, but she had honored Martha's request--Anne's if one believed Martha's letters--and resisted the temptation. Now that her own journey had begun, she could wait no longer and opened the first pages of Anne's diary.

Diary entry by Anne Hopkins, April 18, 1899

Has my journey really begun? It seems so incredible after so many frustrations and false starts! Yet, here I am, gazing upon such formidable mountains, I wonder how I shall ever get over them. They are like the walls of a great fortress, only they are made of stone and ice. And such a vision they make! They are magnificent and frightening at the same time. My Tibetan traveling companion and guide, Tenzin, assures me he knows the way through them, and I must put myself in his strong, capable hands. Accepting one's fate has a certain calming effect on the heart and mind. I stand here, and I am not afraid, even though the idea of scaling the Himalayas' treacherous passes frightens me.

I confess that I begin my journey with a heavy heart, but I must not let it weigh me down. My daughter, Serenity, is gone, taken from me in the bloom of her youth. Small pox is such a barbaric way to die, and to think my husband blames me for her death! His cruelty is beyond words. If he had not abandoned Serenity and me, leaving us to fend for ourselves, perhaps things could have been different. Well, it is over now, and I must not dwell upon it. I am alone in the world and about to enter a forbidden new one. I am on my way to Lhasa, and if I reach the holy city, I shall escape my pain and fulfill my destiny. I shall disappear within my own karma. I am certain of it.

A pocket of air turbulence jarred Sigourney, causing her to look up. She listened to the faint whine of the jet's engines and thought about the anguish Anne must have felt over the loss of her daughter and her husband. Sigourney had no way of knowing how long Anne had been married, but she sensed her sorrow. There was a knot in her stomach where Anne's pain reached down and mingled with her own. How alike their experiences were! Both had learned that nothing lasts forever. Not marriages. Not families. In the end, they only had themselves.

In case this diary survives and I do not, I shall explain myself. I am a Buddhist, you see, and I am convinced that if I complete my pilgrimage to the Holy City, I shall fulfill my quest to achieve Nirvana. My spirit shall be released forever, and I shall end my cycle of deaths and births. Unfortunately, the Tibetans do not believe me! They think I am simply another Western adventurer who wants to reach Lhasa and lay claim to being the first to do so. To become famous. I have no interest in fame. If I do succeed, no one shall even know of it! I shall sneak in and out of the city like an insignificant mouse and be on my way. Only my diary will chronicle my story. For if I brag about my accomplishments, I shall be vain and impure, and my spirit will never reach Nirvana. My quest is a holy one, and I must remain worthy of it.

Many have tried to reach this hallowed city, both men and women, but no one has succeeded. I have spoken to two such travelers. They survived bandits, terrible snow storms, frostbite and other physical hardships, only to be found out by the Tibetans and turned back. The Tibetans guard their borders and have an amazing ability to spread the word when a foreigner attempts to invade their country.

I have disguised myself as a pilgrim and shall act as the humble wife of my companion and friend, Tenzin. My outfit is modest. The cloth I wrap around my head is a dull, uninviting gray, as is my woolen jacket. Under the jacket, I shall wear layers of vests and skirts to protect me from the cold. I must keep my face and hands smudged with a mixture of cocoa and coal from our fires, so that my white skin is masked, and since I do not speak fluent Tibetan, I shall let my "husband" do the talking. I shall pretend I have lost my tongue.

It is quite common for pilgrims to travel throughout Tibet visiting monasteries and other holy sites, so we hope to go unnoticed. If anyone's suspicions are aroused, it will be difficult to reach our goal. Once the word is out that a foreigner has entered the country, officials watch the roads very closely. Many pilgrims travel with no money and rely on alms they receive. We have brought some coins with us, but we shall pretend to be penniless and appeal to the charity of others. Only under extreme circumstances, when we cannot find a helping hand, will we use our money. I have been warned that it is not wise to show you have wealth when traveling alone. There are many bandits that wait to plunder such people. So, I have sewn the coins into my many layers of clothing where they will be safe from detection.

It is only the first night, and my arms and shoulders already ache. Tenzin is much stronger than me, but I must carry my share of our meager belongings. These include tin cooking utensils, plates and cutlery, a teapot, spare clothing, knives for cutting firewood, needles and thread and a medicine kit. Many of these items are not carried by poor pilgrims, and we shall have to keep them hidden from inquiring eyes. Our first meal is typical of what I can expect for the next few months, for we shall eat as the Tibetans do. We are having tsampa, which is a roasted barley flour, dry meat and butter tea. I shall miss my crumpets, fresh beef and evening sherry.

We are still at a low altitude, and the landscape is glorious. Ferns and vines grow everywhere in marvelous profusion. The hillsides are lush, and a nearby stream babbles to us like a newborn child. We shall soon leave these green surroundings as we work our way to higher altitudes. Eventually, we shall reach the Tibetan plateau, where the altitude will be over thirty-six hundred meters and the oxygen much thinner. Not much plant life to be found there, I expect.

It is time to sleep, so I shall close this first entry. I look forward to tomorrow with great expectations.

Sigourney tried to visualize the beginning of Anne's journey. Her hopes and fears were clearly expressed in those opening pages. They weren't too different from her own: hoping to return the manuscript undetected and fearing she might be caught. It must have been frightening to look up at those imposing mountains. Sigourney had seen photographs of the Himalayas, and they did look terrifying with steep, craggy slopes and snow-covered peaks. In two more days, she was going to get her first look at them. And she would have the luxury of traversing the mountains in the comfort of a van. The idea of climbing over them made her shudder.

She couldn't resist reading a bit more and opened the diary to the second entry.

Diary entry by Anne Hopkins, 1899
It is only the first week, and already disaster has nearly undermined my efforts to sneak into this distrustful country. Tenzin and I have been climbing steadily. Our disguises seem satisfactory, but we are trying to avoid showing ourselves anymore than is necessary, until we reach the Tibetan plateau. So, we sleep during the day and travel at night.

We were not more than a few days into our trek when we nearly walked right into a group of soldiers who were bivouacked alongside the trail! We heard low, chatting voices just as we were about to turn a corner and stumble into their camp. We were so close, I could smell the smoke from their fire! We had no idea what they were doing so far down the mountain, but we did not dare let them discover us so near the border. We tried to beat a quiet retreat, but I stumbled and sent loose rocks chattering down the mountainside. The soldiers heard us and two of them came to investigate. We had to throw ourselves into a tangle of thorny bushes that snagged my hair and clothes while we sought a place to hide. The soldiers strolled past us along the trail at a leisurely pace. They were so near, the dust raised by their boots tickled my nose, and I had to bury my face in my clothing to keep from sneezing. It seemed an eternity before they returned to their camp. Once they were gone, we clambered over an outcropping of sharp rocks that nipped at my hands and feet like a dog's fangs, until we were a long way from the trail and well hidden. It was a cold night, but we dared not light a fire. We had no choice but to remain in our little hideout without benefit of such warmth.

We watched the soldiers searching along the trail the next morning, looking for whoever they had heard. They left at last, but we did not dare show ourselves before nightfall. Then, we moved cautiously, knowing they were somewhere ahead of us. I was desperately afraid they would lay a trap for us, and our venture would be finished. Thank goodness, we never saw them again.

Our schedule has become routine. We rise in the late afternoon and start a fire to heat water for tea. We eat our tsampa and dried beef, then pack things up and wait until dark. Walking at night makes it easier to keep warm without a fire. However, I am beginning to feel the effects of the altitude. We are climbing steadily higher, and I am tiring rather easily, requiring us to stop and rest more frequently. The altitude does not bother Tenzin. He has lived above three thousand meters most of his life. Still, I find myself adapting to the thinner air and feel I shall cope.

An hour before dawn, we stop and search for a likely spot to camp. This forces us to leave the trail and stamp around in the dark in some very rough terrain. Last night, I had no notion where I was and nearly stepped off a cliff! Tenzin grabbed my hand and pulled me back just in time. Our bodies met, and I blush to think of the warmth I felt from our brief contact.

After we are secluded, we wait for sunup to start a small fire for our meal and tea. Then, we roll out our mats and sleep. My slumbers have been deep and dreamless, the result of exhaustion no doubt. If Tenzin did not wake me, I fear I should sleep into eternity.

One day, I was rudely awakened by the rumbling of a landslide. I could feel the rough rhythm of boulders tumbling into a stream below us. What started it I could only guess at, but it was not hard to imagine what would have happened to us if we had stood in its way. I was much too upset to close my eyes again, so I sat with my garments pulled around me and listened to the small cries and snapping sounds of the day. I meditated for some time, which relaxed me, and I recalled with pleasure the purpose of my journey. The tensions caused by the cat-and-mouse game Tenzin and I were playing had kept me too occupied to reflect on my quest. Perhaps, the landslide had happened for a purpose. It gave me time to pause and think.

Such pleasant thoughts soon had the effect of a sleeping potion. The next thing I knew, Tenzin was shaking me awake to begin another night's journey.

Sigourney closed the diary and returned it to the valise. A movie had started on the screen at her seat, but she turned it off. She thought about her daughter, instead, and hoped she was doing okay at her father's.

In the end, Debbie hadn't been keen about going, but she'd kept her tough exterior intact and brazened it out. Roger had looked tense and harried when he came to collect his daughter, and Debbie sensed it. She had given her father a half-hearted hug and quickly withdrawn from him. Roger's attempted kiss on her cheek had landed clumsily on her left eyebrow. Debbie had given Sigourney quick, darting looks, while everybody shifted their feet and tried to think what to say.

Sigourney had been surprised by Debbie's lack of enthusiasm. There were many possible reasons for her reaction: facing Bethany, leaving familiar surroundings, maybe even missing her mother more than she cared to admit. Sigourney knew her daughter must be feeling quite lost, just like her. Debbie's hesitancy gave Sigourney hope that their relationship was not damaged beyond repair.

She took a picture of Debbie from her wallet and touched it with her fingers. The picture was taken a year ago, when Debbie was still a smiling, happy-go-lucky girl. Pangs of guilt swept over her. Roger had tested Sigourney's faith by lying to her about his infidelities, and she had eased her pain by burying herself in her research. She had rationalized her retreat from her family by telling herself the university expected her to research and publish. Publish or perish was the common phrase used to describe the life of a university professor.

That meant traveling to Europe, which was ironic in a way. Normally, it was the father who was gone too much, but Roger taught in the English department and had little need to travel. He had been there for Debbie when Sigourney wasn't. It was no wonder Debbie preferred Roger's company to her own and felt so much closer to him at this critical juncture in their lives.

Once again, she was leaving her daughter at a critical moment, only this time it was to reclaim herself. She had to find herself if she hoped to help Debbie do the same. Looking at the photo reminded Sigourney of the pain they were both feeling, and she put it away.

CHAPTER SIX

It was six in the morning, when Sigourney and her fellow travelers loaded their bags into the back of the van that would take them to the Tibetan border. Sigourney had already stored her suitcase but held onto her valise containing the copy of the diary and manuscript. Its weight caused the strap to dig into her shoulder, but she would have to get used to it. She was determined not to let the valise out of her sight. Her hands fidgeted with the strap, as restless as a butterfly's wings. In a few hours, she would face her first test of courage: crossing the Tibetan border. Images of snarling guard dogs and unsmiling Chinese inspectors preyed on her mind.

Someone called Sigourney's name, dispelling these unpleasant thoughts, and she turned to see Henri hurrying towards her waving a piece of paper in the air. She sensed from his quick strides and stern expression that something was amiss, and she instinctively touched the valise still hanging from her shoulder. Henri pushed the wild hair off his forehead as he came to an abrupt halt in front of her. "You've just received a fax." Concern furrowed his brow, and his wide, dust-colored eyes burned into hers. "I couldn't help glancing at it. I hope you're not doing something that might jeopardize the group." He thrust the fax into her hand but didn't budge from his spot.

Henri's suspicions surprised her, but when she read the document, the hairs rose on the back of her neck. She could see why he was so concerned.

Dear Sig:

Bad news, I'm afraid. Brad saw my memo to file regarding your trip. He's quite upset. Thinks you betrayed his trust. Sorry for the mishap. I'd keep an eye out. No telling what he might do. Wouldn't put it past him to alert the Chinese authorities, although he disclaims any such intention. I hope you get this before you leave Kathmandu. Let me know when you reach Lhasa. They tell me there is no way to contact you until then.

Good luck,
David

Sigourney clutched the paper, aware that Henri was waiting for an explanation. Damn it, she thought, how could David have been so clumsy? Smuggling the manuscript into Tibet already had her on edge, and now *this*.

Henri cleared his throat. Sigourney raised her head and met his challenging gaze. She had no choice but to lie to him. She feared it would be the first of many, but if she could fool him, hopefully she could do the same with the Chinese guards. "I have an unpublished diary of a woman who claims to have entered Tibet a long time ago. I wish to verify her story. It has nothing to do with the Chinese or illegal contraband." Sigourney pulled the copy of the diary from her valise and handed it to Henri.

He flipped through a few pages, but stopped when he saw the opening inscription. He whistled. "You think this date is legitimate?"

"I don't know. If I can prove it, I will have made an important discovery. I believe you know I'm a historian. You can see my interest."

Henri's soldier-like posture relaxed. He handed the diary back with a smile. "I shouldn't volunteer to show it to the Chinese," he offered in a conspiratorial tone. "They might confiscate it. But I agree, it isn't something likely to cause trouble." He touched her hand. His fingers were surprisingly soft. "I would like to know what you find, if you don't mind telling me when you return to Kathmandu." He gave Sigourney a friendly nod that told her he was interested in more than the diary, but all she wanted was to get as far away from him as possible.

The van carried Sigourney and her tour group out of Kathmandu, back along the same road she had taken the day before to reach the lookout point at Nagarkot. It was early morning, and the lighter traffic was a blessing. Nepal had not addressed the problem of air pollution, and the country's trucks and busses poured out excessive amounts of diesel fumes. At this hour, the air was much fresher, and Sigourney inhaled a few deep breaths as she observed the verdant countryside.

Pockets of mist clung to the valley floor, stubbornly resisting the sun's efforts to dissolve them. The valley undulated in waves of rolling hills, giving the appearance of a vast ocean with thin veils of fog obscuring the horizon. Farmhouses speckled the landscape like drops of paint scattered by a giant brush. Sigourney stared out her window at the now familiar scenes of farmers harvesting their fields of wheat, barley and rice and thought about Brad Paxton, whose arrogant face smirked at her through the morning mists. She feared his vindictive nature and knew he would disrupt her plans if he could. She prayed he wouldn't interfere before she completed her mission.

Just as the van turned south on the road leading to Tibet, a lonely tree with long, weeping boughs appeared beside the road. Sigourney gaped in disbelief. It was filled with white birds! They reminded Sigourney of a snow storm that had magically eluded the valley's warm climate and blanketed the tree in a feathery blizzard. She pressed her hand against the window. First the white dove in the university cafeteria, and now this. Anne Hopkins' words rushed back to her. Were their spirits connected, after all? *No. Surely not.* Yet, she couldn't help wondering. The birds filled her with the same excitement and foreboding Anne had described in the opening pages of her diary. I'm becoming bewitched, she thought. I'm a scholar acting like a silly school girl who believes in mysticisms. As she watched, one of the birds spread its wings and lifted off its perch. The others followed, filling the sky with soaring snowflakes.

It took several hours to reach the Nepalese border town of Kodari, where a long line of open bed lorries waited for permits to carry their loads into Tibet. Everyone tumbled out of the van to stretch cramped legs and search for a bathroom. Henri told them to wait in a local restaurant while he processed their paperwork. The restaurant was a dark, roughhewn place consisting of wood-paneled walls and picnic-style benches and tables. Soup was being cooked over an open fire in one corner, creating an unappetizing, smoke laden atmosphere that discouraged Sigourney from trying the steamy brew. She decided to eat one of her snacks and take a quick look at the town, instead.

Kodari consisted of a single, dusty street lined with two-story buildings, where shopkeepers stood chatting in doorways while waiting for customers. Several women passed with wicker baskets strapped to their heads. The baskets were similar to the ones Sigourney had seen children carrying in the fields, but these were filled with bricks and other building materials, and their weight bent the women over like trees in a heavy wind. As she wandered down the street, weathered faces and inquisitive looks beckoned to her like long-ago acquaintances. Men sat in the shade drinking tea and gesturing to one another, drawing her into their timeless embrace. The farther she walked, the more engrossed she became in their curious world. The scenes seemed so familiar. Where had she seen these people before? She couldn't say.

A sudden swirl of wind whipped dust into her eyes, breaking her mood. She looked at her watch and realized nearly twenty minutes had passed. How had time passed so quickly? Sigourney's head felt like a dank cellar filled with cob webs and dark corners. She closed her eyes and waited for her mind to clear. When she opened them, she saw John Henley emerging from a tiny shop just ahead of her.

"Hello," he said with a friendly smile. "You decided to skip the soup as well, I see. Probably a wise decision."

Sigourney's shoulders stiffened as he approached, just as they had at the Stupa the day before, but his smile disarmed her and she relaxed. No reason to condemn the man just for being sociable, she thought. "I couldn't get much of an appetite in that place." She held up a bag of mixed nuts and dried raisins. "Thought I'd eat these, instead. Want some?"

"Thank you, no. I have a good cache of things to nibble on. Perhaps we can share in a few days when we're tired of our own food."

"Good idea." Sigourney studied John out of the corner of her eye while they walked. His unassuming manner had an odd charm about it. She suddenly had a mild attack of nerves and regretted not putting on a little eye liner and lipstick. She'd never paid much attention to skin creams, moisturizers and the finer points of makeup, but now that she was becoming a single woman again, she realized she should consider using them. Not that it mattered in John's case. The wedding band on his left hand indicated there was a wife somewhere. Back in England, she supposed. Sigourney glanced at her own barren hand where wedding rings had nestled for so many years. Her finger looked naked without them. A telltale strip of white skin was the only evidence the rings had ever existed at all, and the fierce Tibetan sun would soon take care of that. It will disappear just like my life, she thought. Just like my husband. Looking at the offending hand depressed her, and she shoved it into her pocket.

John broke the silence between them. "It looks like our adventure is about to begin. No second thoughts after yesterday's episode at the temple, I hope." His eyes twinkled with humor, but she could see the curiosity in his face.

"None," Sigourney responded emphatically, "but adventure

seems to be the appropriate word, based on what Henri told us. I meant to apologize, by the way, for leaving the Stupa yesterday without saying good-bye. That crowd of Tibetans got me a bit rattled."

"Yes, that was an odd incident wasn't it? They seemed to be quite interested in your bag."

Sigourney instinctively touched the valise hanging from her shoulder. Before she could think of a reply, she saw Marie-Rose walking towards them.

"May I join you?" she asked.

"We'd be delighted," John responded.

Marie-Rose's smile was much too pretty, and Sigourney felt a sudden twinge of jealousy. Her cheeks burned at the idea that she would consider Marie-Rose a rival for no other reason than the fact that they were two unattached women talking to a man. She didn't like the emotions roused by being single again, and she promised herself not to become obsessed with "meeting men."

"Are you excited?" Sigourney asked in an effort to make conversation.

"*Oui*. I have wanted to travel through Tibet for many years. I only wish the trip would last longer." Her accent had a rhythmical quality that made it sound like she was singing. Sigourney couldn't help liking her. Marie-Rose made her feel comfortable, perhaps because they were both a little shy.

Everyone's luggage was gathered outside the restaurant when Sigourney and her companions returned. Henri distributed temporary visas, which would allow them to cross the border. "I must leave you at this point," he told them. "Your Tibetan guide will meet you in Zhangmu." He waved goodbye and hopped into the van, which quickly departed. Sigourney watched it disappear around a bend in the road. Like the life I'm leaving behind, she thought. In a few more minutes, it'll be gone.

Sigourney fell in line with her suitcase and valise. She walked past the line of waiting lorries onto the Friendship Bridge. The bridge spanned a small river that tumbled through a steep, fern-lined gorge below. Two Chinese guards stood with their rifles at the far end of the span, reminding Sigourney that Tibet was no longer an independent country. Her heart began to thump as she walked towards them. She had reached the point of no return. She was about to face her first test and become irrevocably committed to her quest. John and the others were ahead of her, and she had to resist the urge to run after them.

The American couple, Cameron and Beth, were the first to reach the other side. Sigourney stopped and watched in horror as the guards demanded to see their bags. The two men were opening luggage, and it wasn't a random search! Jenny and Erica were halted, as well. The guards were looking for something. Brad Paxton *had* alerted the Chinese. Panic seized Sigourney. She looked behind her, wondering if she should turn back and knowing she only had a few seconds to decide. The guards seemed to be ignoring Jenny's handbag. Perhaps, they would ignore her valise, as well? The hammering sounds of the river pounded inside her head. Her eyes ached with tension as she riveted them on the guards. They were watching her, waiting for her to take those fateful steps that would seal her doom. She stood there, immobilized, not knowing what to do.

A sudden noise behind her, the sound of pounding feet and loud voices, brought Sigourney to her senses. The guards had dropped the suitcases they were inspecting and were running towards her, shouting and brandishing their guns. Sigourney threw herself to the ground, sprawling awkwardly on the hard cement and scattering her valise and suitcase. She pressed her face against the bridge's gritty surface, conscious of the semi-sweet odor of motor oil mixed with the foul smell of her own fear and sweat. Squeezing her eyes shut, she waited for the guards to grab her and drag her away. But the guards ran past her, their voices mingling with the ones she had heard moments before. When she dared to look, she saw two Tibetan men in woolen jackets and caps struggling with the Chinese guards, who beat the two men with their fists and pushed them backwards. Both men were staring directly at Sigourney. One of them called out a single word to her: *Sakyamuni.* All at once, the Tibetans gave up their resistance.

Their shoulders sagged, and they let the guards march them back to the line of waiting trucks.

Sigourney sat in the middle of the bridge, too dazed to move. She looked down and saw to her dismay that the valise had opened, partially revealing the manuscript and diary. Hastily, she shoved them back into the bag just as John appeared beside her. She threw him a wary look but saw only concern etched in his brow. He gripped her arms and lifted her to her feet. His hands were gentle, not like the rude hands she had just witnessed pummeling the Tibetans.

"What happened?" she asked. Her whole body trembled as she struggled to regain her balance. "What did they say?"

"Those Tibetans jumped out of their trucks and started running across the bridge. I thought the guards were going to shoot them." He held her arm for support. "One of them shouted the word *Sakyamuni.* Buddha is worshipped by that name. I wonder why they were calling the name of Buddha."

Julie shook her head and said nothing. Sakyamuni was the name the monk in Kathmandu had mentioned to her. She could still feel the two men's eyes boring into hers. They were running towards *her.* They were calling to *her.* God, what was going on? What devilish spirits were being unleashed by the manuscript she carried? The valise felt uncomfortably warm where it rested against her body. When she touched it, a vibration raced through her fingers. "I'm going mad," she whispered.

"What did you say?"

"Nothing," she murmured.

John retrieved her suitcase. Her legs were still rubbery, and she leaned against him for support as they hurried towards the porters waiting for them on the far side of the bridge. The porters quickly stowed the luggage in an open bed lorry before the guards could return and helped Sigourney clamber over the open tailgate in the back.

She stared at the tangled growth on the mountainside ahead of her and marveled at her good fortune. The Tibetans had distracted the guards long enough for her to avoid them. Their efforts had saved her. She thought about their tense expressions when they looked at her. They had known she carried something precious in her valise. Just as the worshippers at the Boudhanath Stupa had known.

Sigourney's agitation was slowly replaced by relief. She was in Tibet. She had faced her first test, and survived…for now.

There were no seats in the lorry, so Sigourney and the others stood around in the bed of the truck looking like confused cattle. No sooner had the tail gate been slammed shut than the lorry lurched forward, causing everyone to frantically grasp for hand holds along the metal cross bars overhead. Sigourney gripped one of the bars and braced herself against the truck's violent rocking motion on the rutted, dirt road that led up the mountain. The cross bars were meant to support a canvass covering to protect the truck's contents during foul weather, but none was attached. Sigourney noted with discomfort the thick layer of black clouds forming ominously overhead. Did the clouds symbolize the dangers that lay ahead? She hoped not.

"I believe it's beginning to look like jolly old England," John commented, and everyone laughed nervously.

Soon, large dollops of raindrops tumbled out of the dark sky, and Sigourney found herself being pelted by a cold, driving rain that quickly soaked through her clothing. Her only comfort was the knowledge that her valise was water proofed and the manuscript safe. She tried holding the valise over her head to fend off the water, but it did little good. Soon, the road turned from dust to mire, and the rain settled into a steady downpour.

John pulled a jacket over his head and bravely faced the unwelcome elements. Sigourney appraised him with sidelong glances. Her fear on the bridge had paralyzed her ability to think or act, until he stepped forward and helped her to safety. His calm repose had comforted her and given her strength, but it couldn't lessen her disappointment in herself. She had survived her first test, but she had panicked. Not very encouraging, she thought. She'd have to do better, if she wanted to succeed in her quest.

By the time she reached Zhangmu and received her visa, Sigourney was shivering and miserable, but her spirits lifted when she was introduced to the group's new guide, a Tibetan named Jigme. He greeted everyone and led them to a warm van, which would become their home for the next five days. Sigourney climbed into its protective womb and curled up in the first empty seat she could find behind the driver. The American couple sat across the aisle. She was pleased to see John sitting directly behind her. After the incident on the bridge, she felt more comfortable in his company. Marie-Rose and the two other women sat towards the back.

It took only minutes to drive up the hill to their hotel, a rather sterile looking building that reminded Sigourney of a military barracks. The clouds had passed, and afternoon sunshine poured down on the semi-tropical flora surrounding the town. It was a lovely setting, but Sigourney was much too tired and wet to appreciate it.

Jigme spoke in mumbling, and strained English, while placing unusual emphasis on certain syllables or words, making the rhythm of his dialogue disjointed. He sounded like the percussion section to Marie-Rose's violins. Everyone gathered in the hotel lobby while Jigme explained their schedule. They would have the afternoon to rest and clean up, then meet at five o'clock and walk to a local restaurant for dinner.

Sigourney pulled Jigme aside after the meeting ended. "We were told there would be a random search of our luggage, but the guards at the Friendship Bridge were inspecting everybody's bags, until an incident stopped them." Her voice trembled with anxiety. "Was that normal?"

Jigme hesitated. She could feel him assessing her with his frank stare. Deep lines carved his face into crevasses much like the ones she had seen in the Himalayas, testimony to his many years spent under the harsh, Tibetan sun. Silence deepened between them. She heard the soft squeak of someone's rubber-soled shoes crossing the tile floor behind her.

"I am surprised at what you tell me," he said at last. "Luggage is not inspected at the border. We must stop at a police station tomorrow night, before we reach our next hotel. They only open one or two bags, so there should be nothing to worry about." His reply was a statement, but his inquisitive eyes made it sound like a question.

"I was just curious," Sigourney remarked as casually as she could. She turned and hurried away.

Sigourney's room was sparse, but very clean. The promised thermos bottle filled with hot water sat on the night stand by the bed, along with a single cup and two tea bags. The draperies were open, revealing a panorama of terraced hillsides and gentle mountain slopes. To her right, a row of concrete buildings clung to the side of the mountain like shipping containers. Debris lay scattered on the steep slopes below the buildings, but it was quickly swallowed by the lush plant life growing down the mountain. A lone farmer tended his crops along a series of stone terraces. Below her, wisps of smoke rose from a tiny house nearly hidden among the trees. It was a landscape filled with the promise of eternal spring.

No one could see into her room, so she left the draperies open while she stripped off her wet clothing and unpacked fresh underwear and her robe. Before putting on the robe, she stopped and appraised herself in a small mirror above the sink. Her short-cropped, lunch-bag brown hair still retained its natural color. No signs of gray. She had never liked her breasts, which she considered too small for her lanky body. Her brown eyes desperately needed some eyeliner, and her pale face cried out for a little blush on her cheeks. All-in-all, it wasn't a very attractive sight, at least not in her eyes. She wondered how men looked at her. Her closeted anxieties from her younger, single days reached out and tugged at her. How, for instance, did John Henley see her? Not that it mattered, but she couldn't help being curious.

Wrapping the robe around her, Sigourney lay down on the bed. She was exhausted from the long trip and the wet, rodeo-bucking ride up the mountain, and soon drifted into a fitful slumber filled with visions of Chinese guards, white birds and falling rocks.

Her eyes blinked open for a moment while she thought about the latter image. Tumbling rocks made no sense to her, but she was too tired to think about it. She turned over and went to sleep.

*****

Zhangmu was nothing more than a muddy border town that clung to the mountain's slopes for a mile on either side of the road. Its tumbled down images stood in sharp contrast to the lush hillsides and valley Sigourney had admired from her hotel window. Shanty-town structures with corrugated roofs gave the place a look of impermanence, like a mining town that would disappear once the ore ran out. The place could have folded up tomorrow, and no one would have been the wiser.

The rain had turned the road into a series of mud puddles and slick goo, which was crisscrossed by ruts from the tires of passing lorries. Sigourney and her group picked their way through the puddles as they followed Jigme to a restaurant in the middle of town. Downtown consisted of bars, pool halls, shops and local restaurants of doubtful quality. All the buildings displayed Chinese signs. The few Tibetans she saw were truck drivers waiting for loads to carry into the country's interior.

They climbed a narrow stairway and entered the main room of a Chinese restaurant that looked more promising than the ones Sigourney had seen from the street. A few local people in worn coats and mud-caked boots sat scattered among the tables. A large, round table with a reserved sign had been set aside for the group. Soon, bowls of steaming soup appeared, followed by plates of rice, mushrooms, vegetables, shrimp and other Chinese delicacies. Sigourney attacked her food with the vigor of someone ending a hunger strike. Everyone was ravenous after the long day and the questionable lunch offered them in Kodari.

Conversation was light as people began the process of getting to know each other. Sigourney had never traveled in a tour group before--her research trips had always entailed a private driver and guide--and she was fascinated by the dynamics she could already see emerging. The young woman, Jenny, was outgoing and quickly engaged others in conversation, although she spent most of the time talking about her own experiences and ideas rather than listening to others. She had the kind of firm body that suggested plenty of exercise, but a small bulge in her stomach showed that she was beginning to gain unwanted weight. She made quick gestures with her hands as she spoke and often fiddled with her arrow-straight hair.

Jenny's travel companion, Erica, was the opposite of her friend. She spoke quietly and asked questions of the others. Erica didn't compete with Jenny for attention, which was probably why they were friends. She was slimmer than Jenny but had less sparkle. Jenny was the flawed, but glittering diamond set against Erica's black-star sapphire.

The American couple introduced themselves as Cameron and Beth Mitchell. Cameron was tall and thin and had one of those leathery faces that grew more handsome with age. Beth had a stout figure and a pretty face that showed few wrinkles. She was either younger, Sigourney speculated, or she'd already had a face lift. Cameron had the disturbing habit of glancing about him, giving him a sly look that Sigourney found uncomfortable. He tried to wrest the conversation away from Jenny, and a friendly verbal competition quickly flared between them. Every time Cameron said something witty, Beth rewarded him with a loud, barking laugh that jarred Sigourney's eardrums.

John was polite and reserved, adding comments when appropriate but not attempting to engage the group unnecessarily. Marie-Rose ate her dinner in relative silence.

"Okay, everybody," Jenny announced, tapping her water glass with a spoon. "I propose we play a game to get better acquainted. Everyone tell the group three things about themselves: what they do for a living, what they're most passionate about, and what is the top item on their 'to do' list."

Erica groaned and laughed at the same time. "You must forgive my friend. She always does this. Jenny, you can be a real pain. What if people don't want to talk about themselves?"

Jenny pinched her face at Erica. "Nonsense. I'm not asking for deep, dark secrets." She had an infectious grin, and Sigourney found it hard to be annoyed at her brash behavior. "Let's just break the ice a little," Jenny continued. "I'll go first. I teach art at an inner city school in New York, and I've got to tell you, there's nothing more challenging than trying to get some kid interested in Picasso who's drugged up half the time and more interested in scoring on some chick than getting a passing grade. My greatest passion is painting, which I'm not very good at, and my top 'to do' item is to attend the art academy in Paris. Oh yes, while I'm there, I want to run down the stairs of the Eiffel Tower without any clothes on! Of course, I'll do it at night when no one can see me."

Cameron laughed and immediately waved his hand like an eager child. "I'm a computer software consultant. My greatest passion is golf, and I want to play eighteen holes at Pebble Beach without losing all my balls."

This elicited a loud, barking whoop from Beth, who clearly doted on her husband's every word. "Honey, you never told me you were worried about losing. . .oh, never mind." She laughed again. "Well, I run the marketing department for a new computer software company. My greatest passion is cooking and someday I want to prepare dinners in a five-star restaurant under a famous chef."

John sat next to Beth and agreed to go next. "Nothing too exciting, really. I work for the British government. My passion is my family, and I want to see my son and daughter graduate from school with honors."

John's simple comments brought a sober tone back to the group. Sigourney had been uncomfortable with the direction the conversation was taking, and she silently thanked John for his thoughtful insights, which were more in rhythm with her own mood. Before she knew it, she was raising her hand. "I teach European history at a university. My passion is my research, and my goal is to see my daughter safely through her teenage years."

Erica said she was a nurse in an emergency ward in Seattle. Her passion was traveling, and she wanted to go on a real safari in

Africa. Marie-Rose was reluctant to talk about herself, but she finally admitted to being a staff writer for a woman's magazine in Paris. "I will interview you, Jenny, after you run down the Eiffel Tower," she added with a hint of a smile. She wouldn't talk about her passions or wish list, and Sigourney thought she saw a hidden tear in her eye.

Sigourney hated to admit it, but Jenny's little exercise worked. Conversation around the table picked up noticeably.

After dinner, Sigourney walked back through the town in the waning light. One of the bars had left its doors open, and an old juke box boomed out a Neil Diamond song she hadn't heard in years. It seemed strange to hear Western music so far from home. The song reminded her of long-ago days when she and Roger were young and in love. Had he ever loved her, she wondered? It was a disturbing question. Losing a man's love was heartbreaking; never being loved was devastating. Never being loved said there was something wrong with *her*. Sigourney pushed the thought aside as she picked her way through the mud, but by the time the group reached the hotel, she was fighting a deepening depression.

A heated discussion between Jigme and a Chinese official was taking place in the lobby when Sigourney and her companions arrived. Their conversation ended abruptly, and the official stalked away, leaving Jigme looking visibly upset. He nodded to everyone and followed the official from the room without a word. Sigourney forgot her own worries as she watched the guide depart. He looked as helpless as she felt, and she sympathized with him.

"That was odd, wasn't it?" John commented. "Rather a harsh exchange from the looks of it."

"Jigme didn't look very happy," Sigourney agreed. Her thoughts skipped back to the manuscript and the looming threat of Brad Paxton. It wasn't likely the argument had been about her, but that didn't prevent an attack of anxiety from pricking her skin.

Sigourney could still hear the bar's music when she returned to her room. She lay on the bed and listened to songs that kept reminding her of a time when she was in love and looking forward to a happy future.

To keep herself from becoming too melancholy, she propped her pillow against the headboard and opened Anne's diary.

Diary entry by Anne Hopkins, 1899

I thought last night would see the death of me! What a harrowing adventure for myself and poor Tenzin, who ended up carrying both our packs and very nearly me. We faced our first real mountain pass, and while we knew we must make our ascent in daylight, we wanted to avoid local Tibetans as much as possible. Once we traversed the mountain, Tenzin said it should be safer to travel in the open, but we were still too close to India's borders at this point to feel comfortable.

This meant waiting until the afternoon to begin our climb, after most people would be off the mountain. It was well past lunch time when we started, and we pushed very hard to reach the top as quickly as possible. We wanted to descend the other side before dark. Such a hurried ascent at such a high altitude was nearly too much for me, and I felt myself growing steadily weaker as we approached the summit. My lungs gasped for breath like someone with an advanced stage of consumption, and I had to rest more frequently. Tenzin was very patient, and after awhile he took my pack and slung it over his free shoulder. Being rid of that heavy weight was a blessing, and I found I could walk more steadily again. But I felt terrible for my poor companion.

We both pushed bravely onwards and reached the summit by late afternoon, where we found many small piles of rocks, called chortens, stacked on the ground and a few prayer flags, which were nearly torn apart by forceful storms. The winds had increased during our ascent and now blew so hard, we had to lean well into them to make headway. The summit was too exposed to rest, so we began our descent.

Black clouds followed us up the mountain, and they now threw themselves upon us with great violence, unleashing hail and pellets of snow. The wind-driven snow stung my exposed cheeks with such force, that it brought tears to my eyes. We soon found ourselves in a blizzard that obscured the trail and forced us to seek shelter among some large rocks. It was a poor hiding place, for the boulders afforded us little protection from the storm's assault. We decided to keep moving down the mountain in hopes of finding a cave where we would be safer. In no time at all, the light began to fail, making our climb down the steep slopes increasingly difficult. I missed my step on some loose rocks and fell, sliding some distance on my back down a particularly steep incline while frantically trying to find some purchase with my hands and feet. At last, I landed in a snow drift miraculously unhurt, except for some cuts and bruises. Tenzin hurried down to me, and we lay together in the snow, too exhausted to move.

In spite of the biting, cold wind and blasts of snow, I was beginning to feel pleasantly warm. This, I realized with alarm, was the first sign of freezing! Thank goodness Tenzin had enough strength left to pull me to my feet and half-drag me down the mountain. Otherwise, I believe I would have quite happily lain there and died.

We managed to stumble into a small cave where we were protected, but it was still freezing cold. Since we had no wood to light a fire, we had no choice but to huddle together until the storm passed, which it finally did sometime during the night. I had never considered Tenzin in a romantic way, but when he pressed his warm body against mine, I felt urges tingling in me that made me hide my face from him.

When we emerged from our sanctuary, a three-quarter moon was peeking through the clouds overhead. The winds had died to a whisper, and snowdrifts rose around us like sleeping giants. I was bewildered by the feelings I had just experienced in the cave and stood for some time inhaling the sharp, clean air. The rest in the cave had revived me, and I took possession of my pack again, much to Tenzin's relief, I am certain!

Thanks to the moonlight, we were able to pick our way through the heavy snow until we discovered the trail near the bottom of the mountain. We found a small sanctuary among some rocks and bushes, collapsed on our sleeping mats and slept until the morning was well advanced. By the time I awoke, Tenzin had *already boiled water for tea, and I gratefully accepted a cup. We appraised our situation. It was no longer practical to hide and sleep during the day, for our cover of trees and thick bushes was rapidly disappearing as we moved onto the Tibetan plateau. Nor did we care to risk any more passages through the mountains except in full daylight. This meant joining other pilgrims when they presented themselves. We would continue to avoid the villages when possible, but I must depend on my disguise and hope for the best.*

Sigourney shuddered at the thought of being lost in such a storm. Anne's courage had been extraordinary. Sigourney knew she would need Anne's strength to complete her own quest, and she silently thanked the woman who seemed to reach out to her over the span of a hundred years through her diary. Sigourney picked up the manuscript and caressed its scabrous surface with her fingers. I won't fail you, she thought. She didn't know if she was talking to the book or to Anne. Perhaps, she was talking to both.

CHAPTER SEVEN

The next morning, Sigourney was eager to get started, but it was already half-past eight, and there was no sign of Jigme. The lobby buzzed with expectant energy as the group milled around, waiting. Voices echoed off the sterile walls and tile floors with the dissonance of a noisy library. Sigourney paced the lobby, glancing repeatedly at her watch. Images of Brad Paxton and last night's argument between Jigme and the Chinese official kept flashing through her mind. She was sure the images were connected. She just didn't know how.

When Cameron and Jenny began muttering about unreliable tour guides, Sigourney wanted to walk over and smack them both for their insensitivity. Didn't they realize something was wrong? Their complaints only intensified her own misgivings.

Jigme finally strode through the lobby door, and Sigourney smiled with relief. But her joy scattered like a daydream when she saw a man walking beside him with an overnight bag in his hand. The new man's unexpected appearance sucked the air from

Sigourney's lungs. She tried to remain calm, but tiny shock waves pulsed through her body. The man was Chinese. Jigme's demeanor troubled her even more. He stood stoically beside the man. There was no hint of the smile or keen eyes she had seen the day before. His light had been dulled by the intruder's arrival.

"This is Mr. Ho, who will join us," Jigme announced flatly. Sigourney detected tension in his voice, and her own neck and shoulder muscles tightened. "He was looking for a group traveling to Lhasa. It was his good fortune that we came along and have room."

"Thank you for letting me go with you," he said in English, nodding deferentially to the group. He was several inches shorter than Jigme, but his military-erect posture and unblinking gaze gave him a menacing look.

Everyone introduced themselves while Jigme went to get the van. When Mr. Ho greeted Sigourney, his eyes bore into hers until she looked away. The intensity of his gaze reminded her of the Buddha's eyes atop the Stupa in Kathmandu. Except these eyes didn't make her feel peaceful. They filled her with alarm. They told her Mr. Ho wasn't a tourist. He was the cause of last night's argument, and he'd come to spy on the group. If Brad Paxton *had* warned the Chinese authorities, he'd come to spy on her! She shivered at the idea and instinctively touched her valise.

When they boarded the van, Mr. Ho sat in the very back. Sigourney could feel him watching her. The back of her neck burned like a piece of old wood filled with hungry termites. She couldn't shake her apprehension about him. It was more than just her nerves. Jigme's face had told her the man didn't belong there. When she finally dared to look behind her, she caught him watching her. He smiled and closed his eyes, as if in meditation.

John intercepted her gaze and leaned forward. He spoke in a soft voice. "A bit odd, isn't it, for somebody to join us after we've entered Tibet? I wonder what he was doing in Zhangmu without an approved group. Shouldn't think it's the sort of thing the Chinese normally allow."

"I was wondering the same thing. He makes me nervous."

Sigourney was starting to feel more relaxed around John, and she enjoyed sharing a conspiratorial moment with him. Conversing with him made her feel better. "Perhaps, I'm just being silly."

"Perhaps." John sat back without saying more.

Sigourney's spirits rose as they rode up the mountain, and she put aside her concerns about Mr. Ho. She looked forward to seeing her first real images of Tibet and to traversing her first sixteen-thousand-foot mountain pass at Lalung La, a prospect that was both exhilarating and intimidating. She imagined herself a young bird about to leave its nest. Just like the chicks she and Debbie had watched leaving their nest all those years ago. She was crossing a spiritual divide within herself that would redefine who she was. Once she flew away, she would never return.

The van lurched as the driver shifted gears and began a tortuous climb above the tree line along a rocky road that was literally carved into the face of the sheer, granite cliffs. Jigme sat beside the driver in a free-standing, metal chair that wobbled with each gear shift. The chair's right, rear leg danced within inches of the stairwell used to exit the van. At any moment, Sigourney expected to see the guide tumble down the steps, but he maintained his balance as gracefully as a ballerina.

The terrain quickly changed from lush flora to steel-gray, slate walls and metamorphic rock. Icy, cold air seeped through the windows, chilling Sigourney's hands. The abrupt transformation reminded her of a theater intermission, when stage hands changed the scenery for the next act. The mood shift was completed when the bright, morning sun slunk away behind a blanket of cheerless clouds that looked like the bottoms of old cooking pots.

Sigourney had never feared heights, but when she looked down at the wild river running through the canyon hundreds of feet below her window, she became disoriented. Boulders the size of houses churned the river where they had come to rest after tumbling from the cliffs above the narrow road. The van's tires danced like Jigme's chair within a few feet of the abyss. One false slip would send the van tumbling over the side and into the frothing waters.

Sigourney's head began to spin, and she drew back from the window. She thought about the courage it must have taken for Anne Hopkins to traverse those mountains on foot. Thinking about Anne caused a warm sensation to surge through her body like a shot of strong whiskey. Sigourney leaned back in her seat, surprised and shaken. Peering down the steep gorge had spooked her, but that wasn't what affected her now. It was the feeling that Anne's spirit was reaching out to her over the span of a hundred years. An absurd idea, she thought, but she knew it was true. The vibrations tugged at Sigourney with the impatient urgings of a child. She sat very still and concentrated on them, trying to understand their purpose. Were they comforting her or warning her of danger? The warmth faded away without revealing its message.

The van rounded a curve and came upon a lonely, stone bridge spanning a small ravine. Most of the bridge's railings were broken or missing, offering mute testimony to the violence regularly visited upon it by falling rocks. Rubble from rock slides was piled along the side of the road like snowdrifts.

"We must walk across on foot," Jigme announced as the van halted. "Many rocks have hit the bridge. It may be too weak to carry our weight with the van."

The bridge did look like it was living on borrowed time, and Sigourney quickly fled the van along with the others, then stood nervously and watched as her lifeline to the outside world inched its way across the span. A small rock picked that moment to slide down the slope behind her, destroying any sense of security that might have lingered in her mind.

John joined her. "I read about this place, actually. Someone died here just last year from falling debris. Best to keep one's eyes open."

Sigourney ignored him. Images of white birds and falling rocks were swirling through her mind. She could feel the rock slide Anne Hopkins had described in her diary. Anne's presence in the van *had* been a warning. The ground vibrated beneath her feet causing her to tremble, but no one else noticed.

John looked at her quizzically. "Is something wrong?"

She gazed at the contorted rocks clinging to the slopes above her. They were starting to move! Nobody saw the danger but her. How could that be?

"There's going to be a landslide," she shouted as she pointed to the cliff. "Those rocks are about to fall. Run!" Sigourney grabbed John's arm and yanked it. He hesitated. Everyone was looking in disbelief. Nothing had happened, yet. Sigourney could already visualize the rocks crashing down on them. Then, a heavy rock shifted ominously, causing smaller ones to chatter down the slope above their heads. The rock hung suspended for several heartbeats, until the unyielding force of gravity tore it loose from its perch and sent it rumbling towards them. Jenny gasped and Beth screamed as everyone turned and sprinted for the bridge. Boulders thundered down the slope and smashed onto the road where they had been standing. The ground shook under Sigourney's feet with such violence, she feared the bridge would buckle. When she reached the far side, she stood hands on hips, puffing from her furious exertion and staring at the cloud of dust rising behind her.

Marie-Rose ran towards Sigourney like a frightened mouse, and they embraced. Cameron stumbled forward with Beth holding his arm. Sigourney looked around for John, and was relieved to see him escorting a shaken Jenny and Erica across the bridge. Mr. Ho followed them at a brisk pace with his hands clasped behind his back. He reminded Sigourney of an angry general surveying his retreating troops. The filmy cloud of dust rose into the sky, showering Sigourney and the others with powdery particles of earth. The road had disappeared under the pile of debris.

Everyone was coughing and breathing heavily. Sigourney saw looks of amazement on her companions' faces. They murmured to one another and stared at her in disbelief. How had she known, Erica asked? Sigourney licked the dust from her lips. It tasted like unbaked bread. She nervously brushed her hair from her face and looked away. She had no answer for them, at least not one she could share. She couldn't tell them about Anne Hopkins's spirit or her warning.

Jigme hurried over to them. "Is everyone alright?" Anxiety creased his face. "Please, hurry to the van. This is a dangerous place. We should leave at once."

Sigourney piled into the van behind the others, praying that the thin roof over her head would offer adequate protection. Once in her seat, she squirmed with the desire to reread the passage in Anne's diary about the rock slide, but she could feel the termites at work on the back of her neck and clasped her hands in her lap, instead. She knew Mr. Ho was watching her, and she had to keep the diary and manuscript hidden from his inquiring eyes.

At the mouth of the gorge, they came upon a small glacier that stretched across the road. Enterprising Tibetans had chopped a passageway through the wall of living ice, clearing sufficient space for one vehicle to pass through at a time. However, several vans and lorries were stopped, and no one was moving. It didn't take long to discover the reason for the delay. A lorry with a full load of wooden crates had buried its right-front wheel in a pothole in the middle of the icy passageway. It leaned drunkenly to one side, its cargo resting precariously against the glacier's wall. Traffic was blocked in both directions. Several Tibetan drivers were squatting beside the truck smoking cigarettes, while one man tossed rocks into the pothole around the trapped wheel. The clacking sound of the rocks ricocheted off the ice walls with the staccato beat of cawing crows.

When Sigourney got out to look, the raw air whipped through her sweater, and she hurried back to the van to retrieve an extra jacket. Her chill deepened when she discovered Mr. Ho rummaging around in the back.

"Forgot my camera," he offered with a smile. He held up a battered Canon and left. She looked about her with suspicion. Everything seemed in order, but she couldn't help wondering if he was really looking for his camera or snooping through people's belongings. She was thankful she had kept the valise with her.

John walked over to the stranded truck and inspected the damage. "It's going to take more than a pile of rocks to dislodge that lorry," he announced when he returned.

"What'll they do?" Beth asked.

"Wait for a lorry with a heavy enough load to haul this one out of its predicament, I should imagine. What do you think, Jigme?"

Jigme concurred. Many lorries carried chains for such emergencies. It was simply a matter of waiting for the right one to appear.

The Tibetan drivers were unfazed by the delay. Time was of little consequence to them. They had no watches, but Sigourney noticed several of her fellow passengers glancing warily at theirs as they sensed their journey floundering like a ship lost at sea. It was past noon, and Jigme had already advised them they would not reach their next hotel before nightfall. Sigourney wondered if they would get there at all.

Her mind wandered back to the fateful kiss Peggy had planted on Roger's cheek. The following day, Sigourney had stopped by the university to drop off some student papers and, on a whim, decided to walk across campus to visit Roger. It was a sunny, December day, the kind that resonated with crisp air and bright promises. It was the kind of day that made last night's fears seem petty and silly, and she wanted to heal the wounds from their fight. It had been months since they had enjoyed lunch together, and she hoped he would be free to join her. She could have called first, but she wanted to see him, to let him know she was no longer angry.

She found his door open, but the office was empty. She was always amazed at how meticulously he arranged his books and papers. By contrast, her office looked like an unkempt bed. Her eyes wandered over the shelves and settled on his calendar, which lay open on the desk. She was disappointed to see that he had already penciled in something for 1:30 p.m., his normal lunchtime. It was a cryptic entry that defied her to decipher it: Gbear - P. The rest of the afternoon was blank.

Sigourney stared at the entry for several seconds before the image of Peggy kissing Roger flared into her consciousness. The "P" stood for Peggy. She was sure of it. He had a lunch date with her, and while Sigourney tried to tell herself it was only an innocent holiday outing, her mind burned with the knowledge that it was something more. The room was becoming hot and confining. She hurried from the office and rushed down the stairs before anyone noticed her.

Sigourney drove home at a frantic pace, swerving from lane to lane in a maniacal race to reach the safety of her home, her safe harbor. Once inside, she grabbed the telephone book and thumbed the pages to the listings for restaurants. There was nothing that started with a G followed by Bear. She saw several Chinese restaurants with Golden in the name--Golden Dragon, Golden Gong, Golden Moon--but no Golden Bear. It dawned on her that the name might stand for something else, and even as her mind cried out against the possibility, she slowly turned the pages to the listings for motels. There it was. The name leapt at her from the thin, yellow page. The Golden Bear Motel on Maple Street.

She sat down to catch her breath. It had to be a coincidence. Gbear could stand for many things. Except, she remembered Roger telling her that morning he would be counseling students in the afternoon and not to expect him until dinnertime. Why was his calendar blank for the afternoon? Why was there no entry after Gbear?

It was past 1:00 p.m., but it wouldn't take long to drive over to Maple Street and have a look around. She started to get up but sat down again. She didn't know if she could face such an awful reality. Besides, she would feel ridiculous lurking around some seedy motel, only to learn that there was a simple explanation.

Sigourney had a sudden urge to treat herself at the beauty parlor. It was a silly reaction to her fears, but the thought of having her hair done was oddly comforting. She called and made an appointment for two o'clock. The parlor happened to be on the way to Maple Street, but she told herself that was just a coincidence.

After the beauty parlor, she had intended to go straight home but found herself driving slowly down Maple Street, instead. She was drawn to the green-trimmed, two-story building with the vacancy sign. It was one of those low-budget motels with a covered driveway leading to a blacktopped courtyard where people parked in front of their rooms. Nothing fancy about the place. Nothing romantic. It was the kind of place where people traveling on a budget would stop for the night, or where a couple might go in the afternoon to have sex.

It was already after three o'clock when she parked across the street, and she chided herself for arriving too late to actually see anyone leaving. She thought about simply driving into the courtyard, verifying that Roger's car wasn't there and going home, but when she reached for the ignition key, she found her hand trembling so badly, she decided against the idea. It was easier to stay where she was. She decided to wait for half-an-hour, and then go home.

Less than ten minutes later, she watched in horror as Roger's red Toyota pulled out of the parking lot, followed by a freshly-washed Ford Taurus. Sigourney recognized Peggy's strawberry-blond hair and black-rimmed glasses as she drove past. At least it's not a faculty member, she thought wildly. It's not someone I'll see socially.

Sigourney thought she was handling the shock quite well, until her body began shaking so violently, she had to grip the steering wheel with both hands to keep from losing control of herself. A teeth-rattling chill swept through her. Nausea rose in her throat. Her body ached as if it had been violated and abandoned. She didn't feel the tears rolling down her cheeks until she tasted their salty flavor on her lips.

She closed her eyes. Memories of her courtship with Roger floated into her consciousness. Memories of their first kiss. How alive she had felt. It had been a shy kiss, more exploratory than passionate, but she had shivered with delight. When the evening was over, she had tossed in her bed, unable to sleep. She had known right then she never wanted to lose him.

That knowledge had remained at the core of their relationship as they settled into their lives together. She had loved the comfortable patterns and routines in their marriage. Living in a college town. Teaching at the same university. Things were steadfast; life was dependable. At least until now.

As Sigourney sat there wiping away her tears, she was amazed to realize she still wanted Roger. Just not under these circumstances. She wasn't going to share him with Peggy Wilcox or any other woman. She would have to confront him, make him decide which was more important, his marriage or a fling with his secretary. Sigourney refused to consider the possibility that it was more than just a fling. That meant facing issues too painful to imagine.

She had never liked confrontations and had avoided arguments with Roger whenever possible. The result had been a reasonably smooth ride through their marriage, but at a painful cost. An ugly silence had grown between them, a silence deflected by small talk about faculty meetings and classes. They stopped sharing secrets. Had they ever shared secrets? She couldn't remember. Maybe, Roger had considered her silence a sign that it was okay to wander.

She looked at the motel's sign and saw that the T was unlighted, transforming the name into the Golden Bear Mo el. It dawned on her that if the sign was lighted, it was getting dark. A quick glance at her watch told her it was nearly five o'clock. She had been sitting there more than an hour. The effect had been therapeutic. She was calm again. Her nerves were back under enough control for her to drive. . .where? Home, she supposed glumly. Where else could she go? She had no idea what she would do when she got there, or what she would say. She'd have to figure that out when the time came.

It was dark by the time Sigourney pulled into the driveway at five thirty. She could see the flickering light of the television filtering through the curtains in the family room and pictured Roger and Debbie happily watching a program together. The image bore into her skull like a dentist's drill, grinding nerve endings and sending hot bursts of pain shooting through her body. It took all her courage to stop herself from turning around and driving away again.

Sitting in the dark car, Sigourney willed herself back under control. She wanted to slip into the house unnoticed, but she knew they'd seen her headlights. They knew she was home.

"Hey, where've you been?" Roger stuck his head into the hallway. She walked past him towards the kitchen without responding. An icy calm had replaced her earlier bout of nausea and uncontrolled hysteria. Roger gave her a worried look and retreated back into the den. Somehow, she managed to heat up enough leftovers for the evening meal, although when she sat down to eat, she couldn't remember what she had prepared.

Sigourney ate in funeral silence. Her goal was to make it through the meal without creating a scene. If she could just do that, she reasoned, everything would return to normal. She knew that was impossible, but it was the only way she could sit there facing Roger without raking her fingers across his lying face. A confrontation was inevitable. She knew that, but her anger boiled too close to the surface to speak now. It was all she could do to suppress a primordial urge to scream, and this wild, new emotion terrified her. Her left hand began to tremble uncontrollably, and she hid it in her lap. Her right hand was fine, which she found oddly comforting.

"Mom, are you okay?" Debbie shifted uncomfortably in her chair.

Sigourney gave her a half-hearted smile. "I'm fine, honey. Just tired."

Debbie's nervous behavior said she knew her mother was anything but fine. She slipped behind her own veil of silence, not certain where the problem lay or whether she was to blame.

"Well, *my* day was a disaster. The staff meeting accomplished nothing and two of my students failed to show up for their counseling sessions." Roger offered a cheerful smile, but he quickly dropped the subject when Sigourney glared at him.

Silence descended upon them.

After dinner, Sigourney retreated to the study, where she pretended to read a book until Roger and Debbie had gone to bed. Then, she roamed through the dark house touching favorite objects with her fingers--the smooth surface of a ceramic vase, the delicate curves of a glass ballerina. Touching their cool surfaces soothed her battered nerves. She paused in the living room and listened to the hallway clock ticking relentlessly towards midnight. She had loved this house ever since they'd pushed their finances to the limit and bought it all those years ago. It was a big, rambling place with delicious nooks and crannies, like the storage space under the stairs that she had converted into a sewing niche, the seating area in the bay window in the den, and the sun window by the kitchen sink that provided such a lovely, open view onto the backyard garden. When Roger had suggested selling the place for a newer home in one of the more desirable neighborhoods, she'd said no. Their home was near the university, and it suited her needs perfectly.

Now, she was having a difficult time remaining there. At any moment, she feared she would run out the front door. What was she going do? Lying in bed next to Roger wasn't an option. She had to think of some way to resolve this crisis, but talking about it didn't seem possible. Not now. That much she knew for certain.

It was after midnight when the solution struck her. She threw on her coat and rushed to her car, which still stood in the driveway. A thin veil of snowflakes was falling, transforming the afternoon's grimy sludge into a pristine world filled with promise. Empty streets and silent intersections greeted her as she drove back to the Golden Bear Motel. She rang the door buzzer incessantly, until the sleepy night manager stumbled into the registration area and let her in. Marching past him, she picked up two business cards from the counter, then turned and left without saying a word. The baffled manager just stared at her, too dumbfounded to protest her unseemly behavior.

When Sigourney returned home, she quietly placed one card on her pillow next to Roger and the second one on the sink in the bathroom. Satisfied, she took a spare blanket from the hall closet and curled up on the couch in the living room, where she was soon fast asleep.

The next morning, the cards were gone, and so was Roger. He had risen earlier than normal and fled the house. Sigourney went through the motions of her day. She taught her course and attended a committee meeting. But she couldn't stop the dull ache that pounded just behind her forehead.

When she saw Roger at home that night, an unspoken truce was established. They followed their normal routine--making dinner, talking to Debbie, and watching the evening news. This relieved Sigourney, who was desperately trying to re-establish some normalcy in their relationship. The pounding in her head continued, however, telling her nothing could be normal until she brought some closure to the ugly breach that had split their lives in two. Her mind spun in frenzied circles as she tried to bring herself to face Roger. She feared she might lose the control she had so carefully maintained last night. Sigourney wanted to bury her head in her hands and wait for the crisis to pass, but she knew that would solve nothing. She needed closure. She needed to stop feeling like a woman who had been violated in a dark alley.

The only way to heal herself was to "have it out" with him. Once Debbie had gone to bed, once they were alone, she inhaled all the air her lungs could hold and tried to subdue the throbbing sounds in her head.

"Roger," she began tentatively, "I need to know . . ."

"Forgive me!" Roger blurted the words out, bursting through Sigourney's jumbled thoughts. "I did something really stupid, and I deserve your anger. But I never intended for it to happen, and it won't happen again. I promise you."

His puppy dog eyes were filled with so much anguish and regret, Sigourney's anger melted away. Instead of violent words, he was asking for her forgiveness, and his pleading expression told her the crisis would pass. She was returning to her safe harbor. Relief swept over her, cleansing her wounds and silencing the drums in her head. It would take time, but she knew she could forgive him.

Her suspicions didn't die easily. During the next few weeks, she found herself checking on him in unobtrusive ways: finding a reason to call his office, or glancing at his appointment book when she dropped by to see him. When no new evidence presented itself, her confidence returned, and she decided it was time to get on with their lives. It was three weeks before she slept with him again. When she did, their love making became much more sensual. They spent more time exploring each other, touching and fondling as they had when they first went to bed together. Sigourney experienced more pleasure than she had in a long time. She hated to admit it, but Roger's sordid affair had breathed new life into their relationship.

It didn't last, and she realized later that she should have known it wouldn't. They slowly slipped back into their old patterns--spending less time together, becoming more absorbed with their work, having less frequent and more hurried sex. Sigourney saw the signs, but she told herself it was her fault as much as his. Their Indian summer quietly slipped away.

CHAPTER EIGHT

More lorries arrived, but none had the weight necessary to rescue the imprisoned truck from the glacier. Engines coughed to a halt, and more drivers gathered on both sides, where they laughed and chatted together as an hour flew by. At last, a lorry appeared on the far side with enough ballast to free the truck. Everyone's spirits rose, only to crash again when they learned the driver refused to help. He remained seated in his cab at the back of the line, content to wait for another rescuer. His fellow drivers joked and cajoled him, urging him to come forward. He sat there talking with them but making no move to come to their aide. Sigourney was fascinated by their exchange. The Tibetans showed no signs of anger at the driver's intransigence. They smiled and laughed with the obstinate man, as if the whole thing was merely a joke. The man finally relented and pulled his truck out of the line. He drove past the waiting vehicles and stopped a few feet from the stricken lorry. A chain large enough to hold a boat's anchor was quickly produced, and several men happily attached it to the axles of both lorries. Amid shouts and much fanfare, the crippled lorry was pulled from its prison with its load still intact.

After more than an hour of mindless delays, it had taken less than five minutes to clear the road through the glacier. The incident reminded Sigourney of her own life, which in many ways was like that truck. She had spent twenty years trying to build her marriage with Roger, only to be abandoned in the blink of an eye. Now, she was damaged goods, badly in need of a tow to pull her out of the hole into which she had fallen.

When her van reached the Tibetan plateau, Sigourney was greeted by a monochromatic landscape of windswept valleys surrounded by bleak mountains. Winter hovered just a few feet above her head, and desolation stretched as far as the eye could see. The country wasn't just barren; it looked abandoned. Tibet was an alien planet void of life. The unpaved road, which caused the van to buck like a wild mustang, became Sigourney's only reference point to life as she knew it. It stretched before her like an umbilical cord, carrying her farther and farther into an unknown world.

Just when it seemed that her world was totally lost, the van rounded a bend, and she saw peasants tilling the arid soil with wooden plows pulled by great, woolly yaks. Everywhere she looked, men and women worked to the churning rhythm of the wooden blades and yak's hooves. Bright bits of red cloth tied to the yaks' horns and a rainbow of colors radiating from the women's skirts created a festive scene set against the valley's bleak backdrop. It seemed impossible to grow anything in such inhospitable soil, but Jigme explained that the glacier-fed rivers flowing down from the surrounding mountains assured the farmers a good harvest of barley, which was used to make tsampa, the Tibetan staple that Anne had described in her diary.

Sigourney saw few structures until they reached the village of Nyelam, where several unattractive concrete buildings housing Chinese immigrants crowded together among timeworn, Tibetan structures. It was a forlorn setting, and the air snapped with a chill that reminded her they were now above twelve thousand feet and very close to the snow line. Another van sat with its hood up in front of a dismal looking hotel, while the passengers stood nearby glancing furtively at their surroundings. John approached the group's tour guide and talked with him. She noticed that he was always in the middle of things. What did he do for the government, she wondered? His manner was unassuming, but his behavior suggested someone used to taking control. She found this reassuring. She might need such a friend before her quest was over.

"What's the matter?" she asked after he had finished his conversation.

"Broken fuel pump, I think. Looks like they're stuck here for a day or two, until a replacement vehicle can reach them. I suggested a few of them could join us, but they all seem to know each other and want to stay together."

"It's not a very appealing place to be stranded." She looked at the bleak buildings and countryside and shuddered.

Jigme joined them as they walked back towards their own van. "It is too bad about those unhappy travelers. One's fate is always a mystery."

"Do you believe their circumstances are caused by fate?" John asked curiously.

"There is something in the group's karma that has caused their misfortune. It is like having an unwelcome spirit flying around and looking for a place to land. While it flies, it can cause great harm."

Before receiving Anne's warning at the stone bridge, Sigourney would never have believed in spirits, but that had changed, now. She was intrigued by Jigme's comments, although a world filled with spirits still seemed beyond her comprehension. As they walked, an old, Tibetan woman bundled in a jacket lined with sheep's wool approached them. She stopped in front of Sigourney and stretched out a closed hand. Thick wrinkles creased her weathered face, and when she smiled, she exposed uneven rows of teeth with a gap in front where two were missing. She spoke rapidly and stared at Sigourney with watery, heavily-lidded eyes that seemed more closed than open.

"This woman says you have a spirit with you," Jigme explained. "She wants to give you a charm to keep the spirit from flying away and harming you."

The old woman's eyes flew wide open giving her an owlish expression that startled Sigourney. Did she mean Anne Hopkins' spirit? No, Anne wouldn't harm her. Cold air brushed Sigourney's cheeks with a wintry breath. She shivered and stared at the woman, who opened her outstretched hand to reveal a small, wooden carving of a Buddha. It looked as old and worn as the woman.

"I can't take that." Sigourney raised her hands in protest. "It should stay here where it belongs."

The woman spoke again.

"She says you must take it for your own protection," Jigme commented.

The woman stepped closer and pressed the statue into the palm of Sigourney's hand. The woman's skin was brittle to the touch. Then, she suddenly pressed her palm to the valise, and her face broadened into a smile, revealing the gap in her teeth. She muttered something to herself, nodded, and walked away.

"Jigme, what did she say?" Sigourney asked in a startled voice. The old woman's behavior had frightened her.

"It was hard to hear. Something about returning Buddha where he belongs." Jigme frowned, his gaze fixed on the retreating figure. He seemed about to say something more, but abruptly turned and walked towards the van, instead.

"What an odd occurrence," John said, eyeing the valise. "You seem to be having quite an effect on these people."

"I have no idea what's going on. I've never been so mystified in my life." Sigourney tried to remain calm, but her mind was whirling in confusion. There had been the incidents at the stupa and on the bridge, and now this. The old woman had deliberately touched the valise, as if she knew what was inside. John had witnessed all of these events and was staring at her with his inquisitive gaze. He wasn't the only one. She felt the termites at work on the back of her neck and turned to find Mr. Ho standing nearby, observing her.

Sigourney nearly ran back to the van, where she flung herself into her seat and looked out the window, her chest pounding so hard she thought it would explode. The old woman had disappeared but not the uncertainty Sigourney had experienced at the idea of a wayward spirit. Unexplainable events were piling up like driftwood around her. Her trip had hardly begun, but circumstances were already spinning out of control. She stared at the wooden object in her hand with a mixture of curiosity and apprehension. She had to consider the possibility that there might be some truth to Jigme's spiritual world. The old woman certainly thought so. Sigourney held the valise to her chest and pondered what else might be in store for her, then hastily shoved it under her seat when she saw Mr. Ho marching up the aisle.

CHAPTER NINE

Nyelam slowly faded to a memory. The van passed whitewashed, stone houses with rust-red stripes outlining the walls and moon-shaped symbols on the doors. They reminded Sigourney of illustrations for a fairy-tale book she had once read to her daughter. The image rekindled the misery she had experienced while handing Debbie over to Roger. The fear of losing her daughter still burned in her like a white-hot coal that never wavered in its intensity. But she knew she couldn't hope to regain her daughter's love if she didn't first renew her faith in herself, and her faith in others. That was the goal of her quest. She mustn't lose sight of it.

She turned her attention back to the houses in order to suppress her painful memories.

"What do you make of those symbols?" she asked John. "They remind me of markings for magic spells."

"Quite interesting, aren't they?" John leaned forward in his seat. "Over the centuries, the Tibetans have blended their faith in

Buddhism with more ancient Bon beliefs, which include worshipping spirits in inanimate objects. Perhaps, these symbols are meant to protect the houses' occupants from ghosts or wayward spirits, much like the Buddha statue you were given in Nyelam."

Sigourney involuntarily touched the wooden object in her shirt pocket. The idea that these strange symbols and the Buddha statue were linked perplexed her. Her mind rebelled against such ideology, but she couldn't shake the feeling that she had entered a world where logic and reason no longer mattered.

Firewood and yak's dung were stacked along the outer walls of the courtyards that enclosed many of the houses. Sigourney couldn't imagine where the wood came from. There were no trees, other than an occasional small grove of spindly, white-bark specimens huddled near one of the houses.

Most of the dwellings sat in isolation or in small groups of two or three. Other than Nyelam, there were no villages or towns, no community centers. The Tibetans seemed to welcome their quarantined loneliness.

The van began to ascend the first mountain range. Sigourney had expected to see cliffs and peaks towering above her, but the slopes rose from the valley floor with little drama. They were climbing steadily higher, however, and the air was becoming noticeably thinner, requiring her to take deeper breaths. The fields of snow now surrounding the van had formed into icy stalagmite sculptures that reminded her of hundreds of ground hogs looking for their shadows. Wintry clouds continued to hover overhead, adding to the monochromatic landscape of muted whites and grays.

The terrain at the summit was surprisingly flat. Only a sudden burst of prayer flags whipping furiously in the wind told Sigourney that they had reached top of the mountain pass. Small piles of rocks--Anne had called them chortens--were stacked in random patterns on the ground. Sigourney knew the flags and chortens had been placed there to appease the ancient spirits and to assure a safe passage. She took the wooden Buddha from her shirt pocket and stared at its cryptic eyes. If there were spirits in this enigmatic land, she hoped they would allow her safe passage to the Samye

Monastery.

The others ventured out into the freezing wind to wander around the mounds of rocks and dancing flags, but the dizzying effects of the high altitude were taking their toll on Sigourney, and she decided to remain in her seat. She sat listening to the wind whooshing past her window and thought about Anne. She now believed in Anne's spirit and felt it close to her. It was time to read more of Anne's diary. Sigourney looked out the window to make sure Mr. Ho wasn't lurking close by and pulled it from the valise.

Diary entry by Anne Hopkins, 1899

We are now trekking along one of the pilgrims' main trails across the Tibetan plateau. The weather has grown a bit more cheery, although when the wind blows, all the layers of clothing I possess are not enough to keep out the chill. We are walking by day, and we encounter many voyagers along our route. Some are traveling from monastery to monastery, just as we claim to be doing. My disguise is working quite well. We have managed to beg for tsampa and butter tea on two occasions without raising suspicion. Tenzin has done the begging, while I hang back. My role is a humble one, but I am rather enjoying it.

These pilgrims are simple folk with little knowledge about people beyond Tibet, so it has been easy to fool them. They have a simplistic view of foreigners. They think we all have light-colored hair, white skin and white eyes, meaning the color of our eyes is something other than black or brown. Fortunately, my hair and eyes are brown, so I have little to worry about there. However, I must be very careful to hide my skin color.

At one point, we heard horns wailing across the valley floor, which told us there was a monastery nearby. I knew monks were less likely to be fooled by my disguise. Many of them have traveled to neighboring countries and met foreigners. We must try to avoid them as much as possible, at least until we are farther into Tibet's interior. The horns' mournful calls echoed off the mountains on either side of the valley, making it impossible to determine their direction or how far away they were. They sounded like spirits that had been held captive for a long time and were now rejoicing in their freedom. We continued our journey without ever discovering their source.

At one point, we passed a finely dressed couple on horseback. The woman wore a great deal of jewelry and was accompanied by four maid servants, who walked humbly behind her horse. The man rode a spirited stallion with a saddle of inlaid silver. I counted ten attendants walking behind him. He gave neither of us so much as a glance. His disdain encouraged me, for these fine people had undoubtedly met foreigners.

Sigourney stopped reading long enough to glance out her window. She watched her fellow travelers bracing themselves against the winds and imagined Anne standing there. What a sight she would have made in her peasant's clothes and charcoal-covered skin. Mr. Ho and the others were still occupied with the chortens and flags. Sigourney read on.

I was anxious to return to the mountains where we could avoid curious villagers, but for the moment, we had little choice but to follow the road where it led us. There was no place to hide on the plains. We faced this very problem the next night, when we approached one of the larger villages in the area, one that included a monastery. We stopped before reaching the village, built a small fire from twigs and yak dung for tea and pretended to rest until dark. We waited until everyone was asleep before attempting to pass through the village. As soon as we entered the main street, however, we roused a large mastiff dog inside one of the compounds. Fortunately, it was leashed so it could not attack us, but it issued a loud, bell-toned bark that was bound to wake the home's occupants. We hurried on, but two more dogs from the monastery joined the first. We knew the barking would soon rouse the whole village. We proceeded to the far side of the town, only to discover a soldier's post there! What should we do? How could we explain why we were traveling at night? We decided to wait until morning before trying to pass the outpost. There was a path leading to a stream, and we followed it, until we reached a rocky outcrop. The night was lighted by a nearly full moon, which helped us considerably. A small cave provided us with shelter, and we bedded down to wait for morning. With luck, there might be a trail that would keep us clear of the soldiers.

By the time we awoke, the village was bustling with activity. I could see one of the mastiffs wandering along the road sniffing our strange scent. He had a formidable appearance. No other trail presented itself, so we had no choice but to return to the village. I trembled at the idea that we might be found out and turned back, all because of those stupid dogs!

One of the villagers stopped Tenzin to inquire about our arrival at such a late hour. Tenzin remained calm. He explained that I had not been feeling well, and it was too late when we arrived to seek accommodations. This story seemed to satisfy the villager, and we proceeded toward the soldier's station. I held my breath, certain we would be stopped and interrogated, but the soldier on duty ignored us as we trudged past. We must have looked very poor and uninteresting to him.

Once we were out of sight, I wanted to dance and sing, but I dared not, lest someone see us. We had passed a difficult hurdle, but we knew there were more to come. It was too soon to become confident.

Sigourney was so absorbed in Anne's story, she didn't realize John had returned to the van, until she saw him looking at her. She hastily slipped the diary back into her valise and glanced about nervously to see if anyone else had spotted her. She was relieved to see no sign of Mr. Ho, but she scolded herself for looking so guilty. She would have to be more careful.

John gave her an unassuming smile and said nothing.

"Is it very cold out there?" she asked lamely.

"Yes, quite bracing." The others were returning, but John hesitated in the aisle. "Are you feeling alright?"

"Oh, I'm fine. Trying to adjust to the altitude. I was a little dizzy and my head was aching, but I'm better now." Sigourney felt stupid about her reaction to John, and she hoped her anger at herself wasn't reflected in her voice.

"It'll be another four hours before we reach our hotel at Shegar. If you'd like some company, I'd be happy to join you for awhile."

John's suggestion caught her off guard. Her fingers tightened around the valise in her lap. She was certain he'd seen the manuscript when it lay exposed on the Friendship Bridge, and he'd witnessed the Tibetans reaching for her valise. Could she trust him, or was he merely trying to discover her secret? She glanced at him suspiciously, but his eyes were focused on her, not the bag.

John did help me at the bridge, she thought, and I have to trust someone. She realized she was hesitating, which was embarrassing him. He shifted his weight and started to move to his own seat.

"Do you think I'm safe sitting with a married man?" she asked with an awkward attempt at humor as she slid the valise under her seat.

"That's a long story," he replied with a slight frown. "Perhaps I should save it for another time."

"No, no. Please sit down." She patted the seat next to her with her hand. "You took me by surprise, and I'm afraid I responded poorly to your suggestion. I'd be glad if you joined me."

John hesitated a moment longer, then slipped into the seat beside her. "This is a bit new for me, and I'm not very good at making small talk with a woman I hardly know. Haven't done much of it in years. Oh, I'm fine in social gatherings, that sort of thing. Just not much good at starting conversations on my own." He gave her an embarrassed smile that disarmed her.

"It must be difficult, traveling without your wife," she replied. John's face flinched at the comment, and she immediately regretted what she had said. "Sorry if I said anything wrong."

"Not at all."

When he said nothing further, Sigourney found the silence awkward. "What do you do?" she asked.

"I'm in the diplomatic corps. It's my responsibility to see that our embassies and consulates are staying abreast of policy changes and not working at cross purposes. I travel a great deal, which gives me little time for a social life." He showed her a whimsical smile, giving Sigourney the impression that this polite gentleman was lonely and vulnerable, both of which she found to be endearing qualities. She began to regret that he was married.

"It must be difficult for your family." Once again, she found herself biting her tongue. Why did she persist in mentioning his family?

"My son and daughter are both away at school, so it's not a problem, although they've had a hard time adjusting to their mother being gone."

"Gone? I don't understand. Has she moved elsewhere?"

"No, she died recently."

The words escaped John's lips and sank like a capsized boat into the sudden gloom surrounding them. Sigourney grasped his hand, and then quickly withdrew it.

"I'm very sorry, John. How recent was it?"

"Just a year ago."

She glanced at his wedding ring, a gold band with three little diamonds twinkling like the stars in Orion's belt. He answered her unspoken question. "I promised myself that I'd wear my ring for one year as part of my mourning. Silly, I suppose, but I felt the need to do it."

"Not silly at all." She looked at the tell-tale band on her own finger where her rings had been. Why hadn't she found someone like that?

"I couldn't help noticing you've been wearing a ring until recently. Don't mean to pry."

Sigourney blushed from a sudden attack of nerves . . . much like the reaction she used to experience around men when she was younger. "It's nothing dramatic. I'm getting divorced. Not my choice," she added hastily. "My husband's found someone else. My daughter and I are trying to sort things out."

John's expression remained implacable. Very British, she thought. Very gentlemanly. "Does your daughter live with you?"

"You could say that. We're more like two warring armies

trying to occupy the same territory. Debbie's fifteen, and she's acting very much like a teenager. It's put quite a strain on our relationship." Memories of a sunny, charming daughter skipped through Sigourney's thoughts. Where had she gone? Jigme said spirits could fly through the air and take possession of people. Perhaps, one had taken possession of Debbie.

Sigourney had always felt inadequate as a parent. Roger, on the other hand, had embraced fatherhood. She had marveled at his willingness to change diapers and warm milk bottles at two in the morning. Sigourney had always believed he did a better job of parenting, and Debbie's rebellious behavior had only intensified her misgivings. She knew her lack of confidence hadn't helped matters.

"Too bad about the heavy cloud cover. Mt. Everest is just beyond those foothills."

Sigourney's thoughts scattered like startled rabbits at the sound of John's voice. She looked around, disoriented, trying to remember where she was. They were down the mountain, and she saw sheep grazing in the brown fields to her right. Everything above the foothills was buried in thick clouds. She noticed the earthen walls of a ruin on a nearby hilltop. It reminded her of a sand castle that had been assaulted by shifting ocean tides, except no ocean had existed here during the history of mankind.

"Are those the walls of an old fortress?" she asked. "They look like they've been there forever."

"Left over from a time when Tibet was ruled by fiefdoms, I imagine. I expect we'll see more of them. Tibet was once splintered into feudal states. Many built fortresses to protect their lands from rival kingdoms."

"You know a lot about Tibet." Sigourney gave him an admiring glance.

"Very little, I'm afraid." John's smooth face widened into a self-conscious smile at Sigourney's compliment. "I managed to do a little reading before I left on this trip."

"I wish I could have done that, but my plans were so sudden." Sigourney fidgeted with a loose button on her jacket. She'd meant to repair it but hadn't had the time. She could feel John's curious eyes scanning her.

"I see you've brought something to read on the trip," he said at last. "Part of your work, I suppose." Evening was nearly upon them, but the wary look she shot him didn't go unnoticed. John laughed. "Now I *am* prying. A bad habit of mine, I'm afraid. Please accept my apologies."

Sigourney smiled. She liked John's affable manner. It was easy talking to him. He focused his attention on her when she spoke. That made her feel worthwhile. Not something Roger had done for a long time.

She looked at the passing landscape, and after awhile she imagined she could see the flowing, ethereal forms of ancient spirits swirling past her window. They danced on the wind's currents like silk scarves, creating kaleidoscopic images in blues, yellows and greens. Handfuls of fluffy snow joined the dancing spirits. The entire landscape was alive in a circus of colors and patterns. Sigourney wanted to run after the spirits, but a light shining in the distance distracted her. It mesmerized her, and she stopped and stared at its yellow glow, until a sudden jolting motion scattered the spirits into the black night. Everything disappeared, except for the light, which still beamed at her.

She opened her eyes and realized she'd been dozing. The van had stopped in front of a small building standing beside the road. Total darkness blanketed the countryside in an ink-black veil, causing the light emitted from the building's open doorway to shine like a beacon. Sigourney remembered the light from her dream. It looked lonely. Her hand brushed the seat next to her where John had been sitting, but it was empty.

Jigme left the van and walked to the building, where a police officer stood in the doorway waiting for him.

"This must be the inspection point Henri told us about," John offered. He had returned to his seat behind her.

Sigourney's pulse quickened. She considered herself to be a reasonably calm person, but she couldn't control the wild beating of her heart as she watched Jigme emerge from the building with two Chinese officials. This was the moment she had been dreading. She had escaped the inspection at the border, but what could she do now? Her only hope was that Brad Paxton had kept his mouth shut. If so, the guards would follow normal procedure--randomly pick one or two suitcases from the back of the van--and she would be safe. If not, Mr. Ho would be waiting to pounce on her.

Sigourney couldn't rid herself of an overpowering sense of guilt. She was starting to sweat, even though the air exposed to the open van door was becoming chilly. She hadn't imagined it would be so difficult to appear innocent while hiding something. No wonder criminals got caught, she thought. Many of them gave themselves away just by the looks on their faces. She was glad the van was so dark. Jigme re-entered the van and snapped on the interior lights. So much for hiding in the dark, she thought with dismay. One of the guards followed him, while the other went to the back of the van and opened the door to the luggage compartment.

"We will be a few more minutes than usual," Jigme announced. Sigourney heard the same tension in his voice as when he introduced Mr. Ho. "There are rumors that someone is smuggling Buddhist propaganda into Tibet, so the police must look through all our bags."

Panic shot through Sigourney like gunfire. They *did* know. The second official was already lifting luggage from the back of the van and opening it, while his cohort walked down the aisle towards the last row of seats. His eyes bore into Sigourney's when he passed. They told her he knew she was the one, and he would reveal her treachery shortly. Her hands shook uncontrollably as she picked up the valise and pressed it to her chest. What could she do? The valise was too large to hide under her seat, and there was no other place to put it.

The guard looked through the smaller bags of Jenny and Erica. Mr. Ho had no luggage at his seat and was ignored, but he watched the proceedings with interest. His bright eyes locked onto Sigourney's. She swung her head back to the front and stared blankly out the window. A sticky sweat was building under her armpits. Her shoulders were rigid with tension, and her hands were so moist they slipped on the valise.

Sigourney was vaguely aware of John rising from his seat and walking to the front of the van, where he conversed with Jigme in a low voice. The guard was looking through Erica's handbag. In another minute or two, it would be Sigourney's turn. Damn it, she thought, why had she agreed to do this? It had seemed such a noble pursuit. Now, it was turning into a nightmare. Her hands fidgeted with the clasp on the valise, and she had to grip them together to keep them still. All she could do was put the valise under her seat and hope it wouldn't be unnoticed. It was a poor plan. The official had moved to Marie-Rose. He was getting closer.

John abruptly sat down beside her. "Please forgive my intrusion," he whispered, "but I have noticed your concern about your travel bag. Perhaps, you should give it to me." His face was tense and serious.

Sigourney blinked, not certain she understood him. "What can you do?" she whispered back.

"Just give me the bag, now," he commanded in a more urgent tone. He pulled a document from his own briefcase. "Quickly, before he sees you."

John had sensed her fear and was trying to help. Somehow, she found the strength to slide the valise onto his lap, although she had no idea why she was doing so. There was nothing he could do. In a few moments, the manuscript would be exposed and her quest would end.

The official stepped forward and faced John and Sigourney. "Your bags." There was nothing kind in the request. Only two words spoken in a heavy, Chinese accent. She held out her hand bag, and he quickly rummaged through it and handed it back. He turned to John. The moment had arrived. Her life was about to change forever, but she couldn't let John take the blame for her. She started to reach for the valise.

"Sorry, old man," John said in a calm, pleasant voice. "Diplomatic immunity, I'm afraid. These two cases are official British government business. Not to be opened until I get to

Beijing. As you can see, they're sealed." Sigourney realized that he had managed to slip a yellow, elastic tape around the briefcase and valise. He handed the official the document he was still holding and planted both hands firmly on the cases.

The official looked puzzled. "Must inspect."

Jigme stepped forward in a very deferential manner and spoke to the official in Chinese. A brief flurry of words was exchanged between them, while the official continued to look at the document. He turned and shouted to the other official, who was still busy pawing through the suitcases in back. More words flew back and forth. Sigourney's whole body was trembling by now.

"Must inspect," the official said again more forcefully.

"Jigme." John directed his attention to their guide, ignoring the official. "Please explain to this man that we do not want an international incident here. If he persists with his illegal claim, I shall have to take his name and report him to Liu Feng's office when I reach Beijing."

Jigme spoke again in a deferential tone to the policeman, who blanched noticeably at the mention of Feng's name. The official hesitated for several agonizing seconds as he studied the British document, then he handed it back to John. "You show in Beijing," he announced and turned to Cameron and Beth across the aisle.

Sigourney sagged in her seat, her despair replaced by exhaustion. Moments ago, her world had nearly disintegrated before her eyes. She had seen herself being escorted from the van in the strong, unforgiving grip of that Chinese policeman and forced into the isolated building outside her window. She had been seconds away from ceasing to be a tourist and becoming a criminal held in custody on the edges of the Tibetan frontier. Her mind had whirled with images of ankle shackles, prison bars and dark cells. But she had been saved from this frightening nightmare by the remarkable man seated next to her.

Neither of them spoke while the two policemen finished their search. At one point, John placed his large, gentle hand on hers. The symbolic warmth of his gesture flowed through her, calming her shredded nerves. At last, the two men departed and signaled to

Jigme to be on his way. Sigourney watched the pale light of the desolate police outpost slip farther and farther behind them. She stared into the black night, her mind as void of purpose or thought as the emptiness beyond her window. She had just looked into the face of hell, and she never wanted to confront such terror again.

At some point, she must have gripped John's hand. He gently released her grasp and handed her back the valise. It was too dark for her to see him clearly, but she imagined the unassuming smile playing across his face. She was starting to realize there was nothing unassuming about him. His powers of observation and decision-making were razor sharp.

"Thank you," she said meekly, breaking their silence.

"That was a bit chancy, wasn't it?" His voice was serious, but there was an undertone of amusement, as if he had just played a practical joke on someone. "I didn't want to pry, but I sensed you had something in your travel bag that you didn't want the Chinese to see. Hope you didn't mind my intervention."

"Mind! You just saved my life! That was the most awful thing I've ever been through. Do you really have diplomatic immunity?"

"Of course not. Not here, anyway. I have no government business in Tibet. Simply on holiday. Those were inexperienced, uneducated young men stuck at a post they hate, with no idea what's really going on in the world. I figured if I looked and sounded important enough, they might not want to confront me."

Sigourney felt an incredible mixture of incredulity and giddy relief at what she was hearing. Had the whole thing been a bluff, after all? "But the tape you slipped around my valise and your briefcase. What was that?"

"I brought some tape from home, in case I needed to bind a souvenir or my cranky suitcase, which is getting rather old. The document was a letter to the British embassy discussing holiday schedules. Terribly important stuff, don't you agree? Liu Feng's name is real enough. He's very high up in China's political circles, and I figured our friend back there would know who he was. Never met the man, nor do I expect to."

Sigourney sat in silence for awhile, sifting through this

surprising information. "John," she said at last, "I do thank you from the bottom of my heart. You're an amazing man to think of such a ruse so quickly. If you insist on knowing what I'm doing, I'll tell you. I owe you that, and I know I can trust you. But, I would rather not say anything, if you don't mind. It's something very important to me, and I would like to keep it confidential, at least for now."

"I didn't expect you to. Glad to be of service. If you *do* feel the need to talk to someone, I'll be happy to listen." He patted her hand.

The earlier tension was gone, and she began to relax. Then, she remembered Mr. Ho. The termites started feeding on her neck, once more. She knew he'd seen everything, and he hadn't been fooled. Whatever his reason for joining the group, his presence hung over her like an ill-omened cloud.

CHAPTER TEN

Jigme had turned out the lights inside the van, plunging Sigourney's world into a black hole where the Tibetan night had no beginning or end. She welcomed the darkness, the way it enveloped her in its inky embrace. Her mind began to drift through the layers of her life, capturing lost images in a web of memories triggered by her close call with those Chinese guards.

To her surprise, she found herself thinking about shopping expeditions with her mother. As a child, she had assumed the solution to any problem was to buy clothes. She had her mother to thank for that.

Got picked on at school? "Come one, honey, I'll buy you a new dress."

Fell and skinned a knee? "A new blouse will fix that."

Feeling depressed? "The shoe store's open 'til six. I'll get the car."

It was a lovely world, where anything wrong could be fixed before dinner. She envied her mother's panache. (Sigourney looked the word up in the dictionary when she heard it used to describe her mom). People watched what she wore, and it wasn't unusual to see similar hats and outfits popping up around town after she bought them. However, Sigourney soon realized that the constant parade of new outfits couldn't give her the same verve or style as her mother. For one thing, she was too tall and thin as a willow. She towered over the other girls and stood taller than most of the boys. Her best physical feature was her long legs. She had once been described in a school yearbook as "legs forever," which the editors assured her was meant as a compliment. She wasn't so sure. Her legs only accentuated her height and made her stand out in a most undesirable way. She was also too plain and too small breasted. There was no reason for the boys to look at her, and they didn't.

Her saving grace was her 160+ I.Q. and straight "A's" through high school. Scholarships through college. PhD in history. Brains didn't win popularity contests or get her invited to the senior prom, but they did help compensate for her feelings of inadequacy.

Sigourney loved the town where she grew up. Things were orderly and predictable there, and she found that reassuring. The streets were lined with mature trees that reminded her of cathedrals spreading their protective arms over her head. Her only regret was that her father owned the local hardware store instead of the drug store. The drug store had an old fashioned soda fountain where the kids hung out after school. She would have been much more popular if her father had owned the drug store.

She didn't blame *him* for her lack of friends, however. Dad was patient and caring. He encouraged Sigourney and took an interest in her world. He solved problems with words, not clothes. Mother, on the other hand, didn't ask about her day or show much interest in her barren social life. She just kept buying, and as credit cards replaced cash, she quickly adopted them. When their town became too small to satisfy her, she dragged Sigourney along on weekend trips to Chicago, where she pillaged the department stores and swank shops along Michigan Avenue. Two hundred dollar shoes, $500 coats, $300 purses and hundreds more on cosmetics rang the cash registers like church bells.

Sigourney hated Chicago. The streets were filled with the constant buzz of traffic and the cry of sirens. Chaos ruled in the city. Tall buildings and glass replaced leafy trees. Nothing was orderly; nothing was predictable. Except her mother's shopping. Sigourney grew to hate that most of all. She could see it was an obsession that dwelled inside her mother, a beast waiting to free itself and hop a cab to the nearest Macy's or Robinson's. Even at fifteen, she understood that a hardware store in a small town couldn't support her mother's addiction indefinitely. Her father said little, but she could see the worry lines spreading like cracked glass across his face.

He economized, but it wasn't enough. Angry voices late at night warned Sigourney that her world was changing. "You'll bankrupt us." "Settled for a hardware store." "Thought you were happy here." "Could've made more of yourself." "Can't make ends meet." "Never should've married you." Sigourney understood the tones of voice, if not all the arguments.

A year later, her mother was gone. Divorce and a wealthy Chicago bachelor swept her away, leaving a forest of unpaid bills in her wake. Sigourney soon learned a new word: infidelity. She overheard two women using the word in reference to her mother and immediately went home to the dictionary. Unfaithfulness. Disloyalty. Adultery. She knew the meaning of those words. It didn't take her long to see that her father had become the laughing stock of the town and that she shared in his misfortune at school. Any hope she had of "fitting in" had fled with her mother.

Sigourney had her choice of universities after she graduated, but she selected one in a town that was small enough to make her feel comfortable. College offered a mixed bag of experiences. She was grateful to find that many of the young men were reaching or surpassing her in height, but that didn't help much. Boys made her tongue-tied, and she found it easier to bury herself in books than to carry on conversations with them. Occasionally, a classmate found her shyness appealing and asked her out. One took her to a fraternity party where she cringed all evening at the sight of so much liquor and the rowdy behavior of both genders. After a few dates, her quiet demeanor lost its appeal, and the phone would go dumb. Things improved in graduate school. She liked her classmates' growing maturity, and she found it easier to talk to them.

No one turned her head or made her heart beat so fast she couldn't catch her breathe, however, until she met Roger on a blind date shortly after receiving her PhD. He was preparing his thesis for a doctorate in English and working as a teaching assistant. She had accelerated through her program and was already a first-year history professor.

When he arrived to pick her up on their first date, she opened the door of her tiny apartment and discovered a slightly rumpled young man with a shy grin and wiry, blond hair. She was relieved to see that he was taller than her, and she smiled when he offered her a small bouquet of flowers. Her pleasant reaction quickly turned to panic when she realized he was alone.

"Where is Jan and Fred?" she blurted out without waiting for him to introduce himself. Their friends were supposed to join them for dinner.

"Jan caught a cold. I guess it's just the two of us." He smiled awkwardly. "I'm Roger Phillips, by the way."

"Sorry." She realized she was acting very rude. "It was just such a shock to see you standing there by yourself. I'm Sigourney Marshall." She accepted the flowers but couldn't think what to do next. She had expected to welcome everyone inside for light refreshments before leaving for the restaurant. However, inviting a man she didn't know into her apartment didn't seem proper. An uncomfortable silence followed while she looked at the flowers.

"If you're ready, perhaps we should go," he prompted.

His suggestion galvanized her into action. "Yes, of course. Just wait here while I put these in water and get my sweater." She hurried to the kitchen sink, abandoning him in the doorway.

Dinner was such a bumbling affair, Sigourney knew there was little chance she would see this likable man again, and that made her more miserable. All her anxieties tumbled out of their secret hiding places and tied her up in knots. She didn't know what to do or say and let him carry the conversation. The result was an evening filled with brief comments and questions followed by even briefer replies. When they returned to her front door, she was prepared to flee inside, but he took her hand and stopped her.

"Look, I know neither of us quite knew what to do or say tonight. I was pretty nervous when I found out Fred and Jan wouldn't be joining us. But I had a good time, and I hope to see you again." She had been avoiding Roger's eyes all evening. Now, she gazed directly into them. She was so overcome by feelings of joy, she found it hard to breathe.

"Yes, I . . . I'd like that very much," she managed to stammer.

"Good, it's settled then. I'll call you tomorrow."

There was no good night kiss, but after he left, she leaned against the door for a long time trying to regain her composure. Her hand burned where he had held it, and her body trembled with an excitement she had never felt before. It seemed a small miracle that he was still interested in her, and she feared he was merely being polite. But he called the next day, as promised, and made a second date.

Sigourney was amazed that he found her appealing--he never called her beautiful, and she didn't expect him to--and she found her self-confidence growing. For the first time in her life, she *felt* like an attractive woman. They boated on the lake, took long walks in the woods and shared picnic lunches in the fields near a local winery. It was the happiest time of her life, but there were little things that gnawed at her and raised bouts of uncertainty. Roger was witty and charming. He constantly quoted Shakespeare or famous poets, and women, especially female students, doted on him. They reminded Sigourney of monarchs fluttering around sycamore trees during mating season. There were odd patterns in their dating, as well. Roger would ask Sigourney out on a Friday or Saturday night, but never both, claiming he needed the time to work on his thesis. Sigourney understood the pressures of completing a Ph.D. and said nothing, but she couldn't help wondering why he insisted on studying alone. As the months passed, she began to worry that she might not be captivating enough to hold onto him. Her initial burst of confidence slid into self-doubt.

One evening, Sigourney was hurrying across campus after working late grading papers when she spotted Roger walking with a pert redheaded student. They looked like the ideal couple, chatting and smiling at each other. When the girl slid her free arm through his and pecked him on the cheek, Sigourney's mind froze. She stood like an old tree trunk that had been split by lighting and watched them disappear around the corner of the library. She told herself that she was overreacting. It was nearly dark. It *could* have been somebody else, not him. Except, she had memorized every detail in his handsome face and sauntering stride. She could have picked him out of a pack of marathon runners just by looking at his wiry hair. A wave of nausea rose in her stomach, and she rushed to the nearest bathroom.

Sigourney drove home in a haze of pain and sorrow. Her life was in tatters. A powerful storm raged inside of her, leaving her too weak to think straight. The image of Roger with that redhead filled her with dread, and she had to fight back the urge to keep driving until she had put the university far behind her.

Her apartment echoed her loneliness. She sat in the dark and contemplated a future without Roger. The winds in her mind had quieted enough for her to confront her fears, and she resolved not to succumb to them. If Roger preferred the company of other women, then so be it. Life would go on without him. She wouldn't give him the satisfaction of breaking off their relationship. When the phone rang, however, her resolve wilted, and she jumped up to answer it.

"Hey, where were you tonight?" His voice was light and cheery.

"What . . . what do you mean?" she managed to ask.

"You were supposed to meet me at the library. I just came from there. I would have called sooner, but I was helping a student with her assignment while I waited for you."

"She was holding your arm and kissing you!" Sigourney

declared in a cheerless voice. "I saw you."

"What? Oh good grief. It's not what you think, Sigourney. She does that with other profs, not just me. Wait there. I'm coming right over." The phone clicked, and he was gone.

Sigourney paced the room, not certain what to do. Her mind and stomach were both churning madly. Was it possible that she had gotten it all wrong? That Roger still wanted her? Everything was in a whirl.

She was a nervous wreck by the time Roger rang her doorbell. He took her in his arms and kissed her with more passion than she had ever known before. "You silly goose," he chided her gently. "I'm not interested in some college sophomore. Don't you know you're the girl I want to marry?"

Sigourney swooned in his arms. Had he just proposed to her? She wasn't sure, but it sounded like a proposal. The storm was gone. His arms were strong, secure. She had sailed into a safe harbor, and she gladly surrendered herself to him.

They were married as soon as Roger finished his dissertation and joined the faculty in the English Department. There was a house for sale near the university they could barely afford, and they set about making a life together. Sigourney cocooned herself in her research, teaching and home life. After Debbie was born, she thought life was perfect. Who could ask for more than a darling baby daughter and a husband who was the man of her dreams?

CHAPTER ELEVEN

It was eleven o'clock when the van finally pulled into the hotel's compound in Shegar. When Sigourney stepped from the van, she was greeted by a blast of arctic air that burned her ears and fingers, and by the time she grabbed her suitcase and hurried into the lobby, she was gasping for breath from the high altitude. She nearly collapsed on her suitcase and blew warm breaths on her hands, but it did little good. The lobby was as cold as the cave Anne had described in her diary.

There were no porters or elevator, and it took all Sigourney's strength to lug her suitcase up the stairs to her room. Tiny beads of sweat formed on her forehead despite the cold, but they quickly froze. She flicked on the room's weak ceiling light and saw her breath making foggy puffs as she labored to draw sufficient oxygen into her lungs. It was a plain little room with a dismal bathroom that was missing many of its wall tiles. She tried the hot water faucet in the sink, but nothing came out. It didn't matter. She was too tired to care. The bed was covered by a thick comforter, which would be her only source of warmth for the night. It was too cold to remove her clothing, so she took off her shoes and slid fully dressed between the icy sheet and comforter, where she rolled up into a ball and shivered while she waited for her body heat to warm her space.

When Sigourney finally felt warm enough, she began to doze but snapped awake again gulping for air. She lay in a drowsy stupor, trying to understand what was happening. Soon, her eyes drooped shut, only to open once more as she frantically inhaled what little oxygen she could glean from the stingy atmosphere. Sigourney repeated this maddening ritual for most of the night. At some point early in the morning, she propped her pillow against the wall and sat up with the comforter wrapped around her. The room was so cold, it felt like the inside of a meat locker, but the comforter was doing a reasonable job of keeping her warm as long as she didn't shift in the bed. The moment she slipped a leg or arm outside her little cocoon of warmth, the icy bedding bit her with the ferocity of an angry pit bull.

Sigourney thought about her narrow escapes at the Friendship Bridge and the police check point. She was still badly shaken, and she knew her good fortune couldn't last forever. The increased security worried her. It suggested they were looking for something more important than the diary, but what? Even if Brad *had* alerted the authorities, he didn't know about the manuscript. Yet, Mr. Ho had mysteriously joined the tour, and Jigme had said the police were looking for Buddhist propaganda. Was someone else carrying Buddhist materials, perhaps from the Dalai Lama, and the Chinese had learned about it? That seemed too much of a coincidence. She couldn't shake the notion that they were looking for the manuscript, which was impossible, unless she accepted the proposition that the book was communicating with the Tibetans. Unless she accepted the idea of Tibetan spirits.

One thing was certain. It was going to be much harder to complete her quest than she originally thought, and she knew she had crossed a line tonight. Turning back was no longer an option. She had passed the point of no return, much like those astronauts years ago who experienced a system failure on their way to the moon and had to keep going, using the moon's gravitational force to swing their damaged spacecraft around and return it to earth. Sigourney felt like she was riding in her own space capsule. She had to keep going and use Tibet's spiritual energy to return her home to her daughter. She must deliver the manuscript and complete her quest. If she didn't, she would fail the Tibetans and herself, and she couldn't let that happen.

Her determination surprised her. As frightening as last night's incident had been, it hadn't deterred her resolve. Such boldness was new to her. She was discovering an inner strength she hadn't known she possessed before her journey began. Changes were taking place in her emotional and spiritual psyche. Sigourney felt akin to the metamorphic rock she had seen during yesterday's dramatic ride up that battered gorge; her own mettle was being transformed from sandy loam to granite. The woman who left her daughter a few days ago no longer existed, and the woman she was becoming wouldn't be whole until journey's end. This idea frightened her a little, but it also brought her comfort. She looked forward to discovering more about herself as she pursued her destiny across the frozen tundra of Tibet.

Her thoughts wandered to John. What an amazing thing he had done! If his bluff had been called, they would have both been taken into custody and interrogated. The more she thought about her British traveling companion, the more she realized he was a man of very strong character. That pleasant, unassuming manner and perpetual smile hid some very interesting qualities, qualities that Sigourney associated with more serious undertakings than delivering embassy vacation schedules. She hoped to get to know him better.

Sitting up was proving to be much more comfortable than lying down. She began to breathe more normally.

Sigourney awoke with a start and found herself still sitting upright in the bed. Gray light filtered through the room, announcing the arrival of dawn. She scampered out from under the warm comforter and put on her heavy jacket. The room seemed even colder than last night. She found a fresh thermos outside her door and quickly poured steaming water over a tea bag in the porcelain cup on her night stand. Probably made in China, she thought, as she lifted the cup and sipped the life-restoring liquid.

The idea of going another day without washing was too much, and she tested the faucet in the bathroom for hot water. The water remained icicle cold. Her only choice was to use the water from the thermos, so she hastily removed her clothing, poured hot water onto a washcloth and soaped and rinsed herself as best she could. By the time she had toweled off and thrown on fresh clothes, her teeth were chattering like angry monkeys.

When Sigourney started to fold the shirt she had worn the day before, she felt a lump in the pocket and removed the small, wooden statue given to her in Nyelam. She stared at its vague features, trying to ascertain its details. The worn face stared back at her with an expression of peaceful meditation. The old woman had said the statue would guard her from harmful spirits. Perhaps, that was what had happened last night. She had dreamt about spirits before reaching the police station. The statue gave her comfort, and she put it in her coat pocket where she could keep it close.

The only way to keep warm was to move about, so Sigourney decided to take a brisk walk before breakfast, but just as she opened the door, she heard the sounds of someone vomiting in the bathroom next to hers. She stepped into the hallway and knocked on the adjacent door. No one responded.

"Hello," she said softly, "it's Sigourney. Are you all right in there?"

After a brief pause, she heard footsteps, and the door cracked open enough to reveal Marie-Rose's pinched face. The woman's pale look worried Sigourney.

"Merci. Thank you for asking. I am fine."

"Do you need any medication for altitude sickness or a bacterial infection?"

"I am good, really. Just a small stomach malady. I am better now." She gave Sigourney a thin smile and closed the door.

Sigourney wished there was something she could do, but she

didn't want to pry.

She wandered down the stairs and out into the unexpected glare of morning sunlight. She had never seen such a brilliant sun. It radiated down on her head like an angry Tibetan spirit. She felt like Icarus flying too close to the sun. At any moment, her waxed wings would melt, and she would plunge into the fiery ball. Even with her sunglasses on, it hurt to stare at the sky for too long. And the sky seemed so close. She wanted to reach up and brush it with her fingers.

Objects contrasted sharply with one another, and the nearby mountains stood out in sparkling clarity. Yet despite the burning sun, the air was chilled to the point of frost, and the snow line on the surrounding hillsides nearly reached the valley floor.

As she walked, she heard murmuring voices swelling from behind an earthen wall located across a tiny creek. She hopped over the nearly frozen water and stepped into a large compound, where she discovered rows of young boys seated on the ground in the glaring sunlight. They were bundled in dirty, woolen garments and sat with their backs against a wall, their legs stretched out before them in the dirt. Each child held a tattered paperback book in his hand. Most wore tennis shoes and had caps pulled over their ears. Some rested the books in their laps; others raised them as protective shields against the dazzling rays of the sun. The students read aloud in unison from their assigned texts, creating a cacophony of chanting voices. The sound reminded Sigourney of troubled bees protecting their hive. The children smiled shyly and stared at her with open curiosity as she walked past them, but they never broke their sing-song rhythm.

Their voices filled her with strength and resolve. If these gritty children could withstand Tibet's harsh conditions, then so could she. The frozen air and gleaming sun tested them, just as last night's incident with the police had tested her. She returned to the hotel with a lighter, more energetic step.

Jigme was standing outside enjoying the morning sunlight. "I am glad you had your charm last night. It protected you." He smiled hesitantly, uncertain how she might react.

Sigourney touched the object in her coat pocket. "You mean the statue? Do you believe it has powers?" She was intrigued that Jigme gave voice to the same thought she had pondered a short while ago.

"If you believe in it, yes. Otherwise, no. There are many spirits in Tibet. Some are peaceful; others can be very dangerous. You were visited by a dangerous spirit last night, but your Buddha protected you. Do not lose faith in it. You may need it again." He smiled once more and glanced at the valise hanging from her shoulder before turning away and entering the hotel.

Sigourney gripped the valise and stared after him. Did he, like the old woman in Nyelam, know she was carrying something of spiritual importance into Tibet? It didn't seem possible, but her belief in Tibet's spirits was growing. *Something* was happening that couldn't be explained rationally.

A battered car stopped on the street outside the hotel. To Sigourney's surprise, the passenger door opened and John stepped out. He said something to the driver before closing the door and tapping his hand on the vehicle's roof. The car sped away, and John disappeared around the backside of the building. Sigourney stood for several moments trying to understand what she had just witnessed. Was John working with the Chinese? Impossible! He never would have helped her, if he was. And the car looked much too wretched to belong to anyone of importance. Then, what *was* he doing so early in the morning riding around the frontiers of Tibet in something that looked like it had been caught in a WWII bombing raid?

She shook her head in puzzlement and followed Jigme back into the hotel. Most of her group were wandering about in a sleepy daze, looking like they had spent the night tumbling inside a dryer at a laundromat. It was clear they had all suffered her fate. Even Beth and Cameron were unusually quiet, much to Sigourney's relief. She spotted Marie-Rose chatting with Erica and was pleased to see that some color had returned to her face.

She greeted Sigourney with a tiny smile when she joined them. "Forgive me for being so nosy this morning. Those walls were so thin, I couldn't help hearing you. I was worried."

Marie-Rose's smile broadened. "I want to thank you, actually, for being concerned. It was kind of you to ask."

"Everything's okay, I hope? You look much better."

"Yes, everything is fine. The malady is in the heart, not the body."

John appeared as if from nowhere. He looked the least bedraggled of the group, but that was only in comparison to the others. "Sleep at all?" His pink skin had a freshly-scrubbed look. Sigourney had a sudden urge to stroke it with her fingers. She blushed at her impulse.

"Maybe an hour or two. Not enough to feel rested." She was beginning to enjoy John's company and found herself looking forward to their conversations. But she also harbored some uncertainty about the scene she had just witnessed out front. Whatever John was doing in Tibet, she was convinced he wasn't "on holiday."

"Pretty much the same for everyone, I expect." She could feel his keen eyes observing the warmth that still lingered in her face. "We'll all sleep better tonight. Did you see the children this morning?"

Sigourney nodded and smiled to herself. She thought she had made an interesting discovering, only to learn that John had been there before her. He missed nothing.

*****

The van jostled its way through the narrow streets of Shegar, and Sigourney settled into her seat in preparation for another day's journey. The town consisted of non-descript concrete buildings built by the Chinese and heavily-weathered Tibetan structures with wooden doors and shuttered windows. Beige awnings covered the windows, reminding Sigourney of little skirts. The wooden trim was often painted with colorful images of clouds or flowers. One door had a white scarf nailed to it. A scruffy, metal teapot sat on the adjoining window sill. They were curious images, which spoke volumes about the simple lives of the Tibetans.

Sigourney was eager to read more from Anne's diary, and now that John knew she had something concealed inside her valise, she was less concerned about him seeing it. She checked to make sure Mr. Ho was preoccupied and pulled the diary from its hiding place.

Diary entry by Anne Hopkins, 1899

I cannot imagine a worse nightmare than what happened to us the past two days! We started off innocently enough and managed to skirt several smaller villages at night by using footpaths in the peasants' nearby fields. Then, we encountered a group traveling by horseback from Lhasa, which included a government official and several soldiers. He stopped and began firing questions at Tenzin, who tried to convince him that we were simple peasants on a pilgrimage. I hid behind my guide, fearful that my disguise would not stand up to the man's scrutiny. After several tense minutes, the official let us pass with a warning to watch out for Khampa who were known to be operating in the area.

Khampa are robbers from eastern Tibet who prey on peasants who cannot afford to hire guards for protection. They work in small bands of a dozen or so. Women and children often accompany them. They set up their yak tents in an area and begin accosting the nomads and pilgrims traveling there, threatening them with swords or pistols.

The official's warning gave us pause to consider out best course of action. We had hoped to avoid this danger, but if the Khampa were operating nearby, there was a good chance we would come across them. I worried about the money I had hidden in my clothing, but I was also concerned for our lives. Khampa were known to kill their victims, if they were angered by meager offerings.

There was greater safety in numbers, and we decided to find nomads who would share their tents with us. We planned to spend the evening with them and slip away at night, when it was unlikely the Khampa would be foraging about. This strategy worked well the first night. We joined a friendly group with three tents and even purchased a little food from them. After midnight, we moved on and walked until dawn, before seeking refuge in some nearby hills.

The second day nearly finished us. We ventured onto the road late in the day and approached two tents where a child was playing and several yaks stood tethered nearby. A woman wearing long, braided hair and many beads around her neck came out to greet us, making the scene seem most innocent. Once we went inside her tent, however, several women and two men entered behind us. The men wore swords in their belts, and we realized to our horror that we had stumbled upon one of the camps of the Khampa! They asked us questions and put their hands on our packs. I decided this was no time to pretend to be a humble wife, and I yanked my pack away from them with as much defiance as I could muster. Tenzin also showed his courage by putting his hand on one of the men and pushing him away.

Our actions surprised them, and they laughed as if it was a wonderful joke. Most of the people finally left, but one man and the woman who had greeted us remained in the tent. They became friendly and offered us food and shelter for the night, but we were certain they were merely waiting for others to return from their plundering before deciding what to do with us. We smiled. Tenzin told them we would be happy to stay, but first we must find our companions who were close behind us on the trail. This caused much consternation and confusion with the couple, who did not want us to leave. When we picked up our bags, they tried to prevent us, and we had to force our way from the tent. We started down the road at a brisk pace.

Our worst fears were realized when we saw the two men following us at a safe distance. The failing light would soon turn to darkness, and we were certain they would pounce on us with their swords. There was little choice but to make a run for it, and once we rounded a bend in the road, we hurried forward until we found a ravine leading up the mountain. We slipped into the ravine and hid behind some large boulders. The men sauntered past our hiding place at a surprisingly leisure pace. Once they were gone, we scrambled up the ravine as quickly as we could. Voices below us on the trail soon told us why the two men had been so casual in their behavior. They were greeting other robbers from the band. If we had continued along the road, we would have been caught in a vise between the two groups. It would not take them long to figure out where we had gone, so we pushed onward until we reached the crest of a small hill.

We were exhausted by our rapid climb, and we sat down to catch our breath. I wasn't sure which had tired me more: the climb up the ravine or the fear of knowing our lives were very likely at stake! We did not tarry long before continuing up the mountain. When it was dark, we stopped to build a small fire for our tea and the yak meat we had purchased from the nomad family. The night was growing cold, and we were both very tired from our trying day, so we snuggled into our bundles of clothing and soon slept.

The next morning brought terrible news. When we rolled out of our makeshift beds and looked back down the mountain, we saw smoke rising from a campfire on the ridge we had passed last night. The Khampa were following us up the mountain! We gathered our things and rushed onward. How were we going to rid ourselves of this menace? Hiding and hoping they missed us seemed too chancy a prospect. We could only hope they would lose interest, but when we looked back, we saw three men working their way up the trail below us. They were no more than a half-mile away and very visible in the morning light, as were we.

Suddenly, they stopped and turned back. I was overjoyed, until Tenzin pointed out the reason for their change of heart. Black, boiling clouds were rising over the mountain pass in front of us, and even as I watched them towering into the sky, I felt the wind growing in intensity. We were about to be hit by a massive storm, and we were completely exposed on the mountain. Now, we scrambled to save our lives from a new, more menacing threat. A storm of this magnitude could last for a day or more and would surely kill us, if we could not find shelter. Our only chance was a cave, but we had not seen one during our climb. We had no choice but to rush headlong into the storm in search of refuge. In less than twenty minutes, the winds reached a velocity that forced us to hold onto boulders and outcroppings of rocks as we climbed. Sleet begin to pelt us, and the storm became so ferocious, I was forced to crawl on my hands and knees. Tenzin went ahead of me. I could no longer see him and feared we would both perish alone on this awful mountain. Then, I heard him shouting and saw him standing near an opening in the rocks. He had found our sanctuary, and none too soon! While I piled our things inside the cave, he moved off to look for brush to start a fire. He returned with such meager offerings, we dared not light it until it got desperately cold. There would be no hot tea today, but at least we were protected from the debilitating effects of the wind.

We sat and talked for the rest of the day, while the wind howled past our little home. When night fell, the temperature dropped precipitously, and we bundled together to keep from freezing. His body warmed mine in a way I could not have imagined before we started our journey. Perhaps, it was the stress of our narrow escapes. The salty aroma of his skin and smoky odor in his clothes aroused my senses, and I found myself embracing him more tightly than was proper. I feared he would be put off, but his hands moved in ways that told me he found me desirable, as well. I shall not talk further about our time together, but I am sure the added heat of our passion protected us from the biting cold that night!

Thank goodness the storm passed by dawn. Neither of us looked at the other while we lighted the meager fire. I felt like an embarrassed school girl and gulped down large quantities of hot butter tea to calm my anxious feelings. I had no idea what Tenzin thought about last night, and I could only hope we had not damaged our friendship. He finally put his hand on mine to let me know everything was all right, and I glowed with joy. It had been a long time since I had felt wanted as a woman, and Tenzin's gentle attentions gave me hope that my life was not yet over.

We warmed our tsampa and ate a hearty meal before going out to face the brilliant, sunny day. Everything was blanketed in white, and the air was as still as a Christmas morning. We stood in a world of deep snow banks and dark, blue skies. I believe it was one of the most lovely mornings I have ever witnessed. We had outwitted the robbers and the storm and found happiness in each other's arms. I stood in the snow triumphant and at peace.

Sigourney stared out the window at the rugged terrain and thought about Anne's amazing story. It was hard to imagine fleeing up a mountain to escape from thieves and sleeping in caves at night. She closed her eyes and tried to visualize disguising herself and trekking across such a vast wilderness with nothing more than a back pack and guide. Could she have done it? She had brown hair and eyes, but she was taller than the Tibetans. "Legs forever" wouldn't help her much there.

Anne's frank description of her tryst with Tenzin surprised her even more, but Sigourney understood her feelings of inadequacy. Could a man ever be interested in me again, she wondered? Could John? The thought of John putting his hands on her made her feel "like a school girl," just like Anne. The more she read Anne's diary, the more she felt her kinship growing with the woman. The more she felt Anne's hopes and hardships as her own.

CHAPTER TWELVE

Sigourney stared out the van's window at a small river flowing along a flat valley floor nearly devoid of life. Copper and granite mountain walls rose abruptly at the far side of the valley, where three horsemen magically appeared, riding past isolated patches of snow that hugged the river banks. The riders were dwarfed to insignificance by the jagged cliffs rising beyond them. Where were they going, Sigourney wondered? There had been no sign of human life for miles, other than the crumbled ruins of earthen castles perched on several hilltops. The ruins reminded her of tattered hawks guarding their realms.

The van turned onto a side road. "We are going to visit the Sakya Monastery," Jigme announced. "It has special significance to Tibetans, because it represents one of the four basic orders that formed Tibetan Buddhism. The monastery was founded in the eleventh century and once consisted of over a hundred buildings."

One central building and a lonely stupa were all that greeted them. Jigme explained that the Red Guards from China destroyed most of Sakya's structures during the Chinese rule of Mao Tsetung's Cultural Revolution. It was a story that repeated itself throughout Tibet. Before China's invasion in the 1950s, thousands of monasteries were sprinkled across the country. After the Red Guard rampaged through the countryside, fewer than four hundred remained.

The monastery stood on a small rise facing a village. Sakya's compound and the walls of the village were painted gun-metal gray and bordered with stark-white and blood-red lines. The bold colors and wild setting seemed better suited to a medieval kingdom than such a sacred institution.

John joined Sigourney as the group walked into the inner courtyard. Rows of brass, canister-shaped prayer wheels, similar to the ones she had seen in Kathmandu, lined one wall. A lone man in a wool cap and yak-hair coat was methodically spinning each wheel with his hand. When he turned the next wheel, Sigourney thought she heard the voices of chanting monks rumbling in her ears. She stopped and listened more carefully, but all she could detect was the wind whistling past the compound's walls.

"Did you hear monks chanting?" she asked John.

"No, did you?" He stopped beside her and listened, as well.

"I guess not. It must be my imagination or the wind."

No sooner had she said this, than the man spun the next wheel and the voices returned. They seemed to be coming from her valise, and when she put her hand on it, she felt a tremor that resonated through her body. *Was* the manuscript possessed by spiritual powers, she wondered? The Tibetans seemed to think so, yet John and the others hadn't heard anything unusual. *I must be going crazy.* Sigourney said nothing more about the voices.

Two monks hurried forward with a handful of keys to unlock the great doors of the monastery. They were agitated and spoke enthusiastically to Jigme, who nodded several times. The air was charged by their excitement. One of the monks stared at Sigourney, and then quickly looked away. Their agitation made her nervous, so she turned her attention to the monastery.

The entrance was covered by twin curtains of interlocking,

brass rings, which were drawn back on either side. The wooden doors behind the rings were badly cracked and weathered from centuries of exposure to Tibet's violent elements. Iron strips had been attached to brace the doors and give them added strength. Sigourney pushed aside her apprehensions about the chanting voices and the monks' stares. She was about to enter her first Tibetan monastery, and the prospect thrilled her.

Light from the opened doorway cast dark shadows across a cavernous room, whose high ceiling was braced by thick pillars placed strategically about the room. Monks' robes lay scattered about on pillows arranged in long rows along the floor.

"The monks kneel here during prayers," Jigme explained.

A stale, musk odor permeated the place. It was an old odor, one that reached back to distant centuries and mingled with the dusty manuscripts that nestled on shelves along the walls. Sigourney inspected the ancient books. They looked quite different than the one she carried. The covers appeared to be made of cloth instead of leather and the books were quite narrow. Were any of them as old as hers, she wondered? She laid her hand on the valise and felt a tingling sensation. She doubted any of the manuscripts chanted the way hers did.

When the two monks lit butter candles, the flickering, yellow light revealed several large statues behind an altar. A photo of the exiled Dalai Lama rested on the altar, along with numerous white scarves that had been draped there by visiting pilgrims.

"The statues represent Buddha and bodhisattvas," Jigme continued. "The bodhisattvas are enlightened ones who have achieved Nirvana but have returned to help others along their spiritual paths."

The man in the knit cap, whom Sigourney had watched turning the prayer wheels in the courtyard, entered the room fingering a strand of prayer beads and shuffled down a dark corridor, disappearing behind the altar. He soon reappeared on the other side. Intrigued, Sigourney decided to follow him. The light was feeble, making it difficult to see, and she nearly stumbled on the uneven floor. The voices of her travel companions faded as a hushed mood descended on her. It felt as if she were riding an ocean wave out to sea, where the horizon blended with the sky and the land behind her disappeared in the sun's reflective light. When Sigourney emerged on the other side, she had to squint her eyes against the light streaming through the doorway.

"You have just completed a lingkor," Jigme informed her. "Tibetans perform such walks to earn merits for their next life. We will see a very popular lingkor when we reach Lhasa."

It felt as though every muscle in Sigourney's body had been kneaded by powerful hands. She thought about the countless number of pilgrims who had treaded along that spiritual pathway and tried to imagine what they had experienced. It was the first time she had known such peace. She wondered why she had never discovered Buddhism before.

Her musings were interrupted by raised voices near the altar. Cameron was waving his hands at the two monks and gesturing to his camera, trying to convince them to let him take a picture. They steadfastly refused, their pained expressions reflecting their discomfort at the scene Cameron was causing. Jigme hurried over and spoke to Cameron, who stalked angrily away. Sigourney felt her own anger rising at his behavior, and she marveled at the patience displayed by the monks.

When she stepped outside, she saw Cameron sulking in the courtyard. His childish pose reminded her of Roger, and she couldn't prevent her own anger from boiling over. She suddenly realized the anger she had carried around the past six months had more to do with being abandoned than it did with Roger's infidelities. It wasn't her anger at Roger that was undermining her psyche. That anger was healthy. It cleansed her soul. But she had allowed him to dump her at the side of life's road like damaged goods, and that anger was eating away at her and ruining her chances to sort out her life with Debbie. This sudden insight left her shocked and trembling, and for one fleeting moment, all her frustrations were focused on the idiotic man standing in front of her.

She marched over and grabbed his arm with such force, he

blinked with astonishment. "Cameron," she said with controlled fury, "I don't wish to be unpleasant, but if you *ever* make a scene like that in a monastery again, I'll slap your face."

His eyes widened with disbelief, then narrowed with the contriteness of a naughty child. She had to turn away to keep from laughing at his unhappy expression, but when she turned back, his look had hardened.

"Don't think you're fooling anyone," he spat at her. "Everybody saw your little charade last night with John at the check point. We know you're hiding something." His face contorted with anger. "Maybe, I'll just turn you over to the Chinese. Then see how high and mighty you are."

Sigourney took an involuntary step backwards at his unexpected assault, but she quickly squared her shoulders and faced him.

"Do what you want. Just don't ever cause a scene like that again." She turned and walked stiffly away, hoping she was hiding the turmoil inside of her. God, why did she have to unleash her frustrations at that silly man? If he said anything, all would be lost. She prayed he was bluffing, playing the role of the spoiled child. From now one, she would keep her mouth shut.

She spotted Marie-Rose inspecting a red door in a wall adjacent to the monastery, and she joined her. They stood quietly side-by-side, looking at an elaborate, tree-shaped design painted on either side of the door, while Sigourney struggled with her emotions.

The surreal images reminded Sigourney of painted scenes of the Garden of Eden. "Remarkable artwork, isn't it?" She commented at last.

Marie-Rose gave her a tight smile and nodded. "The temple is very restful, n'est pas? It makes me want to stay here and meditate for a long time."

Sigourney couldn't tell if she was speaking about an hour or a year. When she looked at her, she realized Marie-Rose's eyes were moist to the point of tears. Sigourney took her hand. "Please don't think I'm prying, but I can tell something is troubling you. Can I help?"

Marie-Rose stared at her with eyes so dark and deep, Sigourney felt she could toss stones into them and never hear the stones hit bottom. "I think people must like you very much, yes? You are so kind. But no one can help me now."

Sigourney thought about Marie-Rose's illness earlier that morning and her comment about a malady of the heart. "Are you pregnant?" She was surprised by her boldness. She never would have dared ask such a thing back home.

"Oui. Two, maybe three months. I have not yet seen a doctor." Marie-Rose's cheeks glistened as the tears finally escaped from their hiding place. "I must decide what to do with my life. With my unborn child. I am thirty-eight, you see, and I may never have another chance for a baby. But, I am afraid to have a baby by myself. How can I raise a baby by myself?"

Sigourney gripped her hand tighter. "I too was afraid when I came on this trip. My husband has left me for a younger woman, and I'm trying to cope with an angry daughter. Fear's a terrible burden, but you mustn't let it control your life."

"You are right, of course, but it is very difficult, is it not?"

"What about the father?"

"He is a married man who has no interest in starting a new family."

Sigourney stiffened at this revelation and thought about Roger. Why were married men so appealing to single women? Marie-Rose noticed her annoyed expression and squeezed her hand.

"I did not know he was married until it was too late. I am sorry about your husband."

Sigourney's anger dissipated when she saw Marie-Rose's anguished expression. The poor woman was blaming herself for her circumstances, just as Sigourney had been doing. Talking to Marie-Rose made her see what a futile exercise it was to blame anybody, least of all herself. It only prolonged the agony and slowed the healing process.

"It's not your fault, Marie-Rose. You must decide what's best for you. You must have the courage to live your life the way you want to. I hope you have the baby, and you'll let me visit you both."

Marie-Rose threw her arms around Sigourney and embraced her. "You give me courage. Thank you for your kindness. I hope we can be friends after our trip is finished."

Sigourney said nothing more. She felt a serene connection to this French woman. Her world had yielded to an inner peace, much as it did when she followed the Tibetan around the shrine inside the monastery.

John fell into step with them as they walked back to the van. "You look cheerful," he commented. "No more altitude problems?"

"None," Sigourney replied with a smile. "This has been a very uplifting day." She hooked her arm through Marie-Rose's as she spoke. Her words surprised her, but she realized she felt very good about herself, not an emotion she had experienced much lately. Cameron's flushed and angry face became a distant memory.

CHAPTER THIRTEEN

"Sit with me for awhile," Sigourney suggested to John when they returned to the van. Her relaxed mood was tempered by her concern about the monks' behavior in the courtyard, and she hoped John could explain why they had been so animated. He eased into the seat next to her.

"Do you have any idea why those monks were so excited when we first arrived? Jigme was agitated as well."

"It seems to be connected to the increased security we experienced at the police station. I asked Jigme about it. From what I can gather, the Tibetans are convinced some of Buddha's teachings are returning to them. They're supposed to be part of the original doctrine detailing the path leading to Nirvana. He says they are very sacred tantras dealing with the whole philosophy of enlightenment. They disappeared from a local monastery a hundred years ago."

A wintry hand brushed the back of Sigourney's neck, sending chills racing to the depths of her soul. It was no coincidence that the Chinese were searching everyone. Somehow, the monks knew about the manuscript, and the Chinese had heard the rumors. "How would they know such a thing?" she asked in a hushed voice.

"That is hard to say. Apparently, it's something they've been expecting for some time. The monks have heard oracles foretelling its return. It's all quite mysterious, but Jigme believes it is happening now."

Sigourney stared out her window while she tried to sort through John's remarks. It *was* her manuscript they were expecting. She thought about the chanting voices she'd heard. Was a message being transmitted to the monks, something they could hear in their oracles? The very idea of it, the possibility that the manuscript could possess such powers, confounded her. She was a researcher and a historian who relied on facts, not fiction, yet she couldn't ignore the reality that some very unusual forces were at work in Tibet.

"What do you think about Mr. Ho?" she suddenly asked.

"I don't trust him. I had a chance to chat with him this morning. The chap is very evasive. He's supposed to have immigrated to London from Indonesia, but he doesn't know London at all. He claims he hasn't lived there very long, but things don't add up. Why, for instance, is he traveling here if he's just immigrated to England, and how did he enter Tibet without a group visa? I'd be careful around him."

"I've had similar thoughts." Sigourney stared at the valise near her feet, and her feelings of inner peace evaporated. She was more convinced than ever that Mr. Ho was a Chinese spy who had been inserted into their group to watch for someone trying to smuggle banned materials into Tibet. Someone like her.

To settle her nerves, she turned her thoughts to the British officer credited with being the first Westerner to reach Lhasa. "How much do you know about Colonel Younghusband's invasion of Tibet, John?"

"Quite a bit, actually. I've studied his military campaign, although I imagine campaign is too strong a term. The Tibetans were badly out-gunned. The British were worried that Tsar

Nicholas II was trying to align Russia with Tibet to gain an advantage over the trade and military routes through Central Asia. Twenty-five hundred British troops were dispatched from India to win Tibet by force. The army was actually led by General Macdonald, who was reported to have been strangely affected by Tibet. Some thought he went a bit mad. Sir Francis Younghusband was commissioned to negotiate the terms of peace.

"The Dalai Lama fled to China for protection, which proved to be quite ironic. Two years later, China's Manchu dynasty used Great Britain's foray into Tibet as leverage to claim sovereignty over the Tibetan region."

"Yes, I remember something about that from my undergraduate studies on England," Sigourney acknowledged. "The Chinese signed a treaty with your government recognizing China's right to govern Tibet. It set the stage for China's invasion of Tibet starting in 1950."

"Correct, but the irony didn't end there. When Younghusband reached Lhasa, he found no evidence of a Russian presence. Instead, he discovered a provincial capital filled with golden Buddhas and fanatical worshippers set against a backdrop of squalid houses and filthy streets. After Younghusband obtained his treaty and took the army back to India, the Tibetans turned their backs on the outside world just as they had done for centuries. Considering all the bloodshed, little was changed by his invasion."

It was late afternoon. Clouds had rolled in, covering portions of the sky and turning the surrounding mountains a premature gray. Suddenly, a ray of sunlight broke through the overcast and crowned a small mountain rising above the valley floor in a dazzling display of sienna and golden colors.

"It looks like the Bon spirits have come out to play," John commented with his usual, dry humor. They watched for awhile in silence. It was nice, Sigourney thought, to share something special without the need for words. How long had it been since she had done that? Had she ever? The sun quickly slipped behind the clouds once more, and the skies darkened.

"You know, John, I think you're more than just a government

employee who runs errands for the embassies." She gave him a mischievous look. "Not that I'm prying, mind you. Just stating my opinion."

John chuckled. She noticed he never laughed outright. It was more of a chortle, as if he were holding part of his laugh inside himself. It was very understated, like everything else about the man.

"And I don't believe you're traveling overland to Lhasa just for a vacation," he responded. "Research, perhaps? Or something more intriguing? Not that I'm meddling, of course." He shot her an amused look that said two could play that game.

Sigourney sighed. It was obvious they both had secrets to hide, at least for now. That was fine with her. It made things more interesting. She suddenly wondered if she would have the nerve to make love to this man. She could feel her face heat up at the idea, and she knew he was aware of it. Well heck, she thought, what was wrong with letting a man know he could make her blush? It had been a long time since she'd done that, and she liked the feeling. She liked being around him, period.

"I hope you don't mind if I compliment you," he said after a brief silence. "I'm afraid I haven't done this sort of thing with any woman other than my wife in over twenty years, and I'll probably be a bit bumbling about it. You're a very attractive woman, Sigourney, and I suspect a very brave one, as well, although I haven't sorted out exactly why, yet."

Sigourney's heart beat faster. How long had it been since someone made her feel this way? Too many years. But, I'm not attractive, she thought. Why would John like *me*? Marie-Rose is much prettier. Is it safe to like this man? To believe him? The questions and doubts ran riot through her mind. She needed to return to her safe harbor, but it had gone missing. It was all about faith and trust; faith in herself, and trust in somebody else. She thought about her advice to Marie-Rose. Sigourney had to find the courage to believe in others, but she couldn't do that until she found the courage to believe in herself.

She took John's hand and looked into his luminous eyes.

"Thanks. I needed that."

They arrived at their hotel in Shigatse just before dark. Shigatse was Tibet's second largest population center, but it looked more like a Chinese town than a Tibetan village. Low, uninspiring buildings with Chinese signs dominated the wide, dusty streets. The Tibetans were hidden behind compound walls near the great Tashilhunpo Monastery, which they would visit the following morning.

Sigourney was fatigued by the long, rough ride and the lack of sleep the previous night, but food was at the top of hers and everyone else's agenda. Jigme took the group to a Chinese restaurant for dinner, where she devoured everything put in front of her.

"The more I see of Tibet, the more I dislike China's presence here," Sigourney said as she walked back to the hotel with John after dinner. "What really makes me mad is I like Chinese food, and the dinner was good."

John chuckled. They were well below the snow line, and it was considerably warmer than Shegar. But the air was still chilly, and Sigourney took John's arm. His warmth radiated through her entire body, making her feel wonderfully alive. She smiled at his words on the van. Attractive and brave. She had never believed she possessed either of those qualities, but she was beginning to believe it now.

When she returned to her room, Sigourney discovered running hot water and immediately filled the tub. She soaked herself, then put on her night gown and dived under the comforter. She was asleep by the time her head found the pillow.

*****

Sigourney awoke early the next morning feeling refreshed and eager to face the day. Early morning light filtered into the room. She stretched and splashed warm water on her face. It was too early for breakfast, so she made tea and settled back in bed with Anne's diary.

Diary entry by Anne Hopkins, 1899

There was another mountain range to cross before reaching the road to Shigatse. I was exhilarated by our close brush with those Khampas, but I hoped we would not have to repeat the experience. I knew once we reached the main road to Shigatse, we would be much safer, for there were bound to be many travelers along that route. Of course, that would also mean more eyes watching us, but such were our choices. One cannot try to predict one's fate. It is best to move along your chosen path and make the best of it.

We climbed the mountain without incident and discovered several dwellings in the next valley. These appeared to be lodgings for nomads who moved their herds to the higher plateaus during the summer months, for the buildings had an abandoned look about them. There was no sign of livestock or smoke from the fireplaces. The compound walls surrounding the three houses were poorly constructed and crumbling in places, and the walls of the buildings themselves were badly weathered.

Tenzin called out as we approached, but no one answered or came out to greet us. We poked our heads inside the first dwelling and found the single room cold and empty. No one had made a fire there in many days. The utensils were gone from the cooking stove. A few crude, wooden shelves were attached to the walls, but they were empty.

A small pile of dried yak dung lay on the dirt floor next to the fireplace, but Tenzin went to gather brush for our fire, so there would be fuel for the owners when they returned. We were thankful to have some better shelter and rolled out our sleeping mats in anticipation of a good night's sleep. But just as we settled down for the night, we heard voices and horses' hooves outside! My first thought was the Khampas. There was no place to hide, and our fire was sending enough smoke up the small opening in the roof to alert passersby.

The door burst open and four men stomped inside. The first held a pistol which he waved about in front of him as we hastily rose to our feet. Tenzin called out to the men, telling them we were simple pilgrims looking for shelter. My heart was beating so fast, I could hardly think. I knew Tenzin's pleas would mean nothing to Khampas. I could only hope these were the nomads who used the dwellings during winter. But why would they be there now? They should have already left with their herds.

Two of the men stepped forward and grabbed Tenzin by the shoulders. I hastily bowed my head in a supplicant manner. The head man angrily asked Tenzin questions. Tenzin repeated his story that we were pilgrims and opened his bag to show his meager belongings. I prayed they would not inspect my bag, for they would find items that could only belong to a foreigner. Once my true identity was revealed, they might set upon us and kill us both, or warn the authorities of my presence in the region. Either outlook was an unhappy one.

Fortunately, no one paid any attention to me, and my bag remained closed. Tenzin pointed out that we had gathered our own firewood, rather than use their yak dun. He told them we were not trying to use or take anything that didn't belong to us.

The lead man continued to scowl and eye us suspiciously for what seemed an eternity, then his face broke into a broad grin, and he shoved his pistol in his belt. I nearly sank to the floor with relief! They were the dwellers, after all, and once they knew we meant them no harm, they became quite friendly. Two women entered carrying loads from the horses, and the men laid their blankets on the ground and settled down to talk and share some chang, a locally brewed beer.

Sigourney stopped reading and thought again about Anne's fortitude. What courage it took to survive the incredible threats and ordeals she had faced! Sigourney wondered how she would have reacted. No one could predict their response in the face of danger, but such a journey was bound to raise one's level of self-awareness and define a person's character in new ways. She had experienced something of the sort at the police check point. Her kinship with Anne Hopkins continued to grow.

Tenzin told me later that they had returned for additional supplies which were stored in one of the other buildings. He also told me that the lead man was married to both of the women, who were sisters. I wasn't surprised by this. Polygamy and polyandry are quite common in Tibet. It's a practical way to reduce jealousies in isolated communities, where the choices of marriage partners are few and the potential for rivalries and conflicts are high.

I could not join Tenzin among the men, so I remained with the two women. I pretended to be dumb, just as I had along the trail. When the women realized I couldn't speak, they went about their business and began preparing food for the men. I knew enough about Tibetan customs to help without seeming too clumsy.

After dinner, the men rolled out their sleeping mats on the floor around the fire pit, and the two women joined the lead man. The rest of the night passed without incident, and in the morning, we were on our way again.

After so many harrowing experiences, I was grateful to find the road we sought in the next valley. What a magnificent valley it was! Winter had departed, and fields of yellow and white flowers shimmered in the daylight. I wanted to rush forward and feel their soft caresses with my hands and feet, but I did no such thing. There were many groups of pilgrims and other travelers on the road who would find such behavior very strange.

We by-passed Shigatse without attracting suspicion and joined the steady stream of pilgrims and caravans heading towards Lhasa. Another large town, Gyantse, lay along our route. I felt much safer traveling on the main road and was reticent to return to the mountains, but getting past towns like Gyantse always presented the threat of discovery. Perhaps, we could slip past the town at night. We would have to decide what to do when we got closer.

I prayed our good fortune would continue. If it did, I would see the famous Potala Palace in Lhasa for myself in less than two weeks. The thought of such a prospect thrilled me, and my excitement grew with each passing step.

Sigourney hoped to reach Lhasa in two more days, completing her own quest to see the holy city. Were her trials over, she wondered? A small voice within told her no. She thought about the monk's warning at the stupa in Nepal and hoped she would have Anne's strength and courage to face whatever challenges lay before her.

CHAPTER FOURTEEN

Tashilhunpo was one of the few monasteries spared the destructive rampages of the Chinese Red Guard, and the scenes Sigourney witnessed were little changed from the 15th century. Maroon colored buildings and golden rooftops rose into the azure sky. Dragon heads snarled from the tips of curved rooftops, where they had been placed to protect the monastery's temples from evil spirits. The sound of whirring prayer wheels filled the air as worshippers shuffled across the main square. Monks walked serenely along the narrow streets that wound through the grounds in maze-like fashion, their sandals slapping against the stone pavement in unhurried cadences. The monastery once housed thousands of monks. Only a handful could be seen now, but the size of the place-- it was larger than many of the Tibetan villages-- told Sigourney it had once served as an important religious center.

"Monasteries like Tashilhunpo were self-contained fortresses," Jigme explained. "The Buddhist monks who lived here held greater power over their subjects than most governments.

Monks made up a significant portion of the population in Tibet. They were not only revered by the populace, they interpreted the oracles and established the order of laws and punishments. Their unquestioned authority allowed them to act as judge and jury. Capital punishment was not permitted, because Tibetans consider all forms of life sacred, but a thief would have a hand cut off and a murderer flogged to the point of death."

Jigme led the group through narrow passageways to an inner courtyard where a steep, wooden staircase rose to a temple's entrance. They stopped at the foot of the stairs and waited as a group of pilgrims in charcoal gray trousers and skirts descended. One woman bent with age leaned on the others as she worked her way down. When she reached the bottom step, she suddenly raised her hands above her head and began shouting.

At first, Sigourney thought she was having a seizure, but as the woman continued to rant, she turned and stared at Sigourney with wild eyes that seemed to pierce right through Sigourney's skin. Sigourney tensed, uncertain what to do. She had no idea what the woman was shouting, but she knew it had something to do with her and the manuscript. The earth tilted beneath her until Sigourney thought she might fall, but she couldn't move her feet. She was immobilized by the woman's hypnotic eyes. Frantically, she grasped the wooden Buddha in her pocket to steady herself and to break the old woman's spell. Sigourney half-expected the woman to advance on her, but she shook her head and turned away, all the while muttering under her breath. Only one word was audible: Sakyamuni. The word flashed through her mind with the brilliance of a shooting star, unbalancing her. Only the reassuring touch of her little Buddha kept Sigourney from tumbling to the ground.

The woman's companions surrounded her and guided her to a gate in the far wall. They spoke among themselves in animated voices and cast furtive glances over their shoulders as they disappeared from the courtyard. Sigourney trembled as she watched them go. It was the second time an old woman had confronted her, but unlike the kindly woman who had given her the

Buddha statue, this one had stripped Sigourney naked with her stormy eyes.

Everyone stood in stunned silence, with the exception of two monks who gestured excitedly to one another and hurried up the stairway into the temple.

"Jigme, what was that was all about?" Cameron asked.

"The woman had a fit in which she heard an oracle," Jigme replied. "She said the spirit of Buddha has returned to Tibet. She could feel his presence in the courtyard."

Sigourney stood in numbed silence. The old woman had repeated the same word spoken by those truck drivers at the Friendship Bridge. Sakyamuni: Buddha of the present. There was no doubt that the word was meant for her.

When Jigme glanced her way, Cameron followed his gaze and locked his keen eyes on hers. She felt like a book they were both thumbing through in search of clues.

"Is that normal, what she heard?" Marie-Rose asked.

"It is most unusual," Jigme replied somberly. "The monks who heard her were amazed and have gone to speak with their elders about it. There are rumors spreading through the monasteries foretelling a great event that will soon occur."

Jigme's words reverberated in Sigourney's ears, where they blended with a familiar sound: praying monks. The monks were chanting again, inside her head, but they were much louder than before. Their voices boomed like war drums. The old woman's crazed face danced before her, and the air in the courtyard grew uncomfortably warm. She could feel the surrounding walls squeezing her until she couldn't breathe.

Sigourney wanted to bolt from the yard, but she forced herself to remain rooted to her spot until Jigme led the others up the stairway into the temple. As soon as they had disappeared inside, she walked quickly to the side gate used by the Tibetans. She was about to exit when she felt the gnawing of little teeth on her neck and looked back to find Mr. Ho watching her from the top of the stairs. His unwavering gaze burned her flesh, and she flung herself through the doorway to escape him.

Sigourney felt feverish despite the chilly air and wondered if she might be ill. Perspiration covered her face, and her breathing had become ragged. She stopped and held a hand to her chest until her breathing returned to normal. The alleyway she had entered was so narrow she could touch both walls with her fingertips. Nothing stirred. The passageway had swallowed the old woman and her companions.

Sigourney set off at a quick pace and strode down the passageway. The physical exertion soothed her taut nerves; the tension in her shoulders lessened. To her relief, the chanting voices faded as she walked, but they were soon replaced by another voice, one that slipped into her consciousness with such stealth, it took a minute to realize it was there. The voice whispered too softly for her to understand the words, but she sensed it was Anne's spirit talking to her, telling her not to be afraid.

At first, the English woman's ghostly presence unsettled Sigourney. She didn't know which was worse, listening to those chanting voices or communing with a woman who had been dead for over half a century. Sigourney wanted to run away from both, but Anne's feathery voice had a soothing effect, and she slowed her pace. The Tibetan sun warmed her face, just as Anne's voice warmed her soul. The voice slowly faded, until all she could hear was the puff of a feathery breeze floating past her.

Sigourney stopped and watched as a man in a grey jacket and wool cap turned the far corner carrying a small boy on his shoulders. They were both smiling with such carefree abandon, she couldn't help but smile, as well. Roger had carried Debbie like that when she was little. As soon as Sigourney thought about her daughter, Anne's wordless message became clearer. Anne had lost her own daughter, but she was giving Sigourney a chance to reclaim hers. Debbie's love represented Sigourney's Nirvana. If Sigourney wanted to recover her daughter, she had to be strong. She had to complete her quest and return the manuscript to its rightful place. Only then, could she hope to find peace within herself and with Debbie.

And somewhere in the midst of these swirling forces, a new

puzzle emerged in the form of John Henley. John had become more than a traveling acquaintance. She found her trust in him growing, and with that trust came interest. And desire. She didn't know where her relationship with John was headed, but she intended to pursue it until she understood it better.

After the father and son had passed, Sigourney continued down the passageway until she reached an open doorway, where she saw a flagstone courtyard whose walls were covered with hundreds of painted Buddha images. Praying voices rumbled from a temple at the far end. When she entered the assembly hall, she discovered dozens of chanting monks kneeling on pillows. She stood entranced, trying to absorb the beauty of the scene before her. Ghostly wisps of smoke from burning incense curled into the air, producing a pungent odor that permeated the room. Giant cloth canisters in brilliant blues, reds and greens hung from the ceiling. Shafts of blue-gray light streamed through windows located high in the walls and mingled with the dancing flames of butter lamps burning near the altar. A golden Buddha statue dominated the temple's shrine.

Two brass horns suddenly blared, filling the chamber with a mournful harmony. They reminded Sigourney of the horns Anne had heard echoing across the Tibetan plains. The chanting abruptly stopped. The monks rose in a chorus of swishing robes and filed past her into the courtyard, their wrinkled faces and silver-white hair gleaming in the sunlight.

Sigourney stared at the golden statue, wondering if it represented the Buddha of the Present the Tibetans kept talking about. She touched her valise, half-expecting the manuscript to vibrate or speak to her, but it remained silent.

"You seem interested in Buddhism. Have you studied it?" A monk stepped out of the shadows and strolled towards her.

Her instinct was to turn and leave before he discovered the mysterious spirit she carried with her, but his serene expression gave no indication that he was aware of the manuscript.

"Very little," she replied, "but I'd like to learn more. Can you tell me something of Buddhism's history in Tibet?"

"Of course. There are four orders of Buddhism. The first, Nyingma, began the monastic system of life based on the teachings of Buddha in the eighth century. Buddhist monks were ordained at the Samye Monastery at that time. Do you plan to go there?" Sigourney caught her breath at the mention of the monastery's name. Was it just coincidence, or did this monk know she wished to go there? His gaze, which pierced Sigourney as deeply as the old woman's had in the courtyard, made her shudder.

"It's not on my itinerary," she responded hesitantly.

"A pity. You should visit it. I imagine you have already seen the Sakya Monastery."

She nodded.

"Sakya was one of the other three orders, which all appeared around the eleventh century. The Sakya order developed texts and monastic institutions and attracted many intellectuals and scholars. The Kagyu order introduced tantras on rituals, disciplines and meditation. Yoga, physical hardship and mental trials were initiated as a way to higher spiritual attainment. The last order, the Geluk, reached out to the spiritual needs of the common people. It brought Buddhism to the center of Tibetan life and allowed all levels of society to join in the process of spiritual attainment." He smiled to indicate his brief lecture was finished.

"You speak very good English. Did you learn it here?" she asked.

"No, my family escaped from Tibet when I was very young. I studied Buddhism and became a monk in India, but I had the chance to go to England to further my studies, which is where I learned my English. I returned to Tibet very recently to help my countrymen in their time of need. A great change is coming, and I wish to be here for it."

He smiled, again, and laid his hand on Sigourney's valise. "I hope you will enjoy the remainder of your journey." His words bathed her skin, and his eyes held hers in a hypnotic trance. There could be no doubt what the monk was telling her. He knew about her quest and was urging her onward.

She was about to reply when she heard hasty footsteps

echoing across the courtyard outside and turned to discover Marie-Rose breathing heavily in the doorway.

"I have been looking for you," she announced between gulps of air. "You must return to the van at once."

"Why?" The urgency in her friend's voice shattered Sigourney's momentary calm. "What's happened?"

Marie-Rose rushed forward and grasped Sigourney's hands. "John believes Mr. Ho has sent Chinese guards to look for you. I overheard John speaking to Jigme about it, and I offered to help."

Sigourney wanted to be brave, but her body quivered like a frightened child's. She gripped Marie-Rose for support. "Is it because of the incident in the courtyard?"

"I believe so, yes. John saw Mr. Ho speaking to an official, who left in a great hurry. I do not know why someone would be looking for you, but I will help you anyway I can." Her eyes darted anxiously across Sigourney's face.

She turned to the monk, "How can I return to the main square without being seen?"

"There is a route not used by tourists. I will take you."

She hesitated, wondering if she should trust this stranger. He could be a spy who would lead her to the guards. She sighed. The circle of those on whom she depended was widening, like ripples in a pond. She would have to trust him. She had little choice.

Sigourney squeezed Marie-Rose's hand and told her to return to the van, then hurried after the monk, who led her along a dark hallway to the back of the temple, where they exited into a shadowy passageway similar to the one she had taken earlier. He proceeded at such a brisk pace, she soon found herself breathing heavily as she hurried to keep up. Several twists and turns brought them to a small square where they emerged into brilliant sunlight. Sigourney blinked at the sudden glare, then blinked again when she realized she'd come face-to-face with the old woman from the courtyard! Sigourney tensed in anticipation of another outburst, but the woman's wrinkled face merely broadened with recognition. There was no sign of the earlier ranting that had so unhinged Sigourney. When the old woman reached out her weathered hand

and touched the valise, however, Sigourney flinched and stared at her nemesis, who nodded and smiled. The gesture was familiar to Sigourney by now, but she still reacted with amazement each time it happened.

Sigourney's momentary respite ended when loud voices coming from the direction of the temple began to echo off the courtyard's walls. The voices, shrill and bloodthirsty, told her the guards had picked up her trail and would soon track her down. She felt like a fox surrounded by howling hounds.

"We must hide." The monk changed his direction and started towards a doorway at the back of the courtyard.

Sigourney stood looking at the old woman in confusion, aware that at any moment she might be caught, yet unable to move. The woman's eyes flashed in the sunlight, warning her to flee; the monk's urgent voice prodded her. Still, she stood there listening to the approaching voices as if in a trance. The old woman reached out again, this time to touch the coat pocket containing the wooden Buddha. Did she know about the Buddha, as well, Sigourney wondered? How was that possible? The gesture sent a spark of urgency flashing through Sigourney's consciousness, and her momentary paralysis vanished. She turned and ran after the monk, stumbling on the uneven stones along the way.

They hurried down a new passageway, climbed a wooden ladder to a roof, and descended another. The voices continued their incessant squalling, screeching like birds of prey, but Sigourney was relieved to hear them growing fainter. When the monk finally stopped, Sigourney's put her hands on her hips and gasped for air. Her side ached and her feet hurt. They stood in the shadows like two long distance runners, chests heaving and beads of sweat spreading across their faces.

"I believe we are safe here," the monk panted.

No sooner had he spoken than two guards turned the corner less than fifty feet away. Sigourney couldn't believe her misfortune. She blinked, half-expecting the men to disappear, but they were very real and already moving towards her. This time, she didn't hesitate. She turned ready to run for her life. As long as she kept moving, she knew she had a chance. Her Buddha statue would save her. Or the manuscript. Or Anne. All she had to do was run! But the monk grasped her roughly by the arm and spun her back towards the advancing guards. Sigourney felt like a swimmer caught in an undertow. She was clawing at the water's surface, struggling to break free, but the grip on her arm was unrelenting. She could swim to freedom if only the monk would let her go! But he held her firmly beneath the waves, letting her drown.

The monk spoke to the guards, who grabbed her arms. Sigourney's legs were suddenly too weak to hold her weight, and she sagged against her captors in a state of shock as they half-walked, half-dragged her down the alley. Anger and frustration boiled inside of her. The monk had been a spy, after all. His offer to help had been a hoax. Her brain pressed against her skull until she thought it would explode. The guards gave her curt looks, their mouths firmly shut in thin lines of contempt. They reminded her of the guards at the Friendship Bridge and at that lonely outpost on the road to Shegar. There was no pity in their faces. No hope. Sigourney was a small animal caught in their jaws. Her mind dulled, and her body slumped in resignation. Her quest was over.

She was pushed into a windowless room filled with manuscripts. The door clanged shut behind her, leaving her imprisoned in darkness. The place smelled like old tires and spilled ink. She leaned against the door, her hand grasping the valise that still hung from her shoulder. The guards hadn't taken it, but they had undoubtedly gone to fetch Mr. Ho. When he arrived, he *would* take the valise and discover the manuscript. The thought of Mr. Ho getting his grasping, little hands on the book made her stomach cramp until she wanted to retch. She had to think of something to foil him, and she had to think fast. It would only be a matter of minutes before he came marching through the door.

Weak light filtered under the door, enough light for the room to gradually take shape. Hundreds of manuscripts lined the shelves along the walls. None of them looked like hers, but hiding the manuscript among them seemed her only chance. Perhaps, Mr. Ho wouldn't notice. Let him find the diary. Without the manuscript, he had nothing. He would have to return her to the van or send her home. The manuscript would remain hidden until the monks discovered it.

She was about remove the manuscript from the valise when she heard scurrying sounds overhead. Her hands froze. Were they rats? She tensed and peered around her. She would rather face Mr. Ho than rats in a darkened room! For a moment, nothing stirred. Then, the silence was broken by a scraping noise on the roof. A patch of light suddenly beamed down on her when a section of the roof was pulled away. Before she could think what to do, a wooden ladder appeared in the opening and slid noiselessly to the floor, followed by the worried face of the monk who had betrayed her! He popped his head into the opening and gestured for Sigourney to climb the ladder.

"Hurry," he whispered. "There is little time."

Sigourney jumped to her feet and ran to the ladder. Could it be true? Was the monk really offering his help, or was it another trap? She hesitated on the bottom rung and looked up, still unsure of the man's motives. His face twitched with tension as he furiously motioned for her to climb the ladder. Should she trust him? Her choice was to stay and face Ho. The thought of his glaring face was all the incentive Sigourney needed, and she scrambled up the ladder.

"I must apologize for my earlier behavior," the monk said in hushed tones as he quietly pulled the ladder onto the roof and closed the trap door. His head was bowed, his expression downcast. "There was no time to run or hide. I had to pretend I was bringing you to them, so they would trust me. I hope you will forgive me."

His words and his woebegone look erased her lingering doubts. She touched his arm in a quick gesture of gratitude. "Thank you for rescuing me."

His face broadened like a forgiven child's, then pinched nervously into a look of concern. "We are not yet safe." He pushed the ladder across the narrow alley behind them to the next roof. Sigourney looked at the ground below and hastily stepped back from the roof's edge. It was less than a twelve foot drop, but that knowledge couldn't prevent her legs from wobbling at the prospect of straddling the ladder to cross it.

"Quickly, before the guards return." The monk held out his hand. Sigourney teetered for a moment on the brink, then reached for the hand and stepped into the abyss. The ladder swayed beneath them like a branch on a windy day, forcing her to grip the monk's hand and concentrate on each rung, while ignoring the yawning chasm beneath her feet.

Once they reached the other side, the monk pulled the ladder after them and abandoned it. He led her down a stairway, and they plunged headlong back into the maze of alleys and courtyards. Robed monks watched her with curious expressions as she passed. She gave them furtive glances, fearful one of them would raise the alarm, but the monks said nothing. She entered a courtyard where a dozen monks sat on the ground cutting sections of meat from a carcass. The raw odors and the sight of blood flowing across the stones nearly gagged her, and then another series of passages swallowed her. She was sweating profusely once more, but this time it was partially from nerves. The thought of being captured again was more than she could bear.

The noonday sun radiated down on her head, telling her that she was very late. What would she do if the van was gone? Or if Mr. Ho was waiting for her there? She remembered her thoughts the previous day about Icarus and flying too close to the sun. How soon would the sun melt *her* wings? When they did, she would plunge into the abyss where Mr. Ho waited for her and be lost forever.

The monk stopped abruptly. "We are there."

Sigourney had no idea where "there" was. She had been turned around half-a-dozen times during her flight.

"The main square is just ahead," he explained. "Wait here while I look."

Sigourney's legs were rubbery from her ordeal, but she was too nervous to rest. She prowled back and forth in the alley like a caged cat. The dour look on the monk's face when he returned told

Sigourney that her worst fears had been realized.

"The van is gone." His tone was grave.

Sigourney hurried forward and peered into the square. A handful of pilgrims wandered peacefully across the stone pavement. Otherwise, the square was deserted. She leaned against the wall and swallowed hard, trying to understand what was happening to her. Why had Jigme and the others abandoned her to the Chinese? Why had John? She was suddenly conscious of a blustery wind blowing down the alley. It whipped her pant legs and crept inside her blouse, chilling her to the bone. How could they just *leave* like that? What was she going to do? She touched the valise, reassuring herself that she hadn't somehow lost it in her frantic rush to return to the van. It was a reflexive gesture by now and unnecessary. The valise had become so much a part of her, she would have felt undressed without it. But what could she do with the manuscript *now*? How was she going to return it?

"Need a lift?" John's pleasant voice drifted to her on the wind, as if in a dream. She knew she was just imagining it, but the sound of his voice made her feel cozy warm.

"I thought it might be best to stay behind. Make certain you were all right." His voice again! So close behind her. Not a dream. She whirled and saw John standing in the alley with hands on hips, looking like a worried parent who has just found a lost child. She threw her arms around him and pressed her head against his shoulder. The musky odor of his jacket reassured her that everything was all right. John had become her safe harbor.

"I thought I was lost," she murmured. "Where are the others? Why are you here?"

"Jigme waited as long as he dared. He's taking the group to Gyantse. I've made arrangements for us to join them there." His voice remained calm, controlled. "No one except Jigme and Marie-Rose knows why you were delayed. The others think you simply wandered off, and I stayed to find you."

Sigourney stepped back and looked at him. His eyes had assumed a steely quality she had never seen before. He looked as unperturbed as someone on a picnic, while her mind fluttered in confusion. Then he smiled at her, and she basked in its warmth. Thank you for sending this good man to me, she thought. She didn't know to whom she was addressing this silent acknowledgement: God or Tibetan spirits. It didn't matter.

"It is not wise to stay here too long." The monk interrupted her rumination. She had nearly forgotten him.

"He's right," John agreed. "I have a lorry waiting for us."

Sigourney took the monk's hands in hers and thanked him for his help. He gave her an embarrassed smile and nodded for her to go. Summoning her remaining strength, she sprinted with John across the square to the monastery's main entrance, startling several pilgrims. There was no sign of the horrid guards or Mr. Ho. John guided her to a battered truck covered by a blue tarp and lifted its flap for her to climb inside.

A strong odor greeted them that reminded Sigourney of her father's compost bin when she was a child. The smell had always pinched her nose, just as this one did now. It was nearly dark under the canvass, but there was enough light to see that the truck was loaded with wooden crates. "What are these?" she asked, sitting down on one of them.

John tapped on the cab of the truck. Its engine roared to life in a burst of coughs and diesel fumes. "Tractor parts." The truck lurched forward, nearly spilling John on top of Sigourney. He quickly sat down beside her. "Yaks are starting to be replaced by farm equipment, I'm afraid."

The lorry rumbled onto the main road. She leaned against the truck's side and gathered her thoughts. John and Marie-Rose were both accomplices now, and Jigme had hinted that he knew the purpose of her journey. Even Cameron had expressed his suspicions in no uncertain terms. Soon, everybody would know about her quest.

"And what about Mr. Ho?" Sigourney was surprised to hear her voice, not realizing she had spoken out loud.

John shifted his weight on the box and braced himself against the rattling motion of the truck. "I've arranged a little diversion for him. Planted a rumor that you're heading back to the Sakya

Monastery. By the time he discovers the truth, we should be in Lhasa. I assume that's your ultimate objective."

Sigourney's eyes had adjusted to the low light, and she studied John's face for several moments before responding. Her right leg had cramped from all the climbing and running, and she stretched it as best she could among the boxes. "John, how have you managed this lorry? And how could you plant a rumor at the monastery? Forgive my curiosity, but it doesn't seem possible for a tourist to arrange these things."

John's neck muscles tightened, the only sign that her questions bothered him. He shifted his weight again. Was she making him uncomfortable? "Yes, it does sound a bit fanciful, I suppose. I think we've already agreed that we have hidden agendas on this trip." He frowned and looked at her with obvious concern. "I haven't wanted to pry, but perhaps it's time you confided in me, that we confide in each other. It's hard to help when I don't know what I should be doing."

Sigourney brushed the hair off her forehead in a quick, nervous gesture. Roger's angry face floated like unwanted flotsam to the surface of her mind, and she recoiled at the image. Not a fair comparison, she realized. Roger represented everything she had come to distrust in men, but there was no longer any doubt about trusting John. This was the second time he had shielded her from danger without knowing the circumstances. If she couldn't trust him, than whom? The answer was no one. She was facing a moment of truth: to trust a man again. Impulsively, Sigourney took his big, warm hand in hers and immediately felt safer. How could his hand do that?

She returned his inquiring gaze and fought to get the words out. "I'm returning the teachings of Buddha," she whispered.

"You're what?" John asked in an uncertain voice.

She touched the valise now sitting on the box next to her. "I'm carrying one of the original manuscripts describing the teachings of Buddha. It was taken from the Samye Monastery a hundred years ago to save it from Chinese agents. I'm returning it to Samye. The Tibetans have somehow learned of its return. The manuscript seems to talk to them. I've heard the sounds of chanting monks coming from it myself. The Chinese have heard the rumors and are looking for it. Once they find it, they'll destroy it, and they'll arrest me."

John stared at her in wonder. "You're trying to do this on your own? There's no one to help you?"

She nodded. "This is a terribly important document, John. I hadn't realized how important when I started this trip, but I do now. The manuscript could help the Tibetans for decades to come. I believe the spiritual forces in it are that powerful."

John squeezed her hand to reassure her. "Why don't you just deliver it to one of the monasteries along our route? We could take it to the monastery in Gyantse."

Sigourney shook her head. "It must be given to the monks at Samye. That's the only place where it'll be safe. Don't ask me why I know this. I just do."

The lorry shook as it hit pothole in the road. John released her hand to brace himself and stared at her thoughtfully. "Well, I suppose we'd better see to it that you get to Samye. How do you propose to do that? The monastery's not on our itinerary."

"I don't know." She felt foolish admitting this. "I'd hoped to hire a driver or find public transportation."

"There are taxis in Lhasa. It shouldn't be difficult to hire one for the day."

"But, I'm still worried about Mr. Ho stopping me before I reach Lhasa. Wouldn't it be safer to just take a lorry there and avoid the tour group?"

John frowned as he thought about her idea. "Sounds tempting, but sometimes it's better to hide in plain sight. Mr. Ho won't expect that. He'll follow your false trail for awhile, long enough for you to reach Lhasa and return the manuscript. Besides, Mr. Ho doesn't know who you are, yet. His suspicions have been aroused by today's incident with the Tibetans and our little confrontation at the police check point, but it's unlikely he'll alert his superiors until he gets a closer look at your valise. He doesn't want to look like a fool.

"There's also the danger of more check points. Jigme's documents protect you in the van. You're part of the group. If we're stopped and discovered in this lorry, the jig is up."

Sigourney rubbed her sore calf muscle while she thought this over. John made sense, and he seemed to know what to do. She hesitated, and then asked the question that had teased her for the past two days. "Will you tell me what you really do?" She gave him a quick smile. "I don't mean to meddle, but after what you've done for me, I can't help wondering."

John's face remained serious. "I've already taken some risk in helping you, but I suppose fair is fair. I did say we should confide in each other, and I trust you. But, you must keep what I tell you confidential."

Sigourney nodded.

"Weapons are being smuggled through Tibet by some enterprising Chinese to a rather nasty group of Maoist rebels in Nepal. I'm gathering information to intercept the weapons before the rebels can get their hands on them and shut down their smuggling operation."

"Are you some sort of agent?"

"Not a spy, if that's what you mean. But I do work for British Intelligence. My role is more administrative, but I participate in field operations on occasion."

Sigourney fiddled with her hands, and then looked at him, "How did your wife die?" she asked softly.

"Cancer." John's simple reply was all that needed to be said. Even in the dim light she could see how his lips trembled and his eyes moistened.

"Just like Martha," she murmured. She saw his inquisitive look. "I had a colleague who recently died of cancer. She's the reason I'm here." She reached out and took his hand, again. "Forgive me for being so nosy."

"No, I'm glad you asked. I haven't talked about it much. Kept it bottled up inside. Your concern is appreciated."

Sigourney admired his courage, but she could see it was a painful topic and decided not to probe the subject further. She listened to the boards creaking beneath her feet and the engine whining when the truck struggled up a steep grade. The compost smell had diminished, but its odor still evoked images of her father, and she fell silent.

John removed his jacket and rolled it into a pillow for his head. "Been a bit busy the past two nights. I think I'll nap." He leaned against the side of the truck and closed his eyes.

Despite her emotional and physical ordeal, Sigourney found the truck's ride too rough to think about sleeping. She saw that John had no such difficulty, however. He was soon breathing heavily beside her. In repose, he looked younger than his years and more innocent. She watched his lower lip quiver slightly as he breathed, and she had to resist the temptation to caress his cheek. She blinked and looked away, embarrassed by the idea that she was somehow spying on him. Which was ironic, since *he* was the spy, although he claimed not to be. Who else but a spy would turn up in a battered car at dawn in a tiny village in Tibet?

To pass the time, she decided to read from Anne's diary by lifting the flap to admit a little more light. She hadn't mentioned Anne Hopkins to John yet, but she would. There was no longer any reason to hide the diary from him.

Diary entry by Anne Hopkins, 1899

We joined a small band of pilgrims on the road to Gyantse, which was both a blessing and a risk. Traveling with them made it easier to blend into the steadily increasing traffic, but it also put us in close proximity with our Tibetan companions, which made it harder for me to hide my identity.

One disaster nearly destroyed my hopes and dreams. We were spending our second day with the group, joining their camp fire and eating and sleeping with them, when I accidentally gave myself away to their eldest member! I had gone down to a small stream by myself to wash utensils after dinner and to clean a few personal items. The old man appeared unannounced and saw my white arms and hands. He also noticed my personal items, which were clearly not Tibetan. I remained seated on my haunches and looked up at him with pleading eyes. He stared at me for what seemed an eternity. I didn't know what else to do, so I lowered my head in deference to him and waited. My heart pounded so loudly it drowned out the sounds of the stream behind me, and I held my breath until I thought my lungs would burst.

He placed his hand on my head and nodded his head in understanding. He was, after all, a simple peasant--Tenzin told me they were   farmers from the North where fewer people resided--and he didn't know much about the outside world. I stood up and bowed to him, expressing my gratitude at his kindness. He walked back to the campsite without uttering a word. I quickly finished my business and covered my exposed skin, then hurried back to camp to see if I was safe. No one paid me any special attention. Tenzin told me later that the man had said nothing.

It was difficult to predict the actions of these people, however, and we decided to move on. We quietly departed that night while every one slept and made a forced march until we had put considerable distance between ourselves and the pilgrims. I spent the next two days looking over my shoulder, certain that officials on horseback would arrive at any moment to arrest me. But no one appeared, and we made our way to Gyantse without further incident. The old man had held his tongue, and I silently thanked him.

The village of Gyantse sits at the foot of a small mountain, the top of which is ringed by the great walls of Gyantse's famous dzong, a fortress overlooking the village and the road approaching the town.

Our arrival coincided with a festival, and the streets were filled with revelers and contestants, who brought much gaiety and color to the drab streets. Those with money were dressed in their finest outfits, which included a variety of colorful silks and jewelry. We learned the monks were about to perform dances in the monastery's courtyard. Tomorrow, men would demonstrate their horsemanship and accuracy with bow and arrow. We had not intended to stop at Gyantse, but I could not resist the festivities. The crowds were so great, there seemed little chance of being detected.

We made our way through the dusty streets to the gated entrance of the Pelkor Chode Monastery. People crowded around us, and the inner courtyard was so full it seemed impossible for anyone else to enter. But the throngs kept pushing forward, and we soon found ourselves pressed against the courtyard's inner wall. We were crushed so tightly, I feared I could not breathe. We moved with the flow of bodies until we reached an area in front of the main temple where hundreds of spectators sat on mats on the rough, uneven stones. A dozen monks were performing a ritual dance in bright, colorful robes. Each wore a flat, oval mask that covered his face. The masks had large openings for the eyes and mouth. Narrow, wooden noses protruded comically from the surfaces. They reminded me of wooden puppets that had sprung to life.

When the ceremony ended, the crowd pushed its way towards the gates we had entered. I lingered so that I could see the remarkable stupa next to the monastery. It had a strange, ribbed design, formed by outside walkways that ringed the building in zigzag patterns. Its most interesting feature was the mysterious eyes that peered down at me from its peak. They seemed to follow me wherever I went. As I looked, a shadow swept over them, and I experienced the kind of teeth-aching chill that comes from chewing ice on a summer day. The eyes were warning me of danger! What it meant I did not know, but I told Tenzin we should leave Gyantse at once.

The streets bustled with activity and purpose as we returned to the main road. Shops and stands on either side were doing a brisk business. A din of babbling voices assailed my ears as Tibetan merchants engaged their customers in the bargaining rituals they loved so much. Even the smallest item required an energetic give and take before the sale was consummated. Many of the Tibetan merchants were young women, whose beauty shone through their dusty faces. They called to me in enchanting voices to buy their butter, meat and vegetables. The peppery aroma of spices blending with the familiar fragrance of butter tea tempted me, but I resisted.

We were dressed as poor pilgrims, and it would look peculiar if we suddenly produced money for their goods.

Suddenly, a haughty man in flowing robes strode through the crowds towards me, followed by a dozen monks. I knew this must be the head monk. His intense eyes reminded me of the stupa's. They bore into mine with such ferocity, I looked away in fear. But, I looked back in time to see the same shadow cross his face, and I knew he was the cause of the stupa's warning. I quickly turned my back, trembling with certainty that I was about to be unmasked, but the monks swept past me without a word. I could feel the air from their swishing robes buffeting me like an ill-gotten wind.

To my joyous relief, we escaped the town without incident and joined the pilgrims heading for Lhasa. Lhasa! Was I really to reach my destination? Or would I be discovered and turned away like so many others? Between us stood two more mountain ranges and many pairs of distrustful eyes. It was not the time to become confident. I could not afford another mistake like the one I made with that old man. I must remain diligent if I am to fulfill my quest.

Yes, diligence. Sigourney would need that as well, especially now that she had Mr. Ho after her. The idea of returning to the van frightened her, but she knew John was right. It was the only way to reach Lhasa without becoming a fugitive. Hiding in plain sight, he called it. What a remarkable strategy. Something she would never have considered. She hoped he was right. She hoped he knew what he was doing.

CHAPTER FIFTEEN

Sigourney heard Beth's barking laugh before she saw the group trooping across the square in front of Gyantse's Pelkor Chode Monastery. She had arrived at the hotel with John and learned where the group had gone. Walking into the hotel had given her goose bumps. Everywhere she looked, she saw accusing eyes and people waiting to pounce on her. The desk clerk looked the most menacing of all, but he checked hers and John's names against a reservation list and handed them their room keys with nothing more than a cursory look. She nearly wept with relief when she realized that she wasn't going to be arrested. Hiding in plain sight might be a good strategy, but it set her teeth on edge.

Now, she stood with John at the entrance to the monastery's grounds cautiously watching for any signs of danger. Everything seemed normal. No guards or Chinese officials were visible. Other than her tour group and a lonely pilgrim prostrating herself on the cold, hard stones in front of the monastery, the square was deserted.

Jenny and the others gave her surprised looks when they saw her. "Got a little lost," she explained with an embarrassed smile. John had suggested she keep her story as simple as possible. "Sorry if I caused any trouble."

Marie-Rose gave her a knowing smile and hugged her. "It is good to have you back," she whispered.

"Hey, do you know what they call a tourist when she misses her bus?" Jenny asked in a bantering voice. "A hitchhiker." Everyone laughed as Sigourney's face reddened. She was about to open her mouth to retort when she looked at Jenny's and Erica's beaming faces and realized they were just as happy to see her as Marie-Rose. Jenny's little joke was just her way of telling Sigourney that she had been concerned for her.

Sigourney felt a warm glow at this revelation, but it quickly faded when she met Cameron's suspicious glare. *His* face said something very different. It said "you might fool the others, but not me." Sigourney did her best to ignore him.

"What happened to Mr. Ho?" Beth asked.

"He has left the tour," Jigme replied. His face remained impassive, but Sigourney could see the glimmer of relief in his eyes. "We have visited the stupa and are about to enter the monastery. Please, join us."

The solitary woman near the entrance continued to genuflect and prostrate herself, but Sigourney hardly noticed. The deep, familiar sound of chanting monks were pulsating in her head, once again, and she gripped her valise to quiet them.

"Monks must be praying inside," John commented. He saw the worried look on her face. "I can hear them chanting."

Sigourney relaxed her grip and smiled. "Thank goodness."

Inside, four elderly monks sat against the far wall beating drums and singing in monotone voices. Only the dim light from a small, dirty window illuminated them, but it was enough to see the deep rapture in their heavily wrinkled faces. Dust raised by their drums floated in the light. Their voices boomed like cannons.

Several younger monks stood nearby conversing among themselves. Sigourney observed the scene with growing discomfort. She couldn't help wondering if the prayers were linked to the manuscript. When John stopped beside her, she jumped like a startled bird.

Jigme chatted with the monks and confirmed her suspicions when he rejoined the group. "The monks say the word of Buddha will soon complete its journey and be reunited with Tibet. They are praying for its safe deliverance."

"How is that supposed to happen?" Marie-Rose asked. Her normally hesitant demeanor had vanished. She leaned forward, eager to hear more.

Jigme rubbed his forehead as he framed his response. "No one can be sure. Some believe Buddha will reappear as the legendary Guru Rinpoche and ride into Tibet on a flying tiger, just as he did in Bhutan in the eighth century. Others say he has entered the spirit of the Dalai Lama, who will soon return to Tibet. Nobody knows just how it will happen, but everyone agrees it will be a great event that will help the Tibetans regain their autonomy." He frowned. "You must be careful what you say about this. The Chinese are worried and are watching everyone closely, especially tourists."

Sigourney's thoughts were flying around insider her head like fireflies. The Tibetans, who were fanatical in their faith, were waiting for her! *She* was the figure riding into Tibet, perhaps not as dramatically as Guru Rinpoche, but with just as much purpose. Their faith in what she was trying to accomplish astonished her. It swept aside her fears about Mr. Ho and gave her courage.

When they exited the monastery, Sigourney turned her attention to the ribbed stupa standing nearby. She stopped in the middle of the square and stared at its compelling eyes. Anne had sensed a warning in them. Was there one for her, as well? If so, it eluded her. All she felt was a state of peaceful well-being, a sensation she hadn't experienced in days. She was becoming lost in the stupa's hypnotic gaze, just as she had in Kathmandu.

She shook her head and was about to turn away, when she saw a deep shadow creep across the stupa's eyes. The shadow Anne had described! She froze and stared at the darkened eyes in disbelief. Her first thought was Mr. Ho, and she whirled around, expecting to find him glaring at her. There was no one except her group walking towards the exit and the lone woman still genuflecting in front of the monastery. When she turned back, the shadow was gone. Was her mind playing tricks? No, she *had* seen something. Perhaps, it was just a coincidence. She stared at the unblinking eyes a moment longer, and then hurried after John and the others.

A powerful wind swept off the Tibetan plains as Sigourney left the monastery's compound and walked down the street leading to the hotel. Dust swirled in her eyes with stinging blows. The street was nearly deserted. She tried to picture the throngs of pilgrims, monks, and merchants Anne had described. What a scene that must have been. They were all gone, now. All that was left were a dozen Tibetan workers who sat together on the sidewalk, huddling against the wind and smoking cigarettes, and a horse with more bones than flesh that stood hitched to a cart. The street looked orphaned.

The memory of the stupa's eyes followed Sigourney through the hotel lobby, haunting her. They were warning her of something, but what? At any moment, she expected to be arrested and dragged to the waiting clutches of Mr. Ho, but the lobby was serenely quiet. She raced to her room and slammed the door. It was a Spartan, unheated room, just like the others, but it protected her. It made her feel safe. She sat on the edge of the bed and tried to calm down. The eyes slowly faded away and her breathing returned to normal.

Sigourney was delighted to discover hot, running water in the bathroom. She immediately filled the tub and plunged in. The steaming water was luxuriously warm and soothing on her skin. It lifted her spirits and restored her optimism. Everything would be all right, she told herself. Her spirits would look after her.

Anne's diary always comforted her, and there was time to read another entry before dinner. Once she was dressed, she took the diary and settled into the chair by her bed.

Diary entry by Anne Hopkins, 1899

I am so bone-weary tired from climbing mountains, all I want to do is lie down and sleep for a week. Our latest adventure began while we wandered along the road from Gyantse. Rumors were spreading that Tibetan officials were watching for foreigners in the next mountain pass at Karo La. My mouth went dry when I heard this, and my body groaned at the prospect of new trials to come. Many questions raced through my mind. Had someone noticed me in Gyantse? Had the head priest? Or, did the old man report me, after all? Perhaps, others were trying to sneak into Lhasa, just like me. What an unhappy coincidence that would be!

Tenzin and I agreed it was too risky to try slipping past alerted guards. There was only one alternative: another wearying climb over the mountains using a more remote route. We would have to expose ourselves to the weather and to the danger of Khampas, yet again. So, we left the trail and headed into the snow-capped mountains, which waited to embrace us in their icy arms.

We came across a great glacier near the mountain peak. It swept towards us like a giant tongue, and I wanted to walk on it. The firm ice would be much easier to traverse than the deeper snow. But, Tenzin cautioned me about the danger of hidden crevasses. It was safer, he said, to stay with our route. At least the mountains were free of wind, and no dark clouds threatened us. It was a peaceful place, where I sensed the Bon spirits were friendly, and my own flagging spirits began to revive.

We crossed the summit and descended the other side without incident. It was growing dark by the time we reached the plateau. We discovered a large, blue-green lake and two small stupas on a hillside, and we decided to make camp beside them. As we prepared our belongings, a young woman appeared like an apparition leading two yaks. She approached us and spoke to Tenzin in a cheerful, laughing voice.

Tenzin whispered that the woman hoped we would share our tea with her, and I nodded yes. It would be awkward to turn her away. Tibetans often shared their camp fires with fellow travelers. This presented a small dilemma, for Tenzin had used up his Tibetan matches, and all we had left were ones we had brought from India. It would seem curious to her, if he used those. We had already gathered firewood, and he began to look for pieces of flint rock to start a fire.

The woman laughed and knelt beside the pile of sticks. She rubbed her hands rapidly together, then pressed them down on the wood. Soon, smoke began to billow between her fingers, and when she removed her hands, a small flame leapt from the wood! Was this magic I was witnessing? Tenzin was as surprised as I. He opened her hands, but there was nothing in them.

While I made the tea, the yak herder chatted with Tenzin with growing familiarity. I did not have to understand her words to know what her sing-song voice implied, and when she moved closer to him, I experienced a most unpleasant churning inside of me. Tenzin and I had not been intimate since the cave in the mountain, but I discovered a strong repugnance at the idea of sharing him! I fiddled with my tea until I thought I would explode, and I was about to move my bedding to the other side of the stupas when Tenzin stood up and politely spoke to the woman. She laughed, but remained seated. Tenzin spoke more firmly. She finally rose with a toss of her head and disappeared into the night with her two beasts.

Tenzin explained that she had, indeed, proposed staying the night, but he told her I would be angry and it was best for her to leave. I bridled at his suggestion that I was his jealous wife and told him he should not have let me prevent him from enjoying himself. Tenzin laughed. He said she was not the kind of woman who interested him, and he had all the wives he could handle on this trip. My anger flew away, and before I knew it we were in each other's arms. It was wonderful to feel a man's desire again! My joy expanded until it filled the sky.

"Care to stroll around the town?" John asked after they finished their dinner.

Sigourney felt a rush of pleasure at his suggestion and thought of Anne. Was it possible to find romance in such an unlikely place, or were they just two silly women starving for a man's affections?

She imagined Anne lying under a starry sky in the arms of Tenzin. She *was* being silly, but that didn't stop her skin from growing warm and her heart from skipping a beat.

"I'd like that very much."

They wandered along the main street in silence. Other than a few Chinese families visiting outside their shops, there was little activity. The Tibetans had retreated for the night behind the compound walls surrounding their homes, and the wind had returned to its own spirit world. The night was hushed. Street lamps had replaced the flickering butter lamps that once lighted the thoroughfare, but when they ventured down a side street, the lamps disappeared, leaving only fragments of light leaking through shuttered, second-story windows to illuminate their way. A stray dog, hoping for a handout, perked up as they passed. Low voices floated over the compound walls like stray puffs of wind. Sigourney threw her head back and stared at an opulent sky, where stars were spread across the heavens in a royal display of necklaces and tiaras. The endless pinpoints of light made her dizzy, and she grasped John's arm for balance.

Her awkward movement broke the hesitancy that lingered between them, and he firmly hooked her arm through his, "It's a bit dicey walking these streets in the dark."

Sigourney smiled at the apologetic tone in his voice and squeezed his arm. She could feel the heat from his body where it brushed hers, and she had to resist the urge to press herself more tightly against him.

Another turn brought them to the street leading to the monastery. Here, a few Tibetans were moving about. A wheel squeaked as an elderly man led his horse-drawn cart down the street. Soft laughter erupted in the shadows, where a young man and woman were engaged in the timeless dialogue of courtship. A door popped open, casting a bright shaft of yellow light into the street, while a woman tossed a pan of water out the open doorway.

"I'm reading a diary by someone who visited here a long time ago," Sigourney said hesitantly. She wasn't sure how to broach the subject of Anne Hopkins. She knew it would contradict John's notions about who reached Lhasa first. "She described a very busy scene here in Gyantse, one teeming with merchants and pilgrims. I would have liked to see it then."

"Is that what you've been reading, a diary?" John glanced at her, sensing her hesitancy. "Whose is it?"

"It's written by a woman who traveled to Lhasa on a pilgrimage."

"Are you referring to Alexandra David-Neel?"

"No. This woman came to Tibet before David-Neel." She held her breath and listened to the cart wheel as if squealed its way around the corner. It sounded like a wounded cat. Silence hung in the air between them. She had just told John she carried something that could change history. Would he believe her? She peered intently at his face, but it was hidden in the murky light.

"You know what you're saying, don't you?" he asked in a piqued voice. "David-Neel is widely accepted as the first Western woman to have reached Lhasa. She arrived there in 1924. Her diary is famous."

"I have even more startling news than that," she said quietly. She began walking again, her hands swinging at her sides. John caught up with her, and when they reached the main street, he stopped her with a gentle touch on her shoulder.

"You've just informed me of an unknown woman who is supposed to have reached Lhasa before David-Neel. What more could you possibly tell me?" A nearby street lamp threw patches of light across his face, revealing a look of intense curiosity.

Sigourney took a deep breath. "In addition to returning the manuscript, I'm trying to verify the diary of an Englishwoman named Anne Hopkins. She's the one who removed the manuscript from Samye. If her diary is correct, she reached Lhasa in 1899." The words tumbled from her with the desperation of a confession. Why did she find it harder to tell him about the diary than the manuscript?

John pursed his lips and stared at her with narrowed eyes, causing Sigourney to look away in an unsuccessful attempt to deflect his unspoken skepticism. She shifted her weight uncomfortably, certain she had just ruined a beautiful evening. All she wanted to do was escape back to her hotel room, but she stood her ground and returned John's doubtful look.

"Before Younghusband?" John responded at last. "Surely that information can't be accurate. People would have known. This Anne Hopkins would have confided in friends, family or associates. She would have been famous in England. It sounds like someone has gone to great lengths to prepare a very good hoax."

Sigourney could see him struggling with the idea, trying to grasp hold of it and understand its implications. She knew history wasn't something etched in stone. It was written by the victors and survivors of epoch events, and it often changed over time. Ultimately, history became what historians chose to say about it, and it could shift as quickly as sand blowing in a desert storm. She could see that for John, however, history was more concrete. It wasn't something left to the whims of people like herself.

"That's what I'm trying to prove," she replied defensively. "Or disprove," she quickly added. "Whether her diary is true. There may be a record of her visit to Samye. I won't know until I return the manuscript."

John rubbed his jaw. "Well, if it *is* true, you'll rewrite the history books. What a remarkable story that would be. Imagine, all those adventurers trying to reach Lhasa, and you've discovered a woman who may actually have done so and never told anyone."

Sigourney nearly fell into John's arms when she realized he wasn't dismissing her claim out-of-hand. The distrust in John's face had vanished. Her spirits soared. She put her arm through his, again, and felt his warmth flowing through her.

When they reached the hotel and stopped in front of her door, Sigourney leaned forward impulsively and kissed him on the cheek, then quickly turned and tried to work the key in the lock to hide her flustered smile. When the door finally opened, she looked back and saw John watching her with a broad grin.

"By the way," he said, "if you're willing to wake up before dawn tomorrow, I'll show you a remarkable sunrise."

"I didn't bring an alarm clock." It was a stupid response, but it was all she could think to say.

"I'll tap on your door." With that, he turned and walked down the hallway to his room. Her emotions tumbled over and over inside her as she watched him go. What was she to make of this man? Why did she get so fuzzy around him? She nearly called him back to her room but knew their relationship wasn't far enough along for that. Not yet. Besides, it was something she wanted him to initiate, when they were ready.

Sigourney was too elated to sleep. She had left Anne on the road to Lhasa, and after her discussion with John, she was eager to learn more. She propped herself up in the tiny bed and opened the diary.

Diary entry by Anne Hopkins, 1899

Tenzin and I are now within striking distance of Lhasa, and my excitement is building with each step. For the first time, I allow myself to believe that I will reach my goal. Our landscape has changed noticeably. Solitude and windswept plains have been replaced by farmlands and more villages. We have slipped over the rim of Tibet's isolated world into the only real concentration of people in this desolate country.

After our glorious night by the two stupas, we reached the main road and immersed ourselves in the steady stream of humanity headed for Lhasa. This included wealthy merchants, farmers with barley and salt to sell, and pilgrims like us. When we entered the Kyichu Valley, I saw the sparkle of sunlight reflecting off distant, golden rooftops. I was enjoying my first glimpse of the Potala Palace. I knew the Potala was home to the God-King, the Dalai Lama, and the religious center of Tibetan Buddhism. It glowed like a great beacon, guiding Tibetans towards its spiritual shores. Its energy surged through my aching body, restoring my fortitude, and I prostrated myself on the chilly ground among the many pilgrims who were seeing this sacred edifice for the first time.

Tenzin and I eagerly joined the growing stream of caravans following the Kyichu River. Merchants called to us from stands along the road. They sold delicacies far more tempting than the tsampa and yak meat we had been eating for the past two months. Tenzin wanted to stop and relish them, but I kept walking with a single-minded purpose, forcing him to abandon his desires and increase his stride to keep pace with me.

The Potala came into clearer view. It rose like a magnificent castle from its perch atop a small mountain overlooking the valley. Its massive, lower walls were stark-white, while the upper portion was painted a deep, reddish-brown. Resting on top like a royal crown were the golden rooftops I had seen from afar. A trader in India had told me the white palace housed the living quarters of the Dalai Lama, while the red palace contained the shrines and Tibetan deities.

At last, we approached the gated entrance to the city itself, which stood between the Potala and a lesser hill called Chogburi. My heart raced so fast I feared I might faint. I was steps away from finishing my quest, and I my legs were as wobbly as a tavern maid's. Then, in the blink of an eye, my world crumbled around me. I stopped so suddenly Tenzin nearly collided with me. Standing by the entrance was the head monk from Gyantse! The menacing shadow covering the stupa's eyes flashed before me, and my joy turned to despair. I now knew the warning's message. If I proceeded, I would be stopped by this arrogant man and denied my chance to reach Nirvana. I nearly sat down in the dusty street and cried.

Tenzin saw the head monk and motioned that we should turn back, but I could feel the monk's glowering eyes and knew if I suddenly reversed my course, I would raise his suspicion. Nor could I remain where I was. People were already pushing past me, making my indecision obvious. As I stood there trying to decide what to do, an invisible spirit began urging me onward. The spirit frightened me. I tried to resist it, but its power was too strong. There was no alternative but to proceed. I braced myself and took Tenzin's arm. My journey was reduced to a handful of steps that were in the hands of my karma. I had no choice but to take them and accept my fate.

As I stumbled towards the gate, a fierce wind suddenly whipped the fine, Tibetan soil into swirling patterns of dust that attacked the eyes of Gyantse's monk and the guards. The monk raised his robes to fend off the stinging blows of Mother Earth, while I hurried through the gates with Tenzin. The little dust storm was as wondrous a miracle as any I had ever read about. It had saved me from detection and allowed me to enter the streets of Lhasa, where I now stood! I wanted to dance a jig and shout with joy, but I restrained myself. I did not dare demonstrate my pleasure while the head monk lurked close by.

Tenzin and I walked briskly through the dungy streets, until we found ourselves standing in front of one of Tibet's most holy monasteries, the Jo Khang. The square in front of the monastery bustled with energy and humanity. Stalls lined the square, where merchants displayed everything from salt, crockery and silk to cooking utensils and tea. Their clamoring voices joined the dust raised by hundreds of customers haggling with them over the prices of their wares. Zesty aromas from cooking fires spiked the air with tantalizing hints of seared meat. Bodies bumped and jostled for space.

My attention was drawn to the pilgrims streaming past the Jo Khang like a mighty river. They were following the Par Kor, an avenue forming a ring around the monastery. We joined the pilgrims and slowly walked along the narrow street. Merchants offered food and drinks. One man cut fresh yak meat on his wooden wagon and sold bloody sections to passing customers. Tibetans often ate their meat raw and demanded that it be fresh. A series of elaborate butter sculptures, shaped in the images of animals and gods, had been erected along the route. Many were as tall as the Tibetans. Tenzin learned these were for a festival and would be reviewed tomorrow by the Dalai Lama. What a sight that would be! We agreed to return to see the living god for ourselves.

Night was quickly approaching, and flickering butter lamps soon replaced the failing light with their uneven, yellow glow. Our walk along the Par Kor had refreshed me, both physically and spiritually, but it was time to think about where we would sleep. I removed a few coins from the pockets sewn in my dirty robes to pay for lodgings and food, and we began to wander through the busy streets near the monastery in search of a likely place. Tenzin saw a hand-painted sign for an inn. The lodgings were very poor, but we learned that the festival had attracted many visitors, and these were the best we could expect. We were shown to a large room where pieces of dirty cloth had been hung from the ceiling to divide off sleeping areas. My little spot was hardly bigger than the narrow bed, and there was no privacy other than the grimy curtains around me. The room smelled of cheap beer, musty corners, and unwashed bodies. I yearned to be outside where I could sleep under the stars, but I knew that would be impossible during our stay in Lhasa. So, I lay down on the bed without complaint and was soon asleep.

Sigourney fell asleep with images of spirits and butter sculptures dancing in her head. A strange sound began to work its way into Sigourney's consciousness. At first, she thought the noise came from a dream. It sounded like a woodpecker searching for insects, but what would a woodpecker be doing in Tibet? She had hardly seen a tree since leaving Nepal. It took awhile for her groggy mind to realize the tapping noise was John knocking lightly on her door. She opened an eye and found herself rolled up in her comforter with her legs against her chest and her arms wrapped around her knees. The tapping persisted. She shook her head to rid the last remnants of sleep.

"Just a moment," she mumbled.

The incessant tapping started again.

"Okay," she called out angrily. The tapping stopped.

Gray light filtered through the thin curtains, telling her that night would soon be banished by the morning sun. The floor was freezing when she hopped out of bed, but she was relieved to discover warm water in the bathroom and quickly washed her face. She fussed briefly with her unruly hair, before giving up any pretense of looking attractive at such an ungodly hour. Her unkempt appearance only added to her ill-tempered mood as she flung open the door.

John stood in the hallway freshly shaved and neatly dressed in a blue, turtleneck sweater and grey trousers, looking for all the world like this was a normal hour to be up and about. Sigourney could smell after shave lotion and the light perfume of hair shampoo, which she found oddly appealing. Her sour mood dissipated.

"Morning," he said with a sheepish grin. His furrowed brow indicated he was aware of her earlier displeasure. "Sorry to wake you, but I believe you'll find it worthwhile."

Guilt pricked Sigourney's conscience, and she managed a weak smile. "You're about to discover I'm not much of a morning person. What you see is what you get."

"I like what I see, but come on. There's something else we must observe before the sun reaches the horizon."

He led her down the hallway to a window near the stairwell. Rising before her less than a mile away were the broken walls and buildings of Gyantse's once-mighty dzong. In the early-morning light, the walls merged so naturally with the mountain they appeared to be carved from the scabrous rocks rather than built upon them. Sigourney could almost hear the voices of Tibet's ancestors echoing along the stony barriers they had built to protect themselves from the Mongolians and other rampaging hordes. What a sight it would have been to see those ancient armies throwing themselves against the dzong's battlements! Gyantse was not a village to be taken lightly. One would have needed a mighty army to capture it.

A beam of sunlight abruptly struck the building at the mountain's peak, sending it soaring skyward in a dazzling blaze of light. Sigourney leaned against John and watched in breathtaking silence as the sunlight marched slowly down the mountain like an invading army breaching the dzong's defenses, until it reached the sleeping town at its base.

"Was it worth getting up for?" John asked hopefully. His voice betrayed his continuing uncertainty at waking her so early.

"I haven't seen many sunrises, John, but this one was

definitely worth it. Thank you for sharing it with me." She took his arm to reassure him. A thought struck her. "Do you know if Younghusband fought here?"

"Gyantse was a pivotal battle in Younghusband's campaign. The dzong had never fallen before, despite assaults by the Chinese, Nepalese, Sikhs and others. The Tibetans believed if the dzong was ever captured, further resistance would be futile. Younghusband attacked the fortress and won a bloody battle inside the dzong's perimeter. The Tibetans were badly out-gunned by the modern rifles and cannons of the British."

Sigourney tried to imagine the British soldiers struggling to find a foothold on the unyielding mountain while the Tibetans fired down on them with their antiquated rifles.

"I do owe you an apology, but the way," John said quietly, interrupting her thoughts.

"Whatever for?" Sigourney was surprised by this abrupt shift in the conversation and turned to face him. He had the troubled look of a school boy who had been caught misbehaving.

"Last night, I rejected your thesis about the diary out-of-hand. That was most inappropriate of me. What you told me might very well be true. For me to call it a hoax was impolite. My reaction was emotional and unwarranted."

Sigourney touched the soft fabric of his wool sweater with her fingers and smiled. It took considerable strength to be so humble, and she found herself drawn to him with an intensity that unnerved her.

"Skepticism is a healthy thing," she responded at last, "but thank you for keeping an open mind. I can't tell you how much I appreciate it."

As much as she had enjoyed her early morning rendezvous with John, Sigourney returned to her room with foreboding. She couldn't erase the memory of the stupa's shadowed eyes, nor shake the feeling that danger lurked nearby. She stood in the middle of the frigid room and rubbed her arms in an effort to warm herself. The termites went to work on her neck, once more, and she whipped her head around, half-expecting to find Mr. Ho standing in the doorway. You're being silly, she chided herself, but the uneasy feeling persisted, and she had no idea what to do about it. Her only hope was that John knew what he was doing and would keep her safe.

CHAPTER SIXTEEN

Subtle changes appeared as the van proceeded towards Lhasa, changes that seemed monumental after traveling through Tibet's desolate vistas for the past three days. The road was now paved, evidence that the twentieth century was creeping across the vast plains. It looked like a black, angry tongue licking at Tibet's painted landscapes and sucking the life from the country's culture and people. More trucks, cars, and vans rumbled along their route. Houses appeared in greater numbers, along with more willow trees and farms. A look of progress, if not prosperity, filled the countryside. There were still stretches of empty landscapes and isolated houses, but life began to look more communal and substantial. Sigourney wasn't happy with what she saw. She sensed that the Tibet she had come to admire was slipping away like sand in an hour glass.

Cameron and Jenny contributed to her sour mood. They began singing songs and sharing stories. Every time Cameron acted up, Beth roared with laughter and egged him on, just as one would an overgrown puppy. The resulting exchanges disturbed Sigourney. They reminded her of the world outside Tibet, something she didn't want to think about right now. But, there was one aspect of her world she couldn't ignore: Brad Paxton. Every time she thought about the shadow crossing the stupa's eyes, she saw his pompous face and shuddered. What was he up to, she wondered? Had she heard the last of him? She feared not.

Sigourney watched the passing landscape but saw little of the raw mountains and broad valleys that defined her route. Her eyes were turned inward, where she considered the forces of darkness that threatened to unmask her. She was riding a whirlwind of invisible spirits and unexplainable events. An excitement was building in the air, a maelstrom that created its own energy, like two colliding stars. Her neck ached and she rubbed it absentmindedly. In two more days her ordeal would be over. Today, Lhasa; tomorrow, the Samye Monastery. She had to stay focused on that.

John sensed her unhappy disposition and remained in his seat. She wished he would join her, even though she wasn't in a very pleasant mood. When they approached the mountain pass at Karo La, he leaned forward and spoke for the first time, "A rather famous battle occurred here. It's the highest recorded military conflict in history."

Sigourney could feel his warm breath dancing like wanton gypsies on her neck, and she began to relax. She patted the seat next to her. "Sit with me and tell me about it."

"Karo La was the last major barrier between the English and Lhasa," he said after settling beside her. "Several thousand Tibetans had dug in there, making a traditional attack very difficult. So, some of Younghusband's troops moved up the mountains on the Tibetans' flanks and out-maneuvered them. Eventually, they overwhelmed the Tibetans. The encounter was typical of the battles throughout the invasion. The British lost a handful of men, while the Tibetans lost hundreds."

The summit was an inauspicious looking place for such a famous battle. Nothing about the mountain pass suggested its strategic importance to the Tibetans nearly a hundred years ago. There were no natural barriers that could be used to stop a modern army.

They descended the mountain and arrived at the shores of a serpent-shaped, emerald-blue lake called Yamdrok Tso. Was it the lake described in Anne's diary, she wondered? When they passed two stupas near the road, she nearly cried out for the driver to stop. She could almost see the yak woman from long ago, who so mysteriously started the camp fire with her hands.

"We will stop here for a brief rest," Jigme announced.

Everyone got out of the van to stretch their legs, and Sigourney wandered down to the shore with John. She was struck by the absence of plant life along the water's edge. The brown, dusty mountains simply sloped into the water and disappeared beneath the unruffled surface. The setting was so peaceful, she had nearly forgotten about her earlier concerns, until Jigme joined them.

"I must talk to you." He hesitated, shifting his weight uncomfortably. His discomfort alerted Sigourney that something was wrong. She stiffened and waited for him to continue. "I believe we will have another inspection on the road to Lhasa." He nodded towards the valise hanging from her shoulder. "If you will trust me, I will put your bag with the driver's. It is not likely the police will bother with him. He is too low in importance."

A heavy silence hung between them. Sigourney tried to reply, but found it difficult to form the words. A dull roar began to resonate in her head, blocking her thoughts and rendering her speechless. She looked into Jigme's unblinking eyes and tried to think what she should do. Accepting his request meant acknowledging that she was smuggling contraband into Tibet, and it would turn her quest into a conspiracy. She had come to terms with her growing faith in John, but should she trust Jigme? He *was* Tibetan. Surely, he wouldn't betray her, but should she take the chance?

"Jigme, could we have a moment alone?" John spoke in that quiet, steady tone Sigourney had come to associate with him when he meant business.

"Of course." Jigme walked quickly away.

"You can trust him," John said. Sigourney started to reply, but he took her hand and shook his head. "I've talked enough with Jigme to know he's trying to help you. He's your best option, until we reach Lhasa."

Sigourney suddenly felt small and lost, her resolve washed away in a wave of helplessness. "All right," she replied in a tiny voice. She turned on shaky legs and followed Jigme towards the van. As she walked, the monks began chanting, and a sense of relief surged through her. The voices were telling her she was doing the right thing. She had to give up the manuscript in order to save it.

Sigourney sat quietly beside John as they drove past more stone houses and farmland. The images Anne had described--caravans of merchants, yaks, and pilgrims trudging on foot towards the holy city--were gone, replaced by lorries and cars. She had expected to be thrilled at the prospect of reaching Lhasa, but all she felt was a heavy lump in her stomach, her excitement dulled in anticipation of what lay ahead.

She had decided to keep her valise, so that Cameron wouldn't become suspicious. That meant revealing the manuscript to Jigme and the driver. When she took it from her bag, Jigme's expression remained implacable, but the driver's eyes ballooned as he stared at the sacred book. The conspiracy keeps growing, she thought, as if it has a life of its own. Jigme slid the manuscript into the driver's sack, a shabby canvass bag that looked like it had been dragged across Tibet by yaks, without a word, and Sigourney fled to her seat.

Now, she stared at the wretched bag jouncing on the floor under the driver's seat and furiously rubbed the wooden Buddha statue in her unsteady hands. Her entire world was inside that bag. Sigourney thought about Debbie and tried to summon up an image of her, but the sun shining face she treasured kept merging with the thunderous scowls that had come to define her daughter's more recent moods. Sigourney knew she had to complete her quest if she wanted to feel whole with her daughter again, and her fate was now connected by a fragile strand of trust to a Tibetan guide and driver, men she barely knew.

The moment of truth came when the van arrived at the Chushul Bridge spanning the Tsangpo River. Several cars and trucks stood waiting their turns at a check point swarming with uniformed Chinese inspectors. It was a chilling sight, one Sigourney watched with growing queasiness. The inspectors were searching every vehicle thoroughly. She smiled nervously at John, who still sat next to her, and sank deeper into her seat.

"I am sorry for the delay," Jigme announced to the group. "This is not a normal check point. It is part of the greater security I mentioned before." He glanced at Sigourney, before returning his attention to the approaching officers.

Cameron mumbled something to Beth and gave Sigourney a hard look. Sigourney ignored him. All her thoughts were concentrated on the driver's bag. The police who boarded the van were older and more experienced than the ones John had foiled on the road to Shegar. They moved through the van with military precision. When one of them stopped at Sigourney's seat and pointed to her valise, she stared at him with all the courage she could muster. Her heart pounded like the dove's wings striking the window the last time she saw Martha. Had that only been a few months ago? Or had an eternity passed since then? The officer looked briefly at the copied pages of Anne's diary, shoved them carelessly back into the bag and moved on.

When the officers reached the front of the van, she sagged with relief, knowing the inspections were finished. But the men didn't leave. They stopped and demanded to see Jigme's and the driver's belongings. Sigourney froze in her seat, her eyes fixed on the battered bag the driver was placing in the lead officer's impatient hands. Jigme's plan had failed! Her little statue's spirit hadn't been strong enough to withstand the powerful forces arrayed against her. She grasped John's arm and clung to it. The roaring in her ears returned, blocking out all other sounds. She was watching a silent movie in which evil was about to triumph, and the heroine would be lost. Sigourney could feel the sharp claws of the officer's hand tearing at her heart as he reached into the bag. But the officer's hand emerged empty! The officers abruptly turned and left the van without looking back. Moments later, the van was rolling across the bridge to freedom.

Sigourney gasped for air. She had been holding her breath ever since the officer reached into the bag, which now bounced harmlessly under the driver's seat, once more.

"Where's the manuscript?" she asked John in a whisper.

"Not sure, but if I had to make a guess, I'd say the driver's sitting on it. See the cushion he uses on the seat?"

Sigourney looked incredulously at the ripped, plastic cushion tucked beneath the driver. She hadn't noticed it before. Silently, she thanked her wooden Buddha. Perhaps, it was only her imagination, but she could've sworn the little statue gave her a tiny smile.

The van entered a long valley ringed by snowcapped mountains. Afternoon sunlight slanted through the clouds, touching first one mountain peak, then another. A feeling of euphoria slowly replaced Sigourney's earlier anxiety. Like Anne, she was on the outskirts of Tibet's Holy City. The only thing missing was a view of the Potala's golden rooftops, but the distant images Anne had witnessed were now obscured by a skyline of colorless concrete buildings sprawled across the valley floor. The gaudy splash of Chinese signs announcing stores and restaurants along the road only added to Sigourney's alienation. Gone were the merchants' stalls Anne had described. Gone were the traders and pilgrims. She might as well have been approaching the outskirts of Beijing.

"Not very inspiring, is it?" John offered. He sounded as disappointed as she was.

"It's depressing. Just imagine what this must have looked like before the Chinese invaded."

"We'll find the real Lhasa soon enough."

At last, the Potala's fleeting image skipped in and out of view among the trees and buildings to her right. It sat in imperial splendor on its hill only a heart beat away. Sigourney's spirits lifted, and she leaned forward for a better view.

When the van reached the hotel, she waited until the others had departed before approaching Jigme, who pulled the manuscript from under the driver's cushion and solemnly handed it to her. Sigourney hugged it like a mother being reunited with her lost child.

"Thank you, Jigme." She hesitated. "I'm already in your debt, but I have one more favor to ask. I must get to the Samye Monastery. How can I arrange that?"

Jigme leaned towards her in a conspiring fashion. "You can hire a taxi to take you and bring you back."

"How long will it take?"

"It is a full day's trip. The taxi will take you to a boat landing where you must cross the Yarlung Tsongpo River and ride a truck to the monastery itself. Tomorrow, we will visit the Potala in the morning. We will be watched when we leave the hotel, but I can arrange for a taxi to be waiting for you at the Potala, if you like."

John was right. Jigme was proving to be a valuable ally. "I would very much appreciate your help, but I hope it won't get you in trouble."

Jigme shook his head vigorously. "Tomorrow will be a great day for Tibet. I am honored to help you."

After Sigourney and her group checked into their hotel, which she was delighted to learn had both hot water and heated rooms, she got her first glimpse of the real Lhasa when they visited Barkor Square. Barkor Square was a microcosm of the Holy City Anne had described: a busy market place and social center filled with lively crowds of Tibetans bargaining and chatting with one another. Merchants' stalls lined the edges of the main square, displaying everything from souvenirs to yak meat.

At the far end of the square stood the Jokhang, one of the oldest and most important monasteries in Tibet. "The Jokhang was built in the seventh century by Songsten Gampo, the king who first introduced Buddhism into Tibet," Jigme explained as the group followed him through the square. "The monastery is often referred to as the Cathedral of Lhasa, because of its unique status. Unlike the other monasteries, the Jokhang is not affiliated with any Buddhist movement or sect. It is used by all Tibetans, regardless of their Buddhist training."

"Like a church where all Christian faiths can come together and pray," Marie-Rose suggested. Sigourney realized that she had been spending so much time with John, she had neglected her new friend. She would correct that oversight once she returned from Samye.

"Very much like that," Jigme replied. "And unlike the other great monasteries where thousands of monks once resided, the Jokhang kept only a handful."

Sigourney watched dozens of pilgrims parading past the Jokhang and down a tiny street to her left. This was the spiritual route Anne described in her diary as the Par Kor! She drifted away from her group and immersed herself in the stream of humanity. Peasants in drab coats mingled with wealthier Tibetans dressed in their finest silk blouses, beaded headdresses, and turquoise jewelry. Some stopped to admire the copper teapots, metal butter lamps, herders' knives and fur hats offered in the merchants' stalls on either side of the narrow street. A hundred years vanished before Sigourney's eyes as she walked in Anne's footsteps. When a crowd outside the doorway of a bar caught her attention, she moved closer and discovered they were watching the miracle of a black and white television set. Anne didn't see *that* during her visit, Sigourney thought with a wry smile.

The leisurely pace also allowed people to visit as they walked. Some stopped in the middle of the street to chat, forcing the crowds to flow around them. The avenue was filled with so many murmuring, cheerful voices, Sigourney soon relaxed; the tension in her shoulders melted away. What a wonderful way to relieve stress, she mused. She promised herself that she would find her own spiritual pathway back home.

A woman's voice broke through Sigourney's thoughts. The young Tibetan was striding alongside her and talking in a laughing voice that reminded Sigourney of the Yak herder in Anne's diary. Two older women joined her. Sigourney assumed they were trying to sell her souvenirs, until she saw the younger woman pointing to the valise. More women crowded around, chattering at her. Hands reached out to touch the valise; warm bodies pressed against her, jostling her and hemming her in. Voices rained down on her until she was drenched in their dissonance. Sigourney had to resist an urge to flail at them in order to gain some space. She grabbed the wooden Buddha statue, instead, and held it above her head. The women smiled when they saw it. The young woman who had started the commotion bowed and spoke in a reverent voice. The others nodded in agreement and dissolved into the passing crowd.

Badly shaken, she retreated to an empty space between two merchant stalls to collect herself. The passion in those women reminded her of the Tibetans at the stupa near Kathmandu. Both had displayed a hunger for the word of Buddha that she found a little frightening. Theirs is a passion bordering on madness, she thought. Once she had steadied her nerves, Sigourney looked up and down the street for any signs of a spy who might have witnessed her encounter, but the pilgrims shuffled past without giving her so much as a glance, as if she had become invisible to the crowd. Sigourney adjusted her coat and hurried on.

When she rejoined the group in the monastery, John was waiting for her with a fresh proposal. "Another sunrise tomorrow morning," he announced with a mischievous grin. "This time from the hill facing the Potala. A colleague of mine told me about it. Said it was quite special."

"John, I've never gotten up so early before in my life. You're going to be the death of me," she responded with a laugh. "But if you say it's worth it, I'm game." She gave him a doubtful look that said she wasn't entirely convinced but didn't want to be left behind.

CHAPTER SEVENTEEN

"Oh, my God," Sigourney exclaimed. She had just returned with John and the others to the hotel lobby and now stood face-to-face with her worst nightmare. Seated on a couch with a grim, half-smile was Brad Paxton. Panic seized her, and she nearly turned on her heels and fled the building. Just the sight of Brad made her skin crawl. What was he doing there? Whatever it was, she knew it didn't bode well for her.

"What's wrong?" John asked, his eyes following hers. "Do you know that man?"

"He's trouble." She touched his arm, never taking her eyes off Brad. "Please excuse me, John. I have some unpleasant business to attend to."

When John hesitated, Sigourney shook her head and motioned for him to go. "Well, you know where to find me if you need me." He squeezed her hand and strode across the lobby.

Brad stood up and approached her with a smooth smile plastered on his face. It was the kind of smile a politician used while working a crowd, and she disliked it. Just as she disliked his slick manners, his carefully combed hair, which never had a strand out of place, and his neatly trimmed mustache. Brad Paxton was the only person besides Mr. Ho who could wreck her plans, and there he was walking towards her like an avenging demon.

"Hello, Sig." Her teeth ground at the sound of that name. She knew he was deliberately using it to annoy her, and it was working. "What a surprise to find you here in Lhasa." There was no attempt at a hand shake or other gesture of friendship. That was fine with Sigourney. She knew this was war.

"I might say the same for you." It was important, she knew, to maintain a level voice. She couldn't let Brad see the turmoil boiling inside her.

"We need to have a little chat, don't you think?" He continued to flash his cool smile.

"What about, Brad? The weather? I don't know why you've suddenly appeared, but it certainly has nothing to do with me," Sigourney's mind raced through her options. Her best hope, she decided, was to put up a brazen front and try to keep Brad at bay, at least until tomorrow.

"Oh, it has everything to do with you, Sig. I tell you about my research plans in Tibet, and suddenly you're investigating some woman's diary. Doesn't that strike you as odd?" The cool smile faded.

Sigourney couldn't think how to reply. His sudden appearance had thrown her out of kilter. She needed to put some space between them; she needed time to think before talking with this weasel.

"I'm too tired to talk now, Brad. Maybe, we should meet in the restaurant for dinner. We can talk then." She studied his face to see if he sensed how rattled she was, but his features were as blank as an unplugged computer screen. He was a master at hiding his thoughts.

"Fine," he responded. "Shall we say in an hour?"

Sigourney agreed and fled to her room. She knew she was at a disadvantage in Tibet. This was Brad's turf. He had many contacts with the Chinese government, and he had worked closely with local officials, currying favors and gaining support for his research. His unexpected arrival showed how upset he was with her project. She knew he'd do whatever he could to block her. Her only advantage was that he didn't know the real purpose of her trip.

She flung her shoes into the room's tiny closet and sank onto the bed like a foundering ship. She needed a plan, if she was going to outwit Brad. Her best hope was to let him focus on the diary while she made her run to the Samye Monastery. That meant stalling him for a day. Let him think she was cooperating. Once she returned the manuscript and verified Anne's story, Brad's interference would no longer matter.

The dining room was crowded when she arrived. Brad was seated at a table along the far wall waiting for her. She glanced around and saw John, Marie-Rose, Jenny and Erica chatting in a nearby booth. Jealousy briefly jabbed at her chest, but John's eyes found hers and reassured her. She gave him a quick smile, took a deep breath, and headed towards Brad's table.

"Have you tried yak meat yet?" He stood up until she was seated. It seemed a polite gesture, but she knew he did it to aggravate her. Her teeth began grinding again.

"No. We've mostly eaten Chinese food on the road."

"You must have some. I've already ordered a few dishes. My treat." Brad gave her a crocodile smile that showed his teeth.

Sigourney knew she was tip-toeing through quick sand, and she wanted to get this encounter over with as quickly as possible. "Brad, let's cut to the chase. What exactly do you want?"

"Frankly, Sigourney, I'm a little upset by your duplicity. Your project could trample all over the research I've so carefully arranged, yet I had to find out about it second hand." She noted that he'd switched to her proper name. He was no longer playing games.

"I don't see how my little diary tramples on your research."

"The Chinese are already skittish about someone trying to sneak a book on Buddhism into Tibet. Your diary could be construed by them as an attempt to bring unwarranted literature into the country."

Sigourney avoided Brad's accusing gaze. He was uncomfortably close to the truth, but she couldn't let him know that.

"What you see as history, they may see as propaganda," he continued. "If they get upset, they could stop all exchanges for awhile, including my project. I don't want you or anybody else screwing up my research." Brad tossed his napkin down on the table to emphasize his point.

Laughter from Sigourney's companions in the booth distracted her, and she yearned to join them. She hardly tasted her food. Talking to Brad about the rumors and the diary made her feel even more exposed than she had at those check points on the road. She had to do something to avoid his unwanted intrusions. Subterfuge was her best chance. Send him in one direction, while she went another.

"Look, Brad, two days from now my group will visit the Drepung Monastery. If the diary is true, I hope to find evidence there. But I don't have your connections. Why don't you meet me at the Drepung, and we can share whatever information we find?"

Brad leaned back in his chair. His mustache twitched. She had clearly surprised him with her proposal. She looked him in the eye, willing herself not to give away her "duplicity," as he called it. Silence grew between them, but she was determined not to say more. It was Brad's move. She held her breath and waited.

"Okay," he responded at last. "That sounds fair enough, but why don't we just go tomorrow?"

"I'm scheduled to see the Potala tomorrow. If I leave the group, it'll look suspicious. It's better to wait, don't you think?"

"You're right. The day after it is." His plastic smile returned. "You haven't eaten much dinner. No appetite?"

When she shook her head no, he reached over with his fork and stabbed a chunk of yak meat. She excused herself and returned to her room.

Sigourney felt like she had been pushed through a shredding machine. She collapsed on the bed, too emotionally exhausted to do anything but look at the cracks in the painted ceiling. She reached into her pocket and retrieved the wooden Buddha statue for comfort. It stared at her with the same conspiring expression she had seen on Jigme's face when she talked to him about Samye.

Her exaltation at reaching Lhasa undetected was rapidly dissolving in a mire of uncertainties. Her quest was far from over. Leaving the group and reaching Samye was going to be difficult enough. Brad's sudden arrival only made things worse. He *had* seemed surprised by her offer, but would her ruse put him off long enough for her to complete her mission? And she still had to worry about Mr. Ho, who was searching for her. Sigourney sat up and stared at the wooden Buddha. I need your help, she pleaded silently. The statue warmed her, yet its surface remained cool against her skin. It was a spiritual warmth, not a physical one, and it radiated through her body, succoring her. She closed her eyes and caressed it with her fingertips, before returning it to her pocket.

Sigourney picked up the diary. She didn't want to think about Brad or Mr. Ho at the moment and reading about Anne would calm her nerves. Besides, she was anxious to learn what happened at the Samye Monastery one hundred years ago.

Diary entry by Anne Hopkins, 1899
How do I describe one of the most compelling buildings in the world? I am talking about the Potala, a massive display of architectural and spiritual prowess. Imposing, powerful and sacred are words that leap to mind. The Potala is comprised of thirteen stories, a thousand rooms, ten thousand shrines and two hundred thousand Buddhist images!

The Potala's greatest importance is its role as home of the Living God, the Dalai Lama. I have learned that the Fifth Dalai Lama started building it over two hundred years ago, but he died during its construction. The project was considered so important, his death was concealed by the elder monks for twelve years until it was finished! They feared news of his death would create confusion, which would delay or even stop the Potala's construction.

When a Dalai Lama dies, his reincarnated spirit must be found. This is a painstaking and mysterious process that can take considerable time. Scholarly monks must search for candidates among young boys aged three to five. Visions and oracles are used. Candidates are studied for unusual spiritual insight, certain physical characteristics, reflections of inner character, and their ability to recognize objects of the previous Dalai Lama. Considering all theses complex rituals and procedures, it is small wonder the elder monks wanted to hide the Fifth Dalai Lama's death until the Potala was completed!

I found the palace to be a dark and mysterious place, a complex maze of rooms, shrines, assembly halls and courtyards. Two hundred years of burning butter lamps had imposed layers of oily soot on the walls. Little natural light entered these murky chambers, creating a somber mood. Everywhere I looked, bronze and silver statues sparkled with highlights of gold and painted murals covered the walls with the images and stories of Buddhism.

Tenzin and I left the Potala and returned to the Jo Khang just in time to witness the Dalai Lama's visit to view the tormas, or butter statues. There was pandemonium in the main square when we arrived. Thousands of Tibetans had turned out to catch a glimpse of their God King, and a contingent of soldiers was trying to clear a path for him. This was a helter-skelter process. The officials took sticks and began beating back the crowds. I was shocked to see such heavy-handed behavior, but the Tibetans took it in stride. Some cried out when struck; others simply laughed and moved away. The Dalai Lama arrived in an exquisitely decorated chair carried by several men. His entourage included a garrison of troops, followed by Lhasa's most noble families and high-ranking monks.

The Dalai Lama was surrounded by so many people, it was impossible to get a good look at him. He disappeared around the backside of the Par Kor and didn't return. The crowd didn't seem to mind. The onlookers merrily joined the stragglers in the parade, and everyone milled about in a happy state. Many of the men and women were drinking beer from large, metal buckets, which increased their boisterousness and gaiety.

When Tenzin and I returned to our meager living quarters, we learned that two of our neighbors were leaving the next morning for a trek to the Samye Monastery. I knew this was a very old and sacred place. Guru Rinpoche was supposed to have visited the monastery shortly after it was founded in the eighth century, and Tibet's first Buddhist monks were ordained there. It was considered the birthplace of Tibetan Buddhism. I urged Tenzin to let us join the pilgrims. When he saw how enthused I was, he agreed.

The most direct route to Samye lay through a mountain range, but we were warned that Khampas often waited along the trails to rob the pilgrims. The other route followed the Zangpo River through the Yarlung Valley. It was a longer, but safer route. Time meant little to Tibetans, so we agreed to follow the river and reduce the likelihood that we would run into more of those terrible robbers! This proved a good choice, and we spent the next few days traveling at a leisurely pace. The Yarlung Valley was filled with monasteries, and I was pleased to see that my disguise went undetected when we visited them.

The river was low at that time of year, giving it a lazy appearance. Many sand bars were visible. A few trees grew along the river banks, giving it the appearance of a lengthy mirage, for the mountains on either side were as void of life as any we had seen during our trek. A full moon greeted us each morning, sitting in the sky above the bleak mountains like a god watching over its domain. It quickly fled as daylight approached, sinking behind the lifeless peaks and yielding its place to the brilliant morning sun.

We reached a loading area where yak-skinned boats waited to ferry pilgrims across the river. The Samye Monastery was located on the other side near the base of some distant mountains. The boats filled rapidly with pilgrims, who bundled up against the cold in their woolen caps and heavy coats. Tenzin and I claimed two seats near the bow of the second boat. We had to tuck our legs up against our chests and brace our backs against our bags to squeeze into the tiny space. The sharp odor of unwashed bodies mingled with the leathery smells of yak's hides used by the pilgrims to carry their belongings. Still others forced their way on board until I felt like a cluster of grapes being pressed into wine. Just as we were about to push off, a young monk ran towards the boat and jumped aboard with the lithe precision of a ballerina.

He squeezed in next to Tenzin, who learned the monk was from Samye and was hurrying back because rumors were spreading of a Chinese plot to steal the monastery's most prized manuscripts. There had been territorial disputes between China and Tibet for centuries, and the two countries had taken turns attacking each other. The Manchus in China were now taking advantage of a political conflict between my country, jolly old England, and Russia over the region. The young monk worried that Chinese spies were going to raid the old monastery in an effort to undermine the power of the Buddhist monks and to discredit the Dalai Lama.

Little did I realize what an adventure this whole mess was going to make for me! I was happily gazing upon the muted landscapes along the shore, blissfully unaware of my fate.

The sand bars I had seen earlier blocked our path, forcing the boatman to steer a winding course up and down the river as he picked his way through these obstacles. It took nearly two hours to complete this slow, tortuous journey, but the Tibetans didn't mind. They smiled happily and chatted with each other, knowing they were about to visit one of Tibet's most precious religious sites.

Once we reached the far shore, Tenzin and I fell in with the others marching along a dusty trail that wound its way towards the mountains. It was a long walk, and by the time we reached Samye's high, gated walls, I was exhausted. We entered the courtyard and sat down to rest. People were wandering about in a state of confusion, and we soon realized something was happening. I recalled what the monk had told Tenzin about the Chinese spies and suggested we enter the monastery to have a look.

Pilgrims were milling about in front of the main entrance, uncertain what to do. Inside, monks were hurrying back and forth with texts, Buddha statues and other religious items. Their urgent voices filled the room with a steady, buzzing sound. They reminded me of bees protecting their queen. The atmosphere was thick with burning incense and dust raised by so many people.

I heard shouts and stomping feet above our heads and decided to climb a wooden ladder to investigate. By the time I reached the second floor, the people causing the commotion had disappeared. There were many interesting murals depicting temples and other scenes on the walls, and I began walking down a hallway to look at them.

I had just stopped to inspect one more closely when the young monk from the boat suddenly appeared at the far end of the hallway and came running towards me. He carried an object in his hands that was wrapped in an old painted cloth called a thangka. He was talking as fast as he was running, but I could not understand a word he said. Fortunately, Tenzin caught up with me and translated. He said the monk was trying to hide Samye's most precious possession, but he feared he would be found at any moment by the Chinese agents who had infiltrated the monastery. He said it was a book of Buddha's original teachings, and it must be saved at all costs. The monk thrust the covered book into my hands and told me to take it from Samye. I was surprised by its heavy weight and looked to Tenzin for help. He started to protest, but the monk shook his head violently and said there was no other choice.

The monk looked behind him, fearful that he would be discovered at any moment. He said he had noticed my white skin where my arms became exposed in the crush of bodies on the boat and knew I was a foreigner. He urged me to hide the manuscript under my skirts and to carry it as far away as possible, to a place beyond the reach of the Chinese invaders. There would come a day, he said, with the book would be needed by the Tibetans. Return it then, he said. Bringing it back sooner would only endanger it.

With that, the monk ran back down the hallway and disappeared around the far corner. My hands shook so badly,

Tenzin had to help me place the bundled object under my clothing. No sooner had he finished than two men in dark robes appeared. They were holding the monk by his arms and marching him towards us. My feet urged me to run, but I knew fleeing was useless. So, I did exactly what I had been doing for the past two months. I humbly walked behind Tenzin, and we wandered slowly down the passageway looking at the wall murals and offering prayers. The two robed men blocked our path and spoke harshly to Tenzin, who bowed with great deference. The monk stared past us as if he had never seen us before. My heart beat so fast, I was sure everyone could hear it, and the sweat from my forehead stung my eyes until I could hardly see. The manuscript felt like a great rock about to slip from my unsteady hands. I was alarmed that my fear would betray my guilt, but the two men ignored me. They pushed us aside and continued on their way with the hapless monk imprisoned between them.

After they were gone, I leaned against the wall and tried to catch my breath. This was far more of an adventure than I had bargained for! Tenzin and I discussed what to do. We agreed we must honor the monk's wishes, and we hurried from the monastery and returned to the boats.

Once we were away from the crowds, I uncovered the manuscript. It was unlike any Tibetan text I had ever seen before, with an old, leather binding secured by a large lock and a strange-looking key. I re-wrapped the manuscript, and we considered our options. Sadly, I realized I dare not return to Lhasa with such a possession. This was terribly disappointing to me. I had so looked forward to visiting more of the monasteries.

However, I had fulfilled my goal by reaching Lhasa, and if this manuscript was so important, my quest to achieve Nirvana would surely be strengthened by taking it to a safe place. Where should that be, I wondered? The monk had said to take it far away. Tenzin and I agreed that meant removing it from Tibet. I had planned a leisurely trip back to India, but we now faced the prospect of a more arduous journey over the Himalayas into Bhutan, which lay to the south and was our most direct route out of Tibet. With luck, we could join a caravan of traders.

My rest has been much too brief. Here we are on the move again. Only this time, we must flee like common criminals, which in a way we are! I only hope I have enough strength left to see this odd obligation through to its conclusion. I shall have to place myself in the hands of the Enlightened One and the Tibetan spirits, and hope for the best.

CHAPTER EIGHTEEN

The tale of Anne's dramatic confrontation and escape from the Samye Monastery restored Sigourney's courage. She paced around the room, her mind fired by the descriptions in Anne's diary. They left no doubt that she had successfully reached Lhasa. Not only that, she had saved one of Tibet's most precious treasures from destruction. The manuscript had remained hidden since then, but never lost. It had merely been waiting for the proper time for its return. The only question had been who would return it and when. That question had now been answered.

Sigourney found her room too confining and abandoned it for the hotel's more spacious lobby, where a few people still strolled or sat reading in one of the couches before turning in for the night. She looked down at the valise dangling from her shoulder as she wandered across the tile floor. It had become so much a part of her, she wondered how she would feel once the manuscript was gone. Relieved? Satisfied? Sorry? She tried to imagine how Anne felt as she fled back into the Tibetan wilderness. Fear perhaps? And uncertainty? Sigourney harbored those emotions herself. She could feel herself sharing them with Anne. Their souls were reaching out over the span of a century and touching one another.

When Sigourney looked up, she found herself standing less than twenty feet from John, who sat on a couch staring at her with his keen eyes. She blinked and gave him an embarrassed smile. How long had he been there? How long had she been wandering so obliviously in her mind?

"You looked so absorbed, I didn't want to disturb you." John returned her smile and rose from his seat.

"I was far away, wasn't I?" She fiddled with her hair, which she knew looked a fright.

"You had a most beautiful smile. Wherever you were, it agreed with you."

"Did I? Did it?" Sigourney was too flustered by John's unexpected appearance to put a coherent thought together. "I . . . I guess . . ." Her voice trailed off. She was acting so silly, she wanted to hide.

"I hope your dinner meeting was satisfactory."

He was standing beside her now, and her body was growing warm, just as it had when she held the wooden statue. But this time, the response was very much physical. She nodded, still too distracted to speak. Brad Paxton was the farthest thing from her mind.

"Come on." John took her arm lightly but firmly. "I think we could both use some of Tibet's brisk air." Sparks shot through Sigourney's skin at his touch.

They walked through the parking lot to the street, where darkness enveloped them with the suddenness of a curtain drawn across a window. Sigourney held John's arm as they wandered along the uneven pavement. The air *was* brisk, just as he had predicted. If there had been enough light, she could have seen her own breath. She pushed her hands deep into her coat pockets and snuggled closer to him. For the first time, he put his arm around her, and she nearly stumbled from the pleasure of its touch.

There was little activity along the street. Occasionally, a car's headlights flared to light their route, and a few bicycles slithered past like furtive animals running for protective cover. Otherwise, the night was still. The stars peered down from the sky like unblinking eyes frozen in a timeless glacier.

Sigourney was bewildered by the electrical charges surging through her body. When they stopped, she pulled her hand from its cozy nest in her pocket and touched John's cheek. It felt arctic cold. His face was hidden in the night's shadows, but she could sense his eyes searching for hers, just as she searched for his. They stood there for an eternity, their minds and bodies floating across the vast expanses of the Tibetan plains, until John lowered his head and touched her mouth with his lips. It was such a feathery kiss, Sigourney might not have known it happened at all, if it weren't for the shock waves of desire it sent burning through her. She pushed her face upward, pressing her lips against his with more passion than she had known in years. The kiss freed her from all the angers and frustrations that had been building in her the past six months. Hot tears rolled down her cheeks, tears of happiness at being released from her emotional prison. When John began to pull away, she gripped him more fiercely, refusing to let him go.

At last, they broke free and gasped for air, but their arms continued to embrace each other. Sigourney felt a great heat rising from John's body, a searing heat that pushed away the cold with the energy of a new-born sun. She basked in it as they rocked in each other's arms.

"Sigourney . . ."

She kissed him before he could say more. "Shhh," she whispered, "There'll be time to talk. Let's just enjoy the silence."

They kissed again, this time more slowly, exploring and tasting each other with their tongues and lips. Then, they turned and walked arm-in-arm back towards the oasis of light that marked their hotel. When they reached her room, Sigourney instinctively knew she needed more time before she shared her bed, but John took her in his arms and kissed her with such force, she nearly wilted on the spot.

He pulled back just in time for her to save herself. "Still on for tomorrow morning?" His eyes gleamed like sapphires, and she had to restrain herself from kissing him again.

"I wouldn't miss it for the world." She brushed his lips with hers and escaped to her room, where she sat on the bed, exhausted and trembling.

Spirits were running riot through her body. Anne's spirit had transformed itself from an eccentric woman to a heroic figure with whom Sigourney identified more and more. John's had changed from a cool Englishman to a mysterious and passionate man, a man who was sweeping Sigourney off her feet. It was impossible for her to know where her feelings for one ended and the other began. They were both part of her now, and she intended to continue exploring her relationship with each of them, until she learned where they were taking her.

Only one cloud darkened her horizon: Brad Paxton. She had entered Lhasa feeling a bit triumphant, much like Anne when she slipped past those guarded gates. She was no longer so confident. Not with her rival breathing down her neck. Sigourney thought about tomorrow with trepidation. She was going to need all her courage when she made her run for Samye.

Sleep was a restless affair, alternating between brief naps and long periods when she stared into the black night surrounding her. She was up and dressed when John knocked on her door, although her body still craved the covers she had abandoned.

John's raised eyebrows registered his surprise when she flung open the door ready to go. He fidgeted, not knowing what to do or say. Sigourney loved his awkward pose but decided to end it at once, before she started acting like a school girl herself. She gave him a firm kiss, then turned and closed her door, knowing he was watching her with his big grin.

"I just wanted you to know last night wasn't a one night stand," she said with a wry smile of her own. "So don't think you're off the hook." She took his arm and started them off down the hallway.

"I'm glad, and I don't." His face broadened, showing his relief at her bold action.

The pre-dawn air was even colder than the night before, and they hurried along the sidewalk towards the Potala. Stars still filled the sky, promising a brilliant morning. A few cars were beginning to appear on the lonely street by the time they reached the ancient gate through which Anne had passed so many years ago.

The first streaks of daybreak revealed the dark hulk of the Potala rising above them. John led Sigourney down a tiny side street that wound past Chokpori, the smaller hill facing the Potala across the main boulevard.

"Perhaps, we should try these steps." He indicated a stone stairway leading up the hill.

The stairs soon gave way to a rocky trail, which passed the gutted ruins of what had once been Tibet's school of medicine. Light was spreading rapidly. Bicycles and pedestrians were starting to make their way along the street below. Brash music suddenly blared from a loudspeaker system, jarring Sigourney and destroying the peaceful silence. She saw dozens of figures exercising to the music in a large square in front of the Potala.

"What are they doing?" she asked.

"The Chinese government wants to undermine the status of the Potala," John explained. "They play music each morning and require local Chinese residents to perform calisthenics there."

Sigourney made a face and covered her ears. "It sounds awful. What a terrible thing to do to such a historic place. How would they like it if the Tibetans did that in front of the Forbidden City?"

"It's quite insulting to the Tibetans." John offered his hand as they started up a steep, rocky slope.

At last, they stood on a knoll with their arms around each other, overlooking the maze of concrete buildings and trees of Lhasa. The Potala loomed before them across the divide. It basked in a hazy, blue light that permeated the sky and turned the mountains behind the palace into a montage of ghostly peaks and ridges. The music continued to howl as cars, busses and trucks rumbled through the streets. All around them, Lhasa was coming to life, but it wasn't the Tibetan life Anne had described. This dawn had a distinct Chinese flavor to it that Sigourney found abrasive.

Smoke was rising from a wood fire near the foot of the palace, adding a misty quality to the uncertain light. The effect on Sigourney was dramatic. There was a spiritual aura about the palace that hadn't changed in over three hundred years. She was watching a piece of history that was timeless. Seeing how the Chinese tried to belittle it only reinforced in Sigourney's mind the importance of the manuscript she was delivering back to the Tibetans.

Her thoughts were interrupted when a finger of sunlight streaked across the sky and bathed the Potala in its luminous glow. The snow-white, blood-red and golden hues of the building and its rooftop sprang to life, as if some wandering spirit had sprinkled the palace with pixie dust. From Sigourney's vantage point, the palace seemed to rise out of the night's shadows like a battleship riding an enormous wave at sea.

"What an inspiring vision." Sigourney hugged John. "Thank you for bringing me."

The irritating music finally stopped as they worked their way back down the hill. Taxis roamed the street, reminding Sigourney of the daunting day that awaited her. "Let's not end this moment too quickly," she suggested when one of the cabs slowed beside them. John nodded, and they walked on.

They were within a block of the hotel when Sigourney spotted police cars parked by the entrance. She stopped in her tracks. "Something's wrong," she whispered.

John put his arm around her and stared thoughtfully at the scene. "Doesn't look promising, does it?"

"Do you think it's Mr. Ho?" Sigourney's stomach was doing flip-flops, again. Her neck muscles twitched, and she reached blindly for her valise. This can't be happening, she thought. I'm too close to the finish line to be stopped now.

"No, he wouldn't cause such a spectacle until he examined your baggage. Why don't you wait here, while I go find out what's going on?" John's voice was all business.

"Please be careful, John. I'm sure they're looking for me, and believe me, I'm scared."

He held her a moment longer. "They may be looking at everybody. Throwing a net over all the fish, so to speak."

"It doesn't matter. Once they find me and search me, I'll be arrested." A wave of nausea swept over her, and she had to fight the urge to throw up whatever remained of last night's dinner. Her resolve and courage were abandoning her, and she quivered in John's arms like a frightened child. She wanted to escape the walls closing around her, but there was nowhere to run.

John watched two more police cars pulling into the parking lot. "I admit it looks serious. If you're determined to return the manuscript, you'll need help." He turned to her with the same steely-eyed expression she had seen at the Tashilhunpo Monastery and took her face between his large hands. "I'll talk to Jigme. You must get help from the Tibetans. Soon, you won't be able to make a move without the Chinese discovering you. Go back to Chokpori Hill and wait for me there. If you stay on the street, you'll be spotted. I'll meet you as soon as I can."

He held her tightly. Sigourney returned his embrace with the hunger of a starving soul. A moment later, he was gone, walking rapidly away from her towards the hotel.

Loneliness swept over her as she watched his retreating figure. It was a gut wrenching loneliness, the kind one experienced when lost at sea or in a vast desert. There was no choice but to follow John's lead. She now trusted him completely, and her fate was in his hands. There was something very special about that unassuming man. He made her feel safer than she had in years, even as her world threatened to come crashing down around her.

She started walking quickly back towards the Potala. Many people were on the street now, mainly Chinese, but also a few Tibetans. A police car approached, and she stepped behind a tree until it passed, then pressed onward as fast as she dared without raising suspicion. The pleasant, pre-dawn stroll she had enjoyed just an hour-and-a-half earlier seemed a lifetime ago. She watched the faces passing her, waiting for someone to recognize her and sound the alarm. Everyone ignored her.

Another police car approached, but this time there were no

trees to hide behind. Desperately, she looked for some cover. There was none. She had no choice but to continue walking. Suddenly, two Tibetan men stepped alongside her and shielded her from the policeman's view. Were they protecting her? She walked beside them in dumbfounded silence as the patrol car slowly passed by. When the car was gone, the Tibetans smiled and continued on their way without a word. How had they known she needed help? It was one more mystery she couldn't answer.

Sigourney could no longer stand the suspense and began to run, not caring if she made a spectacle of herself. All she could think about was getting back to that hill. It didn't take long, however, for the high altitude to slow her down. She was panting heavily by the time she hurried down the little street to the steps leading up the hill. She climbed until she reached the ruins of the medical school, where she plopped down on a large stone to catch her breath.

Scattered thoughts tumbled through her mind. She knew her worst fears had been realized. She was a fugitive in a strange country ruled by an oppressive government that would stop at nothing to get the manuscript. She tried to weigh her options, but there was only one. If John couldn't arrange for help, it was just a matter of time before she was apprehended. What fate awaited her then, she didn't care to think about.

Sigourney looked at her surroundings and tried to keep her mind occupied. It seemed a good place to hide. The ruins protected her from the street, and no one seemed to use the trail. No sooner had she concluded this, than an elderly Tibetan woman stepped out of a crumbling doorway in front of her, spooking Sigourney so badly she nearly jumped up and ran. The woman barely noticed her, however, as she shuffled away with a coarsely-woven, shopping bag in her hand. There were people living in the ruins, Sigourney realized. These were their homes! Knowing she was among Tibetans comforted her, and her heart rate returned to normal.

She sat and waited. Time crawled along relentlessly as the morning shadows grew steadily shorter. It had been 7:30 when she returned to the hill. Nearly three hours had crept by, but there was no sign of John. She worried that someone at the hotel had seen him leave with her. He could be under arrest himself. More residents were coming and going, making her wonder how long she should stay there. They were bound to talk, and the word would quickly spread that a foreign woman was hiding on Chokpori Hill. What a wonderful name for a song, she thought giddily. She was going to go mad if she stayed there much longer. It was time to move to higher ground and find a new hiding place.

When Sigourney stood up, she saw John's reassuring face on the steps below her. She shrieked and threw herself into his arms.

"Oh God, John, I've been so terribly afraid something happened to you and you were arrested because they knew you were with me and I didn't know what to do or where to go." She was sobbing as she spoke. All the fears that had been bottled up for the past three hours came gushing out. John quietly held her until she gained enough control to look up at him and smile. She could see from his frown, however, that the news wasn't good, and she prepared herself.

"I had to stay for breakfast and pretend I was leaving on the tour. I'm afraid your dinner friend turned you in. I take it he doesn't know about the manuscript. He kept talking about the diary. The police were searching everybody's rooms and luggage."

Sigourney grimaced at the news. Outrage boiled in her as she pictured Brad's smug face. "His name is Brad Paxton. He's a colleague of mine at the university. He's not to be trusted, but I thought I had put him off until tomorrow. Obviously, I miscalculated."

"I don't think he was trying to have you arrested. Merely stopped and sent home. But the damage is done. They know you're missing, and they're looking for you. Mr. Ho arrived just a short while ago, by the way. He's revealed his true colors and is leading the search. Fortunately, no one seems to know I was with you this morning. I spoke to Jigme. He'll do everything he can to help you. You're somewhat of a heroine in his eyes. Mine too." He smiled for the first time.

John's words warmed her, but they did little to relieve the growing knot in her stomach. "What will I do? I can't stay here indefinitely."

"Jigme is arranging for a driver he can trust to come fetch you. There's a monastery up in the mountains near Lhasa called the Tsurpu, where the seventeenth Karmapa resides. He's only a boy of fourteen, but in the absence of the Dalai Lama, he's the most important religious figure in Tibet. Arrangements can be made there to return the manuscript to the Samye Monastery."

"Why can't the driver just take me to the Samye now? I can deliver the manuscript and return to the hotel tonight. I'll say I chose to wander around Lhasa instead of taking the tour." Sigourney was tumbling into an abyss, and she was pin-wheeling her arms and legs in a furious effort to save herself.

John heaved a sigh and looked at Sigourney with that steely expression of his. It told her things weren't going to be that simple.

"Jigme says check points have already been set up on all the roads leading to and from Lhasa. He says the Karmapa can see that the manuscript is safely transferred to Samye, but if you insist on taking it yourself, you'll have to disguise yourself and go on foot with Tibetans who are traveling there."

Sigourney absorbed this news with the kind of horrible fascination one feels when witnessing a bad car accident. This wasn't an alternative she'd considered. The prospect of trekking to Samye on foot overwhelmed her. How could she possibly manage the high altitudes and primitive conditions she had seen? Yet, she was drawn to the idea. The irony of her situation was so poignant, she nearly burst out laughing. John was telling her that she would have to assume an identity much like Anne's and follow her path to Samye. Their worlds were separated by a century in time, but their passages through Tibet were becoming more entwined. Their quests were blending into a single journey. Was she capable of such an undertaking? Could she complete such a strange voyage through space and time?

John continued to stare at her with concern. "The problem is what happens after Samye? You won't be able to return here without facing arrest. I can't travel with you. It would be too obvious if two foreigners were seen together on foot, and I must attend a meeting in three days that I can't miss."

This was an even more startling idea: what to do after returning the manuscript? Sigourney had never considered the possibility that she might have to do something more. She had always assumed she would hand over the book and return to her group. Now, flying home was no longer an option. The only airport would be watched just as closely as the roads. How would she escape? All the challenges and hardships she had been reading about in Anne's diary came crashing down on her. It was one thing to join a pilgrimage to Samye; it was quite another to trek out of Tibet.

John took her hands in his and gave her one of his most piercing looks. "If you see the Karmapa, you may want to consider letting him return the manuscript. Jigme says he speaks for all the Tibetans and can be trusted."

Was that possible, she wondered? Would that fulfill her quest? She had always assumed *she* would be the one to take the manuscript to Samye, but it didn't matter who did it, as long as the manuscript was safe.

Before she could respond, a car pulled into the side street and stopped by the steps. "There's your driver to take you to Tsurpu," John said softly. "Are you sure you want to do this?"

She looked longingly at him, knowing his was the last familiar face she was going to see for awhile and fearing she might never see him again. "I've never been so unsure of anything in my life, John. Right now, all I want to do is go home . . . and hopefully see you again. But I must see that this manuscript is safely delivered to Samye. If I think the Karmapa can do it, I'll gladly give it to him."

"You'll see me again, I promise. Here's some money for emergencies and a phone you can use to reach me. It's a secure phone that only works on classified frequencies. You can't make normal calls with it, but if you punch this red button, you'll reach a special operator who can patch you through to me." He handed her a wireless phone no larger than her hand. The unexpected sight of such modern technology distracted her momentarily from her anxieties.

"I have to be in Shanghai in three days for an important rendezvous, and I'm going to have a terrible time explaining how I lost my telephone. They'll reprimand me and give me a new one. But, I want to know you're safe, and if not, how I can help you. Wherever you end up, I'll come to you, that I promise."

John led her down the stairs to the waiting car, where he opened her door with all the pomp and circumstance of a doorman at the Savoy Hotel and helped her in. "Stay out of sight until you're well clear of Lhasa." Before she could say anything more, he closed the door and tapped the roof of the car, which immediately took off down the narrow street. Sigourney looked back and watched John until he disappeared around a bend in the road, then ducked her head below the window and began to cry.

CHAPTER NINETEEN

The deity floated on a throne ringed by fire. His face, which was pinched into an angry frown, displayed large, keen eyes, puckered lips, a flared nose, and enormous ears that stuck out like butterfly wings. His robes and headdress were gaily decorated in a profusion of colors, flowers and beastly images. When Sigourney looked at his feet, she saw the legs and paws of a tiger. She asked the deity where she should go, but a great roaring sound filled her ears, and she couldn't hear his reply. Billowing, white clouds surrounded the deity. She found she could step from one cloud to the next, but when she approached him, he floated away from her. The deity pointed towards a mountain range that had appeared in the distance. Then, he rose into the sky and disappeared.

Sigourney blinked her eyes and shook herself awake. The image of the deity was gone, but not the mountain range. It rose above the valley floor to her left, and she realized that was where they were going. Up there, into those mountains. She was astonished at this revelation and would have liked to ask the driver about it, but he spoke no English. Besides, he was too busy trying to avoid the Chinese authorities to be distracted right now.

It had been a harrowing ride. They had taken endless back streets to avoid the main boulevards where the police were watching. Eventually, they had popped out onto a paved road and they were now roaring along at a swift pace, passing a large monastery that sat like a medieval fortress against a rocky outcrop in the hills to her right. She suspected it was one the monasteries she was scheduled to visit with her group, but that was in another lifetime when she was only a tourist. Now, she was a fugitive, and the idea of exploring monasteries was as elusive as the deity in her dream.

The driver slammed his brakes, sending Sigourney thumping into the passenger's seat in front of her. He pointed at two police cars stationed less than a mile up the road and said something in Tibetan. She didn't need to understand him to know they were in trouble. He turned onto a dirt road and headed for three farm houses grouped nearby. Dust billowed about them when he stopped behind the nearest house. An elderly man emerged from the doorway and spoke to the driver. The situation wasn't good. There was no sign of an alternative road that could circumvent the road block, and there was no place to hide for very long in the flat, open farmland surrounding them.

Sigourney knew she should be more frightened, but her senses had been dulled by the emotional upheavals of the past few hours. At that moment, she wanted nothing more than to find a quiet place to rest her tired body. She briefly considered handing the manuscript to the Tibetan farmer and walking down the road to the waiting police cars. What a tempting thought! It would put an end to her fears and avoid the hardships she knew awaited her. She was astonished to find the idea of surrendering so comforting. Was this how fugitives felt when they were on the run, she wondered? Did they have a subconscious desire to be caught? Probably not. She was just tired, hungry, and dehydrated. She hadn't eaten since last night, nor drunk any water since rising early that morning.

But, she wasn't just hungry; she was alone. John had been her support system, and now he was gone. She looked across the cheerless fields and fought back a sudden urge to weep. She wasn't certain how she was going to face her ordeals, but she knew she must find a way.

An old woman using a crude stick as a cane stepped out of the nearest house and motioned to Sigourney to come inside. She got out of the car and followed the woman into a small room with a cement floor and open stove. The walls around the stove were covered with smoky grime. The woman pointed to a wooden chair and set hot, butter tea and cooked bread dough on the table. Sigourney assumed the dough was tsampa. The unusual taste of the tea reminded her of a rich soup that had just started to turn rancid, but she hungrily devoured it along with the dough, and then looked guiltily at the wrinkled woman standing in front of her. The woman leaned on a handle strapped to the end of her pole and smiled, revealing a mouth missing most of its teeth. Her dirty dress and faded yellow cap told the world how poor she was.

Hastily Sigourney removed some of the coins John had given her and offered them to the woman, but she only laughed and shook her head no. When Sigourney tried to insist, the woman gently wrapped her hands around Sigourney's and pushed the money away. The woman lifted her cane and tapped the valise, which hung from the chair. Sigourney could see in the woman's unwavering gaze that she knew who she was.

Sigourney was tempted to show the old woman the manuscript, but the driver burst into the room shouting and motioning for Sigourney to leave. When she emerged from the house, she saw that the police cars were gone! She waved to the old woman and quickly piled into the car. The driver was already gunning the engine. They shot down the dirt road and back onto the pavement like a cannon ball.

The landscape whizzed past her window. Big, woolly yaks adorned with red ribbons were pulling wooden plows through the rough earth, just as they had done on the vast, wild plains of the Tibetan plateau. That part of her journey was like a dream to her now. A different woman had made that trip, a naïve woman who expected to waltz into Lhasa, deliver the manuscript and fly home. The new Sigourney was scared out of her wits but still determined to fulfill her quest. She pulled John's phone from her jacket and nearly pressed the red button, before remembering he wouldn't have a replacement for at least three days. He was supposed to be her lifeline to the outside world, and she couldn't reach him.

Her thoughts were interrupted when the driver abruptly turned off the paved road onto a dirt one aimed at the mountains she had seen earlier. Their new route was not so much a road as a teeth-rattling series of rocks and cavities which made normal progress nearly impossible. The car banged and thumped along as the driver maneuvered over and around the road's obstacles. Sigourney gripped the seat with both hands and tried to prevent her head from bouncing off the ceiling.

The road became marginally better as they entered a narrow valley and began to pass tiny villages. Goats, pigs, and yaks roamed freely along the lower slopes of the surrounding mountains. Mounds of wheat stood like golden igloos in the fields. Peasants pitched the wheat onto wooden carts, filling each cart until the grain hung over the sides. They reminded Sigourney of the busses packed with people in Kathmandu.

They were climbing steadily, and soon, a thin layer of snow appeared in irregular patterns on the fields. The spring-like morning Sigourney had left behind in Lhasa turned into a bone-chilling, sleet-gray day. The snow line crept relentlessly closer, until the entire valley was blanketed in a winter-white coat. She could see that winter came early to this bleak valley, if it ever left at all. It made her wonder about the journey that lay ahead.

She thought about John sitting behind her empty seat in the van. She should be there with him, instead of plunging into this unknown world. It wasn't too late to turn back. John had said the Karmapa was the most important religious leader in Tibet. She could leave the manuscript with him and return to the hotel. The Chinese might be angry with her, but without the manuscript there was little they could do. She could see John again. She could take a hot bath and forget her fears. It was a compelling idea. She would wait until she met the Karmapa, before making up her mind.

The valley narrowed, and the mounds of wheat were replaced by hundreds of yaks wandering through the snow foraging for food. Near the far end of the valley, a series of prayer flags stretched across a nearly frozen stream, signaling their approach to the Tsurpu Monastery. They rounded a bend, and she saw the monastery's roof line tucked against a hillside of tortured rocks. What a happy sight it was! She leaned forward like an excited child on her way to Disneyland.

To her surprise, the driver stopped the car and signaled for her to get out. When she hesitated, he pointed to his eyes and said something that sounded like "spiis." It took her awhile to understand he was saying spies. He was telling her she couldn't go any further by car, because spies would see her. He pointed to the side of the road. She had to wait there, but for what? For someone to fetch her? For dark? She pulled her jacket around her and looked at the icy landscape outside her window. She had dressed warmly enough to visit the Potala at dawn, but she hadn't prepared herself for this. When she opened the car door and stepped outside, thousands of tiny icicles assaulted her face and lungs. She shivered and frantically looked around for a place to escape the wintry air. The driver pointed to a small cave in the rocks by the stream, and she gingerly made her way down the icy slope to its entrance. Sigourney looked back in time to see the driver put the car in gear and drive off towards the monastery.

Panic flooded her, and she clambered part way back up the slope, before resigning herself to the fact that she had been abandoned. She watched the car disappear around the mountain before returning to the cave. Sigourney peeked into the dark opening, half expecting a bear or other wild beast to leap from the shadows and devour her, but only an eerie silence greeted her. As her eyes adjusted to the low light, she was relieved to see that the cave was empty. Cautiously, she stepped into the small opening and sat down on a rock near the entrance. The air crackled with an icy edge that made her shake uncontrollably, and her breaths hung in the air in a series of ghostly shrouds. She wanted to move about to keep warm, but she had to stay hidden from the road. The cave was too small to walk around in. All she could do was wave her arms and hug her chest.

A grinding noise shattered her solitude, and she heard the whine of a truck's engine being shifted into a lower gear. Her spirits rose, and she poked out her head, expecting to see her driver returning to rescue her. Instead, she saw the mottled green and brown colors of a military truck and quickly ducked back into the cave.

Her shivering finally subsided, and she thought about Anne's experience when she nearly froze to death on that mountain pass. Was that beginning to happen to her? Probably not, she surmised. She was still too miserably cold. Sigourney bent forward, wrapped her arms under her legs, and waited.

Other than a tiny gurgling sound from the nearly frozen stream below her and the occasional whispering of a light, fitful breeze, an incredibly deep silence seeped into the pores of her world. There were no sounds of animals or birds. Nothing moved. The valley was as still as a cemetery.

The white snowscape outside her cave slowly turned murky gray, telling her that dusk had arrived and that night wasn't far behind. Her brain was dulled from the insistent cold, but she had made up her mind. Once it was dark, she was going to walk up the road to the monastery, spies or no spies. She couldn't stay where she was much longer.

A new sound broke through her consciousness, the sound of crunching snow. Someone was slogging through the snow outside her hiding place! No sooner had she realized this than a figure filled the cave's entrance, causing Sigourney to squeak with fright and jump to her feet, banging her head against the rocky ceiling. She froze, her heart hammering like a piston, and waited for the figure to do something.

"Miss Phillips?" a voice breathed into the growing darkness.

Sigourney started at the sound of her name. "Who are you?"

"I am your guide, Sukhang. Come with me, please. We must

hurry to monastery. Many people looking for you."

Sigourney nearly slumped to the ground, thankful that the mental battle she had been waging for the past few hours was over. Someone had come for her. Someone who knew her name and would help her. She still emerged cautiously, ready to retreat back into her hole at the first sign of trouble. *I've become a frightened animal*, she thought as she stretched her stiff back. She had to look closely in the failing light to make out Sukhang's features. He didn't look Chinese--his eyes were too round and his complexion too dark--so she assumed he was telling her the truth, that he was there to help her, not take her prisoner. She had little choice but to follow him. Where else could she go? If she stayed where she was, she'd be dead by morning.

Sukhang handed her some clothing. "Put on over your clothes. Wear this hat. Make you look Tibetan."

Sigourney smiled inwardly as she slipped on two layers of dresses and a jacket with sleeves much too short for her long arms. Each step in her journey was bringing her closer to Anne. All she needed was some oil and charcoal on her face to complete the transformation. The clothes immediately made her feel warmer. She carefully strapped the valise under her dresses, and then nodded to Sukhang that she was ready to go.

"Many soldiers," he told her as they began walking along the road. He took quick, busy steps that gave him the appearance of scampering. "Is the same everywhere, I think. At all monasteries. Everyone looking for you, for your book. We pretend to be peasants but not enter monastery. Go to monks' sleeping rooms."

The weak lights of the monastery half a mile away beckoned to her. Walking felt incredibly good after her cramped isolation, and she quickly fell into a rhythm, matching two of Sukhang's hurried steps to one of her own. Her aching muscles began to stretch, and she felt so warm she couldn't imagine that less than fifteen minutes ago she had been close to freezing to death. Night had fallen around her, filling the road with deep shadows that forced her to keep a keen eye on where she stepped. Sukhang proceeded with the confidence of a mountain goat, and she followed closely behind him. Stars filled the sky like swarms of fireflies, telling her the heavy blanket of clouds that had followed her up the valley was gone.

Three soldiers were talking and smoking cigarettes near the entrance to the monastery. Their casual vigilance gave her hope that she could slip into the monastery unnoticed. Sukhang walked right past the gates without looking at the soldiers. Sigourney remembered how Anne had described her humble demeanor, and she did her best to emulate her. She stuck her hands in her pockets to hide her long arms, lowered her head, and trudged modestly behind her guide. One of the guards said something in Chinese, and his companions laughed raucously. Sigourney understood it was a belittling remark about them, and she had to fight the urge to stop and confront the rude man. Nearby, a group of nomads had set up camp, encircling their campsite with a wall of large, burlap sacks to protect themselves from the wind. The glow of a small fire danced off the interior walls, and murmuring voices floated into the night.

Sigourney was relieved when she turned a corner and lost sight of the guards. Sukhang approached a small door in the wall. It was opened by a monk who smiled and invited them to enter a colorful courtyard lined with potted plants. Half-a-dozen doorways covered by cloth flaps led to the monks' living quarters. Sukhang pulled back one of the coverings, and Sigourney followed him into a smoky sitting room with a metal stove in one corner. Heat radiated from wood burning in a hole at the stove's base.

"You sit there." Sukhang pointed to a wooden lounging chair covered by thin padding. He pushed his hat back and scratched his head near his right temple, as if trying to decide what to do next. It was her first chance to see him clearly. She guessed from his leathery skin that he was middle aged. His face was round, his nose flat. Not a handsome face, but a kind one. His black eyes shone with an intensity that gave him an eager look. He was so much shorter than Sigourney, she had to resist the impulse to rest her elbow on his shoulder.

She sat down where he directed. "What do we do now?"

"Wait for Karmapa. Go to him. It is great honor." Sukhang took an old tea pot, swirled it to check for water and shoved it on the stove.

"Can you tell me about him, Sukhang? Why is he so important?"

"Karmapa complete cycle of births and reach Nirvana, but he come back and help others. Karmapa like Dalai Lama. His spirit move from person to person. This Karmapa's spirit found when he seven years old."

Monks entered the room from time-to-time, and each smiled warmly at Sigourney as they prepared more tea and left. She marveled at how serene they looked, despite the Chinese soldiers outside their door and the harsh climate in which they lived. She needed to find such serenity in her own life. It was something she would work on when she got home. Home. The word brought images of Debbie to mind. Sigourney had expected to see her daughter in three more days. She still could if she left the manuscript with the Karmapa. All the more reason to do so, she thought.

The chair wasn't particularly comfortable, but she found the exhausting day taking its toll, and her eyes closed.

Sigourney became aware of something nudging her shoulder. When she opened her eyes, she discovered Sukhang shaking her.

"It time," he said.

Sigourney looked at him in a groggy state of confusion. Then, she remembered. She was waiting to see a boy god in a monastery somewhere in the mountains of Tibet.

Sukhang handed her a white scarf. "When you see Karmapa, you give this."

She took the scarf and followed her guide into the courtyard. A number of people were entering and leaving through the main gate. She glanced nervously at the soldiers, but they paid no attention to her. A broad stairway led to the monastery's entrance, where a monk waited at the top of the stairs. He greeted Sukhang and led them inside. They passed the deserted assembly hall and climbed a steep, wooden stairway to a small audience chamber on the second floor.

When they entered the chamber, Sigourney saw a teenage boy placidly eyeing them from his seat on a raised platform. Sukhang immediately fell to the floor and prostrated himself. Sigourney wasn't sure what she should do, until she noticed a number of white scarves draped on the railing in front of the platform. She walked forward and added her scarf to the others. The boy stared at her without blinking, his face as impervious as a stone chorten protecting a mountain pass. Only his dark eyes moved as he observed his visitors.

A monk in flowing robes strode into the room just as Sukhang stood up. The monk began talking to him in a strident voice. Sukhang nodded several times before turning to Sigourney.

"Karmapa wishes to know why you come here. Say you bring soldiers. Cause much trouble."

Sigourney looked at the boy in surprise. His eyes burned into hers with such astonishing force, it took all her strength to hold his gaze. Hadn't he been told about her mission, she wondered? About her flight from those very same soldiers? An unexpected tension darted helter-skelter through the room like a wayward spirit. She had expected to be greeted with warmth, or at least understanding. Not such a confrontational remark. She paused for a moment to gather her thoughts. He must know why I'm here, she thought. Perhaps, he wants to hear from me. I must show strength, if I expect his help.

Perspiration damped her brow. An hour ago she had been freezing. Now, she was uncomfortably warm, but she didn't know if she was permitted to remove her jacket. The boy never moved a muscle or changed his serious expression.

Sigourney turned her attention to the monk who had spoken. He stood with hands on hips, making it clear he was unhappy. Instinctively, she knew from his assumption of authority that he must be Tsurpu's head monk. "Please tell the Karmapa it is not my intent to cause trouble," she said in a halting voice. "I am hiding from these soldiers so I can return a very important manuscript to the Tibetan people. To the Samye Monastery."

Sukhang spoke rapidly to the monk, who glared at them both. Sigourney was beginning to feel rather foolish standing there. Surely the Karmapa already knew this. Otherwise, why would he have accepted her visit? And why were they not permitted to talk to him? They were forced to talk to this other monk, instead, and it was clear that he wasn't very sympathetic to her circumstances. To make matters worse, she had no idea how clearly Sukhang was translating her words. She knew enough about languages and interpreters to know the true meaning of a dialogue could easily become lost under such circumstances.

The monk spoke angrily to Sukhang, who shifted his feet uncomfortably. "Karmapa say you leave manuscript with him. He see it get to Samye."

There it was. The moment of truth. The Karmapa was willing to take it off her hands, just as John had suggested. All she had to do was hand it over and high tail it back to Lhasa, before further damage was done to her already fragile situation. She could be home with Debbie in a matter of days. But could she be sure the manuscript would be safe? Sigourney was trying to understand the misgivings she had felt ever since the robed monk had entered the room. She could feel a wayward spirit flying about her, looking for a place to land.

Before Sigourney could decide how to respond, the voices of the chanting monks began to rumble inside her valise. The manuscript was speaking to her, warning her of danger. She watched the Karmapa's eyes. They blinked. He heard them, too! A hint of movement caught Sigourney's attention, and she turned her head in time to see a dark shadow fall across the monk's face. Sigourney tried to breathe but couldn't get enough air. The darting spirit was stealing her air and suffocating her. She opened her mouth and sucked at the oxygen in the room like a baby at her mother's breast. At last, she caught her breath and stared at the monk. The shadow was gone, but she had seen it. It was the same warning Anne had described in her diary! This *was* Tsurpu's head monk, and he was the source of danger she had sensed. In that instant, Sigourney knew her fate was sealed. She had no choice but to continue her quest, to turn away from home and plunge further into the icy unknown. She gripped the wooden statue in her pocket and took several more deep breaths. The spirit had landed, and her breathing returned to normal.

"Please thank the Karmapa for his kind assistance, but I must take the manuscript there myself."

Sukhang hesitated, pushing back his cap and scratching his head. His pained expression made it clear he was uncomfortable with her reply and didn't want to confront the Karmapa. She nodded to him, and he finally spoke in his most beseeching voice.

The monk speaking for the Karmapa glowered at Sigourney and yelled at Sukhang, who hung his head and nodded vigorously.

"Karmapa demand you turn over manuscript now," Sukhang translated. "Say it too dangerous for you to deliver."

Sigourney stared at the monk. His angry posture and haughty behavior told her he wasn't used to being disobeyed. Power radiated from the man. Whatever his motives, he wasn't to be trifled with. Silence grew like a malignant tumor around her. Her nails dug into her palm as she clenched her fist around the statue hidden in her pocket. The voices continued to chant, but she realized the head monk couldn't hear them. Only she and the Karmapa knew of their presence.

What had she gotten herself into by coming here and what should she do? How long could she defy this belligerent monk? Sigourney looked back at the Karmapa and saw a tiny smile playing at the corners of his broad-lipped mouth. He knows the manuscript is warning me, she realized. As soon as Sigourney understood this, another insight manifested itself in her consciousness. The head monk had his own agenda, an agenda that put other interests ahead of hers and the book's, and the Karmapa knew it. She drew another deep breath.

"I want to respect the Karmapa's wishes, but I think it would be more dangerous for monks to transport the manuscript to Samye than it will be for me. The Chinese are watching every monastery and searching every monk. I can go disguised as a pilgrim and slip past them, just as I did coming here. I will cover my skin with charcoal and butter oil and dress as a poor pilgrim who is visiting the monasteries. I will protect the manuscript and never let it out of my sight, just as I have done for the past five days."

Sukhang translated as she spoke, hesitantly at first, then with greater strength as he felt the power of her conviction. When he finished, the head monk opened his mouth to speak, but the Karmapa raised his hand.

"Enough," he said. He spoke English! Had he understood everything she had said? "I know very little English," he continued in answer to her question. "You have honored Tibet and done a great . . ." he turned to Sukhang and said something.

"He say you do a great deed for Tibet," Sukhang translated.

The Karmapa spoke rapidly in Tibetan.

"He say you are wise and brave. He say he trust you. He agree you take book to Samye Monastery. He arrange it."

Sigourney exhaled, releasing the tension from her body like steam from a pressure cooker. Even the glare of the head monk couldn't affect the burst of happiness she felt. She bowed her head and smiled. His smiled broadened in return, and he spoke again to Sukhang.

"We stay here tonight," Sukhang said. "Tomorrow we join caravan. I go with you, be your guide."

Sigourney took another deep breath. There was more she wanted to say, but not in front of the angry monk. "Sukhang, please ask the Karmapa if I may have a private audience with him, with you acting as my interpreter."

Sukhang was so startled by her request, he couldn't speak. She realized she might be committing a serious breech of protocol, but she didn't care. She didn't trust this other monk, and she had to make her feelings known to the Karmapa. She wanted to be sure her quest wouldn't be compromised by spies or hidden agendas. At last, Sukhang spoke, and the Karmapa nodded his head knowingly. He talked quietly to the head monk, who immediately stalked from the room.

Please forgive my impertinence," she said once they were

alone. "I do not know who to trust, other than you. I believe it is best if no one else knows I am here. The manuscript is warning me of danger. I hope you will understand my fears."

"I share them," he said in English after Sukhang had translated. He continued in Tibetan. "The monk you met is very trustworthy but concerned about the dangers the book may bring to my people if the Chinese find it. Only the most trusted monks will help. Tomorrow, you will leave with the caravan camped outside. I will ask them to change their route. They will take you over the mountains to the Samye Monastery, not through the Yarlung Valley. That will confuse any spies. I will say many prayers for you. Once you return the book, your name will be written in our history forever."

With that, the Karmapa rose and strode imperiously from the room while Sukhang prostrated himself once more. Sigourney was amazed that a boy of fourteen could be so mature. His training the past seven years had been very effective.

The head monk returned. His manner was now conciliatory, but Sigourney couldn't shake the feeling of danger surrounding him. He ordered a young monk to take them back to the sleeping quarters, where she was shown to an empty room with a simple bed and chair. The bedding looked old and heavily used. She cringed at the idea of sleeping on it, but she was much too tired to debate the subject. Before she undressed, the young monk returned with butter tea, meat and tsampa. She had been so focused on her meeting with the Karmapa, she'd forgotten all about her hunger, but when she saw the food, her stomach turned summersaults. She devoured the food like a starving refugee and collapsed on the bed without removing her clothes. She was about to drift off when she remembered the manuscript's warning, and she forced herself to get up and look around the room for a safe place to hide the valise. Nothing looked promising, so she removed the manuscript and slid it between the thin mattress and rope webbing under her bed. Then, she placed the valise on a wood stool next to the bed and lay back down. Soon, she entered a dreamless void that was so dark and silent, she couldn't remember anything about it the next morning.

CHAPTER TWENTY

Sigourney looked at the empty stool by her bed and knew the valise was gone. Gone were Anne's wonderful stories. Gone was the tale of her escape from Tibet, which Sigourney had so looked forward to reading. Was the manuscript still safe? She leaped off the bed and lifted the mattress. The cracked and worn binding remained where she had hidden it. She cradled it in her arms, thankful to the fates that had intervened last night, and thankful she hadn't brought Anne's original diary on the trip. She thought about the shadow she had seen on the head monk's face and knew it was his doing. She supposed she should feel outrage at his treachery, but she was so relieved to see the manuscript, all other emotions were swept aside.

She thrust her hand into the pocket of her jacket and was comforted to feel the hard, smooth surface of John's cell phone, her only connection to the world. How she longed to hear John's voice! But that would have to wait until he replaced his phone. Until then, she could just as well be on the back side of the moon.

Morning sunlight streamed through the curtain covering the room's door. Sigourney looked around and tried to decide what to do. She wanted to find Sukhang, but was afraid that someone might see and report her. A basin of water sat on a low shelf in the far corner of the room along with a rough towel and a small bar of coarse soap. She hastily removed her clothing and hand-washed herself. Her skin chafed from being scrubbed in the raw morning air, but she didn't expect there would be many chances to clean herself during the next few days. She threw on her clothes and furiously rubbed her arms, wishing she had a cup of hot tea.

As if on command, Sukhang tapped on the wall and entered with a cup of the steaming liquid. She was quickly getting accustomed to the tangy butter tea. Like developing a taste for olives, she thought.

When Sigourney told Sukhang about the theft, he hurried away and returned with the Karmapa's apologies and a sack made of coarse yak hair for the manuscript. The Karmapa feared the valise had been stolen by spies and suggested she leave at once. The caravan was waiting. She wrapped the manuscript in the sack and secured it under her garments with a rope. Sukhang had also brought her a new coat with longer sleeves, and oily grease along with charcoal to rub on her exposed skin. A tiny mirror completed his package of gifts. She smudged her face and arms until she hardly recognized the dark-skinned woman staring back at her. Her transformation was complete. Sigourney had become the adventurer whose diary she was reading; she had become Anne Hopkins.

Sukhang was waiting for her in the courtyard. No sooner had Sigourney joined him than a sleepy young monk emerged from an adjoining room and slapped his way across the stone walkway in his thongs. Fearing he might be a spy, she turned her face until he passed. Sukhang motioned for her to follow, and they hurried across the courtyard to the side entrance they had entered the night before, only to discover a soldier guarding the doorway. Sigourney tensed at the sight of him and hastily looked about for another exit, but there was none. Where had he been when they arrived, she wondered? Probably visiting with the guards at the front entrance. It didn't matter. He was there now, one more obstacle she must face if she was to complete her quest.

Sensing her hesitation, Sukhang slowed his pace and lightly touched her arm, urging her to keep walking. Sigourney's face burned under the guard's icy glare; her hands trembled so badly, she hid them from view. As much as she wanted to avoid his scrutiny, she knew there was nothing she could do. She had to pass through that doorway, and the only way to do it was to make the guard believe she was an unimportant peasant woman who deserved no more than a passing glance. Taking a deep breath, she hunched her shoulders in an effort to disguise her height and, with her eyes cast down at the ground and her heart thudding like base drum, shuffled past the guard.

With each step, Sigourney expected to hear a sharp command to halt, but the only voices were those of the nomads preparing to depart. Moments later, she was through the gate and standing in the brilliant sunlight of freedom. The sun burned so brightly, it reminded Sigourney of that first morning in Shegar, and she half-expected to find a row of school boys reciting their lessons. Instead, she saw horses and people milling about as the caravan prepared for departure. Several women and men were tying the last of the burlap sacks onto the patient beasts, which appeared quite shaggy and undersized. Everyone was talking and laughing as if they were getting ready for a picnic, rather than a trek through the Tibetan wilderness.

The men wore sweaters under their jackets and baseball-style caps on their heads that might have been purchased at Wal-Mart. The women wore their usual layers of colorfully-striped skirts. Two of them had braided their hair with strands of blue cloth. Their broad, smiling faces were so similar, Sigourney was certain they were sisters. Another had covered her head with a magenta scarf, while the fourth woman wore a silk blouse under her wool jacket and a hat that peaked in front. Several pieces of silver jewelry hung from her neck. Sukhang explained that she was the wife of the lead man, whose name was Tsarong.

Tsarong wore woolen breeches jammed inside knee-length boots made of yak's hide. His sheep skin coat was draped over his left shoulder, leaving his right arm exposed to the chilly air. A silver box dangled from his neck, which, according to Sukhang, contained charms and prayers to ward off evil spirits. Unlike the other men, Tsarong wore a fur hat with ear flaps. He knitted his brows together when he first studied Sigourney, giving him the appearance of a stern school teacher. How much had she upset his travel plans, she wondered? How much inconvenience, even danger, was she creating for him and his companions? Tsarong's severe countenance was suddenly transformed into a warm smile. It was a smile that told her he understood and wished to help.

Three of the horses were outfitted with worn saddles. Tsarong's wife skillfully mounted the second horse. Tsarong motioned to Sigourney that she should ride the third. She had never ridden a horse in her life, and she recoiled at the thought of climbing onto this one. The idea of walking for God knows how many days and miles was even less appealing, however, and she gingerly approached the animal. Sukhang boosted her up so she could swing her right leg over the horse's back. The horse snorted and shifted its weight. She tensed, fearing the beast might bolt down the mountain with her clinging to it, but it settled down again. Grabbing the reigns, she gripped them as tightly as she could.

Tsarong mounted the lead horse in one swift motion and started the caravan moving along a trail that headed deeper into the mountains. Sigourney's initial uneasiness dissipated as she became used to her horse's swinging gait. It plodded along after the other horses without giving her so much as a backward glance. She was in the middle of the caravan, with the silver-jeweled woman in front of her and the pack horses behind. The other men and women walked alongside the animals, chatting among themselves. Sukhang stayed close to Sigourney's side.

They began to work their way through a series of steep gorges that tested Sigourney's ability to remain upright in her saddle. She kept sliding from side-to-side as the horse picked its way along the snowy trails and had to grasp the saddle's horn to steady herself. Tsarong's wife looked back several times and said something that made the other women laugh. Sigourney blushed, knowing they were having fun at her expense. When she caught their eyes, however, they smiled good-naturedly. They were strangers, but their smiles made her feel welcome, and that was all that mattered.

The caravan stopped briefly at the summit to rest the horses after their long climb. The frosty-cold air burned Sigourney's ears, and she pulled the scarf more tightly around them. Thankfully, it was a clear day, and there was little wind. Her throat was parched from the altitude, however, and she gratefully accepted a small, earthen container of boiled water from Sukhang.

The valley spreading below them looked just a desolate as the ones she had seen from her van's window, but she'd never imagined how magnificent everything appeared from the back of a horse. She was surrounded by mountains filled with motley peaks that reminded her of dripping candle wax. The hillsides sloped dramatically towards the valley floor, where they mingled with alluvial fans formed by water runoff during the brief, rainy seasons. The scene was filled with limitless horizons that made her think she was looking into eternity.

Once they started their descent, Sigourney faced a new challenge. The trail sloped so steeply, she had to press her hands against the saddle horn to keep from tumbling over the horse's head. It took several hours to descend to the valley floor, and by the time they reached more level ground, her arms were shaking with exhaustion. When they dismounted, Sigourney found her legs too weak to support her. Sukhang helped her to a rock where she could rest, but her buttocks were so inflamed, she couldn't sit down on it. Her only alternative was to sit in the softer dirt. She was beginning to think walking might not be such a bad idea, after all. When she suggested this to Sukhang, he nodded and agreed it would help to change her routine.

The lower altitude and afternoon sun had chased much of the chill from the air, and Sigourney removed her outer jacket. The women pulled sticks of firewood from one of the horse's packs and started a small fire for tea, then piled stones around the sticks to support two blackened kettles, which they filled with water from an earthen jug. The smoky odor of the fire soon mingled with the sweet smelling Tibetan air. Everyone sat on the ground and chatted while they waited for the water to boil.

Boiling water in Tibet's higher elevations took time, but these wayfaring people didn't mind. Time meant nothing more to them than it had to those lorry drivers Sigourney had observed sitting around that stricken vehicle at the glacier. The Tibetans approached time very differently than she did. It was more circular than linear. There was a rhythm to it. It wasn't something to be hurried or pushed along. The Tibetans moved to the beat of time, rather than trying to dictate it. They were like tiny boats at sea, letting the currents carry them along.

Sigourney had been in a great hurry all her life. She had budgeted time, saved it, run out of it and never had enough of it. Now that she was traveling across the Tibetan plateaus, she found time bending in strange, new ways. It had been less than a week since she entered Tibet, but it felt as though she had crossed an event horizon. A chasm had opened that divided the world she had known for forty-three years from a world she had known only a few days, and the difference in time between them had no relevance. Sigourney watched the women and men sitting so comfortably beside her and found herself identifying with them, as if their spirits had entered her body and were mingling with hers. She was becoming one with her new world. In small, undeniable ways, she was becoming Tibetan. She found this idea startling but oddly appealing.

The water was ready and cups of tea were passed around, along with tsampa. Sigourney devoured her food. She couldn't believe how hungry this country made her. She felt she hadn't eaten for days, although she no longer knew what "days" meant.

When Tsarong signaled it was time to move on, Sigourney indicated she would like to walk for awhile. This brought fresh giggles from the women. One of the sisters put her arm around Sigourney's waist and smiled, telling her without words that they understood. They were laughing with her, not at her. Sigourney noticed the men smiling, also, but they kept their distance. Were they being respectful of her, or did they feel the women's antics were beneath them? She suspected it was the former, for they showed considerable deference towards the women, treating them as working partners rather than just wives or chattel.

Walking across the valley floor proved therapeutic. The pace was easy, and she soon found herself lost in thoughts about Debbie. Had she been absent too often from her daughter? Between her research and papers to present at conferences, she had traveled more than she wanted. She had always felt guilty when she returned and had tried to compensate for being away, but her comings and goings had created too much of an imbalance in their lives. It explained why Debbie had grown so close to Roger. When Sigourney first sensed how close father and daughter were becoming, she had been jealous and uncertain of herself. She had resented their bond, and that had only exacerbated her guilt.

The caravan had nearly crossed the valley floor, and Sigourney's feet were as sore as her backside. She saw with dismay that they were approaching another mountain range, but this one had a much heavier layer of snow covering its peaks, indicating even higher elevations. Her muscles ached, and her body screamed at her to stop punishing it. If she was already this sore and tired, how would she cope tomorrow when they climbed into those white-capped mountains? The late afternoon sky dazzled her with a brilliant display of pink and orange hues, but this did little to ease her doubts about what lay ahead.

The caravan finally stopped, and the men and women began unloading sacks from the horses to build a shelter for the night. They stacked the bags in the same circular wall Sigourney had seen at Tsurpu, creating a barrier that would protect them from the bone-chilling winds that often blew across the Tibetan plateau. She wanted to help them, but her exhaustion stripped her of the ability to even remain standing. She sank onto one of the sacks with a weary sigh, uncertain whether she could ever rise again.

Sukhang hurried over and crouched beside her. "You rest. Others make camp. You feel better soon."

"I don't know Sukhang." Sigourney hung her head and drew deep breaths in an effort to regain some strength. "Right now, all I want to do is crawl off somewhere and die. This may be too much for me." She sounded every bit as discouraged as she felt. Hiking in the "great outdoors" had never been her forte, and this experience made her feel useless. Climbing more mountains or riding all the way to the Samye Monastery seemed ludicrous. She might as well consider swimming across the ocean.

Sigourney wondered if she looked as ridiculous as she felt. What had made her think she could deliver the manuscript herself? She'd been mad to reject the Karmapa's offer. She should be back in Lhasa right now, eating a hearty meal and thinking about making love to John. Or, she could be in a Chinese jail eating God knows what! And she couldn't shake the feeling that if she had handed over the manuscript, it wouldn't have made it to Samye. The shadow on the head monk's face told her he had other plans for it. These thoughts sobered her. There was no turning back, in any case. She had to keep pushing forward, even if it killed her.

"Soon, we make tea. You feel better. You see." Sukhang smiled at her. That was the Tibetan's solution to everything, she thought. Make tea.

The women started a fire for the kettles, while the men tethered the horses and smoked their cigarettes. Sigourney sat on the ground next to the women. They smiled and handed her the first cup of tea. She grasped it with the furtive look of a street beggar and sipped the hot liquid as fast as her tongue would permit. It burned a path down to the place where her life force resided, and her aching body slowly regained its vitality. Sukhang was right. Tea did make her feel better. She didn't know if she would be able to sit on a horse or climb a mountain tomorrow, but at least she would live through the night.

Sukhang joined her, and she looked more closely at the unassuming man who had dropped everything in his life and agreed to trek from Tsurpu to Samye, and perhaps beyond.

"Do you have a family, Sukhang?"

He pushed back his cap and scratched his head. "Yes, yes. My wife good woman. Very strong in spirit. When I drink too much, she hit me on head and make me promise to do better." His head bobbed up and down as he laughed at his joke.

"Do you have children?" Sigourney leaned back on one elbow and stretched her legs. She was amazed at how much better her muscles felt, now that she was resting.

"Two daughters. My wife always excuse herself for no sons. I tell her it all right. My daughters take good care of me. Not hit me on head when drunk."

Sigourney joined his laughter. She tried to imagine hitting Roger over the head when he cheated on her. Would it have helped? Probably not, but it would've been very satisfying. Her mind drifted to John. How she wished he were there sharing her adventure. He would've handled today's trek much better than she did. He would've encouraged her and urged her on. Just thinking about him gave her strength.

Sigourney discovered that her guide had learned English by driving for tour guides like Jigme. He lived in Lhasa in the Tibetan section, not far from her hotel. She wished she'd had the chance to see where he lived but knew that wouldn't have been part of the scheduled itinerary.

She thought about her tour group and realized she missed them, even Cameron's wild antics and Beth's barking laughs. She especially missed Marie-Rose and hoped she was finding some resolution to her personal problems. Sigourney had become quite fond of the French woman and wished her well. She missed John most of all. She touched the cell phone in her coat pocket, and his whimsical smile and brown eyes floated before her like a desert mirage. Had they really kissed with so much passion, or had she imagined the whole thing? She wanted to push the red button on the phone but knew it would do her no good. He was beyond her reach for another day or two, which seemed like an eternity. She would have to be patient, like her Tibetan companions, and not hurry time.

After dinner, the men drank chang, the local Tibetan beer, and smoked more cigarettes, while the women washed the metal plates in the remaining hot water. Sukhang joined the men, and soon they were laughing merrily at each other's stories. The women mostly ignored them as they cleaned up.

When it was time to sleep, the well-dressed woman joined Tsarong under his covers as Sigourney had expected, but she was surprised to see both sisters climb in with one of the other men. She remembered what Anne had said about the Tibetans' practice of polygamy and polyandry. That had been a hundred years ago, but it still seemed to be in fashion. If John were there, she knew she'd slip under his covers without further hesitation, but she wouldn't share him with another woman! Sigourney looked at the millions of stars and promised herself she would be ready tomorrow. That was her last thought before she slept.

She woke during the night with an urgent need to go to the bathroom, something she had failed to do before retiring. The fire had been reduced to a few glowing embers, and the arctic cold chilled her to the bone when she stood up. Her aching muscles cried out to her to lie back down, but she ignored them. Choruses of heavy breathing and light snoring told her everyone was sleeping peacefully. The glow from the coals offered only a weak light, but it was enough to destroy her night vision when she looked at it. She was too disoriented to remember which direction she faced when she went to sleep, and it was too dark for her to see the small opening left in the ring of sacks surrounding her. After nearly stepping on someone, she got down on her knees and slowly crawled to the perimeter, using her hands to guide her around the sleeping bodies. Once she reached the sack wall, she stood up and moved along the perimeter until she found the gap.

A brisk wind knifed through her clothing when she stepped outside the encampment, and she hurried about her business. She was about to hasten back inside when she became aware of a strong odor that reminded her of rotting apples. She looked up and nearly tumbled over backwards. A shadowy figure stood less than ten feet away, staring at her! Sigourney pressed her back against the wall of sacks and fought to control the panic rising in her chest. Anne's run-in with the Khampas streaked through her memory. She wanted to cry out a warning, but her voice lodged in her throat. Her mind screamed for her to run, but her feet were rooted in the ground.

The figure remained motionless, showing no signs of aggression towards her. Curiosity began to overcome her initial fear. The man, if that was what it was, seemed to ebb and flow. One moment she saw him; the next, he was nearly lost in the inky night. The harder she stared at him, the more he dissolved in the darkness, until she wasn't sure if he was there at all. When she looked slightly to his left or right, however, she could see him quite clearly.

"Who are you?" she finally managed to whisper.

The figure spoke to her in a thin voice that was so quiet, she could hardly distinguish it from the wind. She strained to understand him, forgetting that she couldn't speak Tibetan. The words grew softer and softer, until they were gone, along with the figure that vanished completely.

Sigourney stared at the spot where the figure had been, shivering violently from the icy wind and from her ghostly encounter. *Had* she seen anything at all? She couldn't be certain. Then, she remembered the smell of rotting apples. It had dissolved along with her apparition. She hurried back inside the protective wall, half expecting to find the figure waiting for her there, but all she saw were the sleeping forms of her travel companions. She retraced her steps to her sleeping mat and plunged under the blankets, where she replayed the incident in her mind. The figure had been trying to tell her something, but what? She would talk to Sukhang about it in the morning. He would probably think she was crazy, but she had to tell someone.

CHAPTER TWENTY-ONE

Sigourney was anxious to speak with Sukhang about last night's incident, but he was helping the men break down the campsite, and she hesitated to interrupt them. Everyone went about their morning chores with such vigor, she marveled at their energy and cheerful nature. Mornings had never been so spirited in the Phillips' household. None of them had been early risers.

This thought reminded her that she was supposed to leave Tibet today. People would expect her home tomorrow. Roger and Debbie would be the first to realize she hadn't arrived on schedule. How would Debbie react, she wondered? Would she be angry? Worried? Her department head, David, would expect to hear from her. He would try to call her at home when she didn't report in, and then try to reach Brad in Lhasa. The thought of Brad eating his yak meat while she scrambled over mountain passes made her blood boil. The next time she saw him, she wanted to scratch his eyes out for his treachery.

She touched John's phone and thought about trying to call home. He'd said it couldn't be used to make normal calls, but she might be able to get a message to Roger or David through the special operator John had mentioned. Not a good option, she decided. It was a secure line, and she didn't want to get John in trouble. She would wait until she talked to him.

Sigourney accepted a cup of butter tea from one of the sisters and motioned to Sukhang to join her on the frosty ground. She wasn't sure how to broach the subject of last night's strange encounter. It was so bizarre, she was beginning to wonder if she hadn't dreamed the entire episode.

"Sukhang," she began tentatively. "Last night I stepped outside the camp, and I saw a man standing there. At least, I think it was a man. I could barely see him. He seemed to be talking to me, but he whispered and I couldn't make out his words."

Sukhang frowned. "Not understand this word, whisper."

She thought for a moment. "He sounded like the wind," she said at last.

"Did you see his face?" Sukhang's frown deepened.

"It was too dark. But it was more than that. It was as if he had no face. He looked like one big shadow. I was frightened at first, but he never threatened me. After he spoke, he just disappeared."

Sukhang pushed back his cap and scratched his head. "I talk to Tsarong." He rose abruptly and hurried over to where the men were still loading the horses. Sigourney watched as the two men conversed. They both looked at her, and then walked several paces out onto the empty plain. Tsarong seemed to be interrogating Sukhang, who kept nodding his head as he responded. When they finished, Tsarong made an announcement to the others, which caused them to murmur and cast uneasy glances towards Sigourney.

Sukhang hurried back to her. "You maybe visited by Bon spirit last night. It very important to know what it want. We not enter mountains until find out. Otherwise, might die."

Sigourney sat in shocked silence. A Bon spirit? How could such a thing be possible? Even if she accepted the idea--she wasn't at all certain she did--she wasn't Tibetan. Why would such a spirit speak to her?

"What shall we do?" she asked.

"Visit shaman. He has home near here. We go to stupa where he pray. Ask him if it safe to travel through mountains."

This alarmed Sigourney. "What if the shaman says it's not safe?"

"Go back to Tsurpu Monastery. Take new route." Sukhang shifted his attention to a stone he was moving back and forth with his foot. He looked like a boy who was afraid of being scolded by his mother.

Sigourney thought about the head monk and knew that would never do. "I can't do that, Sukhang. If the caravan turns back, I must go on without them." She studied his worried face. Would he go with her?

"Look, Sukhang," she continued, "I realize I don't know about your ancient spirits, but I don't think last night was a warning to the caravan. I believe it was a warning to me. It has something to do with the manuscript I'm carrying. When we see the shaman, I think you must explain that to him. It may help him interpret what the spirit wanted to tell me."

Sukhang nodded. "I not tell Tsarong." He said this as a statement, but she knew it was a question.

"No, you not tell Tsarong. Only the shaman."

The caravan turned away from the mountains she had dreaded crossing and headed up the valley, where they passed isolated houses and peasants tilling their fields. Sigourney decided to try the horse once more. Someone had kindly added a second blanket to her saddle, and the extra cushion helped.

The sun was high above her head by the time she saw a dark patch of people in the distance. The trail widened, indicating many visitors traveled that way. Four monks appeared beside the road. They were seated on the ground with their legs crossed in front of them and their maroon robes pulled over their heads. A tennis shoe peeked out from under one robe, reminding Sigourney that even in this remote valley, the outside world was making its presence felt.

Yellow prayer cloths were stretched on the ground in front of them, and a red bag sat to one side with coins and paper money in it. When Tsarong stopped and dropped a few coins in the bag, the monks began praying.

The dark patch of people grew in size until Sigourney could see dozens of Tibetans sitting on the ground surrounding a small stupa. A large bouquet of prayer flags on long poles blossomed from the top of the stupa. Children played in the dirt, and dogs trotted expectantly among the crowd looking for handouts. Most of the men wore wide-brimmed hats, while the women covered their heads with colorful shawls. A small fire cooked meat and warmed water for tea.

Sigourney's caravan stopped, and her traveling companions joined the pilgrims, while Tsarong and Sukhang approached a figure seated next to the stupa. They crouched down on their haunches and spoke with him. The man sat in the shadows, making it difficult for Sigourney to see his features, but she assumed he was the shaman. After several minutes, Tsarong stood up and walked away, but Sukhang remained seated. He motioned to Sigourney to join them. She had formed a mental image of a wizened old man and was surprised to find herself facing the broad features and smooth skin of someone in his late thirties or early forties. Her shoulders had felt tense all day, but his disarming smile relaxed them.

The shaman spoke quietly to Sukhang, who translated. "He want to know why you think warning meant for you and manuscript."

"Tell him I'm afraid Tsurpu's head monk wants to intercept . . . to steal the manuscript and prevent it from reaching Samye. I believe the spirit was warning me of such danger."

The two men conversed, and then the shaman closed his eyes and began murmuring to himself. He swayed in rhythm to his musical voice, and his murmuring grew louder. Sigourney was mesmerized by his baritone voice. It gathered strength until it echoed across the valley floor with the power of a great operatic aria. The Tibetans stopped their prayers to watch, their eyes fixed on the shaman with respect and devotion. She could see that this was a very spiritual moment, one filled with mystery and meaning.

The shaman suddenly opened his eyes and stared at Sigourney. Everyone sat very still and waited for him to speak. Her heart boomed in the silence, as she, too, waited. The shaman leaned over and whispered to Sukhang, who nodded and signaled to Sigourney for them to leave. She could feel the dozens of eyes following her as she walked with Sukhang back to the horses. No one else moved.

"What did he say?" Sigourney shielded her eyes from the sun and studied his face.

Sukhang made his familiar gesture, pushing back his hat and scratching his head. "Shaman say you very wise. He say spirit warning you not to take planned trail to Samye Monastery. Tsurpu monk have men waiting."

"Where? When? Are we safe here?" She fired the questions at her poor guide so quickly, he threw up his hands to slow her down.

"Shaman say we safe until get over mountains." He pointed to the mountain range they were supposed to have crossed that morning. "Danger come later, after we pass Kyi Chu River."

That made sense. If the monk tried to intervene here, the Karmapa would know he was responsible. If he waited until she was closer to Samye, he could deflect the blame onto others. She remembered the Kyi Chu River paralleling the road on the van's approach to Lhasa. "Is there another way we can go?"

"Once we reach river, we leave caravan. Shaman tell Tsarong to take planned trail through mountains near Samye. We go through Yarlung Valley. Tsurpu monk not expect this."

"That will make Tsarong's journey much more difficult."

"Caravan already know you carry great spirit with you. They want to help. It is their joy and duty."

The caravan members were returning, and Sigourney looked at them with renewed appreciation. Tsarong walked up to her and grinned, as if to answer her concerns. She bowed her head to show her gratitude.

After a brief lunch, the caravan turned around and retraced its route back down the valley. It was late afternoon when they reached last night's campsite, and Tsarong announced that they would remain there one more night. Sigourney welcomed the extra night's rest before tackling the mountains. Her body was slowly adapting to her new, more rigorous routine, and the extra blanket on the saddle had softened her pain. Yesterday, she had been ready to abandon her quest. She knew she would feel differently tomorrow.

That night, Sigourney made sure to do her toilet before going to sleep. As much as she appreciated the spirit's warning, she didn't feel the need to encounter it again. Her body was starting to feel like sandpaper from all the dust on the trail, and she wished she could bathe. It seemed impractical under the circumstances. There were no streams or privacy, and the air was so damn cold, she didn't think she could manage it anyway. She watched the other women, but they went about their tasks and settled down without giving the matter a second thought. She resigned herself to remaining dirty a while longer.

Sigourney woke up the next morning refreshed and eager to begin. This was a new experience for her--she had never been eager to do anything in the morning--and she marveled at it. Could mornings really feel this good? She would have to give them a try, especially if she wanted to be around John. She could tell he was a morning person.

The caravan began climbing a steep, rocky trail that led into the heart of the snow-capped mountains. At first, the ascent proceeded comfortably. The trail was wide enough to accommodate both the horses and those on foot, and Sigourney found the slope manageable. As they worked their way higher, however, the trail narrowed, until the horses advanced nose-to-tail, and the walkers followed. They came to a section where a cliff plummeted into a deep gorge on the left, and there was barely enough room for the horses to find their footing. Sigourney's horse was stepping within a foot of the edge. Her head reeled when she looked down, so she forced herself to stay focused on Tsarong's wife, who still rode in front of her. It was the only way she could keep from falling off her horse.

They left the gorge behind, but the trail continued to grow steeper. Eventually, Sigourney decided to dismount and walk. By the time they approached the snow line, she was puffing so hard Tsarong took pity on her and ordered a brief stop. She plopped down on the ground like an old rag doll, shaking with exhaustion. Her early morning enthusiasm had fled back down the mountain. One of the sisters sat beside her, took her hand and spoke with quiet urgency. Sigourney didn't need to understand Tibetan to know she was getting a pep talk from this smiling woman, whose calloused hands reminded Sigourney of a dry riverbed. The Tibetans were such hardy people, she thought. What she viewed as insurmountable barriers, they saw as everyday challenges. She remembered her initial reaction upon seeing the Himalayas from that hill in Nepal. How she had recoiled at the idea of entering them. How they had reminded her of the barriers she faced in her personal life. But here she was, riding a horse through mountains every bit as terrifying, and she was surviving. No, it was more than survival. She was being reborn, a process that began her first day in Tibet. She was growing in strength and confidence, and she wasn't going to let the mountain defeat her.

Sigourney squeezed the woman's hand and stood up. She nodded to Tsarong and walked with new determination to her horse. It was time to move on.

The trail followed a ridge for awhile, and she was able to ride. Then, another steep stretch approached, and she was forced to dismount. It went on that way--mounting and dismounting--for another two hours. The snow crunched beneath her feet, and the wind blew in arctic gusts that threatened to turn her face into a block of ice. But, she persevered, and they reached the summit without further incident.

One of the men built a small pile of rocks into a chorten, while the others said a brief prayer to the Bon spirits. After Sigourney's encounter two nights ago, she looked at the prayer flags and chortens scattered across the summit with renewed interest. There was more to the Tibetans' beliefs than mere superstition. She knew that now, and she prayed to the spirits in her own way, before joining her companions for tea and tsampa. Even though she couldn't understand their words, she knew by their smiles and their little touches on her hands and arms that she was now part of their group. Their friendship warmed her more than the tea.

Descending the mountain proved just as stressful on her legs and knees as climbing it, but her breathing was becoming more regular, and she knew she could make it to the bottom this time without embarrassing herself. Vistas of farmland stretched across the plains below her in ruffled patterns that reminded her of the Pop Tarts Debbie used to eat for breakfast. Somewhere out there was the Kyi Chu River, which she would have to cross under the nose of the Chinese if she wanted to reach Samye. That would require a fresh coat of grease and charcoal. It felt odd to return to the valley she had so recently traveled through by van, although it didn't feel recent anymore. That journey happened in another lifetime. How many days had it been since she fled Lhasa? Five? Like Anne, she was having trouble keeping track of the days. Days meant nothing in this trackless land where distance was measured in mountain ranges and time moved in circles. Tibet swallowed days and spit back centuries.

They made camp on the plains near the base of the mountains they had just crossed. Sigourney pushed her wobbly legs into action and helped build the rocky fire pit for the kettles. She didn't have the strength, yet, to help lift the sacks off the horses, but the women appreciated her gesture and reassured her with more little touches. She was beginning to treasure their touches.

Black clouds had pushed their way across the sky, chasing away the brilliant sunlight they had enjoyed the past two days. Except for the detour to see the shaman, the trip had gone as planned. Would her good fortune hold? Sigourney prayed it would, but as her world grew darker, she couldn't help looking across the plains and wondering if the clouds were a harbinger of things to come.

It was after breakfast the following morning when it dawned on Sigourney that she might be able to reach John. Instinctively, she thrust her hand into her coat pocket and pulled out the sleek, black phone. The thought of hearing his voice again sent shivery fireflies streaking through her body, but before she could push the red button, Sukhang walked over to inform her that the horses were packed and the caravan was ready to depart. Sigourney blinked back her disappointment as she returned the phone to its pocket. She would have to call him later, that night, perhaps, after crossing the Kyi Chu River.

Sigourney prayed to her bon spirit that the crossing would take place without incident, but when they approached the main road, her worst fears were realized. A road block had been set up less than a mile away, backing traffic in both directions. Police were also stopping those on foot along the road. Everyone's belongings were being inspected. It would be too dangerous for her to attempt to run that gauntlet with the caravan, and she suspected it would by the same elsewhere.

When Tsarong signaled for the caravan to stop, Sukhang joined her. "Maybe, we leave group here. Go further south and cross where there no police."

Sigourney considered their options. Sukhang's suggestion made sense. It would lead them away from Lhasa, where security was tight, back towards the summit at Khamba La, where it was mountainous and easier to hide. She smiled when she thought about traveling in disguise with Sukhang, just as Anne had done with Tenzin. Her transformation from university professor to Tibetan pilgrim was nearly complete.

"What about food and water?" she asked.

"We take enough to reach Samye. Once we cross road and river, we be there in two days."

Two days sounded like an eternity right now. "Can you ask Tsarong to delay his journey for a day? We'll need to get closer to Samye before Tsurpu's head monk discovers I'm no longer with the caravan." She hated to inconvenience Tsarong any further, but when Sukhang spoke to him he agreed at once.

A large bundle was prepared for each of them containing the essentials they would need: small jugs of water, food, sleeping mats and blankets, two tin plates and a tea kettle. It didn't seem like much, but when Sigourney hung one of the sacks down her back, she immediately felt the straps digging into her. By evening, her shoulders would be just as sore as Anne's had been at the start of her journey. The two sisters took turns hugging Sigourney and talking to her in their indecipherable language. She would miss their bright faces. Tsarong gave her a small nod and smiled. She would miss his wise leadership and strength. She had come to enjoy their company more than she could have thought possible.

At last, she and Sukhang turned and walked away. The next challenge in her quest had begun.

They walked at a steady pace along trails bordering the cultivated fields, keeping a sharp eye on the road to their left. They had agreed to cross at once, if they thought it was safe. Otherwise, they would climb into the mountains leading to Khamba La and take their chances there. No opportunity presented itself, and after two hours they approached a side road. Sukhang explained it was a secondary road used to reach Shigatse. It was not as well guarded, and with luck, they should cross it without being spotted. The problem was the river flowing on the other side, which was too deep and cold to wade across. Sukhang told her to rest while he scouted ahead for a boat, and she plopped down in the gritty dirt without argument. Her weary body welcomed the rest stop, even if it was the result of another barrier barring her from her goal.

Sukhang returned with good news. He had found someone with a small boat who would take them across. Sigourney forced herself to her feet and pulled the load over her back, sending a series of sharp pains knifing through her shoulders. They quickly traversed the road and joined a peasant, who gestured towards a leaky, wooden vessel that Sigourney feared would sink before they got half-way across.

"Not Tibetan boat," Sukhang sniffed. "This boat made of wood. Tibetan boat made of Yak hide."

Sukhang's obvious disdain did nothing to allay Sigourney's concerns, but when she hesitated, he urged her forward with a warning that they must hurry before a police car spotted them from the road. By the time she was seated in the rickety craft, her feet were already wet, and she grew concerned for the manuscript still secured beneath her clothing. Before she could change her mind, however, the peasant took a long pole and propelled them into the river. She was dismayed to see that the pole was all he used to guide the boat, and he was only marginally successful in keeping his craft on course. They slipped downstream as he poled, but she was relieved to see them slowly making progress towards the other side. No sooner had she begun to relax, than the boat jerked like a hooked fish against a submerged rock, causing it to list precipitously to one side. Sigourney grabbed the boat and hung on with all her strength until it finally righted itself and buried its bow in the muddy river bank. While she hastily clambered to safety, Sukhang thanked the peasant and handed him a few coins.

It was nearly dark, too dark to enter the mountains, so they made camp behind some large boulders and started a small fire. Sigourney's feet were nearly frozen from the water in the boat, and they burned with relief when she rested them near the flames.

"Do you think we can cross the main road, Sukhang?" she asked as they ate their yak meat and tsampa.

"Many police. Never see this before. I not know." He refused to meet her eyes. The worried lines in his face danced in the flickering light. "If police chase us, you run. I stop them."

Sigourney smiled. It sounded like a futile gesture, but she appreciated his gallant offer. She could no longer contain her desire to hear John's voice, and she pulled the cell phone from her coat pocket. As she did so, her fingers touched the wooden Buddha, and she realized with a shock that she had forgotten about it. She removed it from its dark hiding place. Its solemn face stared accusingly at her, telling her it didn't appreciate being ignored. She rubbed it apologetically with her fingers and set it on the ground in front of her. Then, she eagerly turned her attention to the phone.

Her hands trembled as she pressed the red button. Someone answered on the first ring.

"Control." A male voice, followed by silence.

Sigourney hesitated. "I . . . I want to reach . . . to talk to John

Henley."

"No John Henley here." The phone clicked off. The man had hung up on her! She stared at the phone in disbelief and nearly put it away, but she saw her little Buddha and gathered the courage to push the button again.

"Control." The same voice.

"Look, John Henley told me to use this line to reach him. Please don't hang up on me again."

Silence.

"I'm calling him from Tibet for God's sake!" She nearly cried as she spoke.

"Your name." Not a question. A command.

"Sigourney. Sigourney Phillips."

More silence. She decided to wait him out this time.

"Miss Phillips. Yes. I have your name here." The voice grew friendlier. "Please hold on."

Sukhang stood up and wandered off into the darkness to give her privacy. The silence lengthened. She stared at the Buddha. Please help me, she pleaded. The Buddha looked at her with sympathetic eyes. How could a statue's expression keep changing like that? It made no sense. Nothing made sense in Tibet. Her neck and back muscles were becoming tense from waiting. She wanted to shout at the phone. I'm a bundle of nerves, she thought.

"Sigourney, is that you?" The warm, familiar voice nearly bowled her over.

"John. Oh God, John, I miss you terribly." She was sobbing into the phone. "Why did I leave you? Why did I insist on returning this thing myself?" She was babbling, but she didn't care. His voice was a lifeline drawing her back to the sanity she had nearly abandoned somewhere back there in the mountains.

"Where are you? Are you all right?" There was a worried edge to his voice. She must sound like a raving lunatic, she realized. She had to get a grip on herself.

"I want to kiss you and make love with you," was all she could think to say.

Silence for a heart beat, then two, three. "Thank goodness this is a secured line." His familiar chuckle, warm and affectionate. She had nearly forgotten his chuckle. "I've been worried about you. Tell me what's happened."

"I'm still dodging the Chinese. I've spoken to a Bon spirit, visited a shaman, marched over two mountain ranges and ridden a horse until I couldn't sit down. Now, I'm back at the foot of the last mountain we traveled through on our way to Lhasa. I have to cross the road without the police seeing me. Then my guide, Sukhang, and I will make our run for Samye. He tells me we should be there in two more days."

"You're such a remarkable woman, Sigourney. I never cease to be amazed by you. By the way, is there another name I can call you? A nickname, perhaps? What about Sig for short?" There was a teasing tone in his voice.

"Don't even think about it," she laughed merrily. "It's Sigourney, and you'd better get used to it."

"Is there anything I can do?"

"Just keep me in your thoughts."

"You're there all the time."

"Pray for me."

"I will. Listen, I'll be out of touch for a few days, but I'll call you as soon as I'm able. Probably after you leave Samye."

"Your operator is very rude, by the way. He tried to put me off!"

"Sorry. I should have warned you, but there wasn't time. You just called one of the British government's most sensitive lines. Takes getting used to, I'm afraid."

"Would you call Debbie for me? Let her know I'm all right? I don't want her to worry."

"Of course. What's her number?"

"I don't want to let you go," she said somberly after giving him Roger's phone number.

"But you must. I don't know how much life is left on that phone's charge. I used it a bit before giving it to you. You must conserve the battery, so I can call you."

"You have to hang up. I can't." Tears slid down her cheeks.

"You're nearly done with your mission. Soon, it'll be over, and we'll be drinking wine together. Remember what I told you. Wherever you are, I'll come to you. Don't lose your nerve. You've come too far. Now, I must go, and so must you. I'll talk to you in a few days."

"Bye." She gave the phone a little wave as it clicked off. "I love you," she whispered. Love. The word surprised her. Had she really said that? There was no reply from the disconnected phone. Only a silence so deep she thought Tibet had swallowed her, just like it swallowed the days. She was surrounded by a black veil that absorbed all light. Only her Buddha kept her from feeling completely lost. And Sukhang, who quietly crept back into the camp.

CHAPTER TWENTY-TWO

They had climbed into the mountains in the dim, early-morning light, but by the time they reached the road, daylight had taken a firm hold on the cheerless, windy slopes leading to the pass at Khamba La. A cold wind swirled about Sigourney's face in fierce mini-storms of sand and grit that made her journey even more miserable. They found a likely place to cross the road and crouched behind boulders, waiting for an opportunity to make their mad dash to a deep ravine on the other side. There was no roadblock in sight, but a steady stream of lorries, vans and police cars made the crossing difficult. They could see for several miles down into the valley to their left, but their visibility up the mountain was limited to less than a mile by a bend in the road.

When the fateful moment finally presented itself, Sukhang jumped up. "We go now," he shouted.

They scurried across the rocky slope. The loose footing made it difficult for Sigourney to keep her balance, and she stumbled more than once as she ran. By contrast, Sukhang picked his way

248

like a mountain goat, never slipping or losing his stride. They were less than a hundred yards from their goal when a police car appeared around the bend to their right. Her heart sank. It was too late to turn back, and there wasn't enough time to cross the road and hide. She stopped and looked frantically for someplace to take cover, but the barren hillside left her completely exposed. It would take less than a minute for the police to reach them.

"You run," Sukhang yelled above the rising wind. "I stop them."

Sigourney knew she couldn't outrun the police at this altitude, but she didn't know what else to do and started towards the road once more. Suddenly, as if stirred by a magic wand, the wind began swirling around them, raising a choking veil of dust and sand. She turned back and grabbed Sukhang's hand.

"Run for the road," she shouted. "They can't see us in this wind."

Visibility was nearly zero, but they managed to pick their way down the slope and across the pavement. The ravine on the other side was too steep to maintain their footing, and they tumbled down the embankment to the bottom. Sigourney's face burned from the furious assault of the wind-whipped sand, and her hands and arms stung from various cuts and bruises. She moved her limbs gingerly and was thankful to find nothing broken. Sukhang helped her to her feet and they limped deeper into the ravine, until they reached the protective cover of a rocky outcrop. The wind had diminished in intensity by then, revealing the police car, which had stopped during the dust storm. They watched it proceed past their hiding place and disappear from sight.

"Sand storm save us," Sukhang said in an awed voice.

Sigourney thought about Anne's entrance into Lhasa. How the wind had risen and blinded the eyes of the head monk, allowing Anne to slip through the city's gates undetected. The Tibetan spirits had been with Anne that day, and Sigourney was certain they were with her now. They spoke through the manuscript and produced miracles. She pulled out her Buddha statue and stared at it. Was it her imagination, or did it smile at her? She rubbed its face. I won't forget you again, she promised.

Once they had recovered from their ordeal, they made their way further down the ravine, taking cover behind rocks whenever cars appeared on the road they had crossed. When they finally rounded a bend that obscured them from the road, they discovered the remains of a great earthen castle standing majestically on a rocky hill in the widening arroyo. It was strange to find one of the ancient castles in such a vulnerable place--canyon walls rose on both sides, presenting excellent firing positions for enemy armies--but its location had sheltered it from the wind and kept it well-preserved. Its broken walls and main turret reminded Sigourney of Gyantse's dzong and the extraordinary sunrise she had enjoyed with John. She wished she could climb the rocky escarpment and explore the castle, but she had neither the energy nor the time. They agreed, however, that it was the perfect place to rest and eat.

"What happens now, Sukhang?" Sigourney asked as they drank their tea and chewed on the dried meat Tsarong had given them.

Sukhang tossed small pebbles into the remains of their fire. "We stay in mountains until near Mindroling Monastery. Must cross road going to Tsetang and take boat across Yarlung Tsangpo River."

Another road and river to cross! How much longer could they defy the odds and avoid capture? How much longer could the spirits protect them?

"Will we be near Samye then? Will we take the boats used by the pilgrims?" She remembered Anne's vivid description of her river crossing to Samye.

"Very near Samye. Maybe find another boat. Police might watch pilgrims' boats."

They spent the rest of the day walking through ravines and over a small mountain range, stopping at dusk to camp in a protected canyon. The dark clouds lingered, but the wind faded away, as if understanding it was no longer needed.

"What will the Tibetans do in the future?" Sigourney asked her companion while they ate their dinner. "How will your family prosper . . . improve your living standards?"

Sukhang scratched his head, as he always did when he was thinking. "Not know for sure. We wait for Dalai Lama to return. Without him, we maybe not survive. Tibetans ignore Chinese ways. Chinese want us to forget Dalai Lama. Become Chinese. My daughters taught in Chinese schools, learn Chinese ways. Maybe, they not resist so much when grow up. Maybe, Tibet disappear."

"That sounds terrible. There's so much to admire and respect in your culture. How can China do that?"

"They say better life. Not so much poverty or sickness. I not know." He picked up more of the brush he had gathered and threw it on the fire, raising a storm of embers.

Sigourney hesitated before asking her next question. Sukhang's answer could either validate or undermine the importance of her quest. "Do you think the manuscript I'm carrying can really make a difference to Tibetans?"

"Yes, yes. Make big difference. Bring word of Buddha back to people. Bring new hope. Maybe for many, many years." Sukhang's eyes brightened as he spoke.

Sigourney thrilled at his words, but her joy felt empty, devoid of any pleasure. She could see the pain behind Sukhang's eager response, the uncertainty about his family's and his country's future. A spiritual blight was spreading across his land, a blight that slowly eroded the foundations of his beliefs and values. She tried to imagine a stronger nation invading her country and forcing everyone to give up their religious and political beliefs. Would Americans stand up as defiantly to fifty years of social pressure and propaganda as the Tibetans had done?

All the inconsistencies that now plagued the land struck Sigourney full in the face the next day, when she heard a strange, whining noise coming from the sky and looked up in time to see a commercial jet descending only a few miles away! The metal projectile was so alien to her, so out of place in her Tibetan world, it took a moment to fathom what she was witnessing.

"We near Gongkar airport," Sukhang informed her. "Only airport in country. People use to come to Lhasa."

The plane vanished behind the mountains. She had come to accept cars and trucks as part of Tibet's landscape, but an airplane dropping out of the sky didn't compute. How could she assimilate a jet aircraft with shamans and Bon spirits? She shook her head to rid herself of the image and moved on.

It was late in the day when they entered the dusty, main street of a small Tibetan village near the Mindroling Monastery. Sigourney rested beside an earthen wall while Sukhang made inquiries about a boat to cross the Yarlung River. She marveled at how normal the scenes of Tibetan life now appeared to her. High walls hid the Tibetans' homes from the streets, just as they had in the other villages along her route. She watched a woman hand-spinning wool strands into threads outside the entrance to her compound; and a boy wearing a frayed, mustard-colored jacket and torn pants who walked down the middle of the street carrying a woven basket filled with dried yak dung; and a father hoisting his small son on his shoulders just like the father at the Tashilhumpo Monastery.

Sigourney's peaceful interlude was shattered, however, when a Chinese guide suddenly turned the corner with a dozen tourists trailing behind him. Her face froze in an expression of shock--eyes widened, brows lifted, mouth agape--as she stared at the Caucasians coming towards her, their cameras dangling from shoulders, their eyes hidden behind expensive sunglasses. They looked like people from an alien world. Her first instinct was to conceal herself, but it was too late. The Chinese guide had already seen her. It took a moment to remember that she looked just like the other Tibetans on the street, except for her height. She slumped her shoulders and stared quietly at the ground.

"Just look at all the filth and poverty," a woman with a southern twang remarked as the group strolled by.

"Pretty sad," another chimed in.

Sigourney could tell they were Americans, and she had to bite her tongue to control her rising anger. They were talking about people she considered friends. They were talking about *her*. She wanted to rise up to her full six-foot height and shout at them.

What a surprise that would have been!

The group stopped nearby while the guide talked about Tibetan living conditions. Their close proximity made Sigourney uncomfortable, and she decided to move further down the street. But when she started to walk away, the woman spinning wool approached and began talking to her. She was quickly joined by two other women. Weathered faces smiled at her and hands reached out to touch her bag. It was happening again; the manuscript was calling to the Tibetans, and they were responding.

Sigourney realized with growing alarm that the Chinese guide was watching them. Frantically, she looked around and spotted Sukhang hurrying towards her. "Sukhang," she whispered, "tell these women to leave before they raise that guide's suspicions."

He spoke to the women in a low voice. They glanced over their shoulders and moved away. Sigourney turned her back on the guide's inquisitive stare and followed Sukhang around a corner, where he stopped at a compound shaded by a small tree and knocked on the wooden door. As soon as the door opened, they hurried into the courtyard. Sukhang spoke to the woman and turned to Sigourney.

"I go talk to man in village who has boat. You stay here. I come back soon."

Sigourney followed her hostess into a small, two-room house and sat at a wood-planked table while the woman made tea. Her faded shirt and patched dress were stained from use. A half-dozen plastic bracelets jangled on her left wrist in rhythm to her movements. When she smiled, Sigourney could see that many of her teeth were gone. *Like so many of the others I've met,* she thought. Sigourney guessed the woman to be no more than forty, but her leathery skin made her look much older. When Sigourney saw her through the tourists' eyes, she had to admit the woman did look woeful.

Sitting there, Sigourney realized with a shock that, other than dabbling a little water on herself from a tea kettle, she hadn't washed properly in over six days. She must have looked every bit as dirty and unkempt to those tourists as this poor woman. Her own skin was turning leathery brown and her hair was growing in tangled disarray. It was a sobering realization. The longer she was on the run, the more she looked like and identified with these people. Except for the washing. She was desperate to find a place where she could bathe and clean her hair.

Sukhang burst into the room, scattering her wandering thoughts. "Find boatman, but maybe trouble."

Sigourney stiffened. "The Chinese guide?"

"Yes, yes. He talking to police. I watch them. Maybe looking for you."

"We'd better go while we still can." She was on her feet, ready to flee out the door.

"Better you wait. I arrange. Not leave here." With that, he was gone again.

Sigourney paced the room. What stupid luck to run into that guide, she thought angrily. She was so close to her goal. Surely she wasn't going to be thwarted by such an absurd quirk of fate. Her poor hostess stood near the stove watching Sigourney and wringing her hands, causing her bracelets to clatter.

It was nearly dark when Sukhang returned. "Villagers help. We go now."

At the entrance to the compound she saw a two-wheeled, horse-drawn cart waiting for them. Three men stood beside it looking furtively up and down the street. They said something to Sukhang and waived her into the wagon. Sukhang told her to lie down on her side and pull her knees up to her stomach. When she was in position, the men quickly piled so many sacks of grain on her, she could hardly breathe. It was pitch black under the musty sacks. Dust and fetid odors filled her nostrils, and she had to pinch her nose to keep from sneezing. The wagon started with a jolt and bounced slowly along the road. Beads of sweat began dripping down her face as she grew unbearably warm in the tiny space. Each time the wagon hit a bump, the sacks shifted, crushing the breath from her. The darkness and dank odors imprisoned her. It was all she could do to keep from pushing the bags aside. Sigourney closed her eyes, instead, and concentrated on the muffled voices of her accomplices. She could envision their tense bodies moving cautiously through the empty streets.

A voice barked, suddenly, and the wagon halted. Another voice responded. Sukhang's? Sigourney couldn't tell. This was followed by another sharp command. Sigourney knew it was the police, and if they wanted to inspect the cart, there was nothing the villagers could do to stop them. She would be discovered, and her quest would be over. Now, her hiding place had, indeed, become a prison, and she was trapped inside it, unable to flee. Sigourney squeezed her eyes shut and prayed that the police would let them pass, but no sooner had she done so than the load shifted and grew lighter. Cold air filtered through the dust and stale odors as the beam of a flashlight found its way between the bags. They were lifting the sacks off the wagon! Cringing at her helplessness, she silently cursed the ill-timed arrival of that Chinese guide, dug her nails into the wagon's splintered wood, and waited.

Someone made a remark, and there was laughter. A light chatter followed. Several voices, Tibetan as well as Chinese. Sacks were tossed on top of her again, knocking the wind from her lungs. The wagon was moving! They had somehow passed the police inspection without exposing her hiding place. As the wagon bounced along, someone kindly removed a few of the sacks, permitting her to breathe more easily. Minutes passed. How many, she couldn't tell, but she guessed they had traveled a mile or more before stopping again. The bags were quickly removed, and the sweet, cold air of freedom swept over her.

"We safe now," Sukhang announced.

Sigourney sat up and looked around. Partial moonlight turned the men into eerie shapes that reminded her of Bon spirits. "What happened? How did we get past those policemen?"

Sukhang laughed. "We play good joke. Hide bottles under rice sacks." Someone struck a match to light a cigarette, and she could see one of the men holding two bottles of alcohol. "Let policemen find. Tell them we want drink, but not let women find out, or they hit us on head. Police laugh with us. We give them bottle. They tell us to go."

The other men were laughing, and she began to laugh, too, at first with relief, then with growing enjoyment at their enterprising humor. But her laughter soon turned to tears, and she shook so violently, Sukhang put his arm around her shoulders just like the sisters had done on the trail. She knew this was not something he would dare to do under ordinary circumstances, but nothing about their time together had been ordinary. She was grateful for his gesture. The constant fear, tension, and narrow escapes were taking their toll. She sat there sobbing with anguish, relief, and self-pity. The crying felt wonderful. It released all the pent-up emotions that had accumulated since leaving Lhasa. The tears cleansed her more than soap and water ever could.

After she had regained her composure, she asked Sukhang to thank the brave men for helping her. They smiled and nodded as they turned the cart around and disappeared into the night. As soon as they were gone, Sukhang handed her the familiar backpack, and they were on their way again. He explained they would meet the boatman just before dawn and cross the river at first light. The barges wouldn't be operating at that hour, and the police would be less likely to watch the river. They would cross down river from the barges, where they could avoid many of the sand bars and move more quickly.

They left the dirt road leading to the village and used the faint light of a quarter moon to walk across the fields, until they reached the main road. Sukhang scouted ahead while Sigourney waited. There was no sign of a check point in the area, so they hurried across the road and slipped into a grove of thin, stunted trees growing along the river's edge, where they made their camp without benefit of a fire. Sigourney was cold, but for once she didn't feel hungry. The fear and tension of the past few hours had killed her appetite. She curled up under her blankets and rocked herself to sleep.

Sigourney awoke with a start and discovered a gray-blue light filtering through the trees. Sukhang's belongings were already wrapped in their bundle, but he was nowhere to be seen. When she sat up, she was greeted by an icy-sharp blast of wind blowing off the water. Her stomach growled pitifully, reminding her that she hadn't eaten since yesterday's noon meal. At least her appetite was back, but it was small compensation for her misery. She drew her knees to her chest and wrapped her arms around herself just as she had done in the cave by the Tsurpu Monastery.

She thought about what had happened since her journey began. The people, dangers, and hardships she had encountered were being woven into her life like threads in a tapestry. Every scene added a new meaning to the overall theme; each event added to the texture and colors. Life was a tapestry, she thought. It was created stitch-by-stitch according to the actions one took, the people one met, and the paths one chose to follow. Most people built their life's tapestries slowly and methodically, sometimes making choices that enriched the fabric and other times doing things that weakened it. It was different for those who had great adventures. Adventures accelerated the process. The tapestries grew larger and richer. Sigourney's own tapestry had been pitifully small before Tibet. Now, it was flourishing in astonishing ways. Even her misery was contributing to the richness of its colors and designs. She vowed never to let her tapestry flounder again.

Hurried footsteps announced Sukhang's return. "Boatman ready. We go now."

His words galvanized Sigourney. She gathered up her belongings and followed him along the muddy shore with new strength. She was about to complete her quest, and she thanked the spirits for preventing her from damaging her tapestry by yielding to Tsurpu's head monk.

By the time they reached their rendezvous point, dawn had transformed the morning air into a misty, blue haze that floated on the river's placid waters like a bridal veil. Sigourney was relieved to see that the boat they were to use had no leaks.

"This Tibetan boat," Sukhang explained with pride. "Made of yak hide."

The boatman nodded quietly and fired up a small, outboard engine that promised to make their crossing much faster and safer than their last boat trip. Sigourney recalled Anne's description of a winding course around sand bars, but the water was deep enough here for them to take a more direct route across the river. They kept a keen eye on both river banks, but there was no sign of activity, and they reached the far shore without incident. Sigourney offered some of the money John had given her, but Sukhang shook his head and paid the man.

"Is okay," he said. "Monastery pay."

They scrambled ashore with their bags and moved rapidly into a small stand of trees. The nearby mountains were as barren as a moonscape, but the valley floor was filled with small trees and heavy brush, making it easy to hide.

"We make small fire. Stay here until later in day, then walk to monastery. Enter at night."

"Is it safe to light a fire? Don't do it because of me." Sigourney said this with more bravado than she felt. The thought of a warm fire and hot tea made her shiver with anticipation, but she didn't want to take a foolish risk so close to her goal.

"Small fire okay. Many pilgrims travel here. Make many fires."

Sukhang gathered wood, and before she knew it, they were settled down beside the warm flames waiting for water to boil. It seemed incredible to Sigourney that she was nearly finished with her quest. The idea unsettled her. Everything she had done the past eleven days had been focused on this moment. Every breath she had taken had brought her one step closer to Samye. Now that she sat at the monastery's doorstep, she felt an impending sense of loss. One part of her anticipated the joy of putting the manuscript in the hands of Samye's monks, but another part wished her quest could continue. The idea that she might wish to prolong her discomforts startled her. Was this how Buddhists felt about their quest for Nirvana, she wondered?

She thought about the woman she had seen praying in front of the Tashilhunpo Monastery, how she had endlessly prostrated herself on those cold, hard stones. Sigourney had watched her with detachment, much like those American tourists had stared at her yesterday in the village. At the time, the woman's devotion had seemed like a brave ordeal, one filled with pain and sacrifice. Now, she sensed that the woman had embraced her discomfort, and Sigourney felt like a kindred spirit. She understood the woman's suffering. Sigourney had been doing the same thing. She had been prostrating herself on her own unyielding stones, and she didn't want to stop.

There was still the matter of leaving Tibet, however. Her trials were far from over.

"What will happen once we return the manuscript, Sukhang? Will you continue with me?"

"Yes, yes." He nodded his head vigorously. "I take you through big mountains to Bhutan."

She had been only vaguely aware of Bhutan before now. The country had had little involvement with Europe, and her studies hadn't included it. Bhutan was a blank spot on her world map.

"Tell me about Bhutan. What's it like?"

"Not sure. Never go there. Not as high, I think. More trees. Have king, but no Dalai Lama. Friendly people, I think. Like Tibetans. Maybe wives not hit husbands on head when drink." He laughed at his little joke. Sigourney liked his laugh. It was surprisingly deep for such a small man. It made him sound bigger.

"Will it be dangerous? Are their bandits . . . khampas?"

"No, no." He laughed again. "No more khampas. Maybe storm. We carry yak dung for fire, so keep warm."

"What will you do when you return? Will you be in trouble with the Chinese?" Sigourney hated to think she might cause harm to this man or his family.

"They think I sick. No work. I be okay."

"And your future, Sukhang. What about your future? Will you continue to drive cars for tourists? What will your daughters do?" Sigourney hoped she wasn't overwhelming her companion with so many questions. They'd been piling up inside her, but their frantic journey hadn't left much time for idle conversations.

Sukhang pushed back his cap and scratched his head. The gesture had become so familiar, Sigourney expected it. "I make good living driving car. Do that as long as I can. My daughters finish school, and then marry. Wife and I try to teach them Tibetan ways. Hope they listen." A serious tone crept into his voice when he spoke about his daughters. She could tell he was concerned. It was the same everywhere, she supposed. Whoever controlled the education system controlled what the next generation thought.

Sigourney couldn't resist removing the manuscript from its sack and caressing the cracked, leather binding. It had become an old friend, and she would be sorry to give it up. She worried about the Chinese finding it and confiscating it. After all her efforts, that would be a tragedy. Hopefully, the monks had a safe hiding place for it. The warm fire and difficult trip were taking their toll, and when she found her head nodding, she lay down on her mat to sleep.

They rested until late in the day. Sukhang stoked the fire, and they ate a simple meal. Then, they rolled up their belongings and put them in their bags. Sigourney was used to her load by now. The ropes no longer hurt her shoulders, and the weight was tolerable. She was becoming hardened by her ordeal. Her legs felt stronger. Her feet no longer cried out at day's end. Only the cold still bothered her. She would never get used to the bone-aching chill of Tibet. They followed the shore at first, moving at a leisurely pace, so they wouldn't get too close to the monastery before dark. When they approached the landing area for the public barges, there was a flurry of activity along the river bank, and they stopped and waited out of sight. Pilgrims were stepping ashore and climbing into an open-bed lorry similar to the one Sigourney had ridden with John to Gyantse. There was no sign of Chinese guards on this side of the river, but it seemed wise not to show themselves. Rumors might alert the guards at the monastery.

Once the lorry was gone, they hurried past the landing area and continued on their way. Daylight was fading when they approached the monastery, and Sigourney's heart pounded as she gazed at it. She could feel it calling to her, like a mother calling a child, and she wanted to run into its arms. Steady girl, she told herself. They weren't there yet. She knew there would be Chinese guarding the place. Her quest wasn't quite over.

CHAPTER TWENTY-THREE

Night arrived in the typical Tibetan fashion, swallowing everything and sowing points of light across the sky. Last night's quarter moon had not yet risen, and Samye's walls towered above Sigourney's head like a giant, insurmountable shadow. Every nerve in her body vibrated with tension as she considered their plan. She would wait outside the walls while Sukhang entered the monastery and contacted the head monk. Beyond that, they had no plan. Unlike Tsurpu, there was no side gate that would allow them to slip into the courtyard unobserved. There was only the main entrance, and it was heavily guarded. The monks would have to find a way to sneak her inside.

Sukhang had already disappeared into the darkness. Sigourney crouched in the brush behind the monastery listening for the crunch of footsteps or other signs of danger. The odor of cooking meat wafted over the wall. The smell of food normally made her hungry, but tonight it only magnified the queasiness in her stomach. The ground was hard and cold, yet her body was so hot, she wanted to rip off her outer garments. Her face and neck felt feverish to her touch.

She would learn later that Sukhang didn't attempt to enter the monastery immediately. First, he visited a group of pilgrims camped outside the walls, where he chatted and drank tea while they ate their dinner. When the pilgrims finished their meal, they walked to the monastery's entrance, and Sukhang went with them. Guards blocked their way and asked them where they were from and checked their belongings. One member spoke for the group. Once the guards were satisfied, they let the group enter. In this manner, Sukhang gained entrance without drawing undue attention to himself. He immediately went to the assembly hall and asked for the head monk.

Sigourney's legs were beginning to cramp from sitting for so long. She heard occasional, muffled voices coming from the monastery, but there was no sign of Sukhang. Her mind raced with questions and doubts. What would she do if he were caught? Could she fool the guards by herself? Not likely. She needed Sukhang's help. The prospect of proceeding alone raised a fresh wave of nausea.

The quarter moon had broken free from the high mountains behind the monastery--the same mountains she was supposed to have traversed with the caravan--and she could see more clearly. A sudden scraping noise drew her attention to the wall. A rope ladder had been thrown down the side, and a figure was descending it. She tensed, ready to run, and then relaxed when she saw it was Sukhang.

"Monks lower rope ladder," he whispered. "You climb now, before somebody come."

Sigourney wasn't thrilled at the idea of climbing over the wall on a flimsy piece of rope, but there was no better alternative. She nodded and stood up. Her stiff muscles snapped at her as she hurried towards the wall. The ladder didn't reach the ground, but, for once, her long legs and arms worked to her advantage. She secured the bag holding the manuscript around her waist and reached up to the dangling rope. Once she had a firm grip on the bottom rung, Sukhang knelt down and she used his back to lift herself higher. She began to climb. It was a heavy rope, but it sagged and swayed as she sought new handholds and rungs for her feet, causing her hands and knees to scrape painfully against the rough wall. She winced but didn't stop. Looking down, she saw Sukhang watching her. He was too short to reach the ladder. She hoped he would be able to re-enter the monastery.

Helping hands tugged at her arms as she neared the top, and before she knew it, she was over the wall and standing on a second floor balcony. A monk put a finger to his lips and motioned for her to follow him down a stairway to a courtyard below. They hurried across the open space into the monastery itself. She saw the assembly hall to her left, but they kept moving along a dark corridor until they reached a small chapel lighted by butter lamps. The monk signaled for her to wait there and disappeared.

Silence enveloped Sigourney, broken only by the sounds of her own, hard breathing. Her legs were suddenly too weak to hold her weight, and she slumped down on a stool. Her knees and hands hurt where they had scraped the wall, but she was too tired to care. Now that her quest was almost over, she had no energy left. The manuscript was strangely silent. She thought it would be chanting by now, celebrating its return home after a century in exile. Perhaps, it was waiting until she handed it to the monks. Perhaps, it understood that it still wasn't safe. The room smelled and looked newer than the other monasteries she had visited. Sukhang had told her it was rebuilt after the Cultural Revolution. It lacked the musty odors and discolored walls to which she had grown accustomed.

Footsteps echoed in the hallway outside her room. She held her breath, waiting to see if the intruder was Tibetan or Chinese. Then, Sukhang poked his head into the room. Sigourney was so happy to see him, she couldn't resist hugging him. He blushed and smiled.

"We go see head monk, now," he said. "Everybody very excited."

They slipped through the assembly hall and climbed a stairway to the second floor. Chills raced down Sigourney's spine as she remembered Anne's description of a long hallway similar to the one they now entered. She could almost see Anne standing there, while the desperate monk pressed the manuscript into her hesitant hands.

Light spilling from an open doorway guided them to a room filled with books and a small desk. Three monks with silver-gray hair and timeworn faces stood in the center of the room. Sigourney's mind was floating in a dream-like state, observing every detail with a cool detachment that belied her pounding heart. She felt faint and grasped Sukhang's arm for balance. Was this really the moment? Was she about to fulfill her quest? The setting seemed all wrong. There should have been a sea of monks' faces in the assembly hall. There should have been cheering and jubilation. But that wasn't the Tibetan way, and the danger of discovery by the Chinese loomed just beyond the monastery's walls.

The oldest monk stepped forward, took her hands, and stared intently into her eyes. His were old eyes, eyes filled with ancient wisdom, eyes as old as the manuscript itself. They made her feel that she was peering into a deep well filled with history, a well with no bottom.

The monk spoke directly to Sigourney, and Sukhang translated. "Head monk say you welcome to Samye. Say your journey followed by monks all across Tibet. Say you brave woman. Not take easy way out. Not give book to head monk at Tsurpu. Chinese discover there. Here book safe. Chinese never discover special hiding place."

Sigourney continued to stare into the mysteries of the old monk's eyes. "Tell him I'm pleased to return the manuscript. It has enriched my life. Tell him I'm not a Buddhist, but I believe returning the manuscript has helped me to improve my own life, and I'm at peace." She had no idea how much of this Sukhang could translate, but she saw the monk's eyes gleam with acknowledgement and knew he understood.

Sigourney's hands trembled as she untied the rope holding the bag beneath her skirt. The monk reached out and touched her arm. The warmth of his touch coursed through her body, and the trembling subsided. She released the bag from its binding and pulled out the leather-bound book. All three monks gasped when they saw it. Their eyes widened, and they crowded around her like curious school children. She let her hands linger on its rough surface one final time, touching it with love and reverence, and then handed it to the older monk. Tears were streaming down his face as he accepted it.

The other two monks started praying quietly, but they stopped and listened in awe when chanting voices began praying with them. It was a sound Sigourney had come to know quite well, and she enjoyed watching the monks' expressions as they heard the mysterious voices for the first time. She felt around in the bottom of the bag for the key to the manuscript's lock and handed it to the monk.

There, she thought with satisfaction, I'm finished. My spirit has been freed from its cage. I have completed my own cycle and chosen to be reborn, to return to my world to help others achieve their own inner peace, beginning with Debbie, who I shall love and cherish. These are the first breaths of my new life.

All three monks were crying openly as they took turns holding the manuscript. They hugged each other and Sigourney. Sukhang hung back, but Sigourney pulled him into the happy circle.

When everyone had calmed down, Sigourney took a deep breath and asked the question that could determine the fate of Anne's diary. "Sukhang, please ask the monks if they know the date when the manuscript was taken away from Samye."

Sukhang talked with the older monk. "He say date well known, June 25, 1899. Manuscript given to foreign woman to save from Chinese spies. All documented in book kept here at Samye."

Sigourney cried out with joy. It was true! Anne's diary *was* authentic. She *had* been there, and she had come before Younghusband. Sigourney asked if she could see the actual references in the book's log. The monk said he would bring the book to her tomorrow.

Her next thought was about Debbie, her angry, disheveled daughter with whom she hadn't spoken in nearly two weeks. She told the monk she wanted to call her, to tell her she was coming home. But the monk said the Chinese controlled the international phone lines, which were only available in Lhasa and one or two other towns. It was impossible for her to make such a call. Sigourney's joy fluttered away at the news. She knew everyone would be wondering by now what had happened to her. Hopefully, John had talked to Debbie. It saddened her that she couldn't tell them her good news and that she was safe.

The weight of the last two weeks pressed down on her. Exhaustion had seeped into every pore of her body. Suddenly, she could hardly raise her head. She was taken to the monk's quarters, where she was delighted to find a bowl of hot water waiting for her. A large pan had been placed on the floor for her to stand in, and a sliver of soap sat on the table beside the bowl. A robe and wool night shirt lay on the bed. She ignored the fatigue in her limbs and eagerly stripped off her clothes, clothes she had not removed for the past week. Even the chilly air couldn't blunt the sensual pleasure of hot water pouring over her body. She saved enough water to wash her underwear. It wouldn't be dry by morning, but at least it would be clean.

Sigourney woke in a feverish sweat sometime during the night. She had dreamt she was chanting, but the room was quiet. She felt her lips moving, but no sound emerged. She was ranting in her mind. The sound of little, scurrying feet broke the silence, but when she hastily lit a candle, she could find no sign of the furry intruders. The candle's flame created dancing shapes on the far wall. The shapes looked like Bon spirits. She waited for them to speak, but they remained as silent as the room. She was wet with perspiration, but the moment she removed her blanket, warmth fled her body and was replaced by icy fingers that burned through her skin. She tried to think about her departure, but her mind floated away into dreams of snow-white mountains and angry gods. She thought she heard a telephone ringing, and she eagerly grabbed John's phone in anticipation of hearing his voice. The phone was lifeless. She pulled out her Buddha statue and stared at it, hoping for some guidance about her visions. It was as lifeless as the phone. Now that the manuscript had been returned, its spirit had vanished. It was only a piece of carved wood, shaped into a strange little figure. She would miss the statue's spirit. It had been a constant companion. Sigourney floated wearily in and out of consciousness. At times, she thought she heard someone in the room, but when she opened her eyes, no one was there. She heard little feet scurrying, again. Her head spun when she sat up; her mind was numb.

When Sigourney woke up again, the room was bright with sunshine, and the fever was gone. She struggled from the bed on shaky legs and pulled on her clothing. The underwear was surprisingly dry. A thermos of hot butter tea stood on the table. She quickly consumed two cups. Her stomach growled with hunger, but she wasn't sure if it was safe for her to leave the room. So, she sat down on the bed and waited for someone to come. A short time later, Sukhang tapped on the door and poked his head into the room.

"You get good sleep," he said with his usual smile.

"What time is it?" Sigourney couldn't suppress a yawn. Her mind felt bloated.

"Afternoon, day two. You sleep two days. You eat now. Soldiers gone. Safe to go outside." Sigourney blinked in disbelief. Had she heard correctly? Had she really been sleeping two days? She remembered a burning fever, or had that been a dream? Her mind and body were too drained for her to be certain what was imagined and what was real.

Sigourney followed Sukhang to the main courtyard, where activity buzzed around her. Dozens of pilgrims sat in groups along the walls and steps in front of the monastery eating food they had brought with them on their journeys. Dogs roamed everywhere, waiting for scraps to be tossed their way. The broad, entry gates stood open and abandoned.

"Why have the soldiers left?" she queried.

"Word already spread. Manuscript safe."

She wondered how word could travel so quickly in Tibet. She had seen a few phone lines on the trip to Lhasa, but she suspected those weren't for Tibetan use. Perhaps, the Bon spirits were carrying the message.

They entered a tiny kitchen next to the monastery, where an open fire burned under a concrete-block stove. Sigourney's stomach was doing flip-flops at the thought of food, but when Sukhang guided her towards a wooden table, she hesitated. Black soot and grease covered the walls. A powerful odor of cooked fat and smoke permeated the room.

Sukhang gently touched her arm. "Food safe. Must eat." He motioned again. Hunger triumphed over her concerns about the frontier atmosphere of the place, and she sat down. She was too famished to care, and she didn't have any other options, unless she wanted to join the dogs begging for scraps. Sukhang talked to the cook, who brought her a plate filled with meat and tsampa. The food was well-cooked, and she had to admit it tasted as good as any she'd eaten the past two weeks.

The food restored her vitality, and she returned to the monastery with renewed energy. Sukhang led Sigourney to a room filled manuscripts and ledgers. A monk sat on a stool writing at a small desk, but when he saw Sigourney he jumped to his feet and gestured to a page in a dusty book that lay open on the desk. She looked at the inscribed lettering, but she could make no sense of the Tibetan words. The monk pointed to a line displaying the numbers 25 and 1899. She was looking at the original entry recording Anne Hopkins' visit to Samye!

"Sukhang, please translate this for me," she asked enthusiastically.

Sukhang squinted at the ledger. "Say monk give book from Buddha to foreign lady June 25, 1899. Chinese spies search monastery. Not find book."

There it was, the documentation she needed to validate Anne's diary.

"Sukhang," she said in a hushed tone, "I need to make a copy of this page to take with me. Will you ask the head monk if that's possible? It's very important for my research."

"Head monk already know you want. He say you take ledger.

You return when you can."

Sukhang's words rang in her ears. The ledger was hers! She nearly hugged her companion, but she knew he would be embarrassed and resisted the temptation. Sukhang spoke to the monk, who nodded and handed her the volume. The cycle continues, she thought. I return the manuscript and take away an old ledger, which must be returned someday. By whom? Only time could answer that question. Perhaps, she would leave instructions in her will. The weight of the ledger felt good in her hands. She was pleased she would have something to carry with her, now that the manuscript was gone. She would miss the chanting voices, but the ledger would provide a bridge between her and this remarkable country. It would prove *she* had been there, as well.

"We go make ready to leave, now. Maybe, safe to take barge across river. Chinese still look for you. They very angry. Maybe, they only look at airport and on big roads."

Sukhang's words slashed through Sigourney's reverie and yanked her back to reality. It wasn't possible to just give herself up. The Chinese would probably imprison and interrogate her until she told them where the manuscript was hidden. She had read enough about interrogation tactics--sleep deprivation, loss of time reference, being awakened at odd hours, and the use of psychological, maybe even physical pain--to know it wasn't an ordeal she wanted to face. Sukhang was right. She was rested, and it was time to go. She hurried back to gather her meager possessions and returned to the assembly hall. She was astonished to find it filled with monks, who were kneeling in rows on their prayer cushions and bowing to her. The room was filled with the rustling whisper of their robes, and for a moment, she confused the sound with the manuscript's chanting voices. Tears rolled down her cheeks as she returned their gesture.

The head monk approached, and she thanked him through Sukhang for the ledger. She said it would be returned one day, but she couldn't promise when. He nodded and replied that it had only taken one hundred years for the manuscript to come back. The ledger was not so important. They would be patient.

CHAPTER TWENTY-FOUR

Sigourney scanned the banks of the Yarlung River for signs of police as she followed Sukhang down to a crowded barge and settled on a bench near the back. The boatman yanked on a cord, and an engine sputtered to life. Sigourney could now see the sand bars Anne had described. Some were quite visible. Others lay submerged in the water like crocodiles waiting to pounce. They forced the boatman to make a series of wide arching swings as he maneuvered the barge around them. Half-way across, a passenger called out and the boatman pulled alongside a dry stretch of sand. The man stepped ashore and relieved himself without embarrassment. For some reason, Sigourney found the scene quite comical, and she laughed quietly. The woman seated to her right nodded and laughed with her. Soon, other passengers were laughing, as well, but this didn't bother the man. He joined in the laughter when he re-boarded.

It took an hour to reach the other shore, by which time it was nearly dark. Sigourney was relieved to find the landing area peacefully deserted. The police had abandoned their search around the monasteries, just as Sukhang had predicted. They were undoubtedly focusing their attention on the airport and the roads leading out of Tibet. Nobody expected her to leave the country on foot.

When they camped, Sukhang showed her a crude map he had drawn of their proposed route. They would hike to the Himalayas and climb through a mountain pass that was more than twenty thousand feet above sea level. The idea of climbing so high was perturbing. Sigourney had read enough accounts about mountain climbing to know it was going to be a difficult task, one that would test her fortitude in a new, perhaps more demanding, way.

Sukhang told her they would avoid the villages along the way. When they did encounter fellow Tibetans, she would assume the role Anne had played during her journey: a simple pilgrim who couldn't speak. She smiled at the irony of it. I must write my own diary, she thought, one that describes my experiences and the parallels between mine and Anne's journeys. I'll publish the two diaries together, so that I may pay tribute to my ghostly companion.

Sigourney's thoughts wandered as they walked across the plains. She couldn't remember seeing any birds in Tibet. Perhaps, they didn't fly at such altitudes. Perhaps, she had simply failed to look for them. At times, she felt as though *she* was flying, floating over the barren landscape and rising through lesser mountain passes like a feather lifted by invisible hands.

Time became an illusion. Dark and light no longer measured days. Memories no longer measured years. She didn't know if she was traveling in the right time dimension. She might be behind time, or ahead of it. She might arrive at her destination, only to discover she hadn't left yet. Or that she had already returned. Time was being swallowed by Tibet. Time became a dream.

Dreams soothed her painful body and replenished the soil of her life. Flowers grew in her dreams, flowers with great, orange-and-yellow petals. Birds sang, and butterflies flashed brilliant colors when the sunlight caught their dancing wings. There were moments when Debbie joined her on her journey, a smiling and happy Debbie who forgave Sigourney for her human frailties as a mother. They laughed together and threw flower petals into the air. Sigourney was filled with joy. She felt whole again.

Roger didn't appear, but his girl friend did. The girl told her she wanted Roger and would take him away. The girl's threats filled her with anger and fear, the fear of being alone. She was lonesome in her dreams.

Sigourney traveled with Sukhang in this dream-state for several days. Her feet hurt from trudging over the rocky ground, and her shoulders ached from the weight of the supply sack she carried on her back. Her legs were sore from climbing up mountains and descending them again. Yet, she felt none of these pains. She had wrapped herself in a trance that protected her from the world.

The first day and night passed without incident. They met local peasants but no Chinese officials. They avoided a village by walking through the surrounding farmland at night. The second day, a helicopter appeared while they were traversing a broad valley. There was no place to hide, so they lay on the ground and listened to the thwump, thwump, thwump of the heavy rotor blades pushing through the air above their heads. Sigourney saw that it was a Chinese military helicopter, and she prayed to the Bon spirits to make them invisible. The thwump, thwump, thwump slowly faded away.

The second night they camped in the foothills of a small mountain range. Sigourney heard horses' hooves and voices, but it was a moonless night, too dark to see. The next morning they discovered a caravan of yaks camped less than a mile away. The caravan reminded her of Tsarong and the sisters. She hoped they had made it safely to their destination. She missed her traveling companions.

Sukhang chatted with the nomads and learned they were heading in the same direction, so they joined the caravan for a day and a night, until their trails divided. Sigourney knew enough about camp life by now to help prepare the fire and boil water, while pretending to be dumb. The nomads stared at her unusual height, but they said nothing. They knew she wasn't Tibetan. They told Sukhang a story about a foreign woman who had defied the Chinese and brought the word of Buddha back to Tibet. Tibetans were celebrating this miraculous event throughout their country. They talked about the woman in hushed, revered voices. Some claimed she was a giant. Others said she flew into the country on the back of a tiger. She was already entering their folklore and becoming a legend.

They said the Chinese were interrogating many Tibetans, trying to learn where the manuscript had been taken and where the woman was hiding. The Chinese were threatening the Tibetans with reprisals, but they didn't care. They celebrated and prayed for the woman who had returned their spiritual light. The nomads nodded to Sigourney as they spoke and smiled.

When it was time to say good-bye, they gave Sukhang a large sack of dried yak dung to burn when he couldn't find fire wood in the mountains. Sigourney hugged her new friends and watched as they dissolved into the Tibetan landscape. Then, she squared her shoulders under the weight of the back pack and faced the Himalayas, which now loomed before them. The massive peaks had first appeared when they crossed the last mountain range, and she had been warily eyeing them ever since. The mountains towered above the brown, empty plain like a glacial wall that defied anyone to conquer them. She remembered standing on that small lookout point in Nepal at the start of her journey and trying to catch a glimpse of them. Now, she saw them from the opposite side and wished she didn't have to accept their challenge. Her heart pounded as she studied the precipitous cliffs and lofty peaks.

Sukhang saw her worried expression and tried to encourage her. "We be okay. You see."

She appreciated his reassuring words, but she didn't hear much conviction in them. Sukhang was worried, also.

He gathered as much wood as he could find and tied it into a bundle to hang over his pack. "Use so we save yak dung," he explained.

Sigourney feared he was shouldering too much of the load, and she volunteered to carry the bag of dung. It hung like a sack of rocks on her back. They began climbing, and she soon sensed the difference between this ascent and the others they had taken over the lesser ranges in Tibet. In less than a day, they were in the snow line, and she was already exhausted. They stopped briefly for tea, but had to move on again. It was imperative to make us much progress as possible during daylight but still leave time to find a suitable place to camp, preferably in a cave. No cave presented itself the first night, and they bedded down between several large boulders. They burned firewood, and banked the fire with yak dung when it was time to sleep. The small fire provided some warmth, but they still had to bury themselves in their blankets. The night was clear and breathtakingly cold. Sigourney made a mental note to add more layers of clothing in the morning.

The second day, they reached a ridge, and Sigourney was shocked to realize she was about to lose sight of Tibet. She stood for several minutes looking down at the lifeless, undulating landscape she had come to know so intimately. When seen from this height, Tibet looked like a rumpled carpet that had been flung across the roof of the world. The land was so far-flung, the mountains and valleys couldn't fill its emptiness. There were no signs that people lived there. They became invisible in so vast a place. Like time, they were swallowed by Tibet.

Sigourney thought about returning there. About returning the ledger to Samye. She knew the Chinese would not allow her back for a long time, if ever. She was going to miss Tibet's monasteries, monks, bon spirits, and pilgrims walking their lingkors. Tears froze on her cheeks. She bowed her head to the mysterious, spiritual world she was leaving, then turned away and did not look back again.

Sigourney had expected to see a well-worn track, much like the ones they had followed with Tsarong's caravan. What she found, instead, were vague courses through narrow ravines, where any evidence of trails was quickly covered by the shifting snow. More than once, Sukhang pushed back his cap and scratched his head while he decided which way they should go. When the wind picked up in the afternoon, the temperature plummeted until the air tasted like a giant snow cone. They had been working their way along a natural passageway between steep, icy walls. From time-to-time, she saw blocks of ice hanging from ledges above her head, and Sigourney thought of the avalanche on the road into Tibet. She prayed the ice wouldn't fall. Her breathing became more labored, and she was relieved when Sukhang pointed to a small cave where they could escape the frosty air. Eagerly, she crawled into the cave and collapsed.

The next morning brought their first indication of the dangers they faced. The wind had abated, and a light cloud cover spread itself over the mountain. They had been walking for an hour when Sukhang stopped to study the landscape in front of them. To their right lay a steep ridge that would require considerable effort to climb. To their left, a field of glacial ice covered by snow stretched for several miles towards a mountain pass. Neither alternative looked like a natural trail. Sukhang scratched his head and suggested they try the ice. It would be an easier route. As a precaution, he tied a rope between them.

They hadn't walked more than a mile when Sukhang suddenly stopped and pointed to cracks in the surface just ahead. "Maybe hole," he said, prodding the snow with his walking stick. Sigourney flinched when a large section collapsed, revealing a deep chasm. She inched forward and found herself staring into a crevasse that fell away from her in cascading shades of blues and whites, until it disappeared into the shadows far below. She shuddered to think what would have happened if Sukhang had stepped into that yawning gap. She doubted that she could have stopped his fall with the rope tied around her waist. His weight would have pulled them both to their deaths. Tibet would have swallowed them up, and no one would have ever known their fate!

"Too dangerous," Sukhang said. "We go back."

Sigourney retreated from the edge without a word. By the time they returned to their starting point, two hours had passed, and they had made no progress. They were left no choice but to climb the steep ridge. The wind was blowing in gusts, now, sending puffs of snow into Sigourney's face. She discovered that the boots she had worn to trek across Tibet were less effective for climbing in snow. The bottoms were slippery, and she had to compensate by finding solid hand-holds. To make matters worse, the frigid air had settled into her body, where it slowly numbed her muscles. No matter how warm she felt from her exertion, the chilly undertow inside of her never departed.

When they reached the top of the ridge, Sigourney was relieved to find an easier slope ahead. She had no idea what altitude they had reached, but the inside of her head pounded unmercifully, and now that she was no longer working so hard, the cold asserted itself with a vengeance. She shivered uncontrollably but was determined to hide her discomfort from Sukhang. It was important to keep moving. The sooner they reached the mountain pass, the sooner they could get out of these mountains.

They entered a plateau where icy pinnacles sculpted by the wind rose like silent sentinels around them. It was a curious scene. The ice grew out of the ground like corn stalks, filling the plateau with their alien forms.

The combination of altitude, cold, and steep slopes finally became too much for Sigourney, and she sat down in the snow in a dizzy state of mind. Sukhang looked at her and decided it was time to stop for tea and lunch. He removed a few pieces of yak dung from her bag and built a small fire on the leeward side of a large rock. Then, he put snow in the kettle and waited for it to boil.

Sigourney was surprised at how numb her mind had become. Pleasure and pain were dulled to the point of unimportance, and it took her much longer to think about what she wanted to do. Even simple things, like doing her toilet, began to take more thought. Her energy flagged, as well. She had experienced fatigue on her journey across Tibet, but this was different. Her entire system was moving in slow motion, and it took considerable effort to overcome the growing resistance she felt in her body. Her breathing was becoming more labored, as well. At times, Sigourney felt she would suffocate. She would gasp for air, fearing hyperventilation.

"Do we go much higher?" she asked Sukhang with a feeble smile. She didn't want him to think she was complaining.

"Yes, yes. We go higher. Maybe near mountain top over there." He pointed to a jagged summit that rose in the distance. Its peak had vanished in the increasing cloud cover. Her heart sank as she looked at it; it seemed an eternity away.

"How long until we get there, do you think?" She couldn't hide the dismay she felt.

"Maybe two days. Maybe three."

It sounded like a prison sentence. Sigourney didn't know how she would summon the strength to make it through the afternoon, let alone two or three more days.

She had packed her little Buddha statue in her bag. Now, she wished she had kept it in her pocket. She needed to feel its comforting gaze, even if its spirit had departed, but she was too tired to dig it out, now. Maybe later.

Sukhang tied the rope between them, and they started advancing along a ledge carved into the side of a steep slope. A furrow had been dug into the rocky surface by countless yak hooves, and she was glad to see an actual trail for once. It told her they weren't lost. She was less excited when she saw the heavy snow hanging from cliffs overhead and the sheer walls plunging into the shadowy canyon to her right. She refused to look at either, keeping her eyes focused on Sukhang, instead. By the time they emerged on the other side of the canyon, daylight was failing, and they agreed it was time to stop. No cave presented itself, but they found a rocky overhang that protected them from the wind. They settled down for the night.

Sigourney admired Sukhang's vigor. Even at this altitude--she guessed they were between eighteen and twenty thousand feet--he moved with a surprisingly quick gait. He was used to higher altitudes, of course, but she was still amazed at his unflagging energy. He was very patient with her, which she appreciated. She knew he would like to travel faster, but he never pushed her beyond her limits. It couldn't be a very pleasant task for him, dragging her over these wretched mountains, but he never complained.

She pictured him at home with his wife and daughters laughing at some story. She saw him drinking *chang* with his friends, and then facing his wife's disapproval. It sounded like a simple satisfying life. She hoped he would be compensated for dropping everything and taking her under his wing. Once they reached Bhutan, she would offer him the money John had given her. She wouldn't need it anymore.

That night, Sigourney dreamed about Roger's young paramour, dreamed the girl had the audacity to confront Sigourney in her own home. Except, it had happened. Sigourney had answered the doorbell one afternoon and found a perky girl in her early twenties standing on the porch in a halter top and low-cut jeans, showing off a flat stomach and firm arms. Her skin was porcelain white, giving her the appearance of someone who had spent her life hiding from the sun. Her short, black hair bounced about her head in that casual, tousled way that was popular with many college girls.

Her name was Bethany, and she had come to declare her love for Roger. She was there to claim him, like a disputed plot of land. Sigourney was too shocked at first to speak. It was one of Roger's students, for God's sake, a girl twenty years younger than him. What was he thinking? When she found her voice, she calmly told the girl to leave and closed the door. The girl rang the doorbell, but Sigourney refused to answer. She yelled something Sigourney couldn't understand and finally she went away.

Sigourney's icy calm yielded to a burning rage, and she slid to the floor with her back to the wall. Her stomach churned so violently she thought she would be sick. Take deep breaths, she told herself. She slowly regained control of her emotions. This was the Rubicon, she realized. Roger had finally crossed a line, and there was no turning back. She looked around her at the wood-paneled hallway, comfortable living room and carpeted stairway. They had built so much together, but it had been a house of cards. There had never been an adequate foundation under their life. Even

Debbie hadn't been able to provide that. How much of the blame was hers, and how much was simply Roger's weak, male ego no longer mattered. Their marriage was finished.

By the time Roger arrived home at 4:00 p.m., Sigourney had reached a stage of controlled fury. She had carried most of Roger's personal effects down from the bedroom and stacked them in the living room where Debbie wouldn't see them when she came home. Debbie had bounced into the house half-an-hour earlier and was upstairs in her room listening to music. Sigourney wanted to avoid a scene in front of Debbie, but when she saw Roger's red Toyota pull into the driveway, images of Peggy Wilcox at the Golden Bear Motel flashed through her mind, and she exploded. She began shouting and throwing Roger's clothes and suitcases onto the front lawn. He tried to grab her arms, but she hit him with the small, bronze lamp that stood on the hallway table. Debbie heard the racket and ran down the stairs crying and yelling for Sigourney to stop, but she couldn't. She kept throwing things out the door. Roger began picking up his clothes and carrying them to his car. Debbie ran after him, pleading with him not to leave. Sigourney stumbled up the stairs to her bedroom, closed the door, and sobbed uncontrollably. Her life was a shambles, and she had just done the one thing she had wanted to avoid more than anything, losing control in front of her daughter.

*****

When Sigourney awoke the next morning, the sky looked ominous. Thick clouds pressed down on her head, limiting visibility and erasing landmarks. Sigourney discovered that her toes and fingers were numb, and she wondered if this was one of the early stages of frostbite.

The wind was growing stronger, and snowflakes began falling as she and Sukhang picked their way through a ravine littered with large boulders. When they emerged from the ravine, Sigourney felt the earth tremble and looked back, half expecting to see a giant rock tumbling onto the path they had just followed. But nothing had moved. Still, she could sense that something was about to happen, just as she had at the bridge on the road leading into Tibet. She just couldn't visualize what it was.

"What was that?" she asked.

"Snow falling," Sukhang replied. He looked worried. "Big snow."

"Do you mean an avalanche?" Now, she was alarmed.

"Yes, yes. Big snow."

They were standing at the base of a steep incline, which rose on their left to an outcrop of rocks a hundred feet above their heads. Snow had piled up behind the rocky formation in heavy drifts. It would take mountain climbing gear to scale that incline, and the snow pack above it reminded Sigourney of ripe apples ready to fall. A less demanding slope rose ahead of them to a ridge about half-a-mile away, but an ice wall at its base would make it difficult to climb. To their right, another deep canyon fell away into oblivion. The ridge was their only real choice. She tried to muster the strength she would need to face this new obstacle, but she was too exhausted from the morning's effort. She could feel Sukhang's eyes watching her.

"Maybe you rest. I go look. Be right back." Sukhang dropped the firewood and his pack in the snow and started towards the ice wall.

Sigourney couldn't shake the ill feeling that had crept over her when they emerged from the ravine. She took a few hesitant steps, and then stopped. "Maybe, we should both rest here for awhile," she called after him. "I don't like the looks of this place."

Sukhang smiled and waved, but kept going. She stood watching him, too tired to explain herself. It took all her energy just to think about removing her pack and sitting down. He had gone less than fifty yards when a deep rumbling sound began to reverberate above their heads. The earth shook slightly. Sigourney looked up the mountain with a mixture of fascination and fear. Sukhang had stopped and was looking, as well. At first, all seemed normal, except for the rumbling, which grew louder. The earth continued to tremble. A cloud of snow seemed to be gathering above their heads, and for a moment she found the floating, billowing mass very beautiful. She had never seen anything like it before. Then, she saw to her horror that it was cascading towards them with a deafening roar. She took two steps backwards before she was bowled over by a powerful blast of compressed air and snow. In seconds, the roaring sound swept over her and disappeared into the canyon below.

She found herself lying on her back with only her head and shoulders clear of the heavy snow, which pressed down on her like wet cement. The bag on her back had kept her head above the snow, saving her from almost certain suffocation. Sigourney lay there in a dazed state of confusion, trying to understand what had just happened. She raised her head to look for Sukhang, to ask him to extricate her from her white prison, but he was no longer standing where she had last seen him. A vast wasteland of tousled snow covered the mountain where he had been. Panic flooded her mind. Sukhang was gone! But where? She had to find him.

Sigourney frantically twisted her shoulders in an effort to break free, but the snow refused to yield. I'm going to die on this horrible mountain, she thought. She wriggled harder, rocking slightly on the bag underneath her. Her right arm gained a small space by her side, and she pulled it free with a wild cry of relief. She dug into the snow with frantic, little scooping motions until her left arm emerged. Then, she pushed herself upright and tore furiously at the snow covering her legs. When she looked around, she saw she was on the edge of the slide area. Her life had been saved by a matter of feet. If she hadn't taken those steps backward, she would've been buried so deep, even her backpack couldn't have saved her.

Her initial reaction was one of triumph, but she was quickly overwhelmed by the reality of her situation. She yelled for Sukhang, but the only reply was the flowing whoosh of the wind. Snow was falling in a slanted pattern, covering her in its filmy embrace. She got to her feet and climbed onto the thick layer of snow that now blocked her path, the same snow that had buried Sukhang just minutes ago. It was impossible to know exactly where he had stood. She knelt down and began to dig with her hands in the snow, tentatively at first, then with growing urgency. He had to be there, frozen in place just below her feet, waiting for her to rescue him! She plunged her hands again and again into the tightly packed snow, until her arms were too exhausted to move. Tears formed tiny icicles where they streamed down her face. She lifted her weary arms and pounded the snow, hating it for what it had done. Hating it for taking Sukhang from her. His generous smiles and hurried movements were gone. In Lhasa, his wife and daughters were waiting for him. How long would it be before they knew he wasn't coming home to them? A month? A year? The loss engulfed her. It was more than she could bear. She wanted to sit there and stay close to him. Maybe, the spirits would bring him back, if she only waited.

An icy gust of wind brought her to her senses, and she considered the magnitude of her situation. Sukhang had died quickly, but if she didn't act fast, she was going to join him. At least it was peaceful there, now that the avalanche had passed. Not such a bad place to die. Concentrate, she scolded herself. She had to start walking, but where? Should she try to go back? That seemed a poor choice, even if she could retrace her route, which she doubted. She had to keep pushing forward towards the mountain pass. The peak Sukhang had pointed out had disappeared in the falling snow, but she would find it again after the storm passed.

Sigourney struggled to her feet and walked back to Sukhang's bag and the firewood. She couldn't carry everything. She would have to make choices. The firewood and yak dung were important. She would need fires to stay alive. And matches! Sukhang had carried the matches. Were they in his bag or buried with him in the snow? She tore through the clothing inside his bag, until she found the large, blue box. There was food, as well, and the tea kettle. Guilt gnawed at her as she pawed through his belongings and stuffed the prized items into her own bulging bag, but she knew he would understand. The weight of her heavier bag and the yak dung made it impossible to carry the firewood, so she tied the rope binding the wood around her waist to drag it behind her.

When she was ready, Sigourney looked around at the silent graveyard that had become her companion's resting place. Falling snow was already covering the evidence of the slide that had wrecked so much havoc. Soon, there would be no traces left at all. She gave her friend a silent prayer, adjusted her load, and trudged away.

The avalanche had piled several feet of snow against the ice wall, and she found that once she tossed the bags and firewood over the top, she could scale it. However, climbing the ridge proved to be an ordeal in the growing storm. The wind kicked snow in her face, stinging her eyes and making it difficult to see where to secure her hands and feet. Twice, she slipped and nearly fell to the bottom. The firewood was an anchor weighing her down, and it took all her strength to pull herself upward. When she reached the crest, she lay on the ground gasping in an effort to fill her oxygen-starved lungs.

A less daunting slope lay ahead of her, but she didn't have the strength to climb it. It would take all her remaining energy just to find a place to hide from the wind and start a fire. She spotted a small crevice formed by two outcroppings of rock. It would have to do. She crawled into the space and lay there for awhile, wondering if she could get up again. She dozed, and then woke to the sound of her own teeth chattering. Rousing herself, Sigourney dug a hole in the snow for a fire pit. Her hands shook so badly, it took three matches to start the fire, and she cursed her clumsiness. There were plenty of matches in the box, but they wouldn't last long if she wasted them like that. She laid her mat and blanket on the ground while she waited for the snow in the kettle to melt and boil. By the time she drank her tea and ate some warmed yak meat and tsampa, her head was nodding. She pulled out her other two blankets, curled into a ball and slept.

Sigourney found herself covered in snow the next morning. Her body ached, but she ignored her tired muscles and set about the business of starting a new fire for breakfast. It only took one match this time, which satisfied her immensely. The wind was howling by the time she was ready to start. This raised a new dilemma. Should she venture into the storm, or hole up for another day to gather more strength and wait for the storm to pass? She needed Sukhang's sage advice, but she couldn't have it. The spirits hadn't given him back. She stepped away from her shelter and was hit with a blast of raw wind that immediately discouraged her. But she was even more afraid of running out of matches, fuel or food. Waiting a day seemed an even greater risk, and she decided to move on.

The first slope she encountered was easier than the previous ones, but the wind raked across the open space with the ferocity of a wild animal that sensed her weakened condition and was moving in for the kill. It assaulted her eyes, nose and skin, forcing her to pull her scarf over her face, until only a slit remained for her eyes. Her world was transformed into a swirling, white veil that limited her vision in any direction to a few yards. By the time she reached the slope's summit, she was covered in frost, and deep layers of cold had seeped back into her body. Her feet had become heavy stones that she lifted one-at-a-time and plunged back into the snow, and her mind had stopped thinking about anything except taking the next step. Only her will to survive kept her going.

Sigourney had no idea how long she struggled like this, but she knew the snow was becoming thicker and heavier. She was close to collapse when a small cave appeared through the furious storm. She crawled towards it and pushed her body into the narrow opening, collapsing on the rocky floor. Her shivering gradually stopped, and she felt marvelously warm. She saw a sandy beach. Where was it? Hawaii, she decided. She and Roger had vacationed there many years ago. What a warm and sunny place it was! She could stay there forever. She closed her eyes and snuggled into a ball, thinking about soft, ocean breezes and dazzling sunsets.

Something else registered in her mind as she prepared to sleep, a small voice told her she was going to die. But that was all right. She felt happy and warm. She no longer cared.

CHAPTER TWENTY-FIVE

A phone was ringing, and it angered her. Who would have the nerve to call her at this hour? She waited for the answering machine to take a message, but the machine wasn't picking up the call. The phone just kept ringing and ringing.

Sigourney opened her eyes and looked at the walls of the cave. How had she gotten there, she wondered? The last thing she remembered was sitting on a warm, sandy beach. Slowly, she became conscious of her world. The wind was howling outside, and the temperature inside the cave was so cold, frost had formed on everything. She heard the phone again. How could a cave have a phone? It made no sense. Then, she sat up with a start. It was the phone John had given her. John was calling her! The phone was in her coat pocket, but when she tried to reach for it, she found her motor functions were all askew. It took several attempts before she could pull it out. She saw the red button and managed to push it with her thumb.

"Sigourney. Are you there?" John's voice sounded far away. She realized she wasn't holding the phone to her ear. She lifted it up and tried to speak, but all she could do was mumble.

"John," she finally said with a sigh. "I was in Hawaii."

"Sigourney, are you all right?" His voice grew more urgent and demanding. She didn't like that.

"In a cave. Trying to sleep. Don't want to wake up." She slurred her words but couldn't help it. Her lips felt like snorkeling fins.

"Okay. Help me Sigourney. Tell me what's going on. Where's your guide?" The voice was anxious, now.

"Sleeping in snow."

"Do you mean he's dead? Sigourney, are you alone?"

"Alone."

"You're alone in a cave in the mountains?"

"Alone."

"Sigourney, try to pay attention to me. Do you have a fire?"

"No fire. Have matches, but no fire." She looked at the cave's entrance and saw the bag of yak dung lying just inside the opening. "I have yak dung." She giggled uncontrollably at this comment, then fell silent. It was beginning to register that she was in trouble. Her hands and feet were numb.

"We must make a fire, Sigourney. *You* must make a fire. Will you do as I tell you?"

"Yes. I love you John." She didn't know why she said this, but she was glad she had.

"If you love me, you must keep yourself alive. Where are your matches?"

"In the backpack."

"Pull them out and stack some of the yak dung in a pile."

She fumbled with the bag and pawed through her things. Her hands felt like two tree stumps, and when she found the blue box, it took several attempts before she could pick it up. She had to put the phone down to do this, but she could still hear John's voice encouraging her. A burning sensation in her fingers told her some circulation was returning, but she was still having difficulty grasping something as tiny as a match. After several failed attempts, she put the box down and picked up the phone.

"Can't light the match, John. Hands too cold." Her mind was

as numb as her hands. Each word had to form in her brain before she could speak it. It was like talking in quicksand.

"Do you have any feeling in them at all?" His voice had become steady and calm. She remembered how calm he always was. She liked that.

"Cold. Feet and hands very cold."

"You have some frostbite. Try to move yours fingers, but don't rub or message them. You have to increase your blood flow. Put the phone down and keep trying to move them. You should get some flexibility back."

Sigourney followed his directions until she found she could move her fingers a bit more. She tried to pick another match from the box. This time, she was successful. She leaned over the pile of yak dung and carefully struck the match against a rock. Her hand shook, but she held the match to the dung until it caught fire. It was only then she saw that the match was burning her fingers, but she couldn't feel it. She dropped the match and picked up the phone.

"I've started the fire," she announced triumphantly. Her thoughts and speech were improving.

"Good. What have you got to eat and drink?"

"Let me get some snow for the tea kettle." By the time she had scooped snow into the kettle and put it on the fire, she could feel the warmth of the blaze reviving her. She was starting to feel alive again.

"John," she said anxiously, "I think I was dying when you called. The phone woke me. I'm not sure I would have woken otherwise." Had she really given up? Not her spirit, perhaps, but her mind and body had.

"My God, Sigourney, I don't want to lose you. Tell me exactly where you think you are and what happened. I'm going to walk you through this. You're going to make it."

His resolve gave her courage. She told him about the Samye Monastery, the grueling climb into the Himalayas, and the avalanche that killed Sukhang. She talked about her decision to keep going in the blizzard.

"When I found this cave, all I could do was crawl inside and go to sleep. Nothing else mattered."

"You were starting to freeze to death, Sigourney, but you're recovering now. Keep your hands and feet dry and warm, but don't put them near the fire. Wrap them in dry cloth. It doesn't sound like an advanced case of frostbit. You can still walk out of those mountains."

"How, John?" Now that she was talking to him, her will to live had returned, but she was lost in the middle of a terrifying storm in one of the most unforgiving mountains systems in the world. Getting out alive was a concept she could barely fathom.

"Wait for the storm to pass and regain your strength. Save as much fuel as you can, but keep a low fire going. Drink plenty of tea and water. You're dehydrated and need liquids. You may not feel hungry, but eat anyway." He hesitated. "I know this may sound silly, but can you repeat what I just told you? I need to know if your thought processes have been impaired by the altitude."

She recited his instructions back to him.

"Good girl. Keep repeating them. Don't let your mind wander. You have to stay focused on each thing you do. That will keep you alert. I'm going to hang up now. It's hard to know how much battery life is left in your phone. Eat, rest and try to sleep. When you wake up, push the button you used to call me before. If I don't hear from you in four hours, I'll call again. You're going to make it, Sigourney. I won't let you die. My thoughts are with you. Never forget that."

"I won't, John. Good-bye my love."

There was a click, then silence.

Her last sentence hung in the cave like a puff of air turned to frost. The wind howled relentlessly outside, but inside her cave it was deathly still. Smoke from the burning yak dung drifted in a dirty haze around her, burning her eyes and making her cough. She was alone again. John's voice still echoed in her mind, but he was gone. She sat unmoving, while her mind floated away into a pleasant dream. She was riding in a taxi in Paris and looking at all the elegant stores and restaurants through an open window. The air was warm, and it was strangely peaceful. She couldn't hear the traffic buzzing around her, only the wailing sound of the wind rushing past the taxi as it hurried down the boulevard.

Sigourney snapped awake. The fire had been reduced to a few, glowing embers, and the cave was biting cold again. She was sitting exactly where she had been when she spoke to John. Her desire to sleep had wrested away her ability to function, and she had lost all track of time. She forced herself into action, first adding more dung to the coals, then heating more water. The fire and tea warmed her, but she had to move closer to the mouth of the cave to get relief from the sooty smoke burning her lungs. She pulled some dried yak meat from her bag. John was right. She had surprisingly little appetite, but she forced herself to eat. When she was finished, she crawled closer to the fire and pulled her blankets around her. The wind continued to roar as she drifted off to sleep. Her last thought was to wonder if she would ever wake up again.

A deathly silence filled the cave. It was pitch dark. The silence was so frightful she sat bolt upright, uncertain whether she was alive or dead. Then, she realized what was missing. There was no wind. The storm was gone! So was the fire, although the cave no longer felt quite so cold. There was something in her hand. The cell phone. She had held it while she slept. She felt around her blankets until she located the matches. Rather than waste one looking for fuel, she crawled out of her blankets and searched with her hands until she discovered the firewood. She stacked a generous amount near the cave's entrance and lighted it. The flames leapt eagerly from the dry wood. She was satisfied to see that the cave's opening helped ventilate the smoke outside.

After she put the kettle on the fire, she picked up the phone to call John. Her energy was improving by the minute, and she couldn't wait to hear his reassuring voice. When she pressed the button, however, nothing happened. She tried again, but there was no response. Sigourney stared at the phone with growing alarm. The battery light was out. There was no more power. She struck it with the heel of her nearly frozen hand, sending a stabbing pain streaking up her arm. The phone clattered on the stones when she dropped it.

Sigourney's voice echoed in the cave, and she realized she was shouting hysterically. She looked around with apprehension. The narrow, granite walls looked like a prison. Despair swept over her. She was adrift in an unforgiving world. She needed John's help, but he was no longer there. Her lifeline to him had been severed. She had to resist a powerful urge to curl up in the blankets, again, and ignore the terrifying world that waited outside the cave.

The hissing of boiling water striking the fire brought her mind back to business. As she went through the familiar ritual of making tea, she devised a plan to bolster her courage. John could no longer talk to her, but she would tell him what she was doing and thinking. The idea of talking to John, even if he couldn't hear, raised her spirits. The first thing she told him was that daylight was seeping into the cave. She poked her head outside and was greeted by a pale sky and early morning sunlight.

"It's a beautiful morning, John, and as soon as I eat, I'm getting out of here."

Sunlight dazzled Sigourney when she emerged from the cave. The sparkling light reflecting off the fresh snow nearly blinded her. She shaded her eyes with her hand and scanned the horizon. She was surrounded by a monochromatic landscape of fluffy whites and granite grays. The peak Sukhang had shown her stood out in sharp relief against the sky. It looked tantalizingly closer, but it was still out of reach.

She walked with renewed purpose, but her early burst of energy soon wilted as the altitude and heavy snow sapped her strength. The snow came up to her knees, forcing her to slog through heavy drifts and to stop and rest after every two or three steps. Rocky outcroppings and steep ridges blocked her way, and it took all her concentration to decide which way to go. By late morning, she grew too tired to drag the firewood and cut it loose. She would have to make do with the smoky yak dung and hope she had enough. Sigourney chatted with John until the effort became too great. Then, she lapsed into silence. It took all her faculties to think about where to put her feet. A tempting ice flow appeared on her right, where a glacier snaked down from a high pass, but she remembered the deep crevasse Sukhang had uncovered and shuddered. She ignored the glacier and continued toiling in the snow. Her mind grew as numb as her body. The snow beckoned to her. She wanted to lie down in it, but her survival instincts took over and pushed her onward.

By late afternoon, she no longer knew what she was doing. She collapsed, unable to proceed any further. Every time she stopped to rest, the mountain's silence engulfed her. She began talking to John, again. It felt good talking to him; it took the edge off her loneliness. Sunlight slanted between two peaks, casting long shadows across the white landscape. Only a light wind teased the snow. It had been a good weather day, and in spite of her fatigue, she was pleased with her progress. She couldn't see the peak from her current vantage point, but she knew she was closer.

In this manner, two days and nights passed. On the third morning, Sigourney beheld a series of ridges and valleys below her that fell away like rapids in a river. It took awhile for the view's significance to register, but when she spotted a badly weathered stupa, she knew she had reached the summit. She was looking down into Bhutan from her perch above twenty thousand feet. The news should have thrilled her, but her dull mind couldn't summon up the energy to feel anything except weariness. Her supply of yak dung was dangerously low, her food was rapidly becoming depleted, and she could hardly stand. Worst of all, she was only at the half-way point. She still had to work her way down those God-awful mountains, and she wasn't sure she had the mental or physical stamina to do it. She was having a difficult time simply remembering why she was putting herself through so much torment. She could quite easily have sat down and enjoyed looking at the expanses of snow and ice, until she froze or starved to death. That would have been easier than pushing herself any further.

A tiny corner of her brain told her that wouldn't do, however, not if she wanted to see Debbie and John again. So after a brief rest, she willed herself back to her feet and pushed one foot ahead of the other, just as she had been doing for the past several days.

*****

Sigourney remembered little of her descent. She never knew if her partial amnesia was the result of her brain shutting down, or her mind trying to protect her from memories too painful to recall. She knew she babbled a lot, mostly to John and at times to Debbie. Sigourney had no idea what she said. It didn't matter.

She did have one vivid memory of standing at the top of a cliff that plunged more than a thousand feet down a sheer rock face and toying with the idea of sliding down it to save time and energy. She also recalled losing her footing and tumbling down a steep incline, while she frantically grasped for something to hang onto. She landed heavily against an outcropping of rocks, which stopped her fall less than a hundred feet from a yawning chasm that waited to swallow her.

She thought she remembered singing and crying for no reason, but she couldn't be certain. Her memories swirled like snowflakes. One moment they were clear and distinct, the next blurred and indecipherable.

The last thing she remembered was waking up and looking at a blue sky with fluffy clouds dotting it. She was lying on the ground. Not on snow or ice, but leaves and grass. The air was warmer, and she heard unfamiliar sounds: birds chirping, tree branches creaking in the wind, an animal scurrying into the brush. There were even yellow butterflies flitting around her. She decided she was dreaming. It was a lovely dream, the finest dream she'd ever had, and she wanted to cling to it forever. The face of an angel suddenly appeared. It peered down at her from the sky, and she knew she had arrived in heaven. She couldn't remember dying, so it must have been painless. She hadn't fallen into that yawning chasm or slid down the mountain. Probably froze to death, she thought, which wasn't such a bad way to die.

CHAPTER TWENTY-SIX

Sigourney was vaguely aware of hands gently rubbing her arms and legs. The hands glided over her skin on a film of ointment that filled her nostrils with a pungent odor. She wanted to open her eyes, but they were fused together. The hands stopped. Silence surrounded her. She decided it was a Bon spirit and slid back into unconsciousness.

Later, Sigourney did manage to open her eyes but found herself in total darkness. She decided she was in a cave, because she couldn't see any stars, and there was no wind. She reached out for matches to light a fire, but all she could feel was a rough padding beneath her. She must have fallen asleep on her blanket. Anyway, it was warm enough to forego the fire. She turned over and went back to sleep.

The third time she awoke, she saw a terrifying demon staring down at her, and she sat up shrieking, her heart pounding wildly in her chest. She was certain a spirit had come for her, but she didn't want to go with it. The demon put a hand on her shoulder and smiled at her. His face slowly turned into that of an ordinary man. Perhaps, he wasn't such a horrible spirit, after all.

"Don't be alarmed. My name is Dorje Wangdi. I'm a doctor." He lifted her wrist to measure her pulse. "The peasants who found you called me."

Sigourney couldn't comprehend what the spirit was telling her. Why would peasants have called *him*? His face looked friendly, but spirits could be deceiving. He began probing her hands, which burned at his touch. She flinched at the unexpected pain. He must be a very powerful spirit, she decided.

"What is your name?" he asked. His hands moved to her feet, which burned even more than her hands. Why was he torturing her?

She thought if she answered him he would stop, but her mind was too blurred to remember a name. She looked around and realized for the first time that she wasn't in a cave after all. She was in a room, lying on a bed. This confused her, and she gave up trying to recall who she was.

"Can you tell me your name?" the spirit persisted.

Oh God, he wasn't going to stop bothering her, and his hands were sending sharp pains through her feet. She had to think of something.

"I'm Anne Hopkins," she said at last, looking at him triumphantly.

She had expected this to please the spirit, but it only changed the creases in his face from a smile to a frown. Not the right answer, she decided. She thought some more. Then, it came to her. "No. Not Anne Hopkins. My name is Sigourney . . . Sigourney Phillips."

The smile returned to spirit's face. "That is good news. Search parties have been looking for you."

This information surprised Sigourney and snapped her out of her befuddlement. Images rushed back to her: Chinese officials, Tibetan monks, and snow storms, all whirling together like fruits in a blender. Her mind was speeding through the images so quickly they excited and scared her at the same time. Her mind was telling her she was alive, that the man talking to her *was* a doctor, not a spirit. Was she in Bhutan? She looked at the rough, wood planks on the walls and floor. Not a hospital or a doctor's room, she decided. Someone's home? She studied the doctor. He had Asian features, but his skin was too light to be Tibetan. He also spoke very good English. The doctor stopped massaging her feet, for which she was thankful.

"Why were you looking for me?" she asked. She looked at her fingers and realized several were wrapped in bandages.

"A man from the British government called Thimphu, that's our capital, and reported that you were trekking through the Himalayas from Tibet." The doctor sat down on the edge of the bed. "You've had quite a journey."

"Do you mean John Henley?" Memories of a smiling face flooded her. "Was it John who called?" Sigourney was suddenly taut with anticipation.

"I don't know his name. He said he talked to you on a mobile phone several days ago but lost contact. He was very concerned about you."

It *was* John, and he was looking for her. Thinking about him brought back more memories: amused eyes, firm hands, and warm lips. She exulted at the memories, and her face broadened into a blissful smile.

"Am I in Bhutan, doctor?" She tried to wiggle her toes, but found them bound like her fingers. More bandages?

"Please call me Dorje. Yes, you are in Bhutan. I have been treating your hands and feet for frostbite."

Sigourney shuddered as she thought about the freezing winds and blinding snow storms she had endured. And the avalanche. This made her think about Sukhang, and her joy slid into sadness. "I lost my guide," she murmured. Tears stung her eyes. She thought about Sukhang's wife and daughters. She would have to get word to them.

Dorje told Sigourney what a brave woman she had been to walk from Tibet to Bhutan. He said it was a dangerous trip, one he didn't believe any western woman had made before. One had, she told him. Anne Hopkins. That reminded her of the ledger, and she looked around for her tattered bag. Dorje understood and lifted the bag from the floor. Sigourney smiled with relief when she saw it.

She realized for the first time that her clothes were gone. All she was wearing was a cotton nightgown, and she blushed to think that someone had seen her naked body but immediately cast her modesty aside. It was silly to worry about such things after what she had been through.

"You are in surprisingly good health after such an ordeal," the doctor continued, "but I want to keep you here one more day and night. I will drive you to Thimphu tomorrow. The trip will require many hours, so you must rest." He patted her arm and stood up. "Now, I must alert the search parties that you are safe. And you must sleep. I will return in the morning." With that, the doctor departed.

*****

When Sigourney attempted to stand up the next morning, the room spun in circles, forcing her to sit back down on the edge of the wood-framed bed. She tried to focus on the room's walls, but everything floated around her in a dreamy mist. She was riding on a merry-go-round, and it took all her energy to keep from falling off. Her dizziness gradually subsided, and the room came into focus.

She stood up again. Jabbing pains tore through the souls of her feet, but she forced herself to hobble towards a chair, which she knocked over when she tried to grasp it. The noise brought scurrying footsteps, and moments later, a woman rushed in carrying a yellow, silk blouse and a long piece of plaid cloth decorated in varying shades of brown. She laid the fabrics on the bed, bowed, and clasped her hands together in front of Sigourney. Her deference made Sigourney uncomfortable, and she grasped the woman's hands in hers. The woman smiled, causing her cheeks to crinkle into web-like patterns. She offered Sigourney her shoulder and helped her to a bowl filled with water. Sigourney pulled the cotton garment over her head and tried to wash herself, but the bandages hampered her. The woman took the sponge and gently swathed her body with soap and water. Sigourney grimaced at the amount of grime that was removed. She had never been so filthy in her life, yet until that moment, she hadn't cared. Her journey from Samye had been too exhausting and nerve-wracking for her to worry about anything, not even basic hygiene.

When she was finished, the woman helped Sigourney put on a yellow blouse. Next, she wound the plaid cloth around Sigourney's body and secured it at the shoulders with metal clasps. A wide belt was used to gather the material at her waist. The material was soft against her skin and much finer than the coarse clothing worn by her hostess. Sigourney suspected it was her finest outfit, and she felt guilty wearing it. Still, she couldn't resist looking about for a mirror, but there was none.

Her hostess led Sigourney into an adjacent room, where the only furniture consisted of a few cabinets along the walls. Several pots and a tea kettle had been set on the floor. Three children--a boy and two girls ranging in ages from seven to twelve--were seated on the floor with their legs crossed. They watched Sigourney with frank, curious expressions. The boy, who was the youngest, wore a kimono-style robe decorated in brown and white stripes. The two girls wore blouses and cloths pinned at the shoulders similar to Sigourney's.

Her hostess gestured to a mat on the floor across from the children. Tea cups and bowls were passed around, and the children began transferring handfuls of food from the pots to their bowls. Sigourney was given a wood spoon, which she wielded like a club in her bandaged hands. The food consisted of rice, vegetables in a cheese sauce and meat dumplings. After weeks of dried yak meat and tsampa, the exquisite flavors danced on her tongue.

The children giggled and whispered to each other, while the woman hovered over Sigourney like a worried mother. Sigourney had given up trying to guess what the children were saying when the oldest girl suddenly spoke to her in good English. "You are from America?"

Surprised, Sigourney nodded. "How do you know English?"

"We learn in school," she said proudly. "I hope you are well."

"I am now, thank you."

The other two children giggled. Then, the boy spoke. "Someday, I will go to America." This produced a fresh round of giggles.

"When you do," Sigourney responded with a smile, "you must visit me." She could see from his expression that he was having trouble understanding her. "You come to America and see me."

His face brightened. "Yes. I will come see you."

A car pulled up outside, announcing Dorje's arrival. It was time to leave for Thimphu. Sigourney struggled to her feet and indicated to her hostess that she should change back into her own clothing. She knew this was not a wealthy family, and she didn't want to take the woman's beautiful clothes. But the woman shook her head.

"This is too beautiful for me to take from her," Sigourney protested to Dorje when he entered.

"She wants you to keep it," Dorje replied. "She considers it an honor for you to wear it." The woman smiled and nodded her head.

Sigourney hobbled back to the bedroom to collect her meager belongings and the bag containing the ledger. When she picked up her jacket, she felt the wooden Buddha in the pocket and knew what she must do. The Buddha had been her faithful companion. It had protected her during her quest, but its mission was over. It belonged here with the kind woman who had so willingly given her the clothes off her back.

Sigourney returned to the main room and held the statue out to the woman. To her disappointment, the woman refused to accept it.

"Dorje, why won't she take this? I really want her to have it."

"It is the Bhutanese custom to decline a gift the first time it is offered. You must make the offer again."

Sigourney presented the little statue a second time, and the woman took it with a bright smile. She grasped Sigourney's hands and held them. Sigourney felt she had made a friend she could count on for life. It had been the same in Tibet.

Dorje insisted Sigourney ride in the back seat, where she could lie down and rest when she wanted. She soon understood why the trip would take so long. The road was deeply rutted and filled with rocks and pot holes. It reminded her of the road to the Tsurpu Monastery. Had that only been two weeks ago? It seemed a lifetime. Dorje tried to pick his was around the obstacles, but no amount of twists and turns could save them from a bouncing ride.

Sigourney couldn't get used to seeing so much water. Small creeks crossed the road at regular intervals. She saw prayer wheels turned by water pressure from passing streams. The wheels turned night and day, releasing their prayers into the world. The images sent pangs of nostalgia shooting through her; they reminded her of Tibet. Everywhere she looked, farmers tilled the steep hillsides and valley floors. Red chilies were strewn across rooftops to dry, adding crimson bursts to the green mountains and valleys. Green! Sigourney couldn't remember when she had seen so much green. She had spent the past month traveling through oceans of browns, grays and whites. She had forgotten the color green.

She welcomed the long drive. It gave her an opportunity to reflect on her life. After sharing so many adventures with the Tibetans and surviving a near-death experience, she knew her personal values and goals had changed. Teaching and research were still important to her, but they no longer carried such a high priority. Debbie would be the focal point of her life, now, and she hoped her relationship with John would flourish. She tried to picture a future with him but found it confusing. He lived in England and traveled a great deal, and she couldn't pull Debbie away from her life and friends at such an emotional time. Moving to England didn't seem like a viable option, at least for now. Sigourney sighed. If there was to be a continuing relationship, it would have to be long distance. She would do everything possible to make both relationships work. It was time to put down much firmer roots in her life's soil.

Sigourney discovered that many of her recent memories were as elusive as the Bon spirits. The beginning of her journey stood out in brilliant detail. It was like watching the intricate lines of a wood's grain emerging while rubbing a stain into freshly sanded wood. As the trip progressed, however, as it became more frantic and desperate, the images began to blur. By the time she reached Bhutan, she had almost no memories at all. Only fragments of her last few days in the Himalayas, which were scattered, like shards from a vessel, across those towering mountain peaks.

The ride to Thimphu was as disconnected as her recent memories. Sigourney dozed in the back seat of the car, and then snapped awake to see a large stupa standing forlornly in a field, or two naked girls squealing with laughter as they bathed in a channel of water beside the road. She remembered the car running over bamboo poles left in the road by peasants. Dorje explained the weight of the car splintered the poles, making it easier to strip away the bamboo fibers used to weave mats.

Daylight was fading when they entered a broad valley defined by forested hillsides and distant mountain peaks. Houses began to appear closer together. Farmer's plows and planted fields slowly disappeared as the land was claimed by more buildings.

"We have reached Thimphu," Dorje announced.

Thimphu itself was little more than a few blocks of shops, hotels and restaurants, but enough cars filled the streets to merit three roundabout intersections, each with a policeman directing traffic.

"We tried installing traffic signals," Dorje informed her, "but they confused our drivers, and the king ordered them removed." Thimphu is probably the only capital in the world without traffic lights, she thought.

The long, bumpy ride had taken its toll on Sigourney, and by the time they approached the hotel, she was ready for a hot bath and a good night's rest. That could wait, however, until she called Debbie and found batteries for John's phone. She was so absorbed with these thoughts she didn't see the small crowd milling about on the sidewalk until Dorje stopped in front of the hotel.

"There she is," someone cried. Heads turned. Bodies stiffened in anticipation. Necks strained to have a look. The crowd was transformed into a mob of eager inquisitors, and before she knew it, Sigourney was surrounded by a sea of faces peering through the car's windows. Voices called out to her in English, French and German. Cameras flashed. Questions were flung at her like warriors' spears.

The unexpected frenzy made Sigourney dizzy. Images of Tibetans crowding around and reaching for her valise flashed through her mind. She instinctively reached into her pocket for the little Buddha statue before remembering it was gone.

"Who are these people?" she asked Dorje.

"They must be reporters," he responded hesitantly. "When I called to let the authorities know you had been found, I was told many people were asking about you. I didn't want to worry you. You needed to rest. I never expected anything like this." He looked at her apologetically. "You have become something of a celebrity."

Reporters! Sigourney was astonished to think that reporters would want to talk to her. It had never occurred to her that anyone other than her family and colleagues would be interested in her quest. She was unprepared to face all those people-- to answer God knows what sorts of questions. There was nothing she wished to say to them. All she wanted to do was to slip quietly out of the country and return home, just as Anne had done. It was becoming clear, however, that her wish wouldn't be granted.

"Is the no other way to get into the hotel?" she pleaded. "I can't face these people now."

Before Dorje could respond, a face emerged in the throng, a face framed by tousled hair and a joyful smile. Sigourney thrust the car door open and plunged into the group of reporters. People tried to stop her, but she shouldered past them, her mind spinning with disbelief and her heart hammering so hard, she feared she would faint. The face bobbed in the crowd, disappearing and reappearing in the maddening confusion, and agitating Sigourney to the point of panic. Then she felt her daughter's arms around her, and she pressed her face into the sweet, hazelnut scent of Debbie's hair. She squeezed the tremulous body wrapped in hers until she could no longer breathe.

"Mom, you're crushing me!" A laughing voice. Not a reproachful one. Not one filled with anger and accusations.

Sigourney eased her stranglehold and looked at her daughter with tearful eyes. In that moment everything came into focus with a clarity that astonished her. The last mists of doubt and confusion lifted from her mind. Her future with her daughter became as lucent as springtime. She would never let Debbie go again. "Oh, how I've missed you, honey. You're all I've thought about these past weeks." She kissed her daughter's cheek and hair. "I love you so much."

Debbie's face grew serious. "You scared me mother. When you disappeared, I thought you'd gone away for good. I felt awful about what I'd said. I promised never to be bad again, if only you'd come back." She trembled and gulped air into her lungs.

"You weren't bad honey." She rubbed her daughter's arms. "You were just confused. So was I."

Debbie's face became alarmed when she saw the bandages on Sigourney's fingers. "What happened to your hands?" She gingerly touched the bandages. "Are you okay?"

"Just a little frostbite. The doctor who drove me here is taking care of it." Sigourney continued to touch her daughter's arms and face in disbelief, as if she feared she was seeing a Bon spirit that would suddenly evaporate. "But . . . I don't understand . . . what are you doing here? How did you get to Bhutan?"

"Your friend, John, arranged everything." Debbie pointed over her shoulder.

Sigourney's face flushed as she followed her daughter's finger to the figure standing unobtrusively behind them with a sheepish grin. She stared at those soft eyes, eyes she knew could become as hard as steel when faced with a crisis. Dear God, how magnificent he looked in his pullover sweater and crisply ironed pants! Sigourney cried out--it was more of a gasp mixed with a noise in her throat that sounded like a squeak--and threw her arms open to him. She closed her eyes and inhaled that musky odor she had come to love so much. Her mouth found his and he devoured hers, answering her hunger with such urgency she had to break away, laughing and breathless, embarrassed that her daughter should see her so utterly helpless in this man's arms.

"You took me by surprise," she exclaimed.

"I told you I would come to you. Thank heavens you're all right." He held her a moment longer, then dropped his arms as he became aware of Debbie observing them.

"Thank you for finding me, and for bringing Debbie," she said more seriously.

She looked at Debbie with apprehension, wondering what her daughter made of their exchange and half-expecting to see disgust on her face. She was surprised to find a smile instead, one that told her Debbie accepted John in Sigourney's life. John had obviously made a good impression on Debbie, but that didn't surprise Sigourney. He had a way of doing that. She opened her arms to them both and clung to them, never wanting to let them go.

Sigourney became aware of the incessant babble of voices and cameras flashing around her. The reporters clamored for her to speak, but all she wanted to do was escape them and be alone with Debbie and John. As usual, John took charge, pushing the reporters back and firmly advising them to wait until later, when Sigourney would have a statement for them. She ducked her head and hurried as fast as her swollen feet would carry her into the hotel.

Somewhere deep inside of her a voice cried out with happiness, and she knew it was Anne celebrating Sigourney's triumph. The air surrounding her grew warmer, then cooled again. The voice faded and was gone. Sigourney stopped in the middle of the lobby and listened intently. Anne has left me, she thought. Her spirit has flown away like the white birds in Nepal. Sigourney looked at John and Debbie, who were both eyeing her curiously. And I am reborn, she told herself with a surge of joy. I have chosen to return to earth so that I can help my daughter grow into womanhood and cherish the new love I have found. She knew in that moment that her quest had brought her more than new life. It had brought her Nirvana.

A DIARY OF MY QUEST
By
SIGOURNEY HENLEY

PROLOGUE

Some people might think I have written this book for fame and fortune. That isn't the case. I already have more fame than I want, and I have dedicated the proceeds from this book to organizations that are trying to preserve Tibet's culture and restore its independence. Some might believe I've been too harsh on the Chinese government for its continued subjugation of Tibetans. That may be true, but it's never easy to see the will and freedom of one group of people oppressed by another.

The primary reason I'm writing this book is to pay tribute to a remarkable woman, Anne Hopkins, who made a dangerous journey, even a heroic one, and chose not to tell anyone about it. I have documented her story and published her diary with mine. However, I have edited out all references that might disclose the location of the manuscript that brought us together.

I was astonished upon my return from Tibet to find reporters waiting for me in Thimphu. I soon learned that my disappearance had become an international incident. People expressed concern and ~ no one seemed to know why I had left the tour or The Chinese government tried to downplay the in my situation. They were greatly embarrassed y knowledge of my whereabouts. At the same ns announced that a great book of Buddha's ·d to Tibet. There were rumors that the book was connected to my disappearance, and when I appeared in Bhutan, the world was eager to talk to me. I wasn't nearly so eager to talk to them, but eventually I did.

One piece of news left me disappointed and shaken. Less than a week after I met with the Karmapa at the Tsurpu Monastery, he made a dramatic escape from Tibet, climbing over the same Himalayan Mountains into India that I was traversing into Bhutan. He had lost hope of reaching an accord with the Chinese and had chosen to join the Dalai Lama and thousands of other Tibetans in exile. He was planning his escape when we met, which explains the head monk's odd behavior. The monk must have known the Karmapa's plans and realized his position would be greatly diminished by his departure. Taking possession of the manuscript would have helped the head monk maintain his importance in the Tibetan community.

Not a day goes by that I don't think about Tibet and all the wonderful people I met there, especially my guide, Sukhang. China continues to pursue their oppressive policies, and the Tibetans to struggle against them. Somewhere in that great, mysterious land there is a manuscript that speaks to them and gives them hope. I will never disclose its location, but I will say that delivering it back to its people was one of the most rewarding experiences of my life. Bless you, Anne Hopkins, for giving me that opportunity. Best of all, there are nights when I have just crossed over the threshold into sleep, when my thoughts become dreams, that I still hear the voices of those chanting monks. The manuscript still speaks to me. I believe it always will.

ABOUT THE AUTHOR

Gordon Snider missed becoming a native Californian by 5 months, which may explain his wanderlust. He has traveled extensively throughout the world, including such exotic destinations as Uzbekistan, Patagonia, Amazon, Borneo, Burma and the Himalayan countries of Tibet, Bhutan and Nepal.

After earning his bachelor's degree in business from UCLA and his masters in marketing from California State University Los Angeles, he worked in business for fifteen years before becoming an independent consultant and educator. He has taught at four universities: College of Notre Dame (Belmont, CA), St. Mary's College, University of Phoenix and Cal Poly San Luis Obispo.

Gordon has published numerous magazine articles and two business books. His second book, How to Become a Killer Competitor, was published in 1999 and is still in print. However, it was his interest in photography that led him to write Sigourney's Quest. He began photographing for tour operators, one whom (Himalayan Treasures and Travel) hired him to photograph in Tibet in the 1990s. He was captivated by the region's people, culture and spiritual devotion. But he was dismayed by the effects of China's repressive policies towards the region, including a systematic program to populate the region with Chinese settlers. In the process, China has turned Tibet's villages and its capital, Lhasa, into "china towns" that undermine the Tibetans' way of life.

When it became apparent that the Tibet Gordon loved so much would soon disappear, he became inspired to write Sigourney's Quest, a fictional attempt to keep the world from forgetting these wonderful people.

Printed in the United States
46022LVS00005B/145